MOVING AWAY

The house was called Laurel Villa. It was large, battered, and a lasting testimonial to a lost generation of master craftsmen. Jess only went north to see it in order to tidy up the affairs of her legacy, but from the moment she walked inside she felt a sense of belonging, of coming home.

Douglas, her husband, had made it quite plain he was only interested in the market value of the property, but as she began to go through the old things, the furniture, the jewellery, all the remnants of a Victorian age, she felt it would be a betrayal to sell any of it – that she would be happier living in the old house on her own, than with Douglas who openly despised her.

Finding a courage she did not know she possessed, she decided to launch into a new life – to begin again – a new career – new friends – a different world altogether, a world that was to bring her respect, tragedy, involvement, and ultimately a different kind of happiness.

MOVING AWAY

A WONDERFUL NEW SAGA FROM LOUISE BRINDLEY

MOVING AWAY
Louise Brindley

CORGI BOOKS

MOVING AWAY
A CORGI BOOK   0 552 13289 6

First publication in Great Britain

PRINTING HISTORY
Corgi edition published 1989

Copyright © Louise Brindley 1989

This book is set in Sabon

Corgi Books are published by Transworld Publishers Ltd.,
61-63 Uxbridge Road, Ealing, London W5 5SA, in
Australia by Transworld Publishers (Australia) Pty. Ltd.,
15-23 Helles Avenue, Moorebank, NSW 2170, and in New
Zealand by Transworld Publishers (N.Z.) Ltd., Cnr.
Moselle and Waipareira Avenues, Henderson, Auckland.

Printed and bound in Great Britain by
Cox & Wyman Ltd., Reading, Berks.

For Adrienne
Because. . .

PRELUDE

In that moment, as the lights of some home-going car raked the dark and lonely room, she saw, in fleeting silhouette, the drooping branches of the laburnum in the strip of earth separating this bungalow from the next, and caught, through an open window, the unmistakable tang of autumn in a burnt-out bonfire.

These long sleepless vigils were both pointless and humiliating, and yet she continued to wait and watch in the vague hope that one of these endless nights he would come to her room penitent, unblinkered, and tell her that he had put an end to the affair.

People said that the wife is always the last person to know. She wondered if this was true, and began the old familiar sifting and searching through memories for some forgotten clue which might have jogged her to the realisation of what was happening. But if a woman trusted her husband, and he said he'd been kept late to attend a staff meeting, umpire a cricket match, or that he had been for a drink with colleagues, she believed him – if she was a trusting kind of person. Naive. Gullible?

And yet there had been signs that all was not well. She remembered thinking that he had seemed moodier, more restless and short-tempered than usual before the summer holidays. This she had put down to his worry over exam results: Open Day, the last minute clearing up of books and papers; fretting about the car-ferry reservations; having the car serviced, travellers' cheques, the rate of exchange; knowing that he fussed unneccessarily about such matters.

She accepted his pernickety obsession with travel arrangements, his dislike of human error, his unwillingness to trust other people as part and parcel of the man she had married eleven years ago – a man who kept himself on a shorter, tighter rein than most men, as though waging a constant war with himself to prove his equality with the rest of mankind. A kind of inverted snobbery. She had often thought of him as a prudish Bohemian, unable to equate the meticulous side of his nature with the poetic. He had always been, was still an enigma; uncertain of himself. A misfit.

Eleven years . . . Was it really as long ago as that?

Most men would have suggested dinner, but he had stipulated coffee. She had guessed why. He was too hard up to make the grand gesture. This she had seen as a token of his integrity; the proud Welshman unwilling to live beyond his means: had felt intrigued by him, an abrupt young schoolmaster with unruly dark hair which appeared to have been cut with a knife and fork instead of scissors. Had he perpetrated this outrage upon himself, she had wondered at the time. Had he chopped off his own hair because he could not afford to visit a decent barber?

Commonsense had warned her to steer clear of involvement. He must be at least ten years younger than herself. A rainy evening had almost decided her to stay at home and watch television. And yet, if she failed to keep their appointment, he might take her non-appearance as a slight. He would, she guessed, be easily hurt.

And so she had waited outside the café for a quarter of an hour or so, pacing up and down beneath her dripping-wet umbrella, wishing to heaven she had decided not to come.

He arrived, at last, breathlessly apologetic. The bus he was on had been held up in the traffic, he explained, so he had jumped off at the traffic-lights and walked the rest of the way.

'Well, now that you have come,' she said, glancing pointedly at her wristwatch, 'shall we go inside or stand here freezing to death?' Her pretended coldness a shield against pity.

She had just finished reading Stefan Zweig's *Beware of Pity*: had noticed, as the young schoolmaster hurried towards her, that his glasses were misted over with rain, his hair streaming wet, his sodden jacket clinging abjectly to his thin shoulder-blades.

Obviously he possessed neither a mackintosh nor an

8

umbrella. 'Come on,' she said compassionately, 'before you catch your death of cold.'

What they had said to each other across a shiny-topped table, she now scarcely remembered; the coffee-machine was making such a hell of din. All she did clearly remember was the rain streaming down the windows, and treating him to spaghetti on toast, which he devoured like a starving prisoner in a Dumas novel.

She had taken him back to her flat afterwards to dry his wet shoes and jacket, and drink more coffee. Not fat, lazy Espresso in which the sugar never dissolved properly, but the powdered variety with Coffee-Mate. Tantamount to drinking coffee-flavoured milk-coloured hot water.

Busy in the kitchen she wondered if she was being sensible in taking pity on him. But he seemed so lost, like a child in need of praise and affection. She wondered why this was so, why the bad haircut and frayed shirt cuffs. Poverty. That didn't matter to her. Possibly he was spiritually rich.

Switching on the table lamp, lighting the ancient gas fire, she had suggested he take off his shoes and jacket and put them near the hearth to dry, speaking as dispassionately as an elder sister.

When she came through from the kitchen with the coffee mugs, she found him dipping into her small store of books.

'You obviously appreciate poetry,' he said, turning the pages of her *Oxford Book of English Verse*.

'Yes, but I can't afford to buy many books these days. It's a matter of borrowing from the public library.' She had felt awkward, self-conscious, defensive. She had never liked people making discoveries about her private likes and dislikes. Then she noticed that the jacket, which he had placed too near the fire, was beginning to singe, and rushed to the rescue. 'You'd better dry your hair,' she said, 'no sense in catching cold. Here.' She handed him a clean towel.

'You needn't worry about that,' he said stiffly, ignoring the towel, 'I never catch cold. I used to walk about for hours in the rain when . . . to get away from the house. I would go to what they call "The Top" and stand there looking

ing down at the valley. I liked the feel of the rain on my face, the loneliness; the freedom . . . Do you mind if I read to you?'

'No, of course not.'

He crossed to the fire and the warm pool of light from the table lamp, and knelt down on the worn hearthrug near her chair, holding the book so that the light fell on its pages, and began reading Arnold's 'Dover Beach'.

> Ah, love, let us be true
> To one another; for the world, which seems
> So various, so beautiful, so new,
> Hath really neither joy, nor love, nor light,
> Nor certitude, nor peace, nor help for pain . . .

And she had known that all these things he held to be true. He had a lovely voice, the Welsh inflection adding music to the words. Watching the play of light on his face, the shadowed eyes deeply sunk behind the cheap, steel-framed glasses, the mobile mouth which seemed incapable of laughter, she wondered why there was all this sadness, bitterness and pain in one so young, and noticed that his hands were trembling.

When he had finished reading, she laid her hand on his shoulder, deeply moved by the experience, wanting to say something kind and helpful and generous to make him realise that he was not alone. It was a touch meant to convey sympathy for his spiritual isolation, because she, too, was lonely.

When his lips met hers, she closed her eyes to her surroundings; the shabby, secondhand furniture in that rented flat whose windows overlooked Reading Gaol with its shades of Oscar Wilde, hearing the plopping of the gasfire, the pattering of the rain on the windows, the thumping of her heart as their mouths fastened and held for what seemed like an eternity.

Then, because she had never meant this to happen, deeply ashamed that she had allowed her emotions to overrule her commonsense, she rose quickly from her chair and asked him to leave.

'Why? Because I kissed you?' He had no idea why she was angry.

'It was all my fault,' she said as he laced up his shoes and put on his jacket. 'I'm sorry if I encouraged you to think . . .'

'That we might become friends? What a hope! I've never made friends. Now you know why.'

'I don't understand.'

'People make up their minds about me beforehand. There has always been this feeling of incompatibility. They laugh at me, feel sorry for me. Tell me, have you ever seen pictures of dancing bears?'

'It can't be as bad as all that.'

'How would you know?' He stood there with one hand on the doorknob. Her eyes filled suddenly with tears. He looked so – vulnerable.

'Strangely enough, I *do* know. I don't make friends easily myself.'

'That's why I asked you to have coffee with me. I thought it possible that we might have something in common. Well, I'd better be going.'

'Just a minute.' She could not bear to see him go like this. Not understanding. 'I've enjoyed your company – enjoyed the play-readings.'

'But you won't be going again. That's true, isn't it?'

'Of course I shall. Why ever not?'

'After this fiasco?' He laughed briefly; bitterly.

'Has it really been that?' She knew that she had mishandled the situation, had over-reacted in asking him to leave so suddenly: knew why she had done so – the kiss which had she returned too eagerly. That kiss which had touched hidden depths of awareness of her need to be loved which had seemed, at first, as a bridge flung across a chasm of loneliness, until she remembered the difference in their ages.

Then it had seemed a despicable thing to do, starting an

11

affair which could never come to fruition. A brief, untenable love affair was not the seamark of her utmost sail.

He said hoarsely, 'That play-reading group. The moment I walked into the library that night, my first instinct was to leave as quickly as possible. Then I saw you, and I decided to stay.'

'Why?'

'Because you seemed out of place, too.'

She smiled sadly. 'I felt out of place.'

'Then we started reading, and I knew . . .'

'Knew?'

'That I wanted to get to know you better. I saw you as a rose on a midden.'

She had to say it. 'I suppose you realise that I'm years older than you.'

He looked at her as though he scarcely knew what she was talking about.

'I wasn't trying to seduce you, if that's what you're afraid of. In any case, what does age matter?'

But age had mattered in the long run as, deep down, she had always sensed that it might.

They had left the bungalow early on the first day of the summer vacation to catch the mid-afternoon ferry from Dover to Boulogne; had stayed overnight in a typically French pension near Amiens. She remembered, acutely, the paved courtyard, creaking shutters, that pigeon-breasted patronne who wore a stiff bombazine dress and jabbered explosively in a hoarse patois, directing operations from behind a glassed-in reception desk adorned with a vase of drooping pink roses: the dining room redolent with the scent of garlic and Gauloises cigarettes, a tank full of trout awaiting execution.

After a restless night in a stuffy bedroom with creaking floorboards, a breakfast of croissants, *confiture* and strong French *café au lait* served in thick white cups, they had begun the exhausting drive south, via the dangerous Route Nationale, to Arles with its frying-pan arena, sizzling heat and overtones of cruelty, of death in the sun.

There she had become increasingly aware of her husband's restlessness, his scarcely concealed irritation with her halting French pronunciation, the way she dressed, and drove the car: her dislike of highly spiced cuisine, the way the heat affected her; her listlessness and lack of *joie-de-vivre*.

Nothing she had said or done had pleased him during the first fraught week of sightseeing. He hated her wearing flat comfortable sandals and dirndl skirts, the way her hair – which she was growing at the time to please him – kept on escaping from its army of combs and hairgrips, until she was drawn to the painful conclusion that she was being constantly compared to . . . another woman?

In desperation, she had made a stab at what she believed to be the truth. 'There's someone else, isn't there? You're having an affair?'

They were in the bedroom at the time. He declined to answer at first, had simply stared out of the window at the sun-drenched courtyard with its drooping olive trees and masses of flaming bougainvillea. Then, 'What if I am?' He kept his back to her, easing his shoulder-blades against the sweat patches beneath his armpits and above his waist where his shirt clung damply to his body.

'Who is she?' Her voice had sounded dull, flat, vaguely disinterested.

He laughed briefly. 'No one you know.'

A sudden memory of a white-faced woman wearing a handwoven kaftan came into her mind. 'On the contrary,' she said in a queer, empty voice, 'I do know who she is. The headmaster introduced us at the end-of-term party. Her name is Avril Messiter. Well . . .?'

He had turned then, his face a frowning mask of astonishment and disbelief. 'How the hell did you find out? Has someone been talking?'

'What are you going to do about her?'

'*Do?*' His face darkened. 'I'm not giving her up, if that's what you're driving at. She's different. Exciting. We are deeply in love.' He added, 'Christ, you and your bloody plebeian attitudes!'

Stung to anger, 'Don't start blaming me,' she flung at him. 'Why couldn't you have told me what was happening instead of lying, treating me as a half-wit!'

He paced the room flailing his arms, almost knocking over a small table containing a vase of marigolds. 'And have you sermonising, wringing your hands in despair, going into your tragic, wronged-wife act?'

'That simply isn't true, and you know it. When have I ever . . .?' But what was the use of talking? She turned away from his anger feeling as if she had been bludgeoned, stunned into a kind of frozen immobility, overwhelmed with her sense of failure as a woman, battling against the queer, ringing noise in her ears, the cold, sick feeling which threatened to engulf her – as if her body fluid was slowly seeping away, her veins filled with ice-water. Her face, glimpsed in a mirror, was the colour of wax. 'I don't want to see you get hurt, that's all. I know how important your job is, how hard you've studied to get where you are. For God's sake think twice before you risk throwing it all away!'

'Shit you!' He turned on her, spewing words in a torrent, crushing her beneath the onslaught of his guilt, saying that she had never fulfilled him physically, that he wished to God he had never married her.

Stumbling from the room, covering her ears with her hands, she hurried downstairs to the courtyard. Standing in the full glare of the noonday sun, she retched feebly at the overpowering smell of cooking from the hotel kitchen; the intermingled scents of garlic, herbs, red and green peppers and bubbling meat juices, an aroma she would hate for the rest of her life, as much as she disliked the taste of cheap red wine and strong, bitter coffee.

Now memories gave way to imagination. And this was what she feared most, these excursions into fantasy which stripped her of dignity and decency of spirit. Imagination fed the fire of her distress, the knowledge that somewhere, on the other side of the city, her husband and his mistress were together, making love. Possibly creating a child together.

In the darkness, there rose up before her a vivid mental picture of a naked woman with long dark hair and out-spread limbs laughing up into the face of her lover. A man, erect with passion, flickering his tongue between her pink, wet lips, fondling her eager upthrust breasts.

Sick with jealousy, tired out with all the watching and waiting, she wished that she might fall asleep: wake up in the morning to the sound of her mother's voice calling to her that breakfast was ready and she'd better hurry if she didn't want to be late for school.

But childhood, when one seemed invulnerable to pain or unhappiness, was long since over and done with.

Now the hands of the clock, luminous in the darkness, stood at twenty past two. Sooner or later he would come back to the bungalow, as he always came back – stealthily, switching off the car lights before entering the drive, not quite closing the garage doors, not knowing that she remained acutely aware of his movements however quiet, his tiptoeing footsteps in the hall, the turning on of a tap, the creak of the spare-room bed as lay down to sleep.

But tonight was different.

She got up, shivering. Tonight he had not bothered to switch off the car lights and their brilliance momentarily lit up the room, like a flash of lightning. She heard the slam of the garage doors, and stood there, hands clasped, waiting and listening, wondering why the sudden recklessness which had robbed him of the need to move silently, like a thief in the night.

Mouth dry with tension, she heard the turn of his key in the front door, a heavy footfall. Suddenly the door of her room was flung wide open and he stood there, swaying on his feet, his tall figure silhouetted against the faint light fil-tering into the passage from a yellow street lamp.

He began moving towards her, breathing heavily, the

pale wedge of his face resembling some grinning tribal mask in a Third World museum. She smelt the sour taint of whisky on his breath, and backed away, suddenly afraid, until her shoulders came into contact with the wall and she had no space left in which to manoeuvre.

'For God's sake, don't!' She spread out her hands on the wall in a crucifixion of panic, twisting her head this way and that as he moved closer, face stretched in that purposeful rictus smile. Then, as he stumbled slightly, she saw her chance and ran for the door. If only she could get to the bathroom she could lock herself in. But she had reckoned without his anger, his single-mindedness, his need of physical release.

Recovering his balance, he got to the door first and slammed it shut. Catching hold of her, he began kissing her, digging his teeth hard into her bottom lip, making her cry out with pain, ripping her nightdress, fumbling at her breasts with urgent, ungentle hands.

Tasting blood in her mouth, she beat her fists impotently against his chest.

'No!' She could scarcely speak. 'Please don't! Not like this! You don't know what you are doing!'

'Don't I?' The smile was gone now, replaced by something more chilling, a mindless, automaton expression linked to the icy precision of his hands as he forced her down on the bed and began his clinical exploration of her body. Then, head thrown back, mouth open, he began jerking like a marionette, an athlete doing a series of press-ups.

And she remembered, weeping, as his grunting climax came, the way love used to be in the time of his innocence.

CHAPTER 1

It was not simply the extra-marital relationship, the other woman, or the attendant misery and feeling of failure on the wife's part that broke down a marriage, Jess thought, staring out of the window of the rattling branchline train that was taking her to Bevensea Bay. It went far deeper than that. Trust, once broken, could not be easily restored. Picking up and mending the shattered pieces of one's life was not a rewarding occupation, she had discovered. The cracks still showed.

Avril's image – young, fecund, with broad, child-bearing hips, waist-length black hair cut in a semi-circular fringe above the intense gaze of dark brown eyes set in her curiously colourless, square-chinned face – inevitably clad in hand-woven kaftan; silver hand-beaten amulet nestling between shapely breasts, rose up occasionally to haunt her. Busy about the house, she would catch a sudden glimpse of her husband's mistress in a mirror, a windowpane, a bowl of washing-up water. She had even imagined seeing her get on to the train at the last station.

Jess wore her own hair long enough to scoop up with tortoiseshell combs. Douglas preferred long hair. Most men did in her experience. A throwback to the Stone Age, she supposed, when they dragged women along by their tresses.

She had started using colour rinses from Boots to hide the first sign of grey at the temples, so that her hair seemed tortoiseshell too, stippled mid-brown and dark blonde, the tendrils, straying from the combs, imparting a youthful, gamine look to her pale, heartshaped face with its fine-grained skin and clear blue-grey eyes. She wore glasses when she was alone in the house. Douglas disapproved of her wearing them in public.

A petite woman of forty-three, fragile in appearance, Jess was nevertheless surprisingly energetic and resilient. She'd had to be during eleven years of marriage to an unpredictable husband ten years younger than herself. Childless. At this moment, deeply troubled.

She had caught the early morning train from Manchester, and changed at York with its great curving glass-roofed station and bewildering plethora of glittering lines, had watched for a little while the strutting, wry-necked pigeons foraging for crumbs, before catching the 11.40 sprinter to Scarborough.

There she had drunk a cup of coffee, awaiting the arrival of the branchline train to Hull, gazing from the plate-glass windows of the buffet at the stained cream blocks of the Odeon cinema opposite, and the constant stream of taxis disgorging passengers in the station forecourt, feeling the hot sun on her face, wishing she had worn something cooler. But who could have envisaged that this mid-September day would be an echo of summertime, washed over with the brilliant colours of autumn with yet no feeling of decay or of the inevitable drawing in of the year?

She had never visited this corner of England before, and would not be here now, in this rackety diesel train, had it not been for a letter from a firm of solicitors – Mountjoy, Blair and Hoyle, of Bevensea Bay – requesting a meeting to discuss the terms of her Great-Aunt Jessica's will, indicating that she was the sole beneficiary. The firm had experienced some difficulty in tracing her present whereabouts, the letter concluded. It was signed, 'Yours faithfully, William Hoyle'·

Douglas had raised no objections to being left alone to fend for himself. Not that he would need to do much of that, Jess thought wryly. She had stocked the refrigerator with food that would require nothing more by way of preparation than insertion into a hot oven. Knowing Douglas, even switching on the oven might prove too onerous a domestic chore, and he would simply leave his school essays unmarked and stride down to the pub for a bar meal and a bottle of wine. Left to his own devices, might he not also contact Avril? The worm, once introduced into the apple, gnawed remorselessly at its soft, fleshy heart.

Her husband had made no secret of the fact that he coveted the inheritance. The house alone, he'd surmised,

18

would bring a bomb, and God alone knew what the 'old girl' had been worth apart from that.

But Jess, the compassioniate, could not regard the matter in quite the same light. She had never met her great-aunt, but there seemed something infinitely sad in the circumstances of an old lady living out her days in solitary splendour, nor did she relish the thought of putting up for sale the personal effects of the woman who had hovered ghostlike, shadowy and vaguely unreal on the periphery of the Tidey family for as far back as she could remember; and who had never, for some unfathomable reason, even acknowledged the existence of that family.

And yet at some stage, her great-aunt must have carefully considered the matter of her last will and testament. Had she felt secretly pleased that somewhere existed a child who bore her name? Perhaps William Hoyle would be able to shine some light on the mystery.

The train had been bucketing along for some thirty minutes, stopping at every tiny station along the way — more like a tram than a train, Jess thought, watching passengers board and dismount, most of whom were women humping shopping bags.

Leaning back in her vandalised seat with foam rubber entrails oozing messily from the knife wounds, she closed her eyes against the brilliant glare of the sun, feeling the prickle of heat on her neck from the collar of her neatly tailored wool blouse, and the moistness of a few stray wisps of hair escaping from their imprisoning combs.

She must have fallen asleep, but opened her eyes with a start when the driver sounded a particularly loud and strident warning note at an unmanned level-crossing, seeing not the former tame vista of fields with placidly munching cows and skittering horses, but a great expanse of azure sea spreading to a vast, seemingly endless horizon, a seascape underlined with green-topped cliffs falling away to unseen sand, and seagulls cutting the blue fabric of the sky with white scissor wings. In that instant she realised that she hadn't actually *noticed* anything for a very long time.

Now, as the train jogged more slowly along the track, she could see the beginnings of a town. First a wide esplanade with grey railings fronting a huddle of beach chalets. Next came the rear view of tall, elegant Victorian villas facing the promenade; church spires probing the sky; then the inevitable rash of modern houses and bungalows with washing hung out to dry in flower-filled gardens, soon to be swallowed up by a conglomeration of waste ground, coalyards, and the industrial buildings endemic to most railway sidings.

As the train juddered to a halt and a laconic porter came along shouting, 'Bevensea Bay, Bevensea Bay,' Jess rose hurriedly to her feet, put on her tweed jacket, hauled her case from the rack, and stepped on to the platform.

First she must find somewhere to stay. Not that she envisaged much difficulty about that in an end of season holiday town where every hotel and boarding house displayed Vacancy notices tucked discreetly behind white net curtains.

Hiring a taxi from the station rank, she asked the driver to drop her on the seafront, and walked along from there, glancing up at the Victorian villas she had seen from the train, mentally rejecting those which had been 'tarted up' and given exotic foreign names, striped bonnet blinds and neon signs, whose front gardens had been bulldozed to provide parking space, or white-painted tables and chairs.

Eventually she chose a hotel sensibly named 'Sea View' with plain net curtains to its bay windows and late-flowering rose bushes in well-tended plots, and was shown to a room overlooking the promenade, a spacious room with matching curtains and bedcover, spotlessly clean towels and, blissfully, plenty of hot water.

Washing her hands, she caught sight of her face in the mirror over the basin and noticed that tiny lines were beginning to form on her top lip. She thought, absurdly, that were it not for her lips her skin might start to fray, like soft pink linen, from the curving buttonhole of her mouth.

Drying her hands, she walked over to the window and stood for a little while looking out to sea, unaccustomed to this unfamiliar sense of freedom, safely distanced from the semi-detached bungalow on the outskirts of Manchester where she lived, day in, day out, with a husband who no longer loved her. Disturbingly the thought came that Douglas had never really loved her, that she had simply been necessary to him in the early days of their relationship as a mother figure, a provider, a listener, a prop to his ego. And she had needed someone to care for.

She entered Mountjoy, Blair and Hoyle's offices in Regent Street with the feeling that she had somehow stepped from the twentieth into the nineteenth century.

'I have a five o'clock appointment with Mr Hoyle,' she told the girl behind the reception desk. 'My name is Jessica Carmichael.'

'Oh yes, Mr Hoyle is expecting you. Second door to the left on the first landing.'

Jess liked the feel of the slender, curving banister beneath her hand, the high Georgian window on the half-landing, the polished oak panelling.

'Mrs Carmichael. This is a great pleasure, I assure you.'

Mr Hoyle was tall, immaculately dressed in a lightweight grey pinstripe suit with a crisp white handkerchief correctly arranged in the breastpocket. His eyes were shrewd but kindly behind a pair of half-moon spectacles. 'Please sit down.' He smiled sympathetically. 'May I say how sorry we were to lose Miss Tidey. One of the "old school". A truly remarkable lady.'

'Thank you, Mr Hoyle.'

'Of course, you never met her.' Hoyle coughed slightly and adjusted his spectacles. 'Er – would you care for some tea? We have ours at four o'clock, but my receptionist could easily . . .'

'No, thanks, I had a cup at the hotel.'

'Ah well, down to business.'

Watching his delicate fingers shuffling through a sheaf of

21

papers on his desk, Jess gained a sudden but unmistakable impression that all was not well.

'Naturally you are anxious to learn exactly what your inheritance entails, to view the property and so forth.' Hoyle glanced up at her. 'May I show you round the house tomorrow at, say, ten o'clock?'

'Yes, that sounds fine.' Jess waited expectantly.

'Hmm, what I have to say now concerns Miss Tidey's decline in fortune over a considerable period. Things might have been different had not your grandfather, Miss Jessica's brother, been killed in the Great War. As the elder son, he would have inherited the chain of wine merchants' shops his father had established in York, Ripon, Leeds and Scarborough – thus ensuring the family income. Unfortunately, Donald Tidey's untimely death – and the impossibility the war imposed upon the continuation of supplies of wine from the continent, forced the closure of all but the Leeds shop which your great-grandfather, Joshua Tidey, managed to keep going until after the war.'

Hoyle sighed reflectively. 'I can only surmise that the death of his elder son and the decision of the younger son, Franklyn, to emigrate to America after the Armistice was declared, coloured your great-grandfather's thinking to the extent that he eventually sold that one remaining shop to a well-established brewery.'

'Yes, I gleaned something of the family history from my grandmother, Donald's widow,' Jess said. 'As you probably know, she went back to Reading after the war. My father would have been about three years old at the time.'

'Quite so,' Hoyle nodded.

'My brother and I were born in Reading,' Jess explained. 'My parents, Stephen and I, lived with Grandmother Tidey until her death just before the outbreak of the last war. She left the house to my father.'

'So I understand.' Hoyle re-adjusted his spectacles. 'We knew that address from our records, and assumed that you still lived there – hence the delay in finding you.'

'I moved away shortly after my mother died, when my

father remarried,' Jess said slowly, remembering the trauma of her removal from the old house she had loved as a child. 'When my father died, I discovered that he had willed the house to my stepmother.'

'I see.' Hoyle hesitated momentarily. 'Of course,' he continued, 'Joshua Tidey had invested shrewdly and built a fine house here in Bevensea. After his death, however, those investments dwindled considerably. His wife had pre-deceased him, and so the family home – Laurel Villa – became the sole property of your great-aunt.'

'Who was left with the fine house, and little else besides?' Jess raised an enquiring eyebrow.

'Exactly.' Hoyle seemed relieved that she had grasped the situation so quickly.

'But surely – I mean how did my great-aunt manage to survive without a sizeable income?'

'There was some money, of course, albeit a trickle. Enough to keep body and soul together.' Hoyle sighed deeply. 'The truth is, Jessica Tidey lived in comparative poverty during her latter days. But never at any time would she consider selling her home or any of its contents. She was a very proud, very stubborn old lady.'

'So what you are really saying is that my inheritance amounts to a run-down Victorian villa, and the monies from my great-grandfather's investments which are worth almost nothing these days?'

Hoyle said uncomfortably, 'Not even the latter, I'm afraid. The monies from those investments dried up at source five years ago.'

'And if I decide to sell the house and its contents, how much do you think they'll be worth?' Jess bit her lip. 'I'm sorry, Mr Hoyle, I'm not being mercenary, I assure you. Whatever they bring will come as a bonus to me. I said if I "decide" to sell, but that was an ambiguity, a nonsense really. I have no other choice.'

'That is difficult to say. The house is in a poor state of repair. There is no electricity laid on, although I did prevail upon Miss Tidey to have a telephone installed, for obvious reasons. But you will see for yourself.'

Jess stood up to leave. 'Until tomorrow then. I'll be here at ten o'clock sharp.'

'Thank you, my dear.' Hoyle shook hands with her, obviously relieved that the interview was over. 'I'm so sorry about those investments.'

'You needn't be.' Jess smiled. 'It isn't your fault that the well ran dry. I'm simply touched and grateful that my great-aunt remembered me at all. My father would have been so delighted.'

Hoyle walked with her to the door. 'Have you found a decent place to stay?'

'Yes, the Sea View hotel on the esplanade.' She glanced at her watch. 'Dinner's at 6.30. I'll just have time to walk. The fresh air will do me good, give me an appetite for the roast chicken I noticed on the menu for this evening.'

'You are very like your great-aunt, you know,' Mr Hoyle said unexpectedly. 'I can pay you no greater compliment. She was a charming lady.'

Jess walked slowly along the promenade. The sun had gone down in glory, a great blazing ball of light which set fire to the sea. At the same time, the moon had appeared as a pale ghost amid a welter of diffused clouds, a phenomenon she had never seen – or possibly never noticed before – so that looking at the rapidly descending sun and the slowly ascending moon sharing the same sky, she thought that there was really only this one day which came round again and again in different guises, regulated by different tides and unknown forces, but just this one day governed by the sun, this one night softened by the gentleness of the moon.

Leaning her elbows on the railings, she remembered how, throughout the trauma of the other woman, she had thought of gentle things to ease the pain, and wondered, watching the play of light on the water, if other middle-aged women, faced with a similar situation, did the same thing. If they too conjured up oases of the mind in which to seek refuge. The trouble was, there were so few avenues of escape left open: nowhere to go, except in dreams.

The Victorians had a way of building houses which precluded the possibility of their falling down unaided. It would take a bomb, a bulldozer, or an Act of God to bring down all those lovingly cemented bricks and sturdily erected chimneystacks, Jess thought, as the car bowled up the drive.

Laurel Villa, built on a wooded promontory overlooking Bevensea Bay, must have withstood a century of buffeting by North Sea gales, almost forty years of neglect, and yet it had survived as a testimonial to a lost generation of master craftsmen.

Glancing up at it, Jess was struck by its size and the sheer strength of its russet brick walls. Two jutting bay windows flanked the solid stone steps leading to the massive, brass-letterboxed front door; steps guarded by stone lions, couchant, teeth bared, fangs slightly weathered.

The façade had been banded with lighter bricks set diagonally, reminding her of cream stitchery on a Victorian sampler. This curious architectural embellishment underlined the three lace-curtained first-floor bay windows, above which were set a series of sash windows, similarly shrouded in discoloured Nottingham lace and drawn Venetian blinds with dangling ivory acorns. Above these, half hidden from view behind a stone parapet running the length of the house, appeared the points of the attic dormers.

Great swathes of rustling ivy had thrown long tentacles across the brickwork in places – a thick, dark-green mantle with rope-like stems, whose leaves whorled upwards to the roof.

Miss Tidey, in her declining years, bedevilled by lack of money, must have seen with anguish the broken panes in the conservatory abutting the south wall of the house. Or perhaps it had been vandalised since her death just over a month ago. Unoccupied houses provided tempting targets for the slings and arrows of outrageous juvenile delinquents, Jess realised. And what must her great-aunt have thought of the fine crop of brambles overhanging the steps to the front door, the spotted laurel bushes being slowly strangled by a sea of convolvulus, the branches of a giant elm tree reaching out to touch the windows?

And this was her inheritance, this forbidding relic of a bygone age. And yet, Jess thought, picking her way past the brambles, given a choice at this moment, she would have elected to make her entrance into the world as the cossetted daughter of a wealthy Victorian family, knowing exactly what would be expected of her in any given circumstance: attending church twice on Sundays, wearing a beaver bonnet tied with moire ribbons; kneeling at prayer, voluminous skirts discreetly covering her ankles; not having to think for herself or make her own decisions.

She swore softly under her breath as her nylons caught on a briar. Brambles to her were synonymous with berry-picking expeditions in Berkshire in the far off, happy days of childhood; laughter, and 'purple-stained mouth'; the feel of a warm leather car seat sticking to her tender behind, the curious outdoor taste of egg and meat-paste sandwiches; quiet lanes and cool, dark woods.

She knew, of course, exactly what ailed her. Faced with an uncertain, loveless future, it would be comforting to slip back into a past where everything seemed tidily rounded off, complete, safely distanced from the often unbearable present. Yet what proof had she that Victorian women were less vulnerable to hurt than their modern counterparts? The Brontë sisters, for instance, had endured more than their fair share of suffering. Perhaps it was simply that the passage of time imbued the past with a spurious glamour, softening harsh reality to the gentleness of a faded sepia daguerrotype.

Glancing over her shoulder, she saw that Mr Hoyle had managed to negotiate the steps without damaging his pinstripe trousers.

'Well, here we are.' His voice held a note of forced cheerfulness. 'Ah, let me see. Yes, here are the keys.'

A trickle of nervous excitement ran down Jess's spine as she stepped across the threshold into a wide dusty vestibule with a tiled floor and stained-glass lights, beyond which appeared double glass-knobbed doors, similarly church-like in concept, with rich blue, red and green panels depicting St Martin offering his cloak to a beggar amid a flurry of stylised Victorian foliage.

Doors closed, the subject matter of the panels was strikingly apparent – opened, St Martin and the beggar parted company. Jess laughed. 'Heavens! I had no idea it would be so – biblical.'

'Hm, one does tend to look round for the offertory-box,' Hoyle remarked drily, 'but then, the house was built to create the grand impression. The Victorians did not believe in hiding their stained-glass lights under a bushel.' He smiled modestly at the mild witticism, and stood aside to let Jess enter, watching the expression on her face with some amusement.

'Oh!' The exclamation was uttered involuntarily at the sheer extravagance of the hall; the broad, red-carpeted staircase rising to a wide upper landing, the fretted arches supported by a lavishly carved central pier.

And yet despite the overall impression of grandeur, signs of neglect were apparent everywhere. The crimson carpet and the red flock wallpaper were faded and dusty, the arches draped with cobwebs, the red velvet curtains at the landing window lighting the turn of the stairs, hanging like tattered battle honours in some ancient cathedral.

In the drawing room, blue velvet curtains, heavily lined and pelmeted, were drawn against the intrusive eyes of the outside world.

Mr Hoyle told her, as he manoeuvred past the furniture to pull the cords, that a man, a part-time caretaker, had been hired by his firm to sleep in the house since the death of his client – a necessary precaution in view of the valuable contents. The same man, Alfred Cornwell, a retired policeman, also made regular daytime visits to keep an eye on the place.

Hoyle sneezed slightly as the curtains glided back to admit the light of day, and carefully dusted his hands with his pocket handkerchief.

Inhaling the musty fragrance of the room, Jess's eyes lingered on its focal point – the fireplace – around which was grouped a velvet-covered sofa and armchairs. A brass fender enclosed the flower-tiled hearth. Above it rose a towering overmantel decked with Goss china ornaments.

Slightly bewildered, she thought she had never seen a room so crowded with bric-à-brac, occasional tables, domed glass cases of stuffed birds and artificial flowers.

Even so, it was a marvellous room, high-ceilinged, with foot-deep skirting boards. The bay window, set within the curve of an ornate arch, overlooked the shrubbery and the driveway with its double iron gates. Cold, as might be expected: smelling faintly of mildew. A perfect setting for Patrick Hamilton's *Gaslight*, Jess thought, examining the photographs on the massive mahogany sideboard.

'Is this my great-grandfather?' she asked.

'No, that is Franklyn Tidey, Joshua's younger son, who emigrated to America after the Great War.'

'What became of him?'

'He went, initially, to Chicago. Afterwards – who knows?'

'You mean – he didn't keep in touch with his family?'

'I believe that he wrote, occasionally, to his mother. Then the letters ceased to arrive: simply – petered out.'

'I see.' Jess turned her attention to another photograph, that of a fresh-faced young man in a captain's uniform. 'I've seen this before,' she said quietly. 'My grandmother used to show it to me – or one just like it. She never really came to terms with my grandfather's death. I wonder if that is why she moved away from here when she knew he'd been killed.'

'Possibly,' Hoyle said gently, rather wistfully. 'One can only guess the heartbreak of that war, the loss of so many fine, promising young men.'

28

'He and Franklyn were very much alike.' A feeling of tenderness for these lost relations of hers touched Jess's susceptible heart. She blinked rapidly. 'And who is this?'

'Your great-grandmother, Clarice Tidey. The child in her arms is your great-aunt as a baby. And this is Jessica Tidey as a girl.'

Holding the photograph, Jess saw a face of no great beauty but immense character.

Here was a serious face with a slightly aquiline nose above a sensitive mouth. A face with a pointed chin held high and proud above a boned lace collar. The eyes were undoubtedly the best feature – questioning eyes beneath strongly marked yet tapering brows.

The cheek bones were high; cheeks slightly hollow. Two swathes of hair were drawn back from a centre parting, the forehead embellished with a cluster of formally arranged pincurls.

Jess set down the photograph, making no comment. Then, 'Which one is my great-grandfather?' she enquired.

Hoyle said, uneasily, 'I'm afraid there are no photographs of Joshua Tidey anywhere in the house.'

'That's odd, isn't it?' She glanced up at Hoyle, wrinkling her forehead. 'The man who built the house?'

'Yes, it is rather. But Miss Tidey was always evasive about her father. I gathered there was no love lost between them, and I did not pursue the matter.' Hoyle shrugged his shoulders and sighed. 'Your great-aunt was, in present-day parlance, a very "private" person. Moreover, she possessed a sharp temper on occasions.' He smiled ruefully at some personal recollection. 'I'm sorry I can't be more helpful.' He hemmed drily. 'Perhaps you would care to look at the dining-room?'

This room overlooked the conservatory and must have been pleasant enough in the old days, Jess supposed, when the annexe, with its glass-panelled connecting door, would have been filled with flowering plants and, possibly, garden furniture. But those days were long gone. Now a vast network of withered stems, resembling the web of some great bloodsucking spider, curtained the cracked and broken panes, imparting a stygian gloom which made her shudder slightly. The long, central table, fashioned from solid mahogany, would have seated a dozen people, possibly more at a pinch.

Counting the chairs arranged around the lack-lustre surface, she thought, inconsequentially, of the Last Supper: Christ and His disciples. Thirteen chairs in all. Twelve disciples and one master. The 'master' the man who would have taken his rightful place at the head of the table as the undisputed head of the household. Her great-grandfather, Joshua Tidey.

The walls were hung with oil paintings in heavy gilt frames; the long marble-topped side-table still bore its adornment of tarnished dining-room silver – a towering epergne, branched candelabrum, and chased-silver water-jugs.

A pendanted gasolier hung massively from a decorative ceiling rosette. The carpet was of Persian design, its once richly glowing colours darkened now with age and neglect.

'The conservatory should have been taken down years ago,' Mr Hoyle remarked, 'although it was a feature of the house in your great-grandmother's time, I believe. Miss Tidey once told me that her mother kept singing birds there, of a tropical variety, that it was she who planted the grapevines. Apparently the grapes were quite good.' He glanced distastefully at the piles of rubbish – broken plantpots, rotting seed boxes and rusted garden implements – littering the tiled floor.

'Oh, but that would be terribly sad – if the conservatory were demolished. It could still be a feature of the house if it were cleared out and repaired.' Poor house, she thought wistfully, rather like an old person dying of neglect.

The realization that all this – these solidly cemented bricks enclosing, encompassing the museum-like display of Victoriana – now belonged to her, had not so far sunk in. She felt like a tourist being shown round a folk museum by an efficient curator.

'This was your great-grandfather's personal preserve,' Hoyle led the way across the crimson carpeted hall, 'his study-cum-library. Nothing has been changed since his death. Some of the books are, I believe, first editions, worth a good deal of money.'

Jess crossed over to the vast mahogany desk near the bay window. Everything upon that damp-blotched surface – silver inkstand, leather-bound blotter, letter-opener in the shape of a dagger – gave the impression of power, of purpose; a brooding quality which had remained trapped within those four walls was an almost tangible presence; the essence of the shrewd and wealthy businessman who had been her great-grandfather, whose books were locked away in the towering glass-fronted cases reaching up to the heavily embossed ceiling.

It was not a comfortable room, she decided, despite the richness of its furnishings, the solid leather armchairs flanking the mottled marble fireplace, the gilt-framed sporting prints, and heavy crimson curtains. Unaccountably depressed by the sheer weight of the library and its trappings, she closed the door with a sense of relief to be out of it.

Hoyle, who evidently shared her dislike of the room, said gently, 'I think you will find this more to your taste. This was your great-grandmother's sanctum – incidentally your great-aunt's favourite retreat. She spent much of her time here before she became bed-ridden.'

'Ah yes.' Jess smiled. 'This feels lived in.'

The tentacles of power had not invaded this small, neat parlour with its rosewood furniture. There was a feeling of peace here, of quiet industry: a workbox on the table, pink and white china in a glass-fronted cupboard, a tarnished silver tea-kettle on the sideboard, samplers on the walls, and pale, delicate watercolours.

'The ladies of the parish met here, in the old days, to sew and knit for the poor families of Bevensea,' Hoyle said quietly. 'Your great-grandmother did a great deal of good work for charity, I believe.' He wrinkled his forehead apologetically. 'Now for the kitchen quarters. I'd better warn you, they're in a sorry state of repair.'

Jess stared round in dismay. The walls were flaking: spotted like leprosy. There was a huge stone sink with sagging draining-boards. A greasy alcove harboured an enormous kitchen range, rusted now with age and neglect. The central wooden table was littered with a strange variety of domestic objects – a broken basket, copper jelly-moulds, a china hen sitting on an empty nest. A built-in dresser contained the household china. Mammoth willow-pattern meat-dishes, tureens and gravy-boats bore silent witness to those days when the place would have been a hive of activity; the cook hauling tins of roast meat from the oven; some poor drudge doing the washing up.

Kitchen implements – pans, colanders, sieves, and copper skillets – were stacked upon a series of open shelves near the sink. The windows were curtainless, barred halfway on the outside, like a prison.

A passage led to what must have been the butler's pantry, the coal-store, wash-house, and possibly the housekeeper's room, chock-a-block now with sagging chairs and bamboo tables.

The thought of her great-aunt moving feebly down the passage, attempting to bring in scuttles of coal from the freezing cold fuel-store, filled Jess with a burning sense of indignation, laced with pity.

'How my great-aunt managed to cope by herself in this – this mausoleum, I cannot imagine,' she flared. 'Presumably she had a doctor. What was he thinking about in allowing a woman of her age to remain here alone?'

'A district nurse came in daily to wash her and give her the necessary injections.'

'But what about food?'

'Mrs Cornwell, the caretaker's wife, came in two or three times a day to make sure she had all she wanted. She would heat soup for her, make cocoa, or cook her an omelette . . .'

'In *this* kitchen! My God, it's a wonder she didn't die of ptomaine poisoning! Why didn't the doctor have her admitted to hospital or a nursing home?'

'He did of course suggest that, but Miss Tidey wouldn't hear of it. Dr Sanger judged, quite rightly in my opinion, that the old lady would have pined away in a strange environment.' Hoyle frowned. 'To put it more bluntly, Miss Tidey would have been totally out of her element in the geriatric unit of the local hospital. She was, as I have tried to explain, a proud, stubborn, self-willed lady, with all her faculties. On the other hand, she lacked the resources necessary for accommodation in a private nursing home.'

'She could have sold a few of those first editions!' Jess bit her lip. 'I'm sorry, I didn't mean to say that. After all, what right have I to criticise? I who did nothing at all to help her.'

They walked slowly up the wide, dusty staircase. 'This was Miss Tidey's room,' Hoyle said gently, understanding her distress. 'She died quite peacefully in her sleep, and she was not alone at the time. Dr Sanger, the district nurse and Mrs Cornwell were with her.'

'*I* should have been with her. I would have been if I had known, if I had realised . . .'

Hoyle shook his head. 'You don't understand, my dear. She would not have wanted that. Even if you had come, I doubt if she would have seen you. As you know, Miss Tidey severed connections with her family a long time ago.'

'Yes, but *why*? If she had only known, only realised my father's concern that she never replied to any of his letters!' Frowning, searching her memory, Jess said haltingly, 'It's all so strange, so puzzling. Looking back, my grandmother, Donald's widow, would never speak of her. Whenever I asked questions about Great-Aunt Jessica, a queer, closed look came over her face, and she would change the subject. I was only a child at the time, but children are quick to notice. I gained the distinct impression that asking questions about my great-aunt was strictly taboo. And yet she left me – all this. To be honest with you, Mr Hoyle, I wish she hadn't.'

She stared out of the window at the great elm tree,

33

absent-mindedly noticing the way the warm September sunlight filtered through its branches; the crochet-work design dappling the flaccid leaves of the laurel bushes in the garden below.

'Tell me truthfully, Mr Hoyle,' she said, turning to face him, 'was my great-aunt – mad?'

A smile touched the lawyer's lips. 'Far from it. A little eccentric perhaps. But – mad? No! My own guess is that she came to the conclusion, during the last months of her life, that she did not want strangers, outsiders, meddling with her personal belongings after she was dead.'

'And yet *I* was a stranger to her,' Jess reminded him.

Jess watched, from the window, Mr Hoyle picking his way past the brambles, hurrying down the steps to his car, on his way to another appointment. Or perhaps he had simply conjured up an excuse to leave her alone in the house, to wander at will through its neglected rooms.

When he was gone, she turned to look at the high, valanced bed in which a lonely old woman had died, remembering a photograph she had once seen, in a magazine, of Queen Victoria, in death, lying as tiny and shrivelled as a mummified child, beneath a drift of white veiling.

Very slowly, she walked round the room, lightly brushing the furniture with her fingertips.

Opening a drawer of the rosewood dressing-table, she felt suddenly like a voyeuse, an interloper, seeing there the neatly folded undergarments which had clothed the flesh of a woman of a different age, a different generation.

Everything in the house now officially belonged to her, and yet she experienced a curious reluctance to pry. Even so, all these clothes would have to be gone through sooner or later, got rid of, packed in boxes and despatched to various charities. The enormity of the task seemed suddenly daunting.

What an incredible house it was to be sure. Apart from her great-aunt's room on the first landing, there were two others of equal size and importance, one of which had surely belonged to Joshua Tidey; filled with towering furniture – a monolithic wardrobe with mirrored doors, an enormous bed, and several chests of drawers on which were set out leather stud and collar boxes, various rather ugly ornaments, and ivory-backed hair-and clothesbrushes. Glancing in the wardrobe, she saw that it contained rails of suits and overcoats of the finest quality. All were immaculately tailored, and reeked of mothballs.

Next to Joshua's, its window overlooking the rear garden and the stable-block, was a more feminine, much prettier room, filled with furniture of a lighter wood – beech or maple – Jess could not decide which, but she knew that this had been her great-grandmother's room, that every item had been chosen with considerable care.

The dressing table was set out with a rose-patterned china tray and matching accessories – powder bowls, candlesticks, and ring-holders.

The mantelpiece, of lightly-veined white marble, was crowded with silver-framed photographs, a pair of alabaster vases, and two white china swans. Above the mantel hung a framed watercolour of the rear garden as Clarice Tidey would have seen it from the window, as it must have looked in her time – with smooth green lawns and well-tended borders filled with lupins, delphinium, lavender, and crimson peonies – not rank with overgrown nettles and dog-roses.

A cretonne-covered armchair stood near the fireplace with its high brass fireguard. Another chair, such as a nursing mother might use, had been placed near the pinkcurtained window. This was a delicately balanced room, Jess thought, smoothing the bedcover, a room which had housed a gentle spirit.

Further along the landing was a bathroom, grandiosely appointed, the bath mounted on claw feet, the windows of stained and frosted glass.

On the upper landing was a similar bathroom and three more sizeable bedrooms, all of which were sparsely furnished and shrouded in dust sheets, as if their occupants had long since gone away. And yes, Jess thought, with a tug of pity, the occupants of two of these rooms, Donald and Franklyn Tidey, *had* gone away, never to return.

She came upon the servants' staircase behind a green baize door near the bathroom, and wondered what life had been like in those affluent days when servants, as cheap and plentiful as ripe blackberries, scurried about the house lighting fires, dusting and polishing, carrying cans of hot water to the bedrooms, cooking the food, waiting at table.

Had they, at times, bitterly resented the difference between their own and their masters' standard of living; their box-like rooms beneath the slates, narrow iron fireplaces, horse-hair mattresses, cracked ewers and basins? The chill of drudgery seemed still to pervade these servants' quarters with their cheap, varnished furniture and strips of haircord carpet.

In one of the rooms she noticed a thick black book on a bamboo table. Picking it up, she read on the fly-leaf: 'Annie Petch, her Bible. From Mam and Dad, January 1st 1890'. Poor Annie Petch, whoever she was.

Walking downstairs, hand trailing on the mahogany banister, Jess wondered who would buy such a barn of a place, and what they would make of it – a country club, a hotel, a school?

Deep in thought, she went out by the front entrance, past the trailing fronds of bramble, and walked towards the stable-block with its wide arched entrance set in a high brick wall. The yard was cobbled. Just inside the arch stood a rusted drinking-trough dedicated to 'The Glory of God for His Dumb Animals'.

A flight of stone steps led to an apartment over the stables where, presumably, the groom had once lived. But the door was securely locked and, on the bunch Mr Hoyle had given her, she could not find a key to fit.

The stables, however, were accessible, and she entered that world of diffused sunlight, stout oak beams, stalls and mouldering mangers, with some trepidation, afraid of mice – or worse. But nothing stirred in the musty building apart from the dust motes dancing in the shafts of light from the high, barred windows.

She felt suddenly at peace here, safe and secure, as if this place with its faint but unmistakable odours of linseed-oil and leather, hay and horseflesh, had wrapped a comforting cloak about her shoulders. An oasis of the mind, she thought. There had been nowhere, no one to turn to for comfort during the past twelve months.

She had promised Mr Hoyle that she would come to his office at four o'clock to discuss the sale of the property. This was Tuesday. She had also promised Douglas that she would return home on Saturday in time to see to the weekend shopping.

Douglas!

This one day which came round again and again, governed by the one sun which, mysteriously, governed time itself – and all the long, empty days of one's life, shorn of love. The seasons changed, of course. Spring turned into summer, autumn to winter – and people changed too; grew older, more afraid of life. And life, once lost, would never come again. Time. This one day. This one life. Her life, moving inexorably away from her, day by day, bereft of happiness.

'Milk or lemon?' Mr Hoyle asked pleasantly.

'Milk, please,' she replied.

'Biscuit?'

'No, thank you.'

'About the house. We usually deal with Grant and Son, the auctioneers. A trustworthy firm.'

'Yes, I'm sure they are.'

Jess smiled as Mr Hoyle handed her a cup of tea. The cup, she noticed, was Crown Derby, patterned in delicate shades of blue and orange. Her glance strayed to the windows. Regent Street, now a pedestrian thoroughfare, had become the province of the town's elite professional businessmen: lawyers, dentists, doctors, photographers, whose names had been stencilled in gold lettering on

Georgian windowpanes. Her mind drifted. The room was warm; sunlight slanted on to the desk behind which Mr Hoyle was seated.

'Mrs Carmichael . . .'

'I'm sorry, Mr Hoyle. You were saying?'

'I asked how long you intend staying in Bevensea.'

'Until Saturday. My husband expects me home then.'

'Ah yes, of course.' Mr Hoyle coughed discreetly. 'A pity he could not have come with you.'

Jess overcame a sudden desire to blurt out the truth. Douglas was not interested in the house apart from its value at auction. She, on the other hand, had fallen under the spell of its faded grandeur.

Looking out of the window just now, her thoughts had strayed from the Georgian to the Victorian era, to all those people who had gone before her, whose blood flowed through her veins too. Her shrewd and prosperous great-grandfather, Joshua Tidey, his gentle wife, Clarice, who had loved singing birds, and sewn garments for the poor. Her grandfather, Donald, who had married before going off to the war, and left a pregnant widow to mourn his passing. Her great-uncle Franklyn, who had emigrated to America to make a new life, and had been swallowed by that vast, amorphous country., Her great-aunt Jessica, who had lived and died in poverty rather than part with her inheritance of bricks and mortar, tarnished silver, and poignant memories.

She set down her cup and saucer, feeling that some explanation was necessary. 'My husband couldn't have come with me anyway. He's a teacher. The autumn term has just begun.'

'I see.' Hoyle nodded thoughtfully – so thoughtfully that Jess wondered if he had guessed the truth, if something in her voice or manner had betrayed the fact that her marriage bore the hallmark of failure.

Easing her shoulders slightly, relieving the tension in her neck muscles, she remembered that she had rung Douglas three times last night – at eight o'clock, ten, and again at well past midnight. There had been no reply.

'Since your time here is somewhat limited,' Hoyle continued, 'it might be advisable to begin sorting through some of Miss Tidey's more personal belongings. There may be certain items that you would feel reluctant to sell.'

'The truth is, I feel reluctant to sell anything at all,' Jess admitted. 'It seems like a – betrayal. You understand?'

'Only too well, my dear.' William Hoyle thought how unhappy she looked, and wondered why.

'Of course I must be practical.' Jess spoke hesitantly. 'I just wondered – would it be possible for me to stay at the house? It seems a waste of precious time ferrying backwards and forwards to the hotel.'

'What a splendid idea!' Hoyle beamed at her. 'Of course, arrangements will have to be made. A bed aired for you. Which room would you occupy?'

'Oh, that's easily decided. My great-grandmother's room.'

'Quite so.' Hoyle caught something of her inner excitement. Miss Tidey would have approved of this great-niece of hers. This quiet, charming woman with her candid blue eyes and delicate bone structure. What a pity it seemed, in retrospect, an old woman's stubborn refusal to acknowledge that she was lonely and frightened. Yes, frightened. He had known that towards the end of her life.

There were so many imponderables. Why, for instance, had Mrs Carmichael seemed so tense at the mention of her husband, so guarded and defensive?

Forty years in the legal profession had imbued William Hoyle with a deep insight into human nature, had taught him the value of discretion, of patience, the establishment of trust between himself and his clients.

'I will contact Alfred Cornwell immediately.' He made a note on his desk-pad, 'ask him to light fires; air the rooms . . .'

'Alfred Cornwell? Oh, of course, the ex-policeman you mentioned, who has been sleeping at the house since my great-aunt died.'

'Ah, yes – in a sleeping bag on the drawing-room sofa, but that would be scarcely fitting in your case.' Mr Hoyle glanced whimsically over his spectacles, 'No, no, we must make quite sure that you are comfortable. After all, m'dear, it *is* your house.'

Her house. Jess dwelt lingeringly on the concept of ownership; pride in her family, her deep, inexplicable links with the past which had touched her almost to tears in those silent dusty rooms where they had lived, moved, and had their being. She, who had owned nothing of value in her life before, wanted to come close to the house and its ghosts, however fleetingly, before it was sold to the highest bidder.

'If there is anything at all I can do to help you, please don't hesitate to ask.'

Jess rose to her feet. 'Thank you. You have been more than kind and helpful as it is.'

'Ah, one more thing. You'll need some tea-chests.' He made another note on his desk-pad. 'I'll contact Grant at once; ask his men to deliver them first thing in the morning.' He smiled. 'Well, good luck, my dear. Oh, by the way, have you a hot-water bottle?'

Jess laughed. 'No, but I'll buy one on my way to the hotel.' On an impulse, standing on tiptoe she kissed Mr Hoyle warmly on the cheek. 'Goodbye, and again, thank you.'

This was a pleasant town, she decided, with its central square and interesting blend of buildings ancient and modern, interspersed with a wide variety of restaurants, bars and cafés, the atmosphere lightened, made exciting by the sound of the sea in the background, the knowledge that it was there, shining and shimmering in the warm September sun. Rounding corners, one came upon it, inevitably, as the focal point on which revolved Bevensea's popularity as a holiday resort.

Walking slowly round the square, looking in shop windows, she passed the usual department stores and supermarkets, cheek-by-jowl with smaller boutiques, florists' and antiques shops, snack bars, and hairdressing salons.

A notice, 'Appointments not always necessary', caught her attention. Dare she? No, of course not. Douglas would be furious. She turned away from the hairdresser's window and marched quickly into Boots to buy a hot-water bottle. And yet the idea persisted. After all, why not? Would Douglas really care if she had her hair cut off?

Possibly her gesture of defiance had something to do with the sweet, clean smell of sea air, the way the sunlight dappled the pavements. Deep down, she knew it was more than this.

Sitting under the dryer, her newly styled hair done up in pink rollers, she wondered if Douglas had spent the night with Avril, or if they had simply made love at her flat before his return to the bungalow in the early hours of the morning.

She had known, last night, listening to the ringing of the telephone in an empty house, that the affair was not over. Despite all Douglas's angry assurances to the contrary, the other woman still held sway.

CHAPTER 2

Alfred Cornwell walked with the measured tread and upright carriage of a former police sergeant. Over six feet tall, with piercing grey-blue eyes beneath jutting brows, and a shock of wiry grey hair, Jess thought, as they shook hands, that the presence of this man on the premises might well have deterred the villainous-minded youths of Bevensea from their nefarious pursuits. A force to be reckoned with, his handshake made her wince slightly.

Alerted by William Hoyle, Cornwell had been out in the garden lopping wood for the fires, deriving keen pleasure in clearing overgrown branches from the thickly crowded trees shutting out light to the kitchen windows.

Retirement sat uneasily on his massive shoulders. He had received his presentation carriage clock, and the good wishes of his colleagues, more stoically than gratefully. But Dora had needed him at home during the last painful months of Geoff's life.

Grief over that episode, the loss of his son, and concern for his wife, had seamed Alfred's face with deeply scored lines. His skin resembled tooled leather, reminding Jess of a proud, grim-faced Indian chief suffering the injustice of a government reservation.

'I'm afraid I'm putting you to a great deal of trouble,' she said, discreetly massaging her right hand.

'No trouble.' He spoke gruffly, carrying a basket of logs as effortlessly as if it were filled with shavings. 'My wife and I were fond of Miss Tidey.'

'You did a lot for her, and I'm grateful.'

Jess wondered if the Cornwells had ever questioned the lack of family involvement in her great-aunt's life. It must have seemed odd to them, even heartless, that the old lady's only surviving relative had not put in an appearance before she died. But how could she explain the circumstances to a stranger?

The fact remained that her father had tried repeatedly, during the years prior to his death, to keep in touch with his Aunt Jessica. None of the cards and Christmas presents he had sent her was ever acknowledged, nor had she bothered to reply to his letters informing her of the birth – first of a son – then of a daughter who would bear her name.

Memory flicked back to a scene in the kitchen of the Reading house. She must have been about eight at the time, too young to grasp the significance of her father's despair, her mother's anger, but she did clearly remember that the row had started when her father said, 'I can't understand why she hasn't kept in touch. She may be ill – in trouble . . .'

'*Trouble! We're* the ones in trouble! You make me sick and tired, Frank Tidey, forever sucking up to that bloody old autocrat! Wasting our hard-earned money on presents when we need every penny we've got right now! When will you get it through your head that she doesn't want to know us?'

Jess had always remembered her mother's bitter retort, the way her lips had folded together like a shut purse as she began rolling pastry: remembered it because she had never heard the word 'bloody' from her mother before, or known her so angry.

Her brother, Stephen, had been in hospital at the time. Her mother must have been worried sick, her father too. She could see her mother now, pale and drawn; hair pushed back anyhow, the laughter gone from her eyes, their berry-picking days all over and done with. She remembered thinking about those days, when Stephen died; crying because they would never come again.

'By the way,' Cornwell said, breaking into her reverie, 'the auctioneer's van delivered half a dozen tea-chests before you arrived. I've taken them upstairs. Did I do right?' He was standing in the kitchen, still holding the basket of logs.

'Yes, thank you.' Jess turned her attention to the box of groceries she had brought with her, surprised to find that her hands were shaking. 'I – I bought a jar of coffee on my way here. Would you like a cup?'

Setting down the skep, Cornwell dusted his hands on the seat of his trousers, and squatted on his haunches beside an ancient black cylinder. Ignoring the question, he said offhandedly, 'I'd better show you how this thing works. It's a bugger to light. No wonder! The damned thing's been obsolete for the past thirty years.'

'What is it for?' Jess leaned forward to watch as he swung out a slender metal rod at the base of the contraption, fiddled with a box of matches, and lit the gas-jet.

'Domestic hot water. Baths, washing-up, and so-on.'

Conversation was tough-going, but Jess persevered. 'I gather you live close by.'

'Next door, in a manner of speaking. A hundred yards or so down the road.'

'Oh, I see. I haven't quite got my bearings . . .'

'This house marks the end of the esplanade,' he explained grudgingly. 'There's nothing beyond the stables except the coastguard station, then it's open fields down to Broscombe Bay.'

'How far is that?'

'A couple of miles.'

Jess straightened up. The boiler emitted a low, roaring sound. Smiling pleasantly, determined to converse with this strangely abrupt caretaker, 'Are you a family man?' she asked.

'I was. My son died a few months ago.' A shutter came down over his face. He said harshly, 'Well, that's that. I'd best be seeing to the fires.'

'I'm so sorry – about your son.' Jess could have bitten her tongue out. Why hadn't she left well enough alone?

I've hurt him, she thought despairingly, as Cornwell bumped through the door with his burden of logs. In trying to make things better between them, she had done the exact opposite: had thrust up an insurmountable barrier between them.

She knew exactly how he felt. He could not bear to talk about his son just as she could not have borne to engage in casual conversation about Avril. Perhaps they were both afraid that compassion might undermine their willpower to go on surviving.

Emptying the wardrobe in her great-aunt's room, Jess realised that six tea-chests could not possibly contain so many clothes, which she felt reluctant to cram in anyhow.

Easing her neck muscles, she gazed perplexedly at the mountain of garments she had laid on the bed; voluminous dresses, of the finest quality, with stiffly boned collars; wide-brimmed hats; an Indian lamb jacket with a nipped-in waist, frogging, and carved jet buttons; richly beaded shoulder capes with stand-up fur collars.

Lovely clothes such as these belonged in a museum, or to a West End company engaged in Victorian revivals – *The Importance of Being Earnest* sprang to mind – and, of course, *Gaslight*. She couldn't very well stuff them into six tea-chests and send them to Oxfam.

The Tideys, wealthy, influential members of the community, would have received countless invitations to local functions. She could imagine her portly, affluent great-grandfather, immaculate in evening dress, his slim wife and shy young daughter stepping into their carriage, bowling along the esplanade to the Town Hall.

Opening drawers, she came upon nightdresses of finest handsewn lawn; lace boudoir caps; embroidered shawls swathed in tissue paper; fans – some lace, others of stiff rice paper exquisitely painted with birds and flowers: long buttoned gloves; handkerchiefs, lace trimmed, in lavender perfumed sachets.

A carved wooden box containing a bundle of invitation cards lay hidden beneath a pile of ribbon-threaded chemises. Invitations from august local bodies – the Mayor and Corporation of Bevensea, The Ladies' Guild, The Worshipful Company of Silversmiths, The Concertgoers' Society; requesting the pleasure of Councillor and Mrs Joshua Tidey's company at various dinners and charity balls. Then the wording had changed subtly to: 'Request the company of the Mayor and Mayoress of Bevensea, Councillor and Mrs J. Tidey.'

So the old dog had become mayor, had he? Jess smiled. Of course, a man of his standing in the community would have been certain, sooner or later, to wear the chain of office. She must find out more about that. But how strange that none of the invitations, except one, had so far included Miss Jessica Tidey.

Of course, how stupid of her! The vast array of garments heaped on the bed could not possibly have belonged to her great-aunt. Fashions would have altered considerably by the time Jessica was old enough to accompany her parents to balls and dinner parties. These were Clarice's dresses, Clarice's hats, gloves, fans, shawls and shoulder capes, lovingly cared for by her daughter.

It occurred to Jess that the whole house had been kept as a shrine to the memory of Clarice Tidey. A puzzling thought.

She started slightly at Alfred Cornwell's knock, and looked up to see him standing on the threshold, obviously ill at ease.

His manner had changed. 'I just thought that you might like to come home with me for a bite to eat. The wife and I usually have a meal about half-past twelve.' He smiled briefly. 'How are you getting on?'

'Not very well, I'm afraid. I didn't realise how much stuff there'd be. Just look! What on earth am I going to do with it all?'

'Hmm. I see what you mean.' He edged further into the room for a closer inspection.

'I can't see any of the Third World countries wanting this lot, can you?' She laughed at the absurdity of the notion.

'No, to be quite honest, I can't.' He scratched his head thoughtfully. 'Would you like my wife to lend you a hand, after lunch?'

He hadn't been too sure about Mrs Carmichael at first; had harboured some resentment towards her – the old lady's great-niece appearing from nowhere after other people had done all the unpleasant things connected with her illness, death, and the funeral.

He had thought she might be high-handed, dismissive, ungrateful, but she wasn't any of those things, just a nice, pleasant, ordinary woman towards whom he had been deliberately hostile.

'Are you quite sure your wife wouldn't mind?' Jess responded gratefully to Cornwell's offer of help.

'I'm certain she wouldn't. As a matter of fact it would do her good to get out of the house for a while.' He paused. 'You'll come to lunch, then? Mind you, it won't be anything fancy. Cold meat and chips as likely as not.'

They walked down the drive to where the esplanade ended and the road curved down to a series of semi-detached houses flanking a tree-lined thoroughfare. 'Well, this is it. No. 1 Lymington Road,' Alfred said, pushing open a wrought-iron gate.

'Oh, you're thinking of moving?' Jess noticed the For Sale sign in the front garden.

'Yes, well, for Dora's sake, really. She can't seem to settle since our son died.' Gruffness crept back into Cornwell's voice. 'Before we go in, please don't mention our selling the house. It's a touchy subject.'

'Of course not.'

He sighed deeply. 'I don't particularly want to move. I'll miss the garden, but my wife has her heart set on a flat. Oh, excuse me just a second.'

Hurrying back to the gate, he engaged in a few minutes' conversation with an elderly man carrying a walking-stick – a rather distinguished-looking man, Jess thought, with a studious air about him, a mane of greying hair brushed back from a high forehead, and a delightful smile.

'Sorry for the interruption,' Alfred apologised afterwards, 'but I always make it my business to have a word with Mr Sloane. The poor old boy seems like a fish out of water since his wife died.'

Inserting his key in the lock, Alfred continued, apropos

of Mr Sloane, 'One of the nicest, gentlest men you could wish to meet. He worked all his life at Somersets, the gents' outfitters, until his retirement last year. Then, just when he was looking forward to a bit of home life, his wife took ill and died. A rotten world, at times, isn't it?'

'Yes, indeed it is.' Jess followed the gallant, retreating figure of Mr Sloane with compassionate eyes as Alfred pushed open the front door and called out to his wife that he had brought someone to see her. 'She'll be in the kitchen,' he explained.

'Oh!' Mrs Cornwell appeared from a door at the end of the passage, drying her hands on a tea-towel, a thin, faded woman with enormous brown eyes, and greying hair which had been, in her youth, a deep, glowing auburn.

'This is Mrs Carmichael — Miss Tidey's great-niece,' Cornwell explained gently, 'I've brought her for a bite to eat.'

'How do you do?' Dora's mouth lifted in a brief, uncertain smile. She glanced up at her husband as if willing him to tell her what to do next, as if she had lost the power to act on her own initiative. She had, Jess thought, the bewildered look of a hurt animal. The pain and grief she had suffered recently was evident in the lines and shadows of her face.

'I hope I'm not being a nuisance,' Jess said quietly.

'A nuisance? Oh no. I'm pleased to see you. Alf knows I like company.' Her voice trailed into silence. She shook hands, and then continued picking at the tea-towel, carefully pleating the edges.

'What are you giving us to eat, Mother?' Cornwell spoke as if to a child; instilling confidence, placing a protective arm about her shoulders.

'I've made a salad,' Dora said vaguely, 'and there's some cold lamb. Will that be all right?' Her face puckered with anxiety. 'I hope there'll be enough to go round.'

'Let's go and see, shall we?' Alfred drew his wife towards the kitchen.

'May I come too? Perhaps I could help,' Jess said.

Cornwell nodded his assent. 'By the way, Mother, Mrs Carmichael wondered if you could give her a hand, after lunch.'

'Really?' Dora's face brightened. 'Yes, I'd like that.'

The salad and slices of cold meat were set out on the kitchen table. 'I would have laid the table in the other room if I'd known we were having company.' Dora fetched another plate from the dresser. Then, 'Yes, I think it would be more fitting if we ate there. It won't take a minute. Besides, it will be warmer near the fire.'

'Really, Mrs Cornwell, I don't mind in the least . . .'

'Leave her be,' Alfred suggested quietly as his wife trotted off, 'she's better when she has something definite to do. That's what she's been missing lately. Our son relied on her for everything. Geoff was born handicapped, you see, both physically and mentally.'

'I'm so sorry. Thank you for telling me.'

'Perhaps we'd better have a few chips to eke out the meat.'

'Here, let me.'

Cornwell handed Jess the peeler. 'Funny, we always thought of Geoff as a child, but he was going on thirty when he died. The doctor wanted us to put him in a home, but Dora wouldn't hear of it. She worshipped that boy.' His face clouded. 'That's why she wants to get away from this house. Too many painful memories.' He stared out of the window as if he could see, in the garden, the figure of a severely handicapped man-child in a wheelchair, his face uplifted to the sun.

When Alfred told Dora about his meeting with Mr Sloane, 'Oh dear,' she murmured contritely, 'you should have asked him in.'

'I don't think he expected an invitation . . .'

Dora went on, reflectively, 'His wife was such a nice woman. Her death must have come as a terrible shock to him. It was so sudden, so unexpected. The first I knew about her illness was when Mr Sloane told me that Maisie

– that was his wife's name – was going into hospital for tests. Dr Sanger suspected a stomach ulcer. I don't think Mr Sloane was unduly worried at the time. When I met him, that day in the chemist's, he was buying things for her to take into hospital. You know, toothpaste, talcum powder, cologne, that kind of stuff. I remember him saying that Maisie was particularly fond of eau-de-cologne . . .

'I told him to give Maisie my love, and said I hoped she'd be out and about again quite soon, and he said he felt sure she would be. Then, about a fortnight later, I met him in the supermarket. Naturally, I asked him how Maisie was getting on, if she was home now. Well, you can imagine how I felt when he told me . . .' Dora's eyes filled with tears. 'It wasn't a stomach ulcer after all. She had cancer.'

'Now, Mother, don't upset yourself. Mr Sloane would understand that you hadn't seen the announcement of her death in the evening paper,' Alfred said quietly.

'I suppose you are right. Well, you know, Alf! I told you, at the time, how dreadful I felt, that we would have attended her funeral, sent flowers, if we knew what had happened . . .'

Dora's soliloquy continued. 'There wouldn't have been all that many people anyway. At the funeral, I mean. They didn't mix much, did they? Simply lived for each other; seemed content with each other's company. A pity they had no family. No children. Poor Mr Sloane must feel very lonely now, all alone in that big house . . .'

Later, over coffee, Jess sketched in briefly something of her own background, making the bungalow in Manchester seem almost idyllic; skating over the thin ice of her life with Douglas, pretending, as usual, that they were a normal, happily married couple.

One had made this gesture, this pretence of happiness, to save face at school functions, open days and prize-giving: eternally acting out a lie.

Above all, one trooped the colours at those dreadful 'at home' sherry parties the headmaster laid on for members of staff and their partners, when one stood, in an over-crowded sitting-room, a kind of idiot grin soldered to one's lips, sipping sickly Bristol cream sherry: listening to school-talk; being offered, by the headmaster's buxom wife, soggy Ritz crackers piped with cream cheese, and undercooked convenience sausage rolls with particles of ice still clinging fondly to the inner layers of puff pastry.

It was at one of those ghastly sherry parties that she had first met Avril Messiter, when the rapidly balding headmaster, intent on making one happy family of his minions, had said jovially, 'Oh, Jessica, I don't think you've been introduced yet to our new handicrafts' mistress.'

They had shaken hands. And Jess had been instantly aware of the younger woman's sexual magnetism, the curious, still intensity of her square-jawed, milk-white face beneath the heavy curved fringe of lustrous dark hair; her lack of warmth and response, a kind of veiled insolence in her glance, a calculating coolness which had deeply disturbed her.

Afterwards, remembering the curious encounter, Jess thought that Avril Messiter resembled a high priestess in her white surplice-like kaftan and the great silver cross she wore dangling between her firm, untrammelled breasts. Even her perfume was exotic – musky – like incense.

After lunch, Dora appeared wearing a flowered overall and carrying a shopping bag containing dusters and polish. 'That room you're going to sleep in will need a good going over,' she said, settling her hat more firmly on her head.

When Jess remonstrated gently that she had not meant her to do any cleaning, 'But I used to polish round for Miss Tidey when I popped in to do the cooking,' Dora explained. 'I didn't mind, I enjoyed being useful. That's what life's all about isn't it, being useful?' She blinked rapidly. 'I tried to have a go at the kitchen more than once, but Miss Tidey didn't like that: said it was the servants' job. Poor old soul, she got a bit hazy towards the end.'

As they walked up the hill together, 'You'll be putting the

villa up for sale, I suppose?' Alfred said. 'Seems a pity. It's a grand house. The old lady set great store by it.'

'You must have thought it odd that I never came to visit my great-aunt,' Jess said. 'The fact is, my father tried all his life to keep in touch with her – without success, I'm sorry to say. Never once in all those years . . .One drew the obvious conclusion, that she did not wish to be kept in touch with.'

The Cornwells exchanged glances, and Jess knew that they had wondered, had probably discussed the lack of family involvement. 'Aye well,' Alfred said expansively, 'old folk have queer ways. Miss Tidey was what you might call a recluse. Mr Hoyle had tried to persuade her to let Dora and me see to her when she was taken ill. And what a tussle Dr Sanger had with her over the district nurse. Remember, Mother?'

Dora nodded. 'Don't I just. He told her straight, in the end, that it was a toss-up between being looked after at home or going into hospital. Mind you, it wasn't all that easy for us, was it, Alf? Quite off-putting she was at first. You could tell she didn't like interference in her private affairs; wasn't used to having people in the house. Well, that's all in the past now.'

The villa felt warmer already, Jess thought, from the fires Alfred had lit. Now she could hear him whistling about the garden as he tackled the elm tree, and Dora moving about in Clarice's bedroom.

Kneeling beside a cretonne-covered ottoman, Jess came across the jewel boxes unexpectedly: hidden beneath a pile of blankets.

There were several velvet-lined morocco cases containing both precious and semi-precious stones: garnets, aquamarine and turquoise, opals. Matching sets comprising rings, brooches, pendants, ear-drops, pearl chokers, a sparkling ruby and diamond necklace, ruby and emerald bracelets. Beads, too, of coloured glass; coral and amber, such as a child might wear, flung haphazardly into a carved wooden box, as if the wearer had grown tired of them, had cared little about them, or had simply put away childish things.

Sitting back on her heels, Jess stared perplexedly at the treasure trove. Had Mr Hoyle known about these jewels, he would, she felt certain, have prevailed upon her great-aunt to put them into safe keeping.

Fingering a charming ruby and pearl brooch in the shape of a leaf, her thoughts flew to Dora Cornwell who had done so much for Great-Aunt Jessica. If anyone deserved recognition of her kindness, it was she.

Heart beating swiftly with excitement, Jess closed the box containing the brooch, and slipped across the landing to the pink room where Mrs Cornwell was rearranging bedding on the fireguard.

'Oh, I didn't hear you come in.' Dora turned; cheeks flushed with the heat of the fire. She was smiling, obviously revelling in her new-found usefulness.

'Your bed should be nicely aired by tea-time,' she said. 'Alfred has taken the mattress downstairs to the drawing-room fire. After all, we don't want you catching pneumonia. Heaven alone knows how long it is since this bed was slept in.'

Touched by the Cornwells' concern for her welfare, Jess felt the prickle of rising tears. She had grown unaccustomed to simple human kindness.

'I just thought. That is . . .' She handed Dora the box. 'I'd like you to have this.'

'What is it?'

'Open it and see.'

Dora's face was a study. 'But I couldn't possibly,' she faltered. 'It – it's far too valuable.'

'Nonsense. Of course you must have it. I want you to.'

Tears trickled down Dora's cheeks. Overcome with emotion, she sank down on the edge of the bed, clutching the box to her breast.

'I'm sorry,' Jess said, 'I didn't mean to upset you.'

'I'm not. I mean – you haven't.' Dora felt in her overall

pocket for a handkerchief. 'It's just that I haven't been able to cry since – since our son died. I couldn't. I felt all frozen up inside. But now . . . I don't know. It's not just the brooch, it's feeling – wanted again . . .'

'I know.' Jess sat down beside her, and slipped her arm round Dora's shoulders. 'It will do you good to cry.'

She knew exactly how Dora felt. She too had experienced the terrible weight of unshed tears, the same frozen feeling when she had discovered that Douglas was having an affair.

When Dora was all cried out, and had trotted off to show Alfred the brooch, Jess found Mr Hoyle's number in the telephone book in her great-aunt's room, dialled his office, and explained briefly why she was ringing.

'Jewellery!' Hoyle's voice held a note of surprise. 'I had no idea! I'll come at once; take it to the bank. Yes, that would be best.'

'It makes my blood run cold thinking what might have happened if anyone had suspected; if there had been a break-in.'

'Quite so,' Hoyle agreed fervently.

Jess could understand, now, why Great Aunt Jessica had been reluctant to leave the house unattended. Yet what chance would one old lady have stood against a gang of stocking-masked men, strong and intimidating, uncaring of old age and frailty. Then she realised that her great-aunt had relied upon the strength of the house itself to protect her from harm – the solidity of its doors, each one fitted with bolts on the inside.

Jess wished she had known that fragile 'keeper of the flame'. What a proud, indomitable person she must have been.

William Hoyle arrived an hour later.

'It isn't simply the jewellery,' Jess explained, 'I can't think what to do about all these clothes.'

'I shouldn't worry if I were you,' Hoyle said kindly, 'Mr

Grant will put them up for auction, if you are agreeable. By the way, the sale could take place next month, once an inventory has been taken and the event advertised.'

'Next month? Oh yes, that will be fine,' Jess said reluctantly, 'the sooner the better, I suppose.'

They were standing in Miss Jessica's bedroom, the sun filtering lace patterns on to the carpet. 'You look tired,' Hoyle ventured, 'and I can understand why. All this is quite an undertaking.' He smiled sympathetically. 'But I see that Alfred and Dora have been making themselves useful.'

'They've been marvellous,' Jess said, 'I don't know how I should have managed without them.'

Hoyle nodded. 'They're a grand couple. A tragedy about their son. I can never understand why nice, inoffensive people are called upon to endure so much suffering.' He sighed deeply. 'Geoffrey was born crippled. When it became apparent that he would never develop either physically or mentally, Dora devoted her life to his welfare. Of course, she was younger then, fit and active, and the boy was an engaging person, responsive to kindness.' He smiled reflectively, 'I remember Dora once saying that she had been granted the blessing of an eternal baby. Even so, caring for him placed a tremendous physical strain on her, and we're none of us getting any younger.'

Jess thought what a nice man Mr Hoyle was, how fortunate she was to have met him. 'I gave Dora a brooch from my great-aunt's jewellery,' she said, 'and I'm sure to find something suitable, among Joshua's things, to give to Alfred.'

William said gently, 'You must remember, my dear, that all this jewellery belongs to you now. I can't tell you how delighted I am that you made the discovery. Now perhaps I'd better be on my way to the bank before it closes.'

As he gathered together the jewel cases and placed them carefully in his document case, Jess said, 'About the clothes. It may sound foolish, but I'd like to give some of them to a theatre group.' She flushed slightly. Difficult to explain how much the theatre meant to her. Plays, make-believe,

55

were part and parcel of that oasis of the mind – plays, poetry, books, music . . . all those things which had provided comfort and a sense of durability in her loneliest hours.

'That should present no problems,' Hoyle said. 'We are blessed with a fine repertory company here in Bevensea. Would you like me to contact the stage-manager on your behalf?'

'Oh, that would be wonderful.'

'You're fond of the theatre?'

'Yes. I once belonged to a play-reading group – before . . . Well, that was a long time ago.'

Douglas, she thought. She had met Douglas at that play-reading group. Was it possible to fall in love with a voice, she wondered; to imagine, from the sound of a voice, what that person would be like to sleep with – to spend the rest of one's life with? To conjure up non-existent attributes of sensitivity and dependability from a voice speaking words written by others?

Hoyle turned at the door. 'Are you quite sure you'll be all right alone in the house?'

'Quite sure. It's what I want. You understand?'

'Have you a torch?'

'Yes,' she said, 'I bought one in Boots, along with the hot-water bottle.'

Searching through his wallet, Hoyle handed her a card. 'My home address and telephone number,' he explained briefly. 'If you need me, don't hesitate to ring.'

And now she was alone, quite alone in the house; curtains drawn, sitting near the drawing-room fire, hearing the soft plop of the gas-mantles, listening to the rising wind rustling the ivy, thinking about all the people who had lived under this roof, about her own parents too – her mother, Evelyn, who had never recovered from the death of her son, who had changed from a laughing, bright-eyed woman to a pale shadow, forever fretful and fault-finding after that swiftly administered blow which had robbed her of the will to live.

Eventually came the series of minor strokes which had left her feeble-minded and emaciated, clinging to life as a shrivelled winter leaf clings to a tree. Finally came the massive stroke which swept away the leaf.

She remembered kneeling at her father's feet after the funeral, telling him not worry, that she would look after him. And 'No,' he replied, 'you must look after yourself now. Live your own life. You are still young, Jess. Don't waste your time on me.'

'I don't know what you mean. Waste my time?' And then she had known there was something he could not find the courage to tell her. She could read the guilt in his eyes.

'The truth is,' he said after a long silence, 'there's someone else. I should have told you. I – well, you know how it was with your mother and me after Stephen died? She didn't need me any more. I thought you might have guessed.'

'Guessed? About the other woman? No . . .'

And this, she thought afterwards, was what had hurt most. Not knowing. The feeling that her father had gone away from her, secretly, not trusting her. But could she blame him, a man in the prime of life, for wanting love?

None knew better than she the pain of watching her mother slip away from life, the terrible personality changes wrought by her illness; the sheer weight of a sick person in the house, the overwhelming sense of pity and failure.

Her father's life must have been hell. Even so, the thought of the other woman had filled her, at first, with a cold dull feeling of jealousy until, in the early hours of the morning, she had come to terms with the situation.

At breakfast, 'Are you planning to marry her – this woman friend of yours?' Jess asked, deeply aware of the solecism.

'Well, yes. I suppose so, in time.'

Loving her father, wanting his happiness, realising his need for absolution, she said, 'Don't worry, I shan't interfere. I'll find a place of my own. Leave you a clear field.'

The woman, dark-haired, blowsy, with her three children by a previous marriage, had moved in almost immediately. Jess, who had not attended the wedding, read about it in the evening paper: 'Tidey – Collingwood. 27 August at Reading Register Office, Franklyn Brent Tidey to Maybelle Dolores Collingwood – née Delroy'.

That same evening she had walked from her rented flat to join a play-reading group she had seen advertised in the library.

Falling in love with a voice had been easy. Child's play. Nothing to it.

She slept badly, conscious through her uneasy, fitful slumber, of the moaning of the wind, the eeriness of the strange house; awoke at three o'clock to a curious roaring noise somewhere in the distance; the shrill utterance of a barn owl in search of prey. The room felt cold now that the fire had gone out. The low roaring sound persisted.

With a deep sense of relief, she realised that what she heard was the sea.

> Listen! you hear the grating roar
> Of pebbles which the waves suck back and fling,
> At their return, up the high strand . . .

Comforted, she thought about the sea running in on the sand, the eternal, changeless voice of the waves in their ebb and flow, and heard the patter of rain on the window.

Awake again at six, she got up, put on her dressing gown, and padded along the landing to the bathroom. Turning on the tap, she felt, with gratitude, the rush of hot water, and remembered that she had forgotten to switch off the gas under the kitchen boiler.

Strange, one never felt part of a house until one had bathed in it. Now, as the scalding water bubbled into the high-sided bath, she experienced a warm feeling of renewed energy – a kind of baptism.

Last night by the drawing-room fire, in that curiously

evocative atmosphere of gaslight filtered through etched glass shades, listening to the companionable crackle of burning wood had brought release from bitter memories, the initial pain she experienced when she knew that her father had been unfaithful to her mother.

Time had brought about a tenuous truce with the new Mrs Tidey who fed her husband well, bustled him from pillar to post as she did her three, sharp-faced, semi-literate children, and no doubt, gave him the sexual fulfilment he craved. But the light had gone from his eyes. He had seemed to shrink in stature as the years wore on, as if diminished by the constantly scolding tongue of his wife.

Last night by the fire, Jess knew that she had long since forgiven his human frailty, that she had never stopped loving her father; had known, in his last moments, that he had never stopped loving her.

The weather had changed at last. Long grey rollers raced across the bay, harried by the spiteful north-east wind. Watching the grey cavalry charge from the window of her great-aunt's room, Jess experienced the sound and fury – the thrill of the storm.

Nothing in her life had so far matched this feeling of excitement, of fulfilment, in this house, beneath this roof. Rain beat against the windows. Lancing, silver spears bent the heads of the trees in the spinney of birch and alder at the sea-edge of the garden. The wind drove at full force through the branches of the great elm, shaking the leaves. She watched, with a heightened sense of awareness, the sullen downpour drenching the spotted laurels; beating down on the clinging sea of bindweed.

She had dressed warmly in slacks and sweater. There was much to be done. She had decided to clear the rooms of personal memorabilia – family photographs and her great-grandmother's watercolours, which she would keep, along with the china swans and the dressing-table accessories.

Dora had insisted upon giving the kitchen a 'going over' before she and Alfred departed the day before, had scrubbed the working surfaces with hot water and Dettol.

'There,' she said, drying her hands, 'now you'll feel easier in your mind. And I've given the frying pan and saucepans a good wash too, so you needn't worry about being poisoned.'

Dora, in charge, had assumed a protective, motherly attitude towards Jess. 'Now, are you sure you've got enough to eat? You could come round to us for supper, if you like.'

'Thanks, but I'm sure I can manage. I've brought eggs, bacon, bread, cornflakes . . .'

'Yes, well,' Dora nodded, satisfied that her ewe lamb would not starve to death overnight, 'you could always pop round if you're short of anything. Have you got matches, by the way, to light the grill?'

'Yes, I think so. In my handbag.' She laughed suddenly, 'I thought, for one awful moment, I'd have to cook my supper on the range.'

'Huh, *that* thing!' Dora had turned up her nose. 'No. Thank goodness Miss Tidey had the sense to buy a gas-cooker. Mind you, that has seen better days too, but at least it still works.'

Just before they left, Jess gave Alfred a watch and chain she had found among her great-grandfather's belongings.

'It's just a keepsake,' she said awkwardly. 'A bit old-fashioned, but it appears to be in working order.'

She had not been entirely sure that Cornwell's pride would allow the acceptance of the gift. The watch, the guard of solid gold.

She thought, for one awful moment, that he was going to cry. His face puckered. He shook his head bemusedly, lost for words. Then, 'It's grand,' he murmured. 'Look, Dora . . .'

'Eh, fancy you with a gold watch and chain,' she said.

'Thank you, Mrs Carmichael.' He'd smiled suddenly.

'Why not call me Jess?' she suggested, returning his smile.

* * *

Now, even the kitchen seemed less formidable in the light of a new day. Dora had found curtains to hang at the windows, saying it gave her the shivers to think of someone standing among the trees, looking in; had brought along too a red and white gingham cloth and a handful of roses to decorate the table.

Jess made herself a cup of coffee and went through to the drawing-room to rake out the ashes. Alfred had left plenty of kindling – sticks and rolled-up newspapers, had filled the brass coal-scuttle, and brought in a fresh basket of logs.

Arranging a pyramid of sticks and coal, striking a match, watching the paper catch light, curl and blacken, the flames devouring the kindling, she remembered the old house in Reading where, as a child, on wild winter evenings, she would curl up on the hearthrug, conjuring pictures in the heart of the fire. Remembered Stephen, a bright, curly-haired schoolboy, coming in with his satchel of books, her mother setting the table for tea, drawing the curtains; waiting for her father to come home from work.

Sitting back on her heels, she thought how secure her world had seemed then, in that warm back room, the heart of the home with its shabby but comfortable armchairs and dancing firelight, her father's pipes and tobacco-jar on the mantelpiece, her mother's knitting in a bag beside the sofa; Stephen's schoolbooks spread out on the table when the meal was over, her dolls in the wooden cradle her father had made for her. The wireless playing.

Suddenly, the doorbell rang. Startled, Jess scrambled to her feet. A brightly painted van bearing the logo 'Bevensea Theatre in the Round' was parked on the drive. She opened the door to a couple of wet, dishevelled people.

'Mrs Carmichael? I'm Jolyon King. This is Liz Fremont. God, what a morning! May we come in?'

'Of course. Please do.'

Jolyon stamped his feet on the doormat and shook the rain from his shock of dark, tightly permed hair. His smile was dazzling. One had the feeling that an electric bulb, held between his lips, would light up. He wore tightly fitting jeans and a baggy green sweater.

The woman was tall, rangy, imbued with a kind of restless energy and grace. Her hair, worn shoulder-length, was almost the colour of wet sand; amber eyes flecked with green beneath incredibly long black lashes. Those eyes dominated her thin slightly angular face. Her mouth was full-lipped, sensual, mobile. Her voice, when she spoke, was low and vibrant.

She said, 'What marvellous stained glass.'

'Liz has a thing about stained glass,' Jolyon explained. 'She's forever poking round churches, bothering the vicars.' He was fairly dancing to keep warm, shivering, rubbing his hands on the seat of his jeans.

They both looked half frozen, as if a good meal would show. 'I've just lit a fire in the drawing-room,' Jess said. 'Sit down and get warm. I'll make some coffee.'

'God. Thanks!' Jolyon glanced around the hall. 'Jesus, what a house! Yours?'

'For the time being,' Jess said. 'It was left to me by my great-aunt, who died recently.'

'Why for the time being?' Liz tilted her head thoughtfully, a strange expression of longing in her eyes. 'If it were mine, I'd never want to part with it. One has the feeling . . .' She smiled suddenly. 'Oh, nothing.'

'Yes, I have the same feeling,' Jess said softly.

Making the coffee, she wondered what had prompted her reply, why the strange current of understanding – telepathy almost – flowed so strongly between herself and a stranger. Liz Fremont, she knew, had sensed the haunting atmosphere of the house the moment she crossed the threshold – as she herself had done.

Bevensea Theatre in the Round had its roots in the Town Hall basement, they told her, relaxing in the warmth of the fire.

'Money's the biggest bugbear,' Jolyon sighed. 'There never seems enough of the bloody stuff to go round. The financial climate being what it is, and the arts in general coming low on the list of priorities, we're never sure, from year to year, how much the Arts Council will condescend to spend on us. Thank God the local council chips in with a bit of spare cash now and then. Not that they're overly generous either.'

'Maybe not, but the "Friends of the Theatre" have been more than generous up to now,' Liz reminded him.

'Yeah, well, that's because they enjoy the fringe benefits,' Jolyon observed wryly. 'You know, having their names on the programmes; hobnobbing with the actors . . .'

'Don't be so cynical,' Liz said. 'At least they turn out in winter, when the visitors have departed.'

'Hmmm, if there's nowt better on the telly!' Jolyon grinned amiably.

'It must be terribly hard work, putting on a new play every week,' Jess said, enjoying the conversation: wanting to know more.

'We don't. Not in summer anyway,' Liz explained, holding her long slim hands to the fire. 'We work on a monthly rota . . .'

'Yep,' Jolyon butted in. 'Nothing too taxing. Summer visitors don't like being worried with new ideas. They prefer the good old standbys. You know – *Night Must Fall, Time and the Conways, Rookery Nook,* or one of Ayckbourn's earlier efforts. *Taking Steps* always goes down a treat.' He nodded vigorously. 'A good bloke, Ayckbourn. No edge, no side. An actor's writer. Knows the theatre like the back of his hand. He comes over, occasionally, to direct.'

'Do you like the theatre?' Liz asked. 'But of course you do. I can tell.' She smiled gently. 'We're doing *Time and the Conways* this week. Why don't you come?'

'I'd love to.' Jess returned the smile. 'I adore the theatre. But well, I'm afraid there just isn't time. I – I'm leaving here the day after tomorrow.'

'I'm sorry,' Liz said.

'Well, I suppose we'd better be getting on.' Jolyon blew

out his cheeks regretfully. 'Rehearsal's at 10.30. It's nearly that now.' He grinned. 'Seems a pity to leave this lovely fire.'

Jess had almost forgotten the reason for their visit. 'Oh, the dresses! They're upstairs.' She glanced out at the steadily pouring rain.

'Don't worry,' Liz said, reading her mind. 'They won't get wet. We've brought lots of polythene bags in the van.' She prodded Jolyon with the toe of her sandal. 'Isn't it about time you made yourself useful?'

'All right, I can take a hint.' Getting up, he drew an imaginary cloak to his face, and staggered to the door, declaiming, 'Out into the cold, cold night I go, friendless and alone.'

Liz ran her fingers gently over the garments. Her face was incredibly tender. 'They're exquisite,' she said softly. 'But are you quite sure you want to part with them? They must mean a great deal to you. Besides, a collector would pay the earth for them.'

'I know. But – well – I'd like them to be seen, to give other people pleasure. I suppose it sounds foolish, but I want them to go on living.' She flushed slightly. 'Does that seem crazy?'

'Not to me.' Liz smiled wistfully. 'I know exactly what you mean. To dance one moment more among the flowers.'

It struck Jess, as Jolyon came whistling upstairs with the polythene bags, that Liz Fremont was deeply unhappy.

CHAPTER 3

She saw him at the barrier as the train drew in, a tall figure, immaculate in brown Harris tweed jacket and fawn cavalry-twill slacks, wearing executive-type glasses; dark hair falling forward on to his forehead in the manner of an undergraduate.

Looking at Douglas objectively, one would never suspect that he had been born and raised among the slag-heaps of a Welsh mining village. Deeply ashamed of his upbringing and of his working-class father, rejecting the 'cloth cap' image as an affront to his intellectual achievements, he had long since severed connection with his parents.

Stepping down from the carriage, racked with the old feeling of inadequacy, Jess wondered what on earth had possessed her to have her hair cut off. Walking slowly towards the barrier, she explored the back of her head nervously with her free hand.

Douglas stared at her coldly. 'Good God! What the hell have you done to yourself? You look like a skinned rabbit!'

Her new-found feeling of independence deserted her completely as he strode ahead of her to the car, his back registering disapproval.

Shoulders rigid, he manoeuvred the green Metro into the snarl-up of late-afternoon traffic, staring straight ahead; exacting silent retribution. Suddenly he blasted the horn at a nervous woman driver.

'*Christ!*' he muttered, jamming on the brakes.

Jess sat quite still, hands clenched, knowing he wouldn't speak to her until he had burned up his angry resentment towards her. Even if she ventured to speak to him, in this particular mood of Murdstone-like displeasure, he would not answer. And so she kept silent.

'Dover Beach,' she thought, striving towards her oasis of the mind. 'Listen! you hear the grating roar . . .' But it was no use. All she heard was the grating roar of the traffic.

She remembered the smell of polish, the hard-backed

library chairs set in a circle, the initial self-consciousness of reading aloud, her acute awareness of the man beside her who had seemed almost tongue-tied with embarrassment.

Watching his thin, knuckly hands fumbling with the pages of the manuscript, she had noticed that his sleeves were frayed at the wrist. And so it had begun: his Petruchio to her Katharina.

> 'Yet not so deeply as to thee belongs,
> Myself am moved to woo thee for my wife.'

> 'Moved! in good time: let him that moved you hither
> Remove you hence: I knew you at the first
> You were a moveable.'

The group-leader had invited them to her home for coffee afterwards. Her little band of misfits. Four earnest spinsters, three students from the polytechnic, two elderly widowers, an enthusiastic married couple who held hands all the time, a shabby, bespectacled young schoolmaster just down from Cambridge, and a lonely secretary whose father had re-married earlier that day.

The supermarket carpark was almost full, as if, Jess thought, the prospect of a provisionless Sunday had goaded last-minute shoppers into a frenzy of buying.

Douglas, as usual, remained in the car, finishing *The Times* crossword, while she wandered bemusedly between the shelves, wheeling her trolley. Meat, frozen plaice fillets, wholemeal bread, polyunsaturated margarine, grapefruit, eggs, cauliflower, onions, lettuce, tomatoes. She knew the list by heart. Habit.

They were standing together – yet apart – in the kitchen. She had made a pot of tea. The food in the refrigerator remained uneaten. The milk was sour.

'I rang you repeatedly. There was no reply,' she said dully.

'Oh God, here we go again!' Douglas raised his eyes in

supplication to the sublime being he had never, so far as she knew, believed existed. 'Always accusing . . .'

'I haven't accused you of anything.' She turned her head away.

'For Christ's sake! You're spilling the tea!' He regarded her coldly. 'You are simply avoiding the issue. I want to know about the money.'

'There isn't any money. Not yet. There won't be any until the house is sold.' She mopped up the spilt tea with a piece of kitchen paper. Her hands were shaking.

'And how much will that bring? You must have some idea. Or did you allow yourself to be conned by some smooth-talking solicitor who knew a fool when he saw one?'

'It wasn't like that at all . . .' Faced with Douglas in domineering mood, Jess felt unable to think clearly, to marshal her thoughts.

'I want to know exactly what happened.' He pushed back the bridge of his glasses with his forefinger, a habit which irritated her past bearing.

'I don't want to talk about it. Please. I'm tired. I had a lot of packing up to do.'

'Oh, I get it. The *Washington Square* syndrome! The revenge of the petty-minded heiress! You intend keeping the money for yourself!'

'That simply isn't true!' Anger bubbled to the surface. He was so sure of himself. So certain of his power over her.

She looked at him as if she had never seen him before. His eyes, the pupils diminished by the thick-lensed spectacles, held no warmth, no sympathy, no humour.

Even his voice failed to move her now as it used to. It was not his real voice at all – the voice of a roughly spoken Welsh miner's son. This was the voice he had cultivated at Cambridge. The voice of a misfit teased by his fellow students because of his sing-song Welsh accent. A voice refined and mellowed by years of practice.

'Do you remember,' she said slowly, 'the night of the last General Election? The old lady who lived in the end bungalow? Mrs Brough? She's dead now.'

67

'What the hell are you talking about?'

'You wouldn't give her a lift to the polling-station when you realised that her vote would cancel out yours. She was all ready, too. Waiting with her hat and coat on. You wouldn't tell her yourself, so I had to go along and make excuses. And you call me petty-minded!'

She picked up the teapot, emptied it, squeezed the tea-bags and threw them into the pedal-bin. The box of groceries was still on the table. She started, from habit, to put away the contents.

'It seems such a waste, buying all this extra food. You haven't even touched the stuff in the refrigerator.' A thought struck her. She said dully, 'I suppose she fed you? Avril? You have been seeing her?' Her voice faltered. 'Sleeping with her?'

His lips curved contemptuously. 'So what if I have? What did you expect?'

Jess ran her fingers wearily through her hair. 'That you would keep your promise not to see her again: remember what might happen if the headmaster finds out. Oh, Doug!'

'And I suppose you are going to make sure that he does?'

'No, of course not. I thought you knew me better than that. Why do you imagine I've kept quiet all this time? Do you think it has been easy for me knowing that one breath of scandal might cost you your job? For heaven's sake, Douglas, I've done my best to protect you: tried to understand . . .'

'Ah, but you don't understand! That's the trouble!' His voice roughened. 'Do I have to hammer it into you?' He leaned forward, hands outspread on the table. 'You're too old, Jess! Too bloody old!'

She stared at him as if he had struck her. Anger faded, giving way to a dull, all-pervading hopelessness and despair. Tears streamed down her cheeks. 'I can't go on any longer,' she said. 'I'm leaving . . .'

'Leaving? Don't be so bloody dramatic! Where would you go? What would you do? A woman of your age – a fool

into the bargain! You have no brains, no creative ability.'
His lips curled in contempt. 'Why not face it? You're useless, Jess. Completely ineffectual both physically and mentally. The squaw type! Thank God you never got pregnant!
You'd have probably given birth to a mongol!'

She had never liked bungalows, the feeling of being pinned
close to the ground like a field mushroom. Living creatures
needed space and air in which to grow and flourish.

Alone in the bedroom, face swollen with weeping, she
heard the unmistakable sound of an angry frustrated man
slamming the door behind him in protest – against what?
The inevitable physical changes which robbed middle-
aged women of their sexuality, their creative purpose in
life?

Staring out of the window, she noticed that all the
flowers, the snapdragons with their funny little bee-stung
mouths, the bright crimson salvias, the roses and rock-
plants she had watered so assiduously in the cool of the hot
summer evenings, were dying now for lack of rising sap in
their stems, and wondered if Douglas would sell the
bungalow when she was gone.

He had not believed her when she said she was leaving.
She had not entirely believed it herself. She wondered why
he wanted her to stay. Because he did want that: had ham-
mered home her ineffectuality, her inability to exist without him, to that end.

The headmaster, of course. The school, his job, his position, his pride. Or perhaps it was simply that Avril had not
yet made her mind up about him. Yes, that would explain
his anger, his need for a whipping boy. But there was more
to it than that. As long as she stayed with him, he could
take refuge in her shadow.

Now, as she began emptying drawers, she felt that someone else, not herself, had taken control, deciding what to
take and what to leave behind. How odd, she thought, that
a woman of her age had garnered so few personal possessions – as if she had scarcely existed at all.

A few precious family photographs. She stared, through a mist of tears, at a snapshot of herself and Stephen grinning at the camera, clutching their pails of freshly picked blackberries. Her mother, sitting on a stile, her father beside her, his arm around her waist.

Six rose-patterned cups and saucers – reminders of Sunday tea; cucumber sandwiches and chocolate cake. A silver coffee-pot and six teaspoons which had belonged to her grandmother. A dozen or so books of poetry. More prosaically, her waterproof mackintosh, boots, sweaters, skirts, shoes. Nothing more.

Above all, she did not want to be here when Douglas came back. There was virtually nothing left to say which had not been said, in different words and varying moods, during the past months. Ever since the affair started.

She rang for a taxi, locked the door behind her, and stood near the gate to await its arrival, shivering slightly in the plangent darkness of the cool September evening, two bulging suitcases and an assortment of plastic carrier-bags at her feet. Not looking back.

'Where to, madam?' The taxi driver was young, dark-haired, clad in jeans and a thick-knit sweater.

'The Station Hotel.'

She had thought, packing her belongings, that she must stay somewhere overnight; begin the long, involved journey to Bevensea first thing in the morning.

Delving in her purse as the taxi plunged into the thick of the traffic, she discovered that she was worth, in hard cash, exactly £10.51. What if the hotel would not accept a cheque?

The fare came to £1.70. The time was one minute past eight. And this was freedom, standing in a draughty station forecourt surrounded by an incongruous assortment of luggage, afraid to walk into a hotel and book a room for the night because she hadn't enough money?

In the unlikely event that Douglas would come looking for her, how gratified he would be to find her standing here, weak and indecisive, just as he had predicted.

70

Noticing an elderly woman near the information bureau, Jess approached her diffidently; asked her if she would keep an eye on her luggage. 'I want to enquire about train times,' she explained.

The woman smiled. 'Not at all. I'm just waiting for my husband.' She had a nice ordinary face beneath the brim of an unfashionable felt hat.

'There's a train to York in ten minutes,' the man at the reception desk told her. 'No, you wouldn't make the Scarborough connection tonight.'

York, Jess thought, making up her mind on the spur of the moment. She would sit all night in the waiting room, if necessary.

The woman was still standing guard over the luggage.

'Thank you so much,' Jess said breathlessly. 'There's a train in ten minutes.' She felt suddenly defeated. 'I don't think I'll be able to make it in time – with this lot.'

'You need a trolley,' the woman said patiently. 'Over there near the barrier.'

'A trolley! Yes, of course! Thank you!'

'I'll give you a hand, if you like.' The woman picked up two of the carrier bags. 'Don't worry. More haste, less speed.'

She bought a ticket, paying the fare by cheque.

Stimulated by the sudden burst of activity, the release of adrenalin into her bloodstream, she boarded the York train with a minute to spare.

Relaxing into a seat, she watched the station lights glide past the windows like pale waterlilies on a gently flowing stream.

CHAPTER 4

Bevensea had a Sunday morning feel to it. A warm autumnal haze lay over the sea, the sand was firm and golden. A small flotilla of yachts, like dancing white butterflies, fluttered towards a marker buoy anchored in the bay. A row of anglers leaned reflectively on the promenade railings near the harbour. The streets lay quiet and sun-dappled beneath a watercolour sky. Seagulls dipped lazily on outspread wings. The sound of church bells drifted dreamily on the honeysuckle air.

Jess had exactly £5.60 left in her purse.

She felt curiously drained and empty: a derelict ship becalmed. Exhausted, all passion spent, lulled by the rocking motion, she had fallen asleep as soon as the train left Manchester. At York, she had made her way to the refreshment buffet; ordered coffee and a packet of tuna and cucumber sandwiches.

Sitting there, drinking a second cup, she recalled the scene with Douglas. The neat kitchen sprang to mind, the flowered curtains at the windows, the bottles of bleach and washing-up liquid on the draining-board, the kettle and food-blender on a blue laminated surface, the ivy plants on the windowsills; Douglas's hands outspread, like talons, on the table. Every word he had spoken was branded into her memory as clearly as pokerwork on a house-name board.

Love, she realised, watching the stains of someone else's spilt coffee spread out and widen upon the laminated table top, changed inevitably with the years; grew stronger, if one was lucky, or faded to indifference.

In her most optimistic moments, she had believed that their love would blossom and strengthen throughout their marriage. But whatever Douglas had felt for her in the early days had not blossomed but withered, and turned into his bitter resentment against her. She knew why. Because of the age gap between them. And yet she had known how much he had needed her at first – this misfit –

this young/old man educated beyond his natural environment.

Academically brilliant, he had nevertheless remained a misfit in the rarefied atmosphere of Cambridge, hampered by his rough working-class background and the contempt of a father who saw his son's intellectual prowess as something to be ashamed of in the working men's club to which he belonged.

'Now then, Dai, how is that boy of yours coming on?' his club-mates would ask snidely, nudging and winking, taking the rise out of him.

'The less said about him the better. Bloody great know-all! Too soddin' clever for his own good if you want my opinion!'

'Wonder where he got his brains from, eh? Not from you, Dai, that's certain!'

She had realised that Douglas was unpopular at school, laughed at by the pupils, looked down on by his colleagues because of his odd, shabby appearance, his inability to socialise; had felt, in those strangely tender days which followed their first meeting, that she had adopted a stray puppy, as there, in her flat, she had fed him sausages and chips – he always seemed so terribly hungry – mended his frayed shirt cuffs, darned his pullover, and listened as he spilled out his bitterness towards his father in particular: the degradation of his childhood upbringing in the two-up, two-down house with no indoor sanitation; a tin bath on a hook behind the scullery door: the humiliation of bath-nights, lacking in privacy, when his father would take a keen delight in reading his paper by the fire while his son sponged himself in tepid water, The whitewashed lavatory across a cobbled yard: the agony of crossing that yard with the neighbours watching his every move: resting their arms on the crumbling walls between the houses, judging the nature of his visit by the length of time it took the lavatory to flush.

She could not quite forget or reject all that he had once meant to her. What she could not endure was that cruelty had entered the arena, that Douglas, who had suffered his own share of pain, cared so little about the pain he inflicted on others.

Now she experienced a lifting of the heart as the cab swept between the gateposts of Laurel Villa.

'Shall I carry your luggage indoors for you?' The driver was elderly, more concerned and courteous than the dark-haired youngster who had dumped her cases in the station forecourt the night before.

'No, thanks, I think I can manage.' Jess paid the fare; watched as the taxi made a U-turn. She had not wanted the man to know she had no keys to the house.

She had handed them over to Mr Hoyle, on Friday afternoon, at his office. Sitting there, sipping tea from the Crown Derby cup, she had told him about the tea-chest she had labelled Personal, the clothes she had donated to the theatre, and he had nodded his head, smiling, saying she had done well, that he was sorry their acquaintance had been so short-lived.

Everything pertaining to the sale of the villa was proceeding apace, he had told her as she gave him the keys. 'Oh, by the way,' he added, as she stood up to leave, 'here is the receipt for the jewellery. You'll let me know what you decide to do about it? Perhaps you would like to have it transferred to your Manchester bank?' And, 'Yes,' she said, 'that might be the best thing to do.'

She had hated leaving Mr Hoyle whom she regarded as a kind father figure; had said goodbye to the Cornwells next morning with the tightness of tears in her eyes, and watched from the train the rapidly dwindling view of the town she had come to like so well, thinking how strange it was that she had felt more a part of this place, in a few days, than she had ever felt a part of Manchester.

And now . . .

She knew that Alfred had a set of keys to the house. Mr Hoyle had told her that the caretaker arrangement would hold good until the villa was sold, its rooms cleared of furniture and effects.

Leaving her luggage in the porch, she gave one of the guardian lions a friendly pat on the head, and hurried down the drive, through the gates, and along Lymington Road to the Cornwells' house.

Dora had stared at her bemusedly, as if she were seeing a ghost, not quite believing her eyes. The Cornwells' house, pervaded by the Sunday scent of roast beef, reminded Jess of the old house in Reading; her mother, happy and smiling, busy about the kitchen.

She had wondered how to explain her sudden reappearance to the Cornwells. Nothing but the truth would suffice, that she had left her husband; not going into unnecessary detail.

Alfred had come in from the garden then; had gone to the villa to take her luggage indoors, while Dora had insisted that she stayed for lunch.

Warmth, comfort, kindliness, had a way of knitting together the frayed edges of life, Jess thought gratefully as Dora bustled the plates on to the table in front of the fire and helped her lavishly to roast beef and Yorkshire pudding.

Passing the cauliflower and cheese sauce, 'Tell Jess about the folk who came to look over our house yesterday,' Dora prompted her husband. 'Huh, a right stuck-up pair they were. Patronising, I call it, poking and prying into everything!'

'Now then, Mother,' Alfred chided gently, 'people have a right to look into things carefully if they're thinking of buying.'

Dora bridled. 'They had no intention of buying, if you want my opinion. They were simply filling in time before the last train.'

'I don't think so.' Alfred handed Jess the gravy-boat. 'The husband told me they'd come over from Leeds especially. Apparently he's being promoted, starting a new branch of a car-hire firm here in Bevensea, so it stands to reason that he and his missus will need somewhere to live.'

At least, Jess thought, enjoying her lunch, Dora appeared to have come to terms with selling this house – which had been her own idea in the first place, although the fiercely proud streak in her nature refused to admit the possibility of anyone else living here.

'Don't forget we've done a fair bit of poking and prying ourselves recently,' Alfred reminded his wife.

Dora pulled a face. 'I know. But I didn't take a tape-measure, or ask to look at the cupboard under the stairs. In any case, I haven't seen anything I liked so far . . .'

Alfred changed the subject adroitly. 'Mr Hoyle mentioned, the other day, that the sale of Laurel Villa is fixed for the 17th of next month.'

'Yes.' Jess wondered how she would feel, watching the auctioneer at work, selling her house, putting up the various lots – the first editions, the silverware, the furniture. Everything down to the last ladle.

And then what? Would whoever bought the house gut the rooms, carve them up into dormitories, self-contained flats, en-suite bedrooms? Would they relegate St Martin and his beggar to the council tip, bull-doze the conservatory, turn the stable block into a snack-bar; pour cement over the cobbles and use it as a carpark?

Later, in bed, listening to the murmur of the sea in the distance, Jess knew that all the thinking, all the soul-searching in the world would not alter circumstances.

At least she would have capital when the house was sold. But capital to do what?

Engulfed by a sudden feeling of despair, she imagined herself sitting alone in some bought and paid for flat: shopping and cooking for herself. Working, perhaps, as a part-time secretary – if she were lucky enough to find a job. Living without purpose, on the periphery of other people's lives: feeling useless, the way Dora had felt when her son died, the way her mother must have felt – her father, too, when he had turned, in his loneliness, to another woman for comfort.

She pushed to the back of her mind the knowledge that she would never now have a baby. And this was the root and branch of her failure as a woman, that Douglas had not wanted her to bear his child.

The pain of the realisation swept over her in a flood. His words: 'You'd have probably given birth to a mongol,' had expressed a long-held belief, a secret, festering fear, which had soured his attitude towards her and made a mockery of their physical intimacy.

If only he had told her the truth, trusted in her compassion, her understanding. Perhaps the old Douglas, the uncertain, sensitive seeking person she had first known, would have admitted his fear. Possibly he had not minded, at first, that she might become pregnant, when physical love had seemed the ultimate release, the dominant act which proved his manhood.

But the dormant cruelty, the harshness, the bullying of which he had proved himself capable, had been implanted at his conception; the genes of the father handed down to the son he had bullied unmercifully as a child. And she had nurtured, nourished and watered the soil in which those genes had lain fallow, not knowing, not realising that they existed.

She knew now.

Mr Hoyle would be in court until lunchtime, the receptionist told her. But she could make a four o'clock appointment, if she wished.

Lighting the drawing-room fire, Jess knew she must tell William Hoyle the truth. She also realised that Douglas might administer the final coup-de-grâce in stopping payment of her cheques drawn upon their joint account. Knowing Doug, he would do whatever seemed expedient to force her to her knees.

The deeds of the bungalow were in his name, the mortgage paid by standing order from his salary. She had had little money of her own when they moved to Manchester, and what little she had saved was soon spent in the soft-furnishing department of a Deansgate store.

Her secretarial job had gone the way of the swallows when they moved away from Reading. At first her time had been fully occupied with the house and garden, sadly neglected by its former owners – an elderly couple who had given up their home to move into sheltered accommodation.

Later, when she had finished redecorating the rooms and putting the garden to rights, she had signed on at a secretarial employment agency – against Doug's wishes. But, she had argued, with Christmas looming, she could not very well ask him for money to buy his own present.

Her first temporary job entailed filing invoices which, she had thought at the time, a child with nappy rash could have done.

None of the jobs had lasted for more than a few weeks. All had contributed more towards Douglas's irritability than her own financial security. She would find herself shopping for groceries during her lunch breaks, spending her own money instead of his, coming home exhausted after the long journey from the city centre; queueing for buses, struggling aboard with her shopping bags and umbrella, arriving at the house to find Douglas in carping, critical mood because of her lateness.

And so eventually, to keep the peace, she had given up the idea of going to work. As Douglas had reminded her, ad nauseam, none of the other heads of department wives felt it necessary to earn a living. His pride had been stung both that his wife felt it necessary to scuttle off to the city each day and by the nature of the work she engaged in, while the other wives played golf and attended women's luncheon clubs.

To fill in time until her four o'clock appointment, Jess began washing the willow-pattern china from the kitchen dresser, plunging the great meat-dishes, tureens and gravy-boats into hot, soapy water.

Handling the pieces, seeing the colours emerge fresh and sparkling, she decided that, during the weeks leading up to the auction, she would make it her business to wash every item of china, clean the silver, polish the furniture, brush down the cobwebs. Her house, her great-aunt's treasures, should not fall neglected into the hands of strangers.

William Hoyle listened in silence as the story unfolded. Sitting upright in his chair, lightly tapping his fingertips; his forehead puckered into a frown of concentration. A flicker of distaste crossed his face when Jess told him, haltingly, about the other woman.

'You realise,' he said, at length, 'that your husband will probably argue that, in leaving the matrimonial home, your action forced the breakdown of the marriage?'

Jess bit her lip. 'So you think I did wrong in leaving?'

'My dear,' Hoyle said gently, 'as your solicitor, it is my duty to point out all the possibilities.' He smiled encouragingly. 'But we mustn't cross our bridges before we come to them. I imagine that your husband will feel reluctant to pile on too much pressure, to risk discovery of his affair. No, that would not sit at all well with the school governors. Now to more immediate matters. Your present financial situation, for instance.'

She said hesitantly, 'To be frank with you, Mr Hoyle, I have less than five pounds between me and starvation.'

The receptionist came in at that moment with the tea things. Comfort lay in the taste of Earl Grey: the japanned tray with its lace-edged cloth, the plate of Osborne biscuits – like coming home from school to find the kettle boiling. Her trust in William Hoyle was absolute.

He said, when the receptionist had departed, 'I'll ring the bank manager first thing in the morning; explain the circumstances; arrange a loan. Yes, that would be best. The jewellery will stand as collateral for the time being. Later, of course, you may wish to sell certain pieces. That is entirely up to you. Meanwhile, I will advance you fifty pounds from petty cash to tide you over.'

Jess searched frantically for a handkerchief.

'You mustn't cry, m'dear,' he said kindly. 'No matter what line of argument your husband chooses to put forward, even if he tries to wriggle out of his financial responsibilities towards you, the fact remains that, when the house is sold, you will find yourself comfortably situated. And you know that I will do everything possible to help you find somewhere else to live.'

And that, Jess thought, was the crux of her distress. She did not want to live anywhere else. Laurel Villa had become a part of her blood, bone and sinew. That great barn of a house filled with the ghosts of her own people, her own forebears.

The manager of Lloyd's, Mr Pender, might have been cut from the same bolt of cloth as William Hoyle, Jess later discovered.

The loan had been arranged as if by magic, she thought, treating herself to a cup of coffee and a chocolate éclair at the Greyfriar's Café.

This was a warm, wood-smoke morning, holding the promise of afternoon sunshine. The café, in an unfamiliar part of town, occupied two floors of a Jacobean building sandwiched between a gents outfitters and a Dickensian-type chemist.

From her table near the window, Jess could see the women of Bevensea busy about their shopping; realised, with a thrill of pleasure, that she could, if she wished, walk into the delicatessen opposite and buy herself a few slices of smoked salmon, a jar of crystallised ginger, or a pot of Patum Peperium. The pristine cheque-book in her handbag had a warm, comfortable feel about it.

Smiling at the absurdity of the notion, dismissing the thought of a self-indulgent spending spree from her mind, she noticed a sleek, chauffeur-driven Rolls Royce nosing through the traffic, and asked the waitress if she knew who it belonged to, imagining some local celebrity; possibly the lord-lieutenant of the county, or visiting royalty.

'Oh, that's the mayor's car. The Town Hall's just round the corner. There must be a council meeting or somesuch,' the girl said, handing Jess her bill. 'Pay at the desk, love.'

Threading her way through the crowd of shoppers, Jess came upon the Town Hall in a square at the end of the street, an imposing, gothic building set in an island of sloping lawns, whose flowerbeds were being stripped in readiness for the springtime wallflowers.

Walking slowly past the privet hedge encircling the lawns, she glanced up at the building's red-brick façade, stone balconies and oriel windows, and wondered if her great-grandfather's name was inscribed on some memorial tablet within those august precincts.

It was then she noticed the entrance to Theatre in the Round; steps leading down to plate-glass doors; a poster announcing that lunchtime snacks were available between midday and two o'clock.

The tickling sensation of pleasure grew stronger; an exciting awareness that this town with its varied architecture, tucked-away streets and busy main thoroughfares, its shops, restaurants and cafés, was hers to explore at will. But not now. Not today. Alfred was coming, after lunch, to clear the shrubbery of bindweed.

Calling at the fishmonger's on the way home, Jess noticed an old woman, wearing a voluminous black cloak, searching desperately in her shabby black-leather purse with trembling fingers. Shaking her head bemusedly, she said, 'I'm certain I had a pound coin with me when I came out shopping.'

'Look, lady. You owe me 10p. Now do you want this fish or don't you? I'm selling it, not giving it away!'

How brutal some men were, Jess thought, feeling in her pocket. Bending down, making a pretence of finding a pound coin, she said, handing it to the old lady in black, 'I think this must belong to you: it probably slipped out of your purse when you opened it.'

Alfred was in the garden when she arrived home, chopping at the convolvulus with a bill-hook, so deep in thought that he did not notice her until she called out to him. He looked worried, grim, the way he had done at their first meeting.

He came slowly towards her, bending to avoid the lower branches of the elm tree. 'What's wrong?' Jess asked.

'I don't know that anything's wrong exactly.' He rubbed his nose with the back of his hand. 'It's come as a bit of a shock, that's all.'

She waited patiently. Alfred was not a man to be hurried.

'Lord,' he said at length, 'if it isn't one thing it's another. Remember the people Dora was on about? The couple who came to look over our house last weekend?'

'Yes, of course. The people who brought a tape-measure? The ones Dora said weren't interested?'

'Ah, well that's just it. Apparently they *were* interested. The estate-agent rang us this morning. They've paid their deposit. Looks like our house is sold.'

'But isn't that what you wanted?'

'Yeah, I suppose so. But that's not all. They want to move in the week after next, so you can see the fix Dora and I are in now. We'll have to up stumps and move somewhere else. The trouble is, we haven't anywhere else to go.'

Jess laughed. 'If that's all that's worrying you, you can stay here, put your furniture in the stables until you have time to look around.'

At that moment the sun broke through the clouds.

'Look, Alfred!' She laughed. 'If that isn't symbolic I don't know what is! Tell Dora you are welcome to stay here – until we all have to move out!'

Alfred uttered a 'phew' of relief. His face relaxed in a slow smile of gratitude at the sudden reprieve. He gripped Jess's hands tightly. 'I'll go and tell her now,' he said hoarsely.

When he had gone, she walked to the spinney of trees near the wall edging the tip of the promontory. The soil beneath the thickly crowded branches of birch and alder exuded the rich scent of fallen leaves – a compost of the years. Suddenly a small grey shape darted up a tree, a squirrel – tail as finely, as delicately constructed as a dandelion clock. Paws held together in a gesture of supplication, it stared down at her with eyes as bright as newly washed amber.

There would be birds here too, Jess thought, busy about their own concerns – the inevitable cycle of mating, nesting, hatching their young; teaching them to fly, to fend for themselves in the world beyond the nest. She must remember to buy nuts for them when the weather turned colder.

Perhaps Alfred would build a bird-table for them, when winter came.

Turning, she looked up at the house – the walls and windows bathed with gentle September sunlight.

A tide of pure joy, of new hope, welled up inside her. The passionate awareness of how much this place meant to her came as a blinding revelation, untinged by doubt or uncertainty.

The past was over and done with. Perhaps if she had fought harder, confronted Avril, behaved hysterically, threatened Douglas, made her voice heard in the land, she might have emerged victorious from the emotional conflict of the past year. To what end? To what purpose?

Had she simply known in her heart that dead love could not be resurrected? She thought of the raising of Lazarus, the horror of a rag-shrouded corpse emerging from its tomb. That story had always frightened her. The teacher had been shocked when she said, in front of a classroom of giggling girls, 'But miss, did they really want him to come to life again?'

'Of course they did, you stupid girl!'

'But why, miss? They had got used to him being dead. And – and – what I mean is, he couldn't live forever. He'd have to die again when the time came.'

She had been too young to frame her thoughts, to say what she really meant, that there came a time to let go. She had often thought about poor Lazarus, called from his rest to face the world again – to face a second death.

Perhaps she had not fought for her marriage with harsh words, with threats and tantrums, because the mere bones of marriage, without love, had held no prospect of future joy or fulfilment. Because she could not bear to face a second death of the heart.

But this place, this house was worth fighting for. This tangible thing that she could touch and care for; bring to life again without pain or heartbreak.

She knew that – somehow – she would still be here when winter came.

CHAPTER 5

Octavious Sloane scattered crumbs for the birds in the crescent garden near his home, and watched, with sad and gentle eyes, the delicately outspread wings of the pigeons fluttering madly against the pale autumn sky.

He had known of course that the day would come – the day he had dreaded – when Mr Somerset would call him into his office for the final, ritual handing over of the keys: the sincere expressions of regret that their long and fruitful business association was over at last.

He had worked at Somersets, the gents' outfitters in the Town Hall square, ever since he had left school at fourteen. Things were very different then. Now the old counters and fittings had been ripped out; the original windows replaced with gleaming plate glass. And yet he had remained there, at old Mr Somerset's request, because what he did not know about his job was not worth knowing. Indeed, Mr Sloane had become something of an institution behind the shop counter.

The older clientéle, those men who, like himself, had fought for their country and returned to civvy street in desperate need of new clothes, had turned to him as an emblem of stability in a rapidly changing world. Then their wives, daughters, and, more recently, their grandchildren, had come to consult Mr Sloane about shirt-collar sizes, ties and socks. And, 'Ah yes,' he would say, 'Major Newsome. Size 16 collar. Regiment, The Green Howards. Yes, madam, a regimental tie would be entirely suitable.' Or, 'No, madam, the Major, I think, would not care for a gift of socks in that particular shade of green. Possibly these socks in grey or navy would be a more suitable choice. Particularly the grey . . .'

And, 'Yes, thank you, Mr Sloane', they would say with a sigh of relief, 'we knew we could trust to your judgement.'

If anyone had noticed that he moved slightly crabwise and more slowly as a result of a war wound – a German bullet in his leg – no one had ever mentioned the fact to his detriment, even though, as he grew older, he had been obliged to walk with the aid of a stout ashplant.

He leaned on that stick now, as he began his slow perambulation of the garden, stopping briefly to speak to people who made a habit of exercising their dogs in the park, wincing at the inevitable question: 'Now, Mr Sloane. Enjoying your retirement?'

He would smile then and wipe his watery right eye with his handkerchief. And, 'Yes,' he would say, gripping hard on his stick, 'very pleasant,' not wanting them to know how much he hated the feeling that his life had ended the moment he had handed over his set of shop keys to young Mr Somerset and limped away carrying his engraved presentation salver in a plastic carrier-bag.

Things would have been vastly different, of course, if Maisie had lived; if they could have done all the things they had planned to do when he retired. A weekend coach trip to London to stay in a nice hotel and see a show. Maisie was always so fond of musicals. How strange, he pondered, all the years they'd been married and talked of going to London to stay in a nice hotel and see a show, and yet they had never done it. Not once. And now it was too late. Nor had they ever built that patio near the back door she was always on about. 'Never mind. We'll do it when you retire,' she would say. 'We'll have all the time in the world then. And just think, Occy, you'll be able to read all those books you've never got around to reading, and we'll be able to stroll along the sea-front on summer evenings, and have ice-cream at Punchinellos, and watch the moon come up over the sea – like we used to when we were courting.' And he had kissed her warm, plump cheek, and said, 'Yes, we'll try that new pistachio flavour. And I'll go down to the builder's yard tomorrow and get an estimate for the patio. We might even have a couple of stone flower troughs. What do you think?'

Then, ten months ago, Maisie was taken to hospital with a suspected stomach ulcer . . .

Walking along the path, Mr Sloane remembered the way

86

the rooms had felt, silent and cold and empty, when he came home from the hospital the night his wife died. And yet he had thought for one brief, hopeful moment, that she would come bustling into the living room to tell him that his supper was ready. He could have sworn he heard her footsteps, the sound of her voice humming a snatch of 'The Merry Widow Waltz'. And then he realised that, no matter how much he might wish to conjure up the past, there would be no more warmth in these silent rooms, as if the fire that had warmed his heart, and the light which had illuminated his life, had suddenly gone out.

One neighbour in particular had busily involved herself in his affairs. Mrs Catskill, an interfering woman whom Maisie had always disliked, had taken to bringing him his Sunday dinner, bustling aside his embarrassment as she uncovered the tray of unwanted food. The Vicar of St Bede's had also called on him several times, since his retirement, sitting in Maisie's chair near the fire, asking delicately probing questions about the future; what he intended doing about the house. Not that he put his questions as baldly as that. He had simply intimated that a man of his age could not continue to live alone in a three-bedroomed house without someone to do the housework and cook him three good meals a day.

When Mr Sloane admitted that he did not feel in need of three good meals a day, that the most he ever wanted, for breakfast, was a bowl of cornflakes and a cup of tea, and Maisie had packed him sandwich lunches to save him walking home from the shop; that their one hot meal of the day had been supper – meat and potato pie, a liver and onion casserole with baked dumplings and mashed potatoes, or Maisie's 'spécialité de la maison', Irish stew – the Vicar, the Reverend Roger Bullivant, had enquired prissily if he – Mr Sloane – ever attempted cooking such meals for himself? No, he'd guessed as much. So what *was* he living on – cornflakes, sandwiches and baked beans on toast? Yes? But did not Mr Sloane realise how little real nourishment lay in what he termed 'convenience food'? Tinned stuff, cereals, and sandwiches were all very well in their way, but he must realise that he would, sooner or later, undermine his constitution with such lazy eating habits.

Perhaps the Meals on Wheels people would be able to help out, since he now qualified as a senior citizen. And possibly what Mr Sloane also needed was a home help, someone to come in two or three times a week to clean for him, check up on his clothing, and do his shopping.

At that moment, Mr Sloane had stood up stiffly, because of his game leg, and said slowly and carefully, not wishing to cause offence to a man of the cloth, 'Why don't you say what is really on your mind, Vicar? You obviously think I am occupying more than my fair share of room on earth, that I am no longer use nor ornament, and the best place for me would be in an old folk's home! But dammit, man (I beg your pardon), I'm only sixty-five! Not quite ready for the knacker's yard yet! You see, I happen to love this house! Oh, I know it's far too big for one person, but it never seemed all that big when my wife was alive, and I'm not ready to relinquish it just yet!'

Now, as he slowly circumnavigated the crescent garden, Mr Sloane knew that, despite his brave words, the day would come when he would have to give in, to move away from his house and all its memories, because the vicar was quite right, he couldn't carry on by himself for very much longer. Thank God he still possessed a coterie of old friends – Alfred Cornwell, for instance – with whom he occasionally shared a lunchtime drink and a cheese sandwich.

Mr Grant's tea-chests had come into their own at last. As Jess packed her great-grandfather's belongings, Dora bustled about the room knocking dust from the cornices with a long-handled brush.

'Well, whoever would have thought that Alfred and I would be sleeping in that bed?' Dora enthused. 'Huh, I'll feel like the Queen of Sheba!' She had her head tied up with a cotton headsquare at the time. 'Eh, it's a grand room, right enough. And what a view!' She paused, brush in hand, to admire the sea thundering in on the shore. 'I just wish that Alf and I could find a flat with a view like that.'

Jess smiled and went on with her packing. The soliloquy continued.

'I wonder what they'll make of this place? A hotel? Or perhaps whoever buys it will turn it into self-contained flats. I wonder how Alf's getting on? He said he would ring the removal people this morning. Funny, we've been in Lymington Road for over thirty years now – since before Geoff was born. I loved that house. Then, when he died, it seemed like a prison . . .'

Self-contained flats, Jess thought. But if she kept Laurel Villa, bang would go her capital.

' . . . I shan't be sorry to leave, though. Not now the time has come. Geoff filled that house. That's the way it is with handicapped people. He needed me – all I had to give from the moment I got up in the morning to the time I went to bed. Ah, but he was lovely. I think people like Geoff bring their own kind of love . . .'

Of course, I could sell those first editions, the silver, the furniture, Jess pondered.

' . . . Perhaps I was wrong in wanting to keep him with me all the time. Dr Sanger said he'd be perfectly happy at one of those special schools. But I don't know. He might have felt I'd deserted him – didn't want the bother of caring for him any longer. He couldn't have *told* me, you see. But I would have seen it in his eyes. I couldn't have borne that. Perhaps I was just being selfish . . .'

Jess wondered how much it would cost to have electricity installed. She glanced at Dora. How strange that the mind could listen to another person and gnaw silently upon its own thoughts at the same time.

' . . . Well, it's all over and done with now.' Dora's lips trembled. 'It's up to Alf and me to make a new life for ourselves. We're sure to find somewhere to settle soon.'

Jess crossed swiftly towards her. 'Of course you will.' She held Dora tightly, imparting comfort, smiling encouragement. 'Now you'll have time to look round properly.'

'We can't thank you enough,' Dora smiled tremulously, 'for what you've done for us – giving us a breathing space.'

'You and Alfred have done much more for me.'

'I wish you could stay on here,' Dora said wistfully, 'I know this house means a lot to you.'

'I've been trying to think up ways and means of doing just that,' Jess admitted. 'But it always boils down to the same thing – lack of money.'

'You could take in summer visitors,' Dora said eagerly, 'or, better still, let the rooms as furnished bed-sits!'

'With no mod cons?' Jess laughed. 'I can't see anyone falling for that, can you?'

'Oh, I don't know.' Dora frowned. 'There must be plenty of nice retired gentlefolk who'd jump at the chance to live in a house like this.'

'I doubt it,' Jess sighed. 'With no electricity, they wouldn't even be able to watch television.'

'No, there is that,' Dora conceded. 'Oh, there's Alfred! I'd better pop down and see what he wants.'

Jess pictured an advertisement in the evening paper. 'Rooms to let. Decaying Victorian villa. Sea views. No mod cons.' The different approach. Anything was worth a try. She must ask Mr Hoyle.

Dora came puffing upstairs. 'The removal's fixed for next Monday,' she said. 'Alf's just gone to the stables to sweep up a bit, if that's all right.'

William Hoyle appeared undismayed. 'You would probably qualify for a grant from the local council,' he said, 'towards the cost of modernisation. You would certainly need electricity laid on. I could make enquiries for you, obtain estimates and so forth.'

'You don't seem in the least surprised,' Jess said.

'That you want to keep the house?' Hoyle smiled. 'Frankly, I would have been more than surprised if you had not.'

'No penny lectures on my foolhardiness? The risks involved?'

90

'I gathered that you had already lectured yourself on that score,' he remarked drily.

'You're right. I have. I've spent sleepless nights mulling it over, trying to convince myself the whole idea is pie in the sky. But the idea of a grant had never crossed my mind.' She squeezed her hands excitedly. 'Wouldn't it be wonderful if I could have the kitchen modernised, the conservatory repaired?'

'I'd better contact Grant,' Hoyle said, 'tell him there's been a change of plan.' He tapped his desk thoughtfully with his fountain pen. 'Yes, I had better do that immediately, before the advertisement for the sale goes to press.'

'Of course I'll have to sell most of the contents to provide a little working capital,' Jess continued, 'the silver and pictures, the more unwieldy furniture. I could make a list.'

Hoyle regarded her amusedly across the desk. 'I hear, on the grapevine, that you have taken Alfred and Dora under your wing for the time being.'

'Yes, well . . . as a matter of fact it was Dora who suggested the bed-sitting-room idea.' Jess laughed as she told Hoyle about the 'No mod cons' advert she had dreamed up.

'I'm afraid I played the devil's advocate in putting obstacles in my own path,' she admitted. 'I kept on thinking about the question I asked the first time I came to this office – how my great-aunt managed to survive without an income. I realise, of course, that no-one could: if I'm to keep Laurel Villa, I must earn a living from it somehow.'

'And you would really rather do that – face all the struggle, hard work and financial worry, than sell it to the highest bidder? And if you were to let all the rooms, have you worked out what your income would be?'

'Now who's playing the devil's advocate?' Jess asked, tongue-in-cheek. She added more seriously, 'You think I'm biting off more than I can chew, don't you? As a lawyer, you are bound to think that.'

Hoyle leaned back in his chair. 'Not necessarily. I have

missed, to some extent, the element of challenge in my own life. My parents decided, early on, that I should follow in my father's footsteps. Actually I wanted to be an engine-driver.' He shrugged his shoulders. 'But there it was. My future all cut and dried for me.'

He took off his glasses; rubbed his forehead – a little wearily, Jess thought, watching him closely.

'I have often wondered what would have happened if I had held out against them, if I had stuck to my guns.' He smiled ruefully. 'Of course the train-driver notion was simply a boyhood dream. But I might, with some encourage-ment, have become an engineer. I think I'd have built some pretty good bridges.'

'There are different ways of building bridges,' Jess said quietly.

'Season of mists and mellow fruitfulness . . .'

Was this blue, hazy autumn, with its clear mornings and starlit nights, destined to last forever? Jess wondered.

She had gone out into the garden early on the day of the removal to open the gates for the van when it arrived. Watching the spread of light on the sea, the diamond bril-liance of its path on the water, she experienced a delicately poised moment of delight.

Joshua's room was ready to receive Alfred and Dora. She had placed a vase of yellow chrysanthemums on the dressing table; set cups and saucers on the kitchen table, understanding that Dora would feel strange, at first, in her new environment, in need of the common touch, the com-fort of a singing kettle, a warm fire, a hot bath at bedtime.

She walked slowly to the stables, jingling Alfred's keys on the cold metal ring. She had forgotten to ask Mr Hoyle for her own set. They had been too busy discussing other things.

Unlocking the stable doors, she wondered if William Hoyle had a wife – children? Strange how people melted, chameleon-like, into their own background. She had never thought, until the other day, that Mr Hoyle had a life outside his office. He had looked different without his glasses. Younger, more vulnerable. But then, in talking about themselves, however briefly, people emerged as human beings, not simply lawyers, schoolteachers or whatever.

For one brief moment she had glimpsed another dimension to William Hoyle. And then he had polished the lenses of his half-moon spectacles, slipped them back on, and they had been, once more, lawyer and client. The boy who had wanted to be an engine-driver had whistled down the wind.

She walked slowly round the stables, jingling the keys, then she emerged into the sunlit yard and stood there for a moment feeling the warm sun on her face. Suddenly she remembered that there had been no key, on her own ring, to fit the apartment above the stables. She mounted the stone steps. Ah. One of the keys fitted. The door swung open. Jess stepped inside.

The main room, long and raftered, had been left neat and uncluttered by its former occupants. The air felt warm and dry. Sunlight spilled on to the dusty floor. The windows overlooked the wide sweep of Bevensea Bay; the small enclosed world of the cobbled yard with its rusted drinking trough.

There was a feeling of peace here, of quiet self-containment. A door at the far end of the room opened into a kitchen with a shallow stone sink, sagging shelves; a blackened fireplace with a hob and side-oven.

The window above the sink framed a view of the cliffs beyond the stables. She could see the coastguard station perched, like a seagull, near the cliffs' edge. In the distance lay a deep cleft with trees, a church spire, and red pantiled roofs. The village of Broscombe Bay, she imagined.

Stairs led up to three smaller rooms with snecked doors and stoutly beamed ceilings – like a country cottage, Jess thought, wandering from room to room.

Suddenly she heard Dora's voice, laced with anxiety, calling up to her, 'Jess! Are you there?'

Glancing down, she saw Alfred swinging back the heavy

stable doors, Dora standing beside him, looking up.

'Here!' She rapped lightly on the glass; beckoned Dora to come up to her.

'The van's just arrived,' Dora said, out of breath with the steps. 'I noticed the door was open. Oh!' Her face softened with pleasure. She stepped across the threshold with the expression of a woman looking at a newly born baby.

Standing beside Jess, she said, 'I never dreamt – I never realised. I've seen this place dozens of times from the outside, but I never imagined . . .' She drew in a deep breath. 'Look! You can see right along the esplanade to the harbour; the whole of the bay!'

'I'll go down and have a word with Alfred,' Jess said, slipping quietly away, leaving Dora to commune with the view.

Alfred was busy unfolding tough pliofilm sheets to cover the furniture when it arrived. 'We thought we'd best get out of the men's way,' he said gruffly. 'You know what it's like, moving house.'

'Yes,' she said wryly, 'I *do* know.'

'What's Dora doing up yonder?' he asked, frowning, catching sight of his wife's face at one of the bedroom windows.

Jess laughed. 'I rather think she's having a love affair with a view. Why don't you go up and see, while I put the kettle on?'

The removal men had finished their work and departed. The furniture had been duly stacked and sheeted. Jess had spread the gingham cloth, heated soup and made sandwiches for lunch. There was a feeling of anti-climax. Dora seemed strangely withdrawn. It could not have been easy for her, Jess thought, having her precious belongings relegated to a stable.

After lunch, Alfred said he would go to the house to take a final look round; make sure the doors and windows were securely locked.

When he had gone, Dora said, 'I've been thinking . . .'

This much was evident. Jess waited expectantly.

94

'It may sound daft, but do you think whoever buys this place would be open to an offer?'

'An offer?' Jess could not quite grasp what Dora meant. 'An offer for – what?'

Dora's cheeks reddened. She twisted her wedding ring with a kind of nervous excitement. 'That place over the stables,' she said. 'I know it sounds silly, but I knew, the minute I set foot in it, that Alf and I couldn't find a place we'd like better if we searched from now till Doomsday.'

Jess looked at her in amazement. 'But . . .'

'Oh, I know what you're thinking,' Dora interrupted eagerly, 'it would want a lot doing to it – the kitchen and so on. We'd have to spend a bit of money . . .' She raised her hands to her burning cheeks. 'Oh, look at me! As nervous as a kitten! But, well, the thing is, we have a good bit of capital now. We could afford to pay a fair price for it, and we'd have enough left over for modernisation. What do you think?'

'What does Alfred think?' Jess asked cautiously.

'The same as me. I didn't even have to say it, he said it for me! "Mother," he said, "this would make a grand little home for us." And Alfred's not a man to say things he doesn't mean. Then we stood and talked about it, and he said it would all depend on the people who buy the house, and not to raise my hopes too high because it might fall through.'

'I see.' Jess felt slightly stunned.

Dora continued, 'We've always liked this area. It was just our house that was getting me down. But up there, over the stables, I could see the chimneys from the windows. I'd still feel that Geoff was with me.' Her eyes filled with tears. She blew her nose hard on her pocket handkerchief. 'And Alf said he could help keep the garden tidy for whoever . . .' She gave up the unequal struggle with her emotions.

Jess sat quite still. The feeling of joy seemed to come from deep inside, welling up like a fresh spring of bubbling water. The tide had turned.

She said, in a low voice, 'I'm so – happy – about the

garden. I couldn't possibly have managed it on my own.'

'You mean . . . ?' Dora's tears were caught suddenly in the upturned corners of her smile. 'Eh,' she murmured bemusedly, 'I don't know whether to laugh or cry. Just wait till I tell Alfred! Where on earth can he have got to? He should have been back ages ago!'

'Don't worry. Here!' Jess handed Dora a piece of kitchen-roll to replace her wet handkerchief.

'Do you think we could take another look at the flat?' Now that her future had been settled, Dora wished to make plans about what would go where, and dream up colour schemes.

'We'll call it Mews Cottage,' she announced breathlessly as she and Jess climbed the steps to the front door. 'Oh, just look at that view!' Laughing now, after the pent-up emotion of the past few weeks, Dora fairly waltzed about the rooms, daydreaming.

Returning to the sitting-room window, 'Ah, there's Alf now,' she bubbled, 'talking to Mr Sloane.' She rapped urgently on the glass to attract her husband's attention. 'It's no use, he can't hear me. I'll just nip down and have a word . . .'

Jess watched as Dora hurried down the drive: saw Alfred turn his face bemusedly towards the stable-block, the slow, dawning smile which suddenly lit up his eyes, and felt a curious empathy with Mr Sloane as he turned away and limped down the road alone. At that moment, Jess felt like running after him, to say – what? Possibly that she understood what it felt like to be lonely.

Pressing her forehead to the glass, she wondered if it were better to have lost a beloved partner, through death, after a lifetime of happiness, to know where that person lay buried, to place flowers on a grave, rather than to live with the knowledge of own's own failure as a marriage partner, with no resting place for the mind, no spiritual repose; no corpse, no grave, no coffin to mourn over. Perhaps Mr Sloane would know the answer. And then she thought, poor Lazarus. Above all, poor Lazarus's wife who would have scarcely known, in the face of a miracle, whether to grieve or rejoice. How must she have felt, living with a resurrected corpse?

There were so many misfits in the world. Suddenly Jess remembered the old lady in the fishmonger's, that bizarre creature, dressed all in black, for whom she had felt an instant compassion, because in the old woman's humiliation, she had sensed a parallel with her own circumstances, her own failures. The pretence of finding a pound coin had been a kind of salute to a fellow misfit.

The woman had known, of course, that the money did not belong to her, that she had never had a pound in her purse, simply a smattering of small change which, she had assumed, would be enough to purchase one measly cod fillet.

For one awful moment, Jess thought the woman's pride would stand in the way. Then she had smiled, and mouthed the words, 'Thank you.'

Thinking about the incident afterwards, Jess wondered who she was. Obviously a lady, by her air of quiet breeding. An eccentric? Oh yes, certainly that, judging by the outlandish clothes she wore – the sweeping black cloak and witch-like hat; mittened hands clutching a worn, black purse. A very lean purse, Jess noticed.

Now, watching Mr Sloane limping away to his lonely house in Lymington Crescent, Jess thought that the misfits, the eccentrics of this world, the lonely people, possessed one thing in common – this recognition of each other's isolation.

Great-Aunt Jessica, too, had been a misfit in a world which no longer made allowances for gentility and pride. Had a lack of understanding and generosity of spirit in her fellow human beings contributed towards that 'last-ditch' stand of hers behind the guardian walls of a decaying Victorian villa? Had she learned to mistrust the hostile world beyond the gates of her own driveway?

CHAPTER 6

A letter from Douglas shattered Jess's optimism. It was an odd letter, accusatory yet conciliatory. People were beginning to comment upon her prolonged absence, he wrote, and this was highly embarrassing. He wanted her assurance that she would return home immediately her great-aunt's property had been sold.

He realised, of course, that one must make allowances for a woman at her time of life. The tone of the letter implied that she was a woman of unpredictable moods and impulses; intolerant and irresponsible. He even suggested that the breakdown of the marriage was all her fault. Burning with indignation, she rang Mr Hoyle's office to make an appointment.

Hoyle read the letter, then laid it aside as though touching it had soiled his fingers. Jess anxiously awaited his comment. Hoyle did not speak for several minutes. Then he looked at her, smiled, and said, 'I gather from this that your husband has been in touch with his solicitor, who doubtless advised him that attack is often the best means of defence.'

'I don't quite understand.'

'Look at it in this light. Your husband, finding himself out on the proverbial limb, worried about your possible line of action, has taken steps to cover himself, to prove, should the need arise, that he had held out the proverbial olive branch.'

Glancing once more at the letter, he went on, 'In the event of your filing a divorce petition against him, and if it came to the question of paying you alimony, it would suit his purpose to argue that he had asked you to return to the matrimonial home, and that you had refused.'

William Hoyle had this knack of putting things into perspective, but Jess, who had never thought in terms of a divorce, division of property, or taking steps against Douglas, felt daunted by the prospect of engaging in a legal battle with her husband. 'I don't think I could face all that,' she said. 'Standing up in court, dragging personal matters into the limelight.'

'Things are different nowadays,' Hoyle said gently. 'I doubt if a court of law would enter into it, unless your husband decided to defend the petition, which, in my opinion, is hardly likely.'

A flurry of rain swept suddenly against the windowpanes.

'Divorce seems such a final, irrevocable step,' Jess said, thinking that the raindrops looked like tears.

'There is no need to do anything in a hurry,' Hoyle reminded her. 'The best advice I can give you is to write to your husband saying you are considering what steps to take. Or perhaps you'd prefer me to do so on your behalf?' He smiled. 'There's still nothing so awesome as a solicitor's letter typed on headed paper.'

'Oh yes, please.' He read relief, gratitude, in her eyes, and thought what a pity it was that she'd had her confidence shaken in this way. She had seemed so happy a few days ago when she came to the office to tell him about the Cornwells' offer for the stable-block, and he had felt happy for her sake, delighted by the news which would enable her to go ahead with her plans even without the council grant he had applied for.

He wondered, not for the first time, why any man in his right senses would wish to apostrophise, to denigrate so lovely a woman.

'Now you really must stop worrying,' he said, as she stood up to leave. 'Trust me to act in your best interests.'

'Of course. And – thank you.'

He walked with her to the head of the stairs. 'You haven't brought an umbrella,' he said anxiously.

'It wasn't raining when I came out.'

'But you'll get wet.' She was standing one step down. He could see the outline of her shoulder-blades beneath her light tweed jacket.

A feeling of tenderness overwhelmed him. 'You must

borrow mine,' he said gruffly. 'It's in the hallstand. The black one with the brown handle.'

She smiled up at him, twisting his heart with regret, and then she was gone, walking away from him into the rain.

Jess had always liked rain. As a child, she had loved rainy mornings, splashing through puddles on her way to school. Her first tiny umbrella had been red, with shiny spokes and a 'monkey up a stick' handle which her father had given her for her seventh birthday.

Afterwards, she had wanted every day to be rainy: could never explain to anyone how secure and happy she had felt in her secret world of plopping raindrops, beneath that glowing umbrella.

She walked quickly along Regent Street towards the Town Hall square, her mind full of the letter. Possibly what Douglas had written was true. Had she given up too easily, behaved unreasonably?

The rain had chilled the air. When the weather turned even colder, she would need a new winter coat: camel, perhaps, or a good belted tweed with a stand-up collar.

Useless to dwell on the past. She must forget about that letter. Mr Hoyle had advised her not to worry. Dear Mr Hoyle, her friend and comforter, a man she would trust to the ends of the earth and beyond.

Dora and Alfred had arranged to see Mr Mountjoy this afternoon, about the purchase of the stable-block.

Not wanting them to feel in any way restricted by her presence, Jess had decided to keep out of the way until the interview was over. She wanted no part of their discussion over money matters. All she wanted was the Cornwells' happiness: the two people who had made all the difference in the world to her own sense of well-being, of belonging.

The woman in the coat department was both kind and helpful, and the coat was exactly what Jess wanted — brown tweed with raglan sleeves, a tie belt and a generous collar.

When the purchase had been made, she wandered through the other departments, thinking how marvellously that moss-green velvet would blend with the dining-room furniture; how wonderful a Chinese lamp with a glowing red shade would look on the carved oak chest at the foot of the stairs.

Emerging from the store, she walked along towards the seafront. It had stopped raining. Turning the corner, she found herself near the harbour.

Most of the snack-bars and amusement arcades were shuttered now against the coming winter. Sand had begun to pile up, in drifts, along the deserted promenade, as though the town were drawing in upon itself to face the onslaught of winter. But the fish-pier was still a hive of activity, with fishing-cobles tethered to iron rings; fishermen swabbing decks, unloading boxes, inspecting the nets, whistling about their work.

She lingered there awhile, enjoying the feel of the salt air upon her face, watching the laid-up yachts and cabin cruisers straining at their moorings as the tide tugged at them, feeling herself an integral part of the swiftly running sea, the raucous cries of the seagulls swooping down to hover, on outspread wings, above the grey harbour walls; knowing that it was here she belonged, now and for all time.

Filled with an unaccountable feeling of joy, clinging to her carrier bag and Mr Hoyle's black umbrella with the brown handle, she walked slowly past the shuttered amusement arcades and noticed a sign with a pointing arrow: 'Bevensea Parish Church'. She began to climb upwards through a maze of narrow, twisting streets, between the pantiled fishermen's cottages of the Old Town of Bevensea Bay; until, at last, she stood upon the town's highest vantage point, misted with rising smoke from the chimneys, and looked back to see the whole town spread beneath her like a child's drawing of a town, blocked in with colourful wedges of pink and blue. It was bathed in mist, with twilight stealing in from the sea, and rainclouds rising, column upon column, from the far-flung horizon, and little pinpricks of early-switched-on street lights shining along the shore.

Walking on, she came at last to a grey wall, a graveyard with lichened stones, a Norman church set against a background of thickly clustered yew trees.

Pushing open the heavy oak door, she saw a blue-carpeted aisle stretching between polished pews to an altar of breathtaking beauty. Breathing in the scent of wax polish and autumn flowers, she noticed, by the dim light burning in the Lady Chapel, the figure of a young woman, standing near a stone pillar, looking up at one of the stained-glass windows. A woman wearing a tightly belted raincoat, whose shoulders were hunched forward slightly beneath a cascade of tawny hair.

Jess could not see her face, but she recognised Liz Fremont in an instant by her hair and the grace of her body, the intensity of her attitude.

Then, when the woman turned slightly and Jess caught sight of her in profile, she knew that she had not been mistaken, and quietly waited until Liz walked up the aisle towards her.

Approaching hesitantly, Jess noticed that the girl's cheeks were wet with tears. She said cautiously, 'Possibly you won't remember me. Jessica Carmichael?'

'But of course I remember you.' Liz brushed away her tears almost savagely, as though ashamed of some inner weakness. 'Laurel Villa. All those lovely dresses! Forgive me, I was lost in thought.'

'Jolyon King said you were interested in stained glass,' Jess ventured, wondering why Liz was so upset; not daring to ask. Yet the telepathy still worked.

'You know as well as I do that I didn't come here to look at the stained glass,' Liz said. She smiled briefly. 'I came here to work something out: something I can't quite come to terms with.'

Jess had gathered as much. 'Would it help to talk about it?' she asked.

Liz lifted her chin. Blinking away her tears, fiddling in

her shoulder-bag for a handkerchief, she said bleakly, 'I'm not quite sure. It's a man, of course. The man I'm in love with. He's gone away.' She laughed bitterly. 'And I thought it would last forever.'

'Nothing lasts forever,' Jess said slowly, intent upon her own memories, as they left the church.

'*Nothing?*'

'I'm sorry. Certainly not the "first, fine careless rapture", at any rate. It seems to me that everything is bound to move on, to move away from the past towards a totally new concept of living.' She lifted her face to the raindrops falling on her cheeks, glad of their freshness, their sweetness, not bothering to put up Mr Hoyle's umbrella.

Liz said hoarsely, 'Do you think it helps to pray?'

'I don't know. I'm not a very religious person. I simply believe in certain precepts of right and wrong, that human life is too precious to waste.'

They walked together between the leaning gravestones.

'I thought you were leaving Bevensea,' Liz said.

Jess smiled. 'I came back. I've decided to keep the house.'

'I'm so glad,' Liz said simply, 'it's such a lovely house – a house full of secrets.' She traced an indecipherable name with a delicate fingertip, 'I felt safe there. Comforted. Sorry, I'm not making much sense, am I?'

The rain was falling more heavily now, as sharp as needles in a pincushion. 'It might help to talk about it,' Jess said.

'Oh, I daresay you've heard it all before.' Liz laughed briefly. 'It's the age-old story of the married man, the "betrayed" woman!' Being Liz, she felt it necessary to clown the scene, to make fun of her feelings.

'Perhaps he'll come back some day,' Jess said.

'No, I don't think so.' Liz flicked back her hair, held it away from her face with both hands, pressing her palms to her temples, revealing her beautifully modelled cheekbones. 'Steen's work here is finished, you see. He's gone back to America – to San Francisco. His wife's name is Dominique. She's Mexican. Very beautiful. He showed me her photograph. Wasn't that kind of him? I say, we're getting soaked to the skin!'

'Sorry.' Jess opened the umbrella. 'My husband's mistress is called Avril,' she said. 'He didn't need to show me her photograph, I met her face to face at a sherry party. She's much younger than he is. Ironic, isn't it? I'm ten years older. He has this thing about age. My age in particular. I think he resented my fortieth birthday, my first grey hairs, my having to wear reading glasses. He wears glasses, of course, but that's different.'

Liz let her hair fall back into place. 'Men,' she said bitterly, 'God, how I hate them!' Then, more gently, 'I'm glad you came back, Jess. The last time we met, you were the one doing the packing up. Now it's my turn. I can't stay any longer at the flat, you see, where Steen and I were happy together. You know how it is when everything reminds you of someone you've lost? That bloom on life that will never come again.'

'What will you do?'

Liz shrugged. 'Oh, I'll probably end up in one of those winter-let flats the papers are full of at this time of year. One room carved up into cubbyholes, a Baby Belling cooker with an oven the size of a postage stamp. To be honest, I don't really care any more.'

Jess spoke without thinking. 'You could come to me, if you like.'

Liz drew in a sharp breath of relief. 'Really? God, that would be simply wonderful.'

The minute the words were out of her mouth, Jess regretted her impulsive offer. Not because she did not want Liz. She did. So much that she hadn't paused to consider the drawbacks of that cold room on the second landing.

She had to be honest with Liz. 'It might not be all that wonderful,' she admitted. 'There's no electricity laid on for a start. You wouldn't be able to cook for yourself.'

'You mean no Baby Belling? Hallelujah, praise the Lord!'

'I'm quite serious, believe me. The room I had in mind is rather big – and terribly cold.'

She had reckoned without the curious empathy between herself and Liz.

'I gather that you are trying to put me off,' Liz said.

'No, not exactly . . .'

'Tell me, is there a view of the sea from the window of this big, cold room of yours?'

'Well, yes, a marvellous view of the sea.'

Liz said wistfully, 'I'd like that. You know, Jess, in the case of that apocryphal Four Minute Warning, if I knew that I was about to die, I'd want to be close to the sea. I think I could bear it then, if I could watch the seagulls flying.' A shudder passed through her. 'If you don't want me, just say so. I'll make out somehow.'

'Of course I want you. I just wouldn't want to mislead you in any way.'

Liz said quietly, 'Dear Jess, I wouldn't want to mislead you either. Before you make up your mind one way or the other, before you rush into something you might regret later, there's something you should know. I'm pregnant!'

There was something unmistakable about October nights, Liz thought. A certain chill which froze the stars. She looked up at them now, far distant rapiers of light in the black arch of the sky above the yellow street lamps. Shivering, she turned away from the window.

This is the end for which we twain are met.

She moved slowly towards the settee in front of the simulated coal fire; absent-mindedly smoothed the crumpled linen cover where Steen's head had rested; imagined the incredible length of him lying there, totally relaxed, arms outstretched to her, lamplight shining on his tousled mass of dark, wet hair; bathrobe damp after showering: wanting coffee, wine, music – 'Adagio for Strings'. Wanting love. Life.

He had left his white towelling bathrobe on the hook behind the bathroom door. Whether by design or accident,

Liz was not quite certain. Possibly he had not wanted to find it among his possessions when he returned to San Francisco.

This flat had been Steen's idea. She hated it now. His presence had filled the rooms. He had left his imprint on everything he used; touched. He was a man who crumpled linen chair covers, sheets and pillowcases, with a careless disregard of who would iron them afterwards, because the things he used were not important.

Only life was important. Ideas, travel, books, music, the theatre, food and drink. His work above all. He was a man obsessed by work – the American link-up with British theatre groups, the interchange of actors; productions. Package deals with hotels and tourist agencies.

Steen Bancroft commuted as easily between England and the States, between San Francisco and his apartment in New York, as effortlessly as English office workers commute between Central London and Welwyn Garden City.

He had left his imprint on Liz.

She had started packing, after the evening performance, wandering aimlessly from room to room, opening and shutting drawers, emptying cupboards, coming across things which had meant little to him: packs of soap in Cellophane, bottles of after-shave lotion, tubes of toothpaste squeezed in the middle then thrown aside.

There were several unopened bottles of wine in the kitchen, she discovered; a freezer full of convenience food, a shelf stacked with herbs and spices – oregano, ginger, cumin.

He had shopped as extravagantly as he lived, bringing in more fresh flowers when the vases were already full to over flowing; stuffing yesterday's flowers into the waste-bin before they were dead.

Had she really believed that their affair would last? Steen Bancroft and Bevensea Bay had not been entirely compatible. The East Yorkshire Coast was, of course, his main centre of interest, within easy reach of so many thriving theatre companies in Leeds, Sheffield, York, Hull, and

Scarborough. But she knew he had chosen Bevensea Bay because of her, because of the instant rapport between them the moment they were introduced.

Thank God she had not told him she was pregnant when she knew he was leaving. She could not have borne that: had convinced herself that it was not important he should know. She had no intention of keeping the foetus, scarcely yet formed as a human being, whose removal would cause her no physical pain.

She was young. Her body would soon recover. The tiny seed of so passionate a love would simply be removed as if it had never existed. There was no other choice, she had known that the moment Steen told he he was going home – back to America, to his wife, Dominique, and their three-year-old son, Miguel. But what of the heart, the mind, the memory of love? The bitterness and the pain of loss?

She thought suddenly of Jess Carmichael; the house with the stained-glass doors and no mod cons: noticed that the simulated coal fire was not working properly. Why was it that one of the revolving discs which caused the fireglow effect always remained static?

She would use Jess's house as a caravanserai until the abortion was over, until she decided what to do next. Come the spring, she might go to New York: might even see Steen again.

Her career came first. She had worked too hard to allow the passion of an unguarded moment to ruin the future she had mapped out for herself.

Hair spilling forward, hands clasped, she experienced once more the familiar tug of ambition, that vital force which sang through her veins like blood.

She had known, as a child, that she wanted to be an actress; had always been a natural for the school plays and pantomines because of her height, her looks, her lack of inhibition. She was lucky, too, in having parents who had recognised and fostered her talent.

Her father worked as a signalman at King's Cross Station, her mother helped serve school dinners at the local comprehensive. They lived in a semi-detached house on a post-war housing estate near Walthamstow. By the time she was fifteen she had gained silver and gold medals for ballet and tap dancing at Miss Daisy Althrop's Academy in Walthamstow High Street, and read Shakespeare, Donne and Shaw from cover to cover in the privacy of her bedroom.

One evening, Daisy Althrop, a stylish blonde, had come to the house for a private word with her parents.

Sitting on the bottom step of the stairs, straining her ears to the sound of voices from the sitting room with its rexine cocktail cabinet, flights of wild duck, and the picture of the green-faced woman, she had wondered, agonisingly, what Miss Althrop had come to say that required so much discussion.

Eventually her mother had emerged, slightly flushed from the three glasses of sherry she had drunk in quick succession. 'You can come in now,' she said fondly, picking a stray hair from Liz's dark sweater. 'We've had a good talk with Daisy, and we won't stand in your way if you like the idea . . .'

'What – idea?'

'Of course, your headmistress might kick up a fuss, but you'll be leaving school next Easter in any case.' Mrs Fremont, slim, with dark, cropped hair, and threadveins which she concealed with heavy Max Factor pancake makeup, burst out laughing. 'Oh, Liz! If you could see your face!'

'Mum! If you don't stop teasing, I'll . . .'

'She wants you to go into a Christmas production of *Alice in Wonderland* at the Theatre Royal, in York! What do you think of that?'

'Oh, *Mum*!' At that moment, Liz had glimpsed the future shining before her as the Golden Road to Samarkand. And that had been the starting point, her initiation into the magic world of the professional theatre. The beginning that would certainly lead her to the Royal Academy of Dramatic Art.

Hedda Gabler, Cleopatra, St Joan. She had wanted to play them all. Ambition seemed, at times, an all-devouring flame burning inside her; hard work the food on which she thrived. The theatre was in her heart, mind, blood; in the air she breathed. Without her work, her ambition, there was nothing.

Now, staring into the dark void of her loneliness, she wondered if Steen had arrived in his windswept city with its Golden Gate Bridge and clanging trolley cars, to find his wife at the airport to meet him. If, making love to Dominique, he had spared a thought for that towelling bathrobe hanging behind the door of a flat in Bevensea Bay.

Dora was helping Jess to strip the dustsheets from one of the rooms on the second landing.

'An actress, you say?' Dora said doubtfully. 'Well, I just hope she won't start throwing wild parties and suchlike.'

'You needn't worry. Liz isn't like that. She's a very private, self-contained person.' Jess bundled up one of the sheets. 'I thought you'd be pleased.'

'Yes, I am in a way, except that . . . Well, what I mean is, if she's renting a room, she'll want to live in it, and I don't see how she can, as things are. She won't want the mess and bother of a coal fire, and I daresay she'll want to boil a kettle now and then, or make a bit of toast when she comes home from the theatre.'

It was obviously Dora's turn to play the devil's advocate. 'And what about that old-fashioned wallpaper and dark brown paint? Not to mention those lace curtains and roller-blinds. The dustbin's the only fit place for them!'

Jess wondered if she had bitten off more than she could chew. Dora was absolutely right. She ran her fingers through her hair.

'Mind you,' Dora went on, hating to see her ewe lamb upset, 'Alf could soon slap on a couple of coats of emulsion. Magnolia's a nice colour. And if you were to buy some material, I could easily run up some new curtains –

chintz or folkweave's not all that expensive.'

Jess had chosen this room for its lack of overpowering furniture. Gazing at the bare walls and mantelpiece, she wondered if her great-grandmother, grieved by the death of her elder son, the emigration of her younger, had simply decided to strip the rooms of their identity. And yet that seemed an odd thing for a mother to do.

'Eh, come on, love!' Dora slipped a comforting arm around Jess's waist. 'Don't take any notice of me saying what I did about actresses. Is she coming to look at the room?'

'No. She's rather busy at the moment.' Jess felt it expedient not to mention that Liz had seemed overwrought when she rang her. 'I just want to get out of this place as quickly as possible.' She'd sounded fraught; tense, irritable.

'Well, this won't buy the baby a new bonnet,' Dora sighed, causing Jess's heart to miss a beat until she realised that this was just one of her sayings. 'I'll go and find Alfred; ask him about the decorating.'

When she pottered away, Jess stared at the empty fireplace. No mod cons, she thought. Rushing in where angels feared to tread had always been one of her failings. Then suddenly . . . of course, why hadn't she thought of it before? She would ring the Gas Board immediately.

Flying downstairs, she bumped into Dora coming up. 'Whatever's the matter?' she asked in alarm.

'It came to me like a bolt from the blue,' Jess laughed. 'You know what you said about the mess and bother of a coal fire?'

'Yes.' Dora stood flattened against the banister, one hand clutched to her breast.

'Well, that's it! Don't you see. We haven't any electricity, but we have got . . .'

'Gas,' said Dora, smiling beatifically.

And so the transformation had taken place. On the day Liz was due to arrive, Jess put the finishing touches to the room; lit the brand new gas fire and placed a little pot of trailing ivy on the magnolia mantelpiece, beneath one of Clarice's watercolours.

The feeling of age and darkness had been dispelled by the fresh creaminess of the new paint, Dora's pink and fawn folk-weave curtains and matching bedspread.

Alfred had fixed shelves in an alcove, and helped Jess to lump upstairs one of the deep leather armchairs from Joshua's study, an oval table from the drawing-room, and a couple of rush-seated chairs from Clarice's parlour. Together they had manoeuvred the wardrobe into a less prominent position near the far wall, while Dora had polished the dressing-table to the patina of newly fallen chestnuts, and shampooed the carpet.

Jess knew that Liz would appreciate the privacy of this landing; her own bathroom. She had not told Dora that Liz was pregnant. That would become obvious in the fullness of time. She wondered what Liz would do when the baby began to show.

Standing near the window, absentmindedly smoothing the edge of a curtain, Jess looked out at the sea rocking gently to the grey blue horizon, and thought about the coming child.

On an impulse, she hurried down to her own room to fetch the nursing chair her grandmother must have used when her son was born, before she left this house to return to her family in Reading.

Suddenly she heard the crunch of tyres on the gravel. Liz had arrived.

Setting the chair in place, Jess gave one final glance round the room, and hurried down to greet her.

'Sorry if I sounded a bit offhand when you rang the other day,' Liz said blithely. 'I wouldn't have blamed you had you told me to find somewhere else to live, and slammed down the receiver.'

'You might have been better off if I had.' Jess handed her a cup of tea. 'I hadn't really meant to start letting rooms until the house was ready. It seemed a bit of a cheek, afterwards, expecting you to muck in here when you might have

111

found something better. It was simply . . .'

'I know. You felt sorry for me.'

'I wanted to help.'

Jess thought, at that moment, they might be rehearsing a scene from a second-rate comedy. Liz's voice sounded as brittle as egg shells. Her laughter rang hollow.

'You have helped – enormously. I suppose I might have gone back to Mrs Ruddle's boarding house where Jolyon and a few of the others hang out. But, well, quite frankly that idea did not appeal to me after . . .' She had been about to say, 'after Steen.'

Her eyes darkened suddenly with pain at the memory of their brief, almost casual goodbye on an early-morning station platform. The comedy scene was over. She stopped pretending.

They were having tea in the drawing-room. Jess had lit the fire and covered a small table with a white cloth, had polished her great-grandmother's silver tea-kettle, and brought out the pink and white china.

Liz glanced up at her. 'I really am sorry,' she said quietly. 'You've gone to a lot of trouble.'

'The trouble hasn't started yet,' Jess said wryly. 'Wait until the plumbers and electricians start ripping up the floorboards. My solicitor rang up this morning to tell me my grant's been confirmed.' Her eyes shone. 'The kitchen's to be given a facelift, and the conservatory repaired. You can't think what that will mean to me. It will be worth all the mess and bother . . .'

'I envy you,' Liz said simply.

'Why me?'

'Because of all this, I suppose.' Liz glanced round the room. 'Because you have the potential for happiness.'

'It's I who envy you,' Jess said. 'You will have the one thing I always wanted and never had. A child. It's too late for me now.'

Liz drew in a deep breath. She had not meant to tell Jess, so soon, about the abortion. Not to do so now would seem a betrayal of her confidence, her kindness. But the words,

'I'm not keeping the baby,' were not easy to say, she discovered. She spoke them in a low voice, shielding her face with her hand, looking into the fire, remembering Steen.

'You can't mean that!' Jess leaned forward urgently. 'This is your child you're talking about. *Yours!* A valuable human life!'

Liz looked up, her eyes brilliant with unshed tears. 'There's no way I can keep it,' she said angrily. 'I'm sorry I told you. I should have known better!'

She rose quickly to her feet. 'I'd better go before I cause you any more distress.' She laughed bitterly. 'You wondered why I was there in church that day. I could read your mind. Well, now you know. I was attempting to strike a bargain with God. "Forgive me this time, and I'll never sin again." Don't worry, I'll see myself out!'

'Very well then, go if you want to. I can't stop you running away. What you do with your life is your own affair. I imagined I could at least provide a roof, a kind of oasis; friendship . . .'

Jess remembered how much it would have meant if there had been someone close to her during the past months. Anger faded. She said dully, 'The offer still stands.'

Liz turned away. Resting her head against the mantelpiece, she began, noiselessly, to cry.

With an effort of will, Jess overcame the temptation to comfort her. In that delicately balanced moment she knew instinctively that one false move might sway Liz's decision to leave, that even a hand on her shoulder, a misplaced word of sympathy might do more harm than good.

She walked slowly to the window.

Shadows were lengthening, merging, blending. The first street lamps blossomed against the dusk of evening. Silently, Jess watched them spring to life along the esplanade, noticing the way the sea caught and held the wavering reflections.

In a little while she sensed rather than heard Liz moving towards her. 'Thank you,' she said simply, 'for letting me be. I couldn't have borne sympathy.'

113

'I know.' Until that moment, Jess scarcely realised that she had been praying inwardly. Her hands were still tightly clenched.

Liz laid a hand on her arm. 'Please forgive me. I must go ahead with the abortion. But I'd like to stay, if you'll have me. I really do need someone, you see. I need *you*, Jess!'

William Hoyle parked his car in the garage, closed the doors and walked slowly towards the house. Glancing up at the Georgian façade, the narrow, twelve-paned windows, the scalloped fanlight above the front door, the delicate tracery of ivy upon russet brickwork, he noticed that the curtains of Beryl's room had been drawn, although it was not quite dark yet.

He stood for a moment before entering the house, looking down the tree-lined road curving towards the heart of the town, seeing, in the far distance, the familiar roofs and church spires as a dreamlike Impressionist painting overlaid with a delicate wash of purple-grey evening mist, pierced with diffused pinpricks of light springing up along the shore.

There on the steps, latchkey in hand, he felt the sourness of age and habit as a presence, a kind of doppelganger which would slip, once the door opened, into his own shoes, to tread the negative pattern of homecoming.

He knew, from long experience, that Mrs Bartram, the housekeeper, hearing his footsteps on the parquet floor, would emerge from the kitchen, glance at the grandfather clock, and say reproachfully, 'You're home early tonight.'

It happened exactly as he knew it would. On this occasion, Mrs Bartram added unnecessarily: 'Madam hasn't been at all well today.'

Hanging up his hat and overcoat, he crossed to his study, shuffled through the pile of letters on his desk, switched off the light and went slowly upstairs to his wife's room.

'You're home early,' Beryl Hoyle said, with a marked lack of enthusiasm, holding up her cheek to be pecked.

'Yes. I finished early at the office.'

'I've had a dreadful day. Simply *awful*'!

She was lying in bed, propped up with pillows, wearing a pink shawl about her soft, plump shoulders. Mrs Hoyle was a lady who liked the colour pink. The bed-cover was pink, the smooth fitted carpet was also pink, with fawn roses. The pink-shaded lamps flanking the padded pink headboard cast a rosy glow over sheets crumpled by restless movement. A white-framed colour television flickered in a corner near the pink-skirted dressing table. Beryl's soft pink hand held the remote control switch as a kind of weapon. Her habit of changing rapidly from one channel to another irritated her husband almost beyond endurance.

'I'm sorry you're not well,' he said. 'What seems to be the trouble?'

'Oh, I don't know. Some kind of bug, I expect.'

'Have you sent for Dr Sanger?'

'No, of course not. You know how much I dislike him.' She had switched channels three times since her husband entered the room.

'Even so, he's a good doctor.'

'He doesn't begin to understand me. Neither do you!'

Hoyle closed the door quietly behind him. He had heard it all before.

He thought, as he went along to his own room to wash and change for dinner, that he had, perhaps, deserved his fate in marrying the wife his parents had chosen for him thirty-eight years ago, that the Meek did not necessarily inherit the Earth.

But why blame them? Taking off his tie, he remembered that Beryl had once been very pretty; charmingly doll-like, with fair hair and a roses and cream complexion. She was also the daughter of his father's closest business associate.

If only there had been a child. But Beryl had not wanted a baby. He wondered, for the thousandth time, if that had been the start of her hypochondria – forever feigning illness as her safeguard against an unwanted pregnancy.

Dinner, which he ate alone in the immaculately appointed dining-room with its bow-fronted sideboard and glossy Regency table, was predictably mundane. Chicken soup, fish pie, and rice pudding. He heard, as he ate, Mrs Bertram going upstairs with his wife's meal on a tray.

Christ, he thought. Christ. Oh dear Christ.

CHAPTER 7

Swirling her Wagnerian cloak about her shoulders, Miss Rachel Sweeting swept grandly from the Adsel supermarket into the cool fresh air of a pristine autumn morning, and walked as quickly as she could past the paper shop, the Green Man public house, and the launderette, before turning into the quiet cul-de-sac where she lived.

There, her heart hammering inside her chest, she slowed down to catch her breath. It had been a bad moment, at the check-out, thinking that she might suddenly feel the weight of a hand on her shoulder, accompanied by a request to step into the manager's office.

Seized with a sudden, almost uncontrollable shaking of her limbs, she clung desperately to the railing on the right-hand side of the steps leading to the front door of her lodgings – seven in all. Inserting her Yale key in the lock, she moved stiffly along the passage to her room overlooking the neglected back garden.

Locking the door behind her, she unpinned her broad-brimmed black hat, unfastened the cloak, and went across to the kitchen to fill the kettle.

Then, crossing over to the high, old-fashioned bed where she had flung her outdoor things, she rummaged in one of the deep inside pockets of the cloak to find the box of tea-bags and the packet of chocolate biscuits she had stolen, and went back to the kitchen recess to prise open the Cellophane with a pair of blunt scissors. She knew she had done wrong, but she had so wanted a nice cup of tea and a few chocolate biscuits for her elevenses.

Waiting for the kettle to boil, she hung up her cloak in the maplewood wardrobe which had been part of her bedroom furniture in the old house in Stickleback Lane.

Closing the heavy doors, she caught sight of herself in the damp-spotted mirror, and paused a while to consider the gaunt stranger staring back at her, the old woman with untidy white hair framing a thin, sallow face with high, jutting cheekbones, dark eyes etched about with a network of lines, and thin, pale lips which, slightly open, revealed the fine, prominent teeth of which she had always taken the greatest care, which, even now, in her seventies, she brushed regularly after meals, and at bedtime.

Her father had been fanatical about his family's health and well-being, encouraging his children – herself, her sister Lavinia, and their two brothers – to run about in the garden and play hide-and-seek in the orchard: to gorge themselves on the apples, plump blue damsons, yellow Victorias, and those deliciously sweet, juicy pears from which derived the name of the house – Pear Tree Cottage.

Not that their home could be accurately termed a cottage, Rachel thought, turning away from her mirrored reflection as the kettle began to boil. No, Pear Tree Cottage was not really a cottage at all, she mused, popping a couple of tea-bags into the pink teapot with the cracked lid, pouring on the boiling water, and setting, upon a Woolworth's plate, three of the stolen biscuits.

Looking back, as she often did these days, since there was little to look forward to except frightening things, Miss Sweeting sat down in the rocking-chair, near the window, to sip her tea and remember the way things used to be when she was a girl.

Pear Tree Cottage had always seemed so warm and cosy despite the smoke which gushed down the chimneys in wintertime. She laughed to herself, remembering how their father would rise up from his chair, waving his hands in mock alarm whenever that happened, and adjure the four of them to wrap up warmly and go for a quick run round the garden to get rid of the smoke in their lungs.

Nibbling a stolen chocolate biscuit, Miss Sweeting wondered whatever became of those lost, happy years of her childhood; why she had ended up like a jellyfish stranded upon a shore of loneliness and regret, poverty and old age.

Gazing about her, she noticed with a dull feeling of sickness and dread, the chintz curtain, on a sagging wire, covering the kitchen compartment; the tiny porcelain sink, gas-ring, and the ancient 'Kool' refrigerator with its crowning spongy circle of what looked like prehistoric pumice-stone, upon which she must pour, in summertime, a daily pint of cold water to make certain that her food remained edible.

What a ghastly room this was, to be sure, apart from one of the beds, one of the wardrobes, and this rocking-chair, which belonged to her. And how she'd had to struggle and cajole the landlady, Mrs Roach, with her black, shoe-button eyes, before the woman would allow the introduction of her own few remaining bits and pieces into what she referred to as her already 'adequately furnished' apartment.

'I mean to say, Miss Sweeting,' Mrs Roach said hostilely, when Rachel had come to look at the room five months ago, after the death of her sister Lavinia, 'there's already a good wardrobe, bed, and armchairs in situ, which I am not prepared to move out for the good and sufficient reason that I have nowhere else to put them.'

'But I am not for one moment suggesting that you should move out your furniture,' Rachel said, appealing to the woman's better nature. 'I'm simply asking that you will allow me to bring in mine.'

And so, after a great deal of grumbling on the part of the landlady, Rachel had ended up in a room containing two beds, two wardrobes, and three chairs — one a Victorian rocker from the old house in Stickleback Lane, the others cheap, mock-leather monstrosities of the post-war era, with hard springs and dark brown cushions edged with fuzzy, yellowish brown piping: a room whose crowded-together furniture and the far from inspiring view of the back garden, had brought to Miss Sweeting the full realisation that life, as she had once known it, filled to overflowing with love, hope and dreams, had utterly failed to bring to a fruitful, happy conclusion, any one of those dreams.

As for love. Well, she had known that was over and done with when she had received a letter from her fiancé's mother saying that her son, Captain Ronald Amersham, had been killed in action at Dieppe, during the Normandy landings. Her two brothers had also been killed during the war. Teddy at Monte Casino; Charles in the North African desert.

She and Lavinia had been left all alone then to manage as best they could. The house in Stickleback Lane had been requisitioned by the Army and sold, when the war ended, for a fraction of its real value; a kind of white elephant which nobody had cared to tackle because of its size, and the amount of money needed to restore the crumbling Victorian brickwork.

And so they had been obliged to rent a basement flat in a far from salubrious area of Bevensea, where the damp conditions had seriously affected Lavinia's health. Perhaps some of that smoke had got into her lungs, after all.

Gradually, as time went by, they had been forced to sell their personal items of jewellery – nothing of any real value – to make ends meet. Most of the Victorian furniture from the old house had been sent to the saleroom long ago. Then, when Lavinia became really ill, Rachel had insisted that she went into a private nursing home as befitted the daughter of a respected family of physicians, using the money which they had put aside as their 'nest-egg' to pay the nursing-home bills.

It seemed a terrible thought that poor Vinnie had died just in time, before the money quite ran out. But when the funeral expenses had been met, there was virtually nothing left for Rachel to live on except her State pension. Now all she had left in the world to call her own was her bed, rocking-chair and wardrobe, apart from a few items of china, photographs, and a host of memories.

Then had come the realisation that she could not, without the indignity of approaching the social-security people for supplementary benefit, begin to afford the small luxuries that made life worth while. And so she had begun to steal. Just small items, of course. Tins of salmon; apples, cartons of cream; biscuits; toothpaste; secreting her ill-gotten gains in the deep inner pockets of her cloak.

Covering her face with her hands, Miss Sweeting began, suddenly, to cry. To think that she, of all people, had resorted to petty crime to shore up her miserable existence. She had no doubt whatever that, sooner or later, would come the hand on her shoulder, the inevitable court appearance, the shame of having her name in the papers. Possibly even the final degradation of a prison sentence; the loss of her liberty – her home. This one room which, no matter how much she might loathe and detest it, was all she had left to cling to. Then what would become of her?

Rising stiffly to her feet, she walked firmly to the kitchen and began crumbling the stolen biscuits. That done, she washed away the crumbs, and stood there, wondering what to do about the tea-bags.

Of course, the answer was quite simple. She would boil the kettle once more, pack all the bags into the teapot, then pour the tea down the sink. But when the moment of truth arrived, when the kettle was boiling, Rachel knew that she was totally incapable of the wanton destruction of a perfectly good packet of PG Tips.

Filled with a burning curiosity about Laurel Villa, Felix Grant came personally to take the inventory, accompanied by his son Ronnie. They arrived almost at the same moment as William Hoyle, who had rung Jess earlier to say that there were a few papers he wanted her to sign.

Jess met them at the door. Dora, fluttering anxiously in the background, put the kettle on for coffee as they filed into the drawing room.

Hoyle glanced round, agreeably surprised. The fretted arches had been swept clean of cobwebs. There were new curtains at the landing window, and the drawing-room had been cleared of the overpowering display of ornaments and domed glass cases.

'I've moved most of the smaller items into the dining-room,' Jess explained. 'I thought it would make things easier for you.'

Grant, in his well-upholstered fifties, with red-veined cheeks, wearing tweeds and a lovat tie, looked more like a prosperous farmer than an auctioneer, Jess thought, while his son resembled one of those smart young executive types in TV insurance ads.

'I thought you'd like some coffee first, before we begin the "grand tour",' she said lightly. 'Ah, here's Dora now.'

The three men rose to their feet as Dora advanced with the tray. 'Allow me,' Hoyle said, clearing a space. 'May I say how remarkably well you are looking?'

Dora beamed. Pleased with the compliment, she set down the tray and acknowledged her introduction to the Grants with brisk handshakes. 'I'm feeling better', she admitted, 'now that everything's been sorted out.'

'You haven't brought a cup for yourself,' Jess reminded her.

'Oh, Alfred and I will have ours in the kitchen. We're in the middle of clearing the storeroom ready for the workmen,' Dora replied airily. 'There's a lot to do before next week.'

'It would be a great help if the removal could take place before the alterations get under way,' Jess said, handing Grant the sugar-bowl.

'No problem.' He waved the tongs dismissively, a man well inured to setting people's minds at rest. 'Once the inventory's been taken, my men can get to work almost immediately. Today's Wednesday. They can shift the stuff on Friday – or Monday. Whichever you prefer.'

'Monday will be fine.'

'Make a note of that, Ronnie,' Grant said expansively, helping himself to the sugar.

Jess smiled to herself, thinking, inconsequentially, of Laurel and Hardy.

She looked as excited as a child at a birthday party, Hoyle thought. Incredibly young and clear-eyed, casually but neatly dressed in slacks and a sweater; a green paisley scarf at her throat.

'I've decided to keep the carpets,' she said eagerly, leaning forward to rescue the sugar-bowl which she passed to William. 'They'd be far too costly to replace.'

Her cheeks were flushed with excitement he noticed;

stained a delicate wild rose colour; her hair, highlighted with silver threads, reminded him of the first traces of frost on an autumn morning.

'And I'd like to keep these chairs and the sofa. But the sideboard can go, and the over-mantel. I think they are too overpowering.'

After coffee, they moved across the hall to Joshua's study. 'I'm not quite sure what to do about this room,' she said, speaking to Hoyle, inviting his comment. 'What do you think?'

Knowing her dislike of the library, he said thoughtfully, 'It might be as well to clear it entirely – apart from the carpet and one of the bookcases. By the way, Felix, I think I should mention that there are several first editions.'

'Really?' Grant raised his eyebrows. 'Make a note of that, Ronnie.'

Hoyle caught Jess's eye, and smiled, warmed by a sudden feeling of comradeship.

'Perhaps we'd better take a look at the dining-room,' Jess said, leading the way.

'My word!' Obviously impressed, Grant stepped forward eagerly. The table, sheeted to prevent scratching, was filled end to end with silverware, china and glass – all sparklingly clean and polished; epernes, candelabra, meat-covers, cutlery.

Even young Ronnie Grant seemed impressed by this massive display of Victoriana, the great willow-pattern dishes and tureens; delicately cut lustres and rose-shaded oil-lamps; spirit and wine decanters.

Jess had set out the Goss china on the side-table along with the domed cases of birds and artificial flowers – which she detested. They looked so funereal.

'My God!' Grant said forcibly. 'Hannah Barlow!' He picked up and examined eagerly one of a pair of vases. 'My dear Mrs Carmichael!'

'You mean they're valuable?' Jess raised her eyebrows.

'Not only valuable but extremely rare.' Grant had taken out his eyeglass for a closer inspection.

'Gosh! I very nearly threw them out,' Jess admitted. 'They were in my great-grandfather's room. I thought how ugly they were.'

Hoyle laughed. Grant looked suitably shocked. Ronnie jingled the dangling lustres of one of the oil-lamps. His father glared at him. Ronnie blushed.

'What about the table and chairs?' Hoyle asked conspiratorially.

'Oh well, I'd better hang on to them, hadn't I, if I'm to become a . . . landlady?'

Hoyle frowned. 'You mean you are thinking along hotel lines? Doing the cooking?'

'There's no alternative,' Jess explained. 'There's no way my guests – always supposing there are any – could cook for themselves.'

'But,' Hoyle said anxiously, 'have you thought of all the hard work that would entail?'

Jess smiled. 'I'm not afraid of hard work. In any case, I would just provide breakfast and an evening meal. I'd enjoy doing that. How else would I fill in my time?'

'Yes, I see.' Hoyle did see. He understood clearly her need to keep busy as a shield against uselessness; he knew because he, too, felt the same need.

There was a great deal to be looked at, gone over and discussed. It had not been easy for Jess to decide what to keep and what to sell. The house was far too big and grand to strip completely. These rooms were not designed for modern, lightweight furniture. It was really a matter of striking a balance in this eponymous guest house of hers.

The people who came to live here would naturally want to bring their own belongings but, Jess thought, to blend in with rather than to swamp the pre-eminently Victorian character of Laurel Villa. Besides, she did not want to let the rooms entirely unfurnished. Dora and Alfred had warned her against that.

In any event, she believed she would know instinctively the kind of people who would merge against this background. Possibly lonely, retired people who had kept a nucleus of solid furniture from their former homes – doctors or dons, elderly widows, schoolmistresses, bank managers, solicitors.

The future had seemed bathed with a rosy glow until she remembered, with a laugh at her own expense, that her first lodger was neither retired or elderly, but a pregnant young actress about to have an abortion. Ah well . . .

But she had long since decided that she would keep Clarice's parlour intact. Great-Aunt Jessica would turn in her grave if that room was disturbed.

Also, she felt reluctant to have her great-aunt's room stripped of its massive bed, wardrobes and chests-of-drawers, but this was possibly the finest room in the house – apart from Joshua's – which presented another problem. She could not very well remove the furniture, leaving the Cornwells high and dry. Or so she thought, until Dora said, 'Oh, fudge! You sell whatever you've a mind to. We'll manage somehow. Don't forget we've got our own stuff stowed away in the stables.'

Hoyle knew exactly how Jess felt when she told Grant to include most of the furniture from those two rooms, in his inventory.

Perspicaciously, 'Have you thought where *you* are going to live?' William asked gently.

Jess glanced at him curiously. 'Well, as you know, I'm sleeping in my great-grandmother's bedroom at the moment,' and then she knew what he meant. Sleeping, not living. 'I'm afraid the furniture up here will not qualify for a sale of importance,' she said when they came to the servants' quarters. 'I only wish that it might.' She smiled wistfully, and picked up Annie Petch's Bible. 'Not for mercenary reasons, simply because of the wretched time they must have endured. As if servants scarcely counted as human beings.'

'Oh, I don't know.' Grant cast an expert eye over the walls and ceilings. 'They're not bad rooms. Remarkably good compared with some I've seen. At least they're light and dry. But you're right about the furniture. It's rubbish!

125

Still, my men can take it along with the rest of the stuff.'

Hoyle knew that Grant's careless remark had hurt Jess. Her knuckles whitened on the book she was holding. 'We'd better go down and take a look at the kitchen quarters,' she said sharply. 'I believe you'll find a lot more – rubbish – there too!'

The barb glanced off Felix Grant's thick hide, but Jess knew that William Hoyle understood her compassionate, possibly ridiculous concern for that lost generation of servants who had lived in poverty under this roof.

When the Grants had whisked away in their silver Mercedes, Jess and Hoyle went back to the drawing-room.

'There's something I'd like to discuss with you, when you've signed these papers,' he said, opening his briefcase.

'Just a sec. I'll need my glasses. They're in my handbag.'

She experienced, as she slipped them on, the old familiar feeling of self-consciousness. 'Douglas hated me in glasses,' she explained. 'I suppose he thought they made me look older.'

'That was short-sighted of him,' Hoyle remarked drily.

Jess laughed. 'Actually he *is* short-sighted: has a bit of a complex about it. Where do you want me to sign?'

As she bent forward, Hoyle added another piece to his mental jigsaw of Douglas Carmichael. The slowly emerging picture was not an attractive one. He had found himself thinking a great deal about Jess's husband recently. It was not unusual for wronged wives to spill out their resentment in a torrent of words and tears. In this case, the 'wronged' wife had uttered no bitter recriminations against her husband, had levelled no accusations, made no demands.

'There,' Jess said, straightening up, 'is that all right?'

'Fine.' He paused.

'Please sit down, Mr Hoyle. I'll put more wood on the fire.'

He watched in silence as she knelt to her task. 'Well now, fire away!'

'This matter of where you are to live,' he said slowly. 'I think it is very important.'

'I hadn't thought of it until you mentioned it,' she admitted. 'I had simply imagined myself flitting from room to room.'

'Yes. But have you thought that when most of the rooms are occupied, you will need a door of your own to close behind you?'

'A kind of oasis?' she said wistfully.

'Yes, an oasis.'

'And you think I should plant my date palms in the servants' quarters. Is that it?'

'It occurred to me that those rooms would convert into a splendid self-contained flat,' he said gently. 'Moreover, you would have your own staircase. You'll need privacy.'

'Privacy,' she said, savouring the word. 'Of course you are perfectly right. But then, you always are.'

He felt the touch of her hand on his. She was still kneeling on the hearthrug, looking up at him; smiling, warming his heart with her new-found happiness.

Hoyle's fleeting moment of joy terminated abruptly as Jess removed her hand to sweep a scattering of ash from the hearth. He cleared his throat in a valiant attempt at a new topic of conversation.

'I – er – noticed you picked up a book.'

'Oh, yes.' Jess laid down the hearth-brush. 'Annie Petch's Bible.'

'Annie Petch?' he mused.

'Probably one of the servants.' Jess scrambled to her feet. 'Would you like to look at it?' She spoke abstractedly, mulling over the idea Mr Hoyle had implanted. An oasis on the top floor. She had the feeling that events were running away with her as she handed him the book: happening far too quickly.

She had repaid the petty-cash and temporary bank loans as soon as the contract with Alfred and Dora had been finalised. Once the heavy furniture had been removed to the saleroom, carpets would have to be rolled up in readiness for the plumbers and electricians. The place would be in chaos. But from that temporary chaos a new life would emerge.

She thought, wistfully, that Laurel Villa seemed like an elderly lady being operated on for her own good.

At least the 'operation' would soon be over. And when the workmen had stitched up the earth-wounds above the newly laid pipes and cables, she could begin the post-operative business of covering the wall-scars with new paint and wallpaper.

There were many of her great-aunt's and Clarice's treasures still left to her – certain pieces of furniture, several paintings and watercolours, items of china, glassware and silver which she would never willingly part with.

She thought, as Hoyle examined Annie Petch's Bible, that when her oasis was ready to move into, she would gather together those nostalgic reminders of the past beneath her metaphysical date palms.

'I've seen the name Annie Petch somewhere before,' Hoyle said, breaking into her thoughts. His forehead puckered in a frown of concentration. 'Ah yes! Of course! The day of Jessica's funeral! I saw that name engraved on a stone in the old Greyfriar's Road cemetery!'

'Really? How interesting!'

'Yes. The inscription struck me as unusual. It read, as I remember, "Sacred to the Memory of Annie Petch. A Devoted Servant and Friend".'

'I have never visited my great-aunt's grave,' Jess said uneasily, 'and that has worried me a good deal. She was buried in the old cemetery, you say?'

'Yes, the family plot. Burials do not normally take place there nowadays, but Miss Tidey left explicit instructions that she wished to be interred next to her mother.'

'I see.' Jess paused, then, 'I should like to go there as soon as possible,' she said quietly. 'Would it be asking too much for you to come with me?'

Hoyle smiled. 'I was about to suggest that in any case. My car's at the door. We could go now, if you wish.'

She bought flowers on the way: a sheaf of white chrysanthemums with curled petals for Jessica; bunches of glowing red dahlias for Annie Petch.

Strangely, she had never found old cemeteries in any way macabre or chilling, rather sad and gentle places. It was the new cemeteries, as harsh and glaring as neon light, that disturbed her: the rawness of white marble arranged in uncompromisingly straight rows. Or perhaps it was simply that time had not softened her grief over the crosses raised to her parents, and her brother Stephen.

In this old Victorian cemetery, however, grief did not seem so recent, so personal, as though the passage of time had softened and mellowed the very earth which undulated softly above the graves.

High wrought-iron gates were set in a brick wall pierced with strengthening ties and bolts. Paths wound intricate patterns beneath trees whose branches were beginning to emerge, as winter skeletons, from the steady drift of falling leaves. As the rain which had threatened all morning began to fall, Hoyle put up his black umbrella with the brown handle.

'Over there,' he said quietly, guiding her footsteps, holding the umbrella over her head, tucking his free hand into the crook of her elbow.

The monument marking the last resting place of the Tidey family dominated the surrounding gravestones. Sculpted from solid Aberdeen granite, it resembled a towering exclamation mark, surmounted by an urn inscribed with the words: 'Lay Hold on Life'.

'Jessica's name will be inscribed later,' Hoyle told her. 'The work has already been commissioned.'

'The wording seems so brief, so formal,' Jess said, staring at the bronze disc set in the obelisk, which gave the names and dates of the birth and death of the people buried there. Nothing more. 'No mention of – love.'

She remembered that Mr Hoyle had once said that there was 'no love lost between your great-aunt and her father'. Looking at that clinical inscription, Jess wondered if there had been any love lost between husband and wife.

129

A rusted vase, long empty of flowers, stood forlornly upon the grave. Her great-aunt's floral tributes had obviously been removed, by the cemetery caretaker, when they were dead. She asked Hoyle how many there had been. 'Five,' he told her, 'from the Cornwells, Dr Sanger, the district nurse, my firm, and myself.'

'Which is tantamount to saying that you sent two wreaths?'

'Well, I wanted to be sure,' Hoyle admitted. 'I had no way of knowing that Sanger and the district nurse would send floral tributes until the day of the funeral.'

Hoyle's concern that a lonely old woman's coffin should not go to its last resting place bearing a single wreath, touched Jess deeply. Thank God it was raining. She bent her head to unwrap her great aunt's chrysanthemums, ashamed of her tears.

'I'll fetch some water for the vase,' Hoyle murmured, turning away, understanding her emotion. 'Here. You'd better hold on to the umbrella.'

When Jessica's flowers had been arranged, she asked about Annie Petch's grave, and Hoyle showed her where it was, half hidden by the lower branches of a yew tree.

The headstone revealed that Annie Petch had died young.

So Annie was not the old retainer of Jess's imagination, but a 30-year-old woman who had, nevertheless, during her brief lifetime, earned the accolade of Friend as well as Servant.

At least poor Annie had merited someone's love. Walking back with Hoyle to the car, Jess wondered whose love – and why.

CHAPTER 8

Johnny McEvoy lay sprawled on the shabby settee in front of the television, his feet resting on a low coffee-table littered with his mother's beauty magazines, bottles of nail varnish, a pair of discarded tights, an ashtray filled with lipstick-smeared cigarette stubs, and a mug half full of cold coffee.

She always got ready for work in the kitchen-cum-sitting room, squinting at the clock, coughing on the smoke from her cigarette; repairing her washing-up-impaired nail-varnish, standing in front of the mirror to drag a wire brush through her tangle of bleached fair hair, raising herself on tiptoe the better to see herself – a tiny figure in the clinging black dress which she referred to as her 'working clobber'; chattering all the while; issuing orders: 'Now don't forget to turn off the fire when you go up to bed. And don't forget to take your dad's supper out of the fridge. You know how he carries on if it's not put on the table in front of him. And make sure Colleen's not fallen asleep with her radio on! Oh God. I'm going to be late again, if I don't hurry!'

It was always the same. Johnny listened with half an ear to the stream of consciousness issuing between her full red lips. And yet he was fond of his foolish impractical mother, whom he regarded as a slightly tatty version of Marilyn Monroe – the screen goddess whose films had been featured recently on TV – Marilyn Monroe playing the part of an ageing cloakroom-attendant in a Newcastle night club.

In his 14-year-old wisdom, he reckoned it must be hard for a woman nudging 40 to keep up the illusion of youth. Most of his school-mates' mothers had given up the unequal struggle long ago. He met them often enough, coming out of the supermarket wearing elastic-waisted skirts and squashed-flat sandals, lumping plastic shopping bags, and smelling unpleasantly of body odour.

His mother, on the other hand, always reeked of scent. Her 'insurance policy' she called it: Coty l'Aimant or her favourite— Estée Lauder's 'Youth Dew'. And she looked smashing when she was ready for work – done up like a dog's dinner in her figure-hugging black dress, dangling earrings, black tights and high-heeled court shoes, with perhaps a scrap of emerald green or scarlet chiffon wound round her throat, which she referred to as 'ringing the changes'.

When she had talked and cigarette-butted her way out of the house, Johnny would watch television for a little while longer, then get up reluctantly to remove from the refrigerator whatever his 'dad' was supposed to have for his supper, which she left on a plate covered with an upturned cereal dish – a hunk of pork pie and a couple of sliced tomatoes, or maybe a chicken portion and a dollop of chutney, which he would plonk unceremoniously on the kitchen-table, along with a sliced loaf, a tub of poly-unsaturated margarine, and a couple of tins of beer – knowing the row there'd be if his mother's husband came home to find that he hadn't been properly catered for.

His mother's husband! Thinking of him as such mit-igated, to some extent, Johnny's hatred of the man his mother had married twelve months ago. But nothing she could say or do would persuade Johnny to change his name to Stubbings. Moreover, he had declared hotly before the ceremony, Colleen wouldn't change her name either. He'd see to that, because he still loved their real father, with his thatch of dark curly hair and laughing Irish eyes, and no fat slob of a Geordie would ever take Rory McEvoy's place.

His mother had clung to him then, tearful and upset, say-ing that she was marrying Bert Stubbings as much for their sake as hers. 'You don't understand,' she'd said bitterly, drying her tears, dabbing on more powder, and lighting a desperately needed cigarette, 'how could you? You're only a boy. But a woman needs security, someone to lean on, and Bert has a good steady job at the leisure centre. Oh that may not mean much to you, but it means a hell of a lot to me. How do you think I've managed all these years since your dad left me? Huh, think a lot of him you do, but you

132

never knew him as I did: lazy, bone-selfish, forever spouting poetry and playing that bloody guitar of his – as if that would put clothes on our backs or food in our stomachs!'

His sister Colleen, dressed for the registry office in a pink satin dress, with gold studs in her puffy pink ear-lobes, clutching a posy of pink silk roses, had begun to cry then. Johnny's anger had almost choked him. 'And yet you found enough money to waste on having Colleen's ears pierced,' he said bitterly. 'A kid of her age! Why couldn't we have gone on managing for a bit longer? After all, I'll be leaving school soon, bringing in my own money!'

His mother had hugged him fiercely then. 'You still don't understand,' she said weepily, 'there's more to it than that. I – love – Bert. I *need* him! Oh Christ, Johnny, it's almost time for us to leave. Don't making things more difficult for me than they already are.'

She'd turned her head away at that moment. 'There's something else, you see. Something I haven't told you. I'm going to have a baby.'

He had stared at her flushed, foolish face as if she had struck him, and struggled away from her, not wanting her to touch him any more, an awkward teenager filled with the shame of knowing that his mother had been messing about with a man; that he would be forced to watch her growing fat and ugly again, as she had done before Colleen was born.

But his mother had lost her baby in the sixth month of her pregnancy. The rows had been growing in intensity about that time. He knew because he had heard his mother and Bert shouting at each other in their room across the landing; saying terrible things to each other, something about that 'tart' Bert was carrying on with, and him coming home 'pissed' every night; Bert telling her to shut her bloody mouth before he shut it for her, and his mother yelling at him to hit her if he dare.

Then one terrible night, hearing his mother scream out in pain, Johnny got up and rushed into their room, shouting at Bert to leave her alone.

She was crouched on the floor, rocking to and fro, doubled up with pain, clutching her stomach, her face the colour of clay. Then Bert, in singlet and trousers, had flopped to his knees beside her, blubbering that he was sorry; that he hadn't meant to hit her so hard; urging her to get up and lie on the bed. And Johnny had stood there watching as Bert hauled her to her feet; had seen, with dreadful fascination, the pool of blood on the carpet.

'You'd better fetch the doctor,' Bert had said, shocked into sobriety at the sight of the blood. But Johnny had known that his mother needed an ambulance, and he had run all the way to the phone box on the corner to dial 999.

Bert had mended his ways after that, and his foolish mother had forgiven him for causing her miscarriage. But Johnny had never forgiven him; would never forgive him until the day he died.

Now, he and his stepfather hardly spoke a word to each other. As soon as his mother had gone to work at half-past ten, knowing that Bert would come in half an hour later from clearing up at the leisure centre, Johnny would simply leave out Bert's grub and go to bed to listen to Radio One, so that he wouldn't have to speak to the fat bastard, or watch him shovel his supper into his mouth.

But there was more to it than that. He had begun noticing lately the way his step-father had started playing about with Colleen, sliding his arm round her waist, fondling her long fair hair and calling her 'Petal'. Then something inside Johnny McEvoy alerted him to danger. In his room next door to his sister's, he would lie all tensed up, awaiting the heavy creak of Bert's footsteps on the stair, ready to do battle if once, just once, those footsteps stopped outside Colleen's door.

CHAPTER 9

When his wife left him for a younger, richer man, Mark Sanger had assumed a defensive attitude towards life. Mentally, he had pulled up the drawbridge.

Many of his former, so-called friends, he had realised bitterly, were simply Margaret's admirers – a coterie of charming sycophants dazzled by her brilliance and beauty. Strange how the wind of change had separated the wheat from the chaff. A mere handful of friends – people whom Margaret had considered boring – were left to him now, William Hoyle among them.

Sanger's house, set in a quarter acre of roughly mown grass with unkempt borders, stood in what the local estate agents described as a 'desirable residential neighbourhood'. The privet hedge, towering above woven larch fencing, almost obscured the brass nameplate affixed to one of the gateposts. The pebbled drive curved to a porch hung with a straggling mass of unpruned clematis, brittle now from the sugar-icing frosts of mid-October. The lawn was messy with unswept leaves.

He had sold, since Margaret's departure, the lease of his former premises in Regent Street, and turned the two main ground-floor rooms of his home into a surgery and waiting room. Pressure of work left him little time to attend to the garden. A part-time housekeeper came in three days a week to clean and cook for him. The rest of the time he managed to survive on convenience food and pub lunches. He could not have borne the presence of a full-time woman.

A faintly aseptic odour pervaded the entrance hall, the walls of which had been papered with a serviceable anaglypta. The waiting room had been partitioned to provide an office for his receptionist. The remaining space was taken up with a circular mahogany table and a dozen dining-chairs with rexine seats.

Flicking over the pages of a last year's edition of *Punch*, Liz Fremont gave up the pretence of reading, glanced impatiently at her wrist-watch, and asked the receptionist how much longer Dr Sanger was likely to be.

The woman smiled and said that the doctor was very thorough. He must be, Liz thought; that strange-looking old lady in a black cloak and hat, who had gone in before her, had been with Dr Sanger more than half-an-hour already.

The receptionist knew Liz by sight, and supposed that actresses were naturally temperamental. Besides which there had been a lengthy discussion about her medical card.

'Medical card? I haven't got one.' Liz pushed back her hair distractedly. 'Does that mean I can't see the doctor?'

'Oh no, I can fill out a temporary card for you. But if you intend to become a regular patient, you must go through the proper channels.'

The thought of going through the 'proper channels' seemd as inimical to Liz as facing a strange doctor and saying she wanted an abortion. The whole situation was abhorrent to her. She wanted the whole thing over and done with as quickly as possible: wanted Steen out of her system, and the child he had so carelessly fathered on her.

When the buzzer sounded, Liz got up, threw down the magazine, and walked firmly to the door. The old woman in black was just leaving. Crying by the look of her.

'Sit down.' Sanger spoke abruptly, not looking up as Liz entered, apparently engaged in making notes in his desk diary, finishing what he was doing before raising his eyes.

'I prefer to stand,' she said coolly, disliking his manner, noticing the strong dark hairs on the back of his hands, the bulldog set of his shoulders beneath his shabby tweed jacket, the foreshortened features dominated by a jutting nose and dark eyebrows which met almost in the middle – a sure sign of a bad temper.

Sanger blew out his lips. 'If you insist upon standing, I shall feel obliged to stand up also. I would rather not. A matter of pride, Miss Fremont. You are considerably taller than I am. Apart from which, I find the idea of conducting a consultation, standing up, somewhat ludicrous.'

Liz sat down abruptly. 'You recognise me?' Her voice was tinged with amusement. What a strange little man, she thought.

Sanger closed the desk diary and laid down his pen. 'I saw you in the Fry play, *The Brontës of Haworth.*'

'Really? What did you think of it?'

He sat back in his chair. 'The constant scene-shifting, though it was cleverly done, detracted from my enjoyment. Lighting would have been more subtle than those blocks of wood they kept heaving about the stage. And I found the constant appearances of "Mrs Gaskell" more than a little irritating.'

'Is that all?'

Sanger considered the question carefully. 'No, the auditorium was so cold, I caught a chill. I complained to the manager half way through, but the damage was done.' He regarded Liz thoughtfully. 'Ah, you want me to say how much I enjoyed your performance as Emily Brontë? But yours was a comparatively minor role. Fry, in my opinion, rather wasted his talent in this direction. The character lacked the necessary touch of vitriol.' His lips quirked slightly. 'However, you died quite prettily upon your horse-hair sofa.'

'Thank you,' Liz said stiffly.

'Well, what can I do for you? If you've come for a bottle of tranquillisers, perhaps I should warn you – I don't believe in them.'

'I haven't.' This, Liz felt, was a man upon whom subtlety would be wasted. She drew in a deep breath. 'I want an abortion.'

Suddenly Sanger rose to his feet, turned his back on her, and began studying a 'Smoking Can Cause Cancer' notice pinned to an aides-memoires board as intently as if he had never seen it before. Hands thrust deep in the pockets of his leather-patched jacket, he said, 'I wonder if it's true that Emily Brontë had a lover. What do you think?'

'Really Dr Sanger, I did not come here to discuss Emily Brontë's love life!' Liz sprang to her feet. It was true what

137

he said. She was at least four inches taller than the brusque little man whose clothes looked as if they had been slept in. 'Do you intend to help me or not?'

'Help you? My God!' He spun round, his face dark with anger. 'Woman! You are young! You have a superb child-bearing body! Have you any idea of the number of women who come to me, frantic because they cannot conceive? And there you stand, asking me to help you abort an innocent life!'

He spoke passionately, contemptuously. 'But then, this is a disposable age we're living in! Disposable nappies! Disposable lovers! Disposable lives! The age of unconsidered sex and its consequences!'

Anger boiled up in Liz. 'If I had wanted a lecture on morality, I would have gone to a parson! I don't need you to search my conscience for me. The reasons why I want an abortion are none of your damned business! If you won't help me, I'll find someone who will!'

Scooping up her handbag, she headed blindly for the door.

'Oh, for heaven's sake let us sit down,' Sanger said wearily. 'It is very much my business to know the reasons. They are manifold, believe me. Often dreary, soul-destroying reasons which someone in your position might find difficult to understand. Malformation of the uterus. Women with more children than they know how to cope with as it is, left alone to fend for themselves for one reason or another. Believe me, I know! Women faced with giving birth to a brain-damaged child, possibly a much wanted child. Women for whom I feel the utmost compassion . . . What are your reasons, Miss Fremont?'

She faced him grimly. 'The father of my child is already married: living abroad. I have my career to think of.'

'Ah yes, your career. That make-believe world of yours.'

'And you consider that unimportant? It may seem so to you. To me it is the most important factor of my life. I've worked bloody hard to get where I am – and this is just the beginning.' Tears sprang to her eyes. 'But what's the use of

138

talking! You think this is easy for me? How dare you assume that my affair meant nothing?'

'And if the father had not been married? If he had not left you – which I assume he must have done – how would you have felt then? Would you have still wanted an abortion?'

'No. Yes. I – don't know.'

Sanger's face softened. 'At least that is honest.'

'I loved him,' she said simply, brushing away the tears. 'I thought he loved me. Enough to . . .'

'Enough to leave his wife? To create more unhappiness? Tell me, is there a child – children – of that marriage?'

'One child. A boy.'

'I see.' Sanger picked up his pen; tapped it thoughtfully on the desk. 'Does the man in question know that you are pregnant?'

Liz shook her head. 'I didn't tell him.' She wondered how long the catechism would continue. She couldn't stand much more.

'Has it occurred to you that he has a right to know? He might not want his child aborted.'

'Oh, for Christ's sake! This is my decision. Mine alone! I have no other choice!'

'You could go ahead with the pregnancy,' Sanger suggested quietly. 'Give birth to the child – have it adopted.' He rubbed his hand across his eyes as if, Liz thought, some facet of their conversation had touched a chord of memory too painful to pursue.

He said slowly, 'There are so many unwanted children in the world, so many childless, unfulfilled women – and yet the scales remain unbalanced. It seems such a waste.'

'Possibly. But that doesn't solve my problem.' Liz squared her shoulders. 'I'm sorry, Dr Sanger. I came here for a specific reason. I need to know whether or not you are prepared to help me. The discussion of generalities seems rather pointless.'

Sanger's lips tightened. 'As you so rightly suggest,' he said briefly, 'I am neither priest nor arbiter in the ethics of human behaviour. There is, however, one point I must make clear. Abortion is not the simple affair that you may have been led to believe.'

'I'm not sure I understand what you mean by "led to believe". I haven't been indulging in heart-to-heart discussions on the matter, if that's what you think.' Liz flicked back a strand of hair with trembling fingers. 'I have had the penny lecture on morality. Why don't you come to the point?'

'Very well then. Since you are determined to go ahead, I will write a letter to the consultant gynaecologist of the Pregnancy Advisory Clinic, stating your reasons for wanting an abortion. An appointment will be made for you to undergo examination and questioning.'

'Questioning? My God! More questioning?' Liz bit her lip. 'But *why*? I thought . . .'

'Yes, I know what you thought. Most women think the same, that all they have to do is say, "I want an abortion," and hey presto! Perhaps you've been reading too many glossy magazines, Miss Fremont.'

'I can't stand any more of this!' Liz got quickly to her feet. 'Do you treat all your patients this way, or are you waging some kind of vendetta against myself in particular?'

Sanger bowed his head, remembering his wife, Margaret; thinking that all beautiful women should carry a Government Health Warning. So too should men soured by the 'fall-out' from such women. He was punishing Liz Fremont for the sins of his wife who had booked into an expensive London nursing home and aborted their child without even telling him.

Looking up, he said quietly, 'I'm sorry. Please sit down. I'll explain things as simply as possible. Can I offer you something? A glass of water, perhaps?'

'No, I don't want anything, except to get this over and done with. The sooner the better. After the gynaecologist, then what?'

'After his examination; after counselling, if he considers that there is no firm medical reason to terminate your pregnancy, he will refer the matter back to me. It will be up to me, then, to make the final decision.'

Liz said bitterly, 'You'll enjoy that, won't you. My life, my future in your hands. I imagine it will give you infinite pleasure to say no, to make me have this baby whether I want to or not! What are you, Doctor, some kind of sadist?'

'No,' he said slowly, 'just a very ordinary medical practitioner trying to prevent unnecessary suffering.'

Liz put Jess in mind of Sarah Siddons as she stalked the room, speaking her mind on the subject of Dr Sanger, unleashing a torrent of pithy comment on everything from his appearance to his out-of-date copies of *Punch*.

'I've never been so humiliated in all my life,' she cried passionately. 'The man should be struck from the Medical Register! All that claptrap about unconsidered sex and its consequences! He's living in the Middle Ages!'

Listening to the tale of woe, Jess remembered a chance remark of Dora's concerning Mark Sanger.

'I gather his wife left him recently,' she said consolingly. 'Perhaps that's why he acted so . . .'

The sentence was left in mid-air. In no mood for mitigating circumstances, Liz snorted contemptuously, 'I'm not surprised. It must have been hell for her living under the same roof as that bloody-minded hypocrite! That puffed-up excuse for a human being! I've never met a man I detested so utterly before!'

'Even so, he bothered to send a wreath to my great-aunt's funeral.'

Liz turned on Jess in a fury. 'Oh, I'd forgotten! Of course, you're on his side, aren't you? You agree with him about the abortion! Why be mealy-mouthed about it? Why don't *you* read me a penny lecture on morality, too?'

Then, realizing that she had gone too far, her anger evaporated suddenly. Sick at heart, she murmured hoarsely, 'Jess! I'm sorry. I didn't mean to say that. I'm so wound up, I scarcely know what I *am* saying!'

And conscience doth make bullies of us all, Jess thought. Conscience – and fear. Doug had been like this, lashing out at her, whenever he could not cope with the weight of his own guilt.

'Why don't you say something – throw something?'

Jess stood up. 'Have you noticed the time? You'll be late for the theatre if you don't hurry.'

Liz glanced at the graceful carriage clock next to the trailing ivy; one of her personal belongings. A present from Steen who had paid the earth for it in a London antique shop – 'To mark our precious hours together,' he'd said.

He must have known then, Liz thought bitterly, that their time would be measured in hours, not years.

Crossing to the dressing-table, she said wistfully, 'Have you changed your mind about coming tonight?'

'Of course not. Whatever gave you that idea?' Jess spoke lightly, more shaken than she cared to admit, racked with pity for Liz. 'I wouldn't miss it for the world.'

Liz raked a comb through her hair. 'The way I feel, I'll probably fluff my lines!'

'Not you. In any case, I could probably step into your shoes if it came to the crunch,' Jess smiled, 'I know *Gaslight* like the back of my hand.'

Liz laid down the comb. 'Have you forgiven me for what I said just now?' She turned away from the mirror. 'It was dreadful of me. I – used you as a whipping boy.'

'Have you thought,' Jess said slowly, 'that Dr Sanger was probably doing the same with you?'

Alarmed by Beryl's condition, William Hoyle called Sanger in the early hours of the morning.

Aroused suddenly from a light sleep, he had raised his head from the pillow to hear his wife, in the next room, vomiting, moaning, crying out for someone to come to her.

Pulling on his dressing gown, he hurried along the landing. The television set was still on, the screen a blur of snowflakes. The control switch had fallen to the floor, Beryl was half in, half out of bed, lying face down, retching violently. The smell of vomit filled the air – a terrible, pungent stench which made him recoil slightly as he found a clean towel to hold to her lips.

At that moment the housekeeper appeared, wearing a padded dressing gown and a slumber-helmet.

'I told you madam hadn't been at all well.' Mrs Bartram clicked her tongue against her teeth in a castanet reproach. 'You'd best let me see to her.' Her tone indicated that this was all his fault.

'I'll ring Dr Sanger.' William dialled the number, and waited.

'Hello! Mark? Sorry to call you so early. It's Beryl. Violent sickness! No, I don't think so. Soup, fish, rice pudding. I had the same. You will? Thank you.'

There had been a great deal of unpleasant clearing up to do after Beryl had been taken to the nursing home. Hoyle had felt almost sorry for Mrs Bartram. By the time he had seen his wife settled and returned to get ready for the office, the housekeeper had stripped the soiled sheets and blankets from the bed, and sprayed the room liberally with a lavender-scented aerosol.

'What did the doctor say?' Mrs Bartram had, by this time, exchanged padded nylon for a flowered overall.

'It's gastro-enteritis. A pretty bad dose, I'm afraid.'

'I told you madam wasn't well . . .'

'So you keep saying.' William felt his patience ebbing.

'Shall I cook you some breakfast?'

'No. No, I couldn't eat a thing.' The intermingled smell of vomit and lavender aerosol very nearly turned his own stomach.

'That mattress will have to be got rid off,' Mrs Bartram said stonily. 'There's no way those stains can be removed.'

'I realise that.' Hoyle glanced at his watch. 'I'll order a new one. By the way, I shan't be home for dinner. I'll have something to eat in town, then go on to the nursing home.'

'How long is madam likely to be away?' The housekeeper regarded him coldly. 'I shall want to clean everything

143

thoroughly before she comes back.'

'I really couldn't say. At least a week, I imagine.'

That was four days ago. He had demurred, at first, when Sanger suggested a visit to the theatre. 'I'd better stay with Beryl,' he said stoically.

'Nonsense!' Sanger raised his eyebrows. 'If I know Beryl, she would much rather watch television than sit up in bed gassing to you.' He had no illusions about the Hoyles' marital relationship. 'It's high time you gained remission for good behaviour. We'll have a meal in town, see the play, then go back to my place for a couple of drinks.' He slapped Hoyle's shoulder. 'Frankly, I could do with a night off myself.'

Glancing up from her programme, Jess was surprised to see William Hoyle and another man edging their way past a row of knees. Mr Hoyle, she noticed with some amusement, appeared to be having difficulty in finding a comfortable position for his legs. She wondered who his companion might be – a thick-set man with a mane of dark hair, wearing a a casual, roll-neck sweater.

They were sitting almost directly opposite. Not wanting Hoyle to catch her looking at them, Jess stared up at the ceiling with its intricate pattern of cables and spotlights. Then the house lights dimmed, the piped music rose from a mere suggestion of sound to a more sinister beat. The audience stirred with anticipation. The lights blacked out suddenly. The spotlights came on. The play began.

Actors were the dream pedlars, the singers of songs, the alchemists transmuting base metal to gold. This was something Jess had always known and respected, the possible reason for her understanding of Liz, despite their difference in age and way of thinking.

She watched intently Liz's performance as Bella, the wife driven to the brink of insanity by a calculatingly cruel husband. The alchemy worked. One sensed that fear, understood the terror of this woman who believed that she was becoming slowly insane: pitied her confusion, her desper-

144

ate, futile desire to please her husband.

Gripped by the power of the performance, Jess subconsciously drew parallels with her own life. She too had experienced this effective sapping of the will. Perhaps all dominant men possessed this running streak of cruelty, engendered by their own greed, fear, or inadequacy.

Leaning forward in his seat, Sanger followed Liz Fremont's every movement with his eyes. The woman was magnificent. He understood now why her career was so important to her. She possessed that intangible star quality which riveted attention to herself, so that her every fleeting facial expression, each movement of her hands and finely honed body, every nuance of her exquisitely clear voice, assumed a fascinating importance and meaning.

He had known, the minute she walked into his surgery, that here was a woman to set the pulse racing, to fire the imagination. And so he had treated her badly, unsympathetically – his own petty revenge against women of her kind who held the power of enslavement – as Margaret had done.

Then, when the shell of his feigned indifference had shattered suddenly to conflict with his passionately held views against abortion as a kind of cosmetic surgery, he had failed to impress her as either man or physician – as he had failed to satisfy his wife's unquenchable thirst for life.

Possibly his failure as a husband had stemmed from the knowledge that Margaret had married him on the rebound from a broken love affair. He had of course closely questioned her motives; had acted the part of inquisitor to such good effect that she had begun to have second thoughts about marrying him. And then he had known that he did not care *why* she wished to marry him, however flimsy the reasons – that she found him amusing, reliable, oddly attractive – he had simply wanted her on any terms. But he had known from the beginning that she was not in love with him, and that had rankled; made him wary, suspicious, jealous of her every move.

145

He also knew, as he watched Liz Fremont's masterly performance, that he had used Hoyle as an excuse to come here tonight – poor old William, for whom he felt a great deal of affection. But friendship had its limitations. Male pride built up certain barriers of reserve. He knew for instance, that Hoyle would never say, in so many words, that Beryl had ruined his life. By the same token, Sanger would never admit that he had allowed a woman to make a fool of him.

William remained acutely conscious that he should have stayed with Beryl. What Sanger had said was true enough. Perhaps she would prefer watching television to holding intelligent conversation, and his presence in her room at the Belvedere nursing home might have acted as an irritant rather than a comfort. On the other hand, Beryl held strait-laced views on the duties and responsibilities of the husband within the framework of marriage – excluding the duty of sharing the same bed.

Beryl liked to be seen in public with her husband. Despite her hypochondriacal tendencies, she enjoyed playing hostess occasionally to her bridge friends and their partners, to establish the status quo.

At those intimate dinner parties, Beryl invariably held court in rose-coloured lace and sparkling jewellery, treating him as a kind of flunkey, trained to fetch a scarf for her shoulders if she felt cold, to mix drinks, to open doors for her, and plump up the drawing-room cushions to place at her back.

Inevitably, she would lead the conversation to the subject of ill-health – the escalating cost of private treatment, the disgrace of nurses haggling over pay-rises, the off-handedness of National Health doctors in general. (Hoyle knew that she meant Sanger in particular.) The care she needed to take of her own health, especially when she and her husband went abroad. One never quite *knew* about the water. As for garlic . . .

Earlier this evening, when he had called at the Belvedere

with fresh flowers, his wife had not been pleased when he told her that he was going, with Sanger, to see *Gaslight*. He had known beforehand what her attitude would be. She had assumed her martyed expression and said coldly that she supposed the nursing home would be able to get in touch with him if she happened to suffer a relapse.

'Actually, you're looking a great deal better,' William said mildly. 'You'll be home in a couple of days.'

'That's where you're wrong! I shall be here for at least another week. Dr Frobisher, the medical director, strongly advises a series of tests. Such a charming man!'

Hoyle had left the nursing home shredded with the old feeling of guilt laced with irritation at his wife gullibility; had eaten his meal, with Sanger, in a downcast mood, and came to the theatre with little prospect of enjoyment until, during the interval, he noticed Jess, sitting alone, her eyes fixed firmly on her programme.

Turning to Sanger, he said boyishly, 'Let's have a drink, shall we? There's someone I'd like you to meet.'

Sanger regarded Hoyle with some amusement. 'Who is she? I assume the "someone" *is* a woman?'

'Well, yes. A client of mine. Miss Tidey's great-niece, Jessica Carmichael,' William said, slightly offended by Sanger's tone of voice.

'Really?' Sanger's interest quickened. 'By all means. It might be interesing to find out why she left the old lady to rot! Oh, come on, Bill, I was merely joking! Do you really imagine I'd start an argument in the crush-bar?'

So this was Dr Sanger, Jess thought, when the introduction had been made, remembering Liz's scathing comments. Certainly he bore little resemblance to any doctor she had ever met before. Nor, she imagined, would his bedside manner be anything to write home about. Liz was right. The man was insufferable, puffed up with a sense of his own importance.

Hoyle had gone to fetch their drinks. All Sanger had said, so far, was 'How d'you do?' And yet she could not

147

help feeling that there was a great deal more he wished to say. It seemed to her as though they were playing a game of cat and mouse – he waiting for her to speak first, laying a mental bet on her opening gambit.

'I understand that you attended my great-aunt during her last illness,' she said, in desperation. And Sanger smiled to himself as though he had won his bet.

'Ah yes. Your great-aunt,' he said mockingly. 'Now, I hear on the grapevine, that you are about to turn Laurel Villa into a boarding-house.'

Jess coloured up. Stung to anger by his contempt, 'That is the last thing I intend doing,' she assured him.

Sanger smiled faintly. 'You are surely not thinking of turning it into an old people's home?'

The barb was direct. The shaft quivered. Jess knew that she was being punished for her neglect of Great-Aunt Jessica.

'I am scarcely qualified for that!' She spoke coldly, defensively.

'How refreshing to hear you say so, Mrs Carmichael. So many people, these days, stand ready to make a killing from the misfortunes of the elderly.'

At that moment, Hoyle came back with the drinks.

Sick with humiliation, Jess slipped out of the theatre before the general exodus began. Walking home along the esplanade, she could not remember ever having disliked anyone as much as Dr Sanger. Liz was correct in her opinion of the man.

Tomorrow, or the next day, workmen would appear to begin tearing the house apart. If only she could get away somewhere, to think; the far-flung Hebrides, or Haworth, set among drifts of lonely moorland.

CHAPTER 10

Dora said it would do Jess good to get away for a couple of days. She and Alf would see to the workmen. 'In any case,' she added, with the air of one inured to the vagaries of plumbers and electricians, 'they'll just swan in tomorrow, pull everything to pieces, then sugar off until Monday, and you'll be back by then.'

Jess remained unconvinced. 'I wonder how we'll manage while the kitchen's being ripped apart.' She looked worriedly at the ancient gas-cooker and the old Equator boiler destined for the council tip. 'And I don't really need a break. I just said that on the spur of the moment.' She had given up the idea of Haworth or the far-flung Hebrides as pie-in-the-sky notions born of fatigue.

But Dora, who had noticed her ewe lamb's pallor, was not to be put off so easily. 'Of course you need a break,' she said briskly, 'what with – you know – *HIM* – making a nuisance of himself. (She had referred to Douglas in capital italics ever since the letter). No wonder you look worn out. And I know how upset you were when the furniture went to the saleroom.'

Dora smoothed her hands down her pinafore, sniffed, and continued, 'Now don't waste time thinking up reasons why you shouldn't have a couple of days off. Take my advice, nip over to Scarborough for the weekend. Book in at a nice comfy hotel, and have a darned good rest.'

Mrs Bartram pointed out that since Madam was not expected back for several more days, she might as well take advantage of the time off owing her to visit her married daughter in Leeds. William made no demur, and told her to go ahead with her arrangements.

'Of course I'll leave plenty of food ready for you,' the housekeeper conceded, as if she were doing him a favour, and seemed annoyed when he told her, cheerfully, not to bother; that he would probably take advantage of the 'lull in the storm' to pay a flying visit to his sister and her family.

Not that he used that particular expression. Nor did he relish the thought of breaking the news to Beryl. But then, his wife had never enjoyed visits to 'Mountain Ash' — George and Adeline's sprawling guest-house at Goathland, and did not see eye to eye with his forthright sister, whose easy style of dressing, and bright, often heedless conversation, annoyed her past bearing. Indeed, Beryl still regarded her sister-in-law's late-in-life pregnancy as nothing short of distasteful. Lina, on the other hand, made no secret of the fact that she saw Beryl as a prude, a frigid woman whose uncompromising attitude towards sexual intimacy had robbed William of the joys of fatherhood.

And so, with diplomacy in mind, Hoyle stopped on his way to the nursing home to purchase a bottle of his wife's favourite perfume, and entered her room with a nonchalant air, feeling like a mutation of 'The Man who Broke the Bank at Monte Carlo', and a Christian about to be thrown to a bad-tempered lion.

Jess thought how subtly the scenery had changed since she had last made this journey. The sky held the misty blueness of a damp watercolour. The grass seemed drained of its former lushness, leaves were more brittle, the morning air as clear as vintage wine — 'Cool'd a long age in the deep delved earth' — giving promise of later warmth, when the mist lifted.

Dora had painted Scarborough, where she and Alfred had spent their honeymoon, in glowing colours. All Jess had seen of the place, so far, was the not very inspiring view of the Odeon cinema from the refreshment buffet window.

Bevensea was comparatively flat, but this town was hilly. The main street meandered down gently to a paved pedestrian thoroughfare with seats and shrubs, where an itinerant street musician, playing a 'honky tonk' piano, belted out a catchy tune evocative of a Judy Garland musical.

The music in the autumn sunshine, the pavements crowded with shoppers, imparted a light-hearted holiday gaiety to the scene. Jess wandered along, pausing now and then to look in the shop windows. Passing a Marks and Spencer store, she hesitated momentarily, wondering whether to continue downhill or turn right into St Nicholas Street. Then, remembering Dora's roughly drawn map of the town centre, and her advice to head towards the St Nicholas Cliff where the best hotels were, she chose the right-hand turning and walked along towards the Town Hall – a red-brick Victorian mansion overlooking the magnificent spread of the South Bay.

Dora was right in her appraisal of Scarborough as a beauty spot. The bay seemed to go on forever. The Old Town, nestling in the lee of the Castle hill, sparkled red-roofed in the sunshine. Looking down through a cascade of trees, Jess noticed that a timber boat was edging into harbour on the full tide, squeezing through what seemed an incredibly narrow space between the grey harbour walls. The sky seemed alive with seagulls, as white as if they had been freshly Snowcemmed, floating down from their nesting places on the rock face of the Castle hill, filling the air with their raucous cries, fanning out in the wake of a flotilla of fishing cobles chugging homeward from the open sea.

Finding a café with a seaview window, she ordered a cup of coffee, and leaned forward in her seat to watch a group of children, on the beach below, dodging the fast-incoming tide.

The catchy tune played by the street musician jingled on in her mind – 'I Can't Give you Anything but Love'.

She had not meant to think about Douglas. Had not wanted to churn through old memories, and yet . . . it seemed that wherever she went, whatever she did, the shadow of a lost love walked beside her.

Foolishly, she had believed that the affair would burn itself out in time. She thought she knew Douglas so well; had believed that sooner or later he would come back to her in need of forgiveness and understanding. But nothing had happened the way she hoped it would. Watching the children dragging a piece of flotsam from the sea, she wondered how she could have been so blind, so stupid as to cling to the floating spars of her marriage long after the vessel had sunk without trace.

Douglas. The name conjured up a state of mind, a sense of frustration, an emptiness, a phase of her life which had left the stamp of impermanence on every other relationship.

There were other people in the café, laughing and talking, not even seeing her. The sense of panic was unlike anything Jess had ever known before, an engulfment by slow waves of rising heat until her clothes clung to her. She sat quite still for little while, trying to master the horrifying fear: the acute feeling of loneliness. It was as though she had suddenly become invisible, as if she had ceased to exist. The panic was akin to staring into an abyss. And nobody knew: no one even noticed.

Getting up, she left a pound coin on the table, and walked unsteadily to the door, gripping the handle of her overnight case, and crossed the road, unseeingly, like a blind woman: blundering into people.

Suddenly she felt a steadying hand on her arm; a familiar voice at her elbow. She could have wept, then, with the sheer relief of seeing a friendly face in a world of strangers.

She scarcely recognised him at first. He looked different wearing a comfortable tweed suit, checked shirt and soft collar. Mr Hoyle, who usually dressed so formally in tailored pin-stripes, with a blameless white handkerchief peeking up from his breast-pocket.

She could not have borne it if he had asked her what was wrong. Hoyle did nothing of the kind. 'You need a drink,' he said firmly. 'We'll go in here. The bar should be open now.'

Jess allowed herself to be led through plate-glass doors, past a reception desk, a branching staircase; flowers in a floodlit niche. Her footsteps dragged on luxuriously soft carpet. 'Here, let me!' Hoyle took her case which he dumped, along with his own green carrier-bag, just inside the door of the cocktail bar.

'I'm so sorry,' she murmured. 'I can't think what came over me.'

'Nonsense! Sit down. I'll fetch you some brandy.'

He had believed, for one heart-stopping moment, that Jess was going to faint out there in the street. Now he noticed, with a frown of sympathy, the smudged shadows under her eyes, the way her fingers trembled on the stem of her glass.

'Feeling better?'

'Much better, thank you.'

'I couldn't believe my luck, bumping into you the way I did,' he said gently.

'It was the other way round, wasn't it? I – blundered – into you.' She spoke stiffly, implying an apology, deeply ashamed of her panic reaction to a nervous frisson born of loneliness.

A couple came into the bar at that moment. The woman, wearing dark glasses, collided with the case and the carrier-bag. 'Damn!' She inspected her stockings for a newly sprung ladder.

'I beg your pardon.' Hoyle moved the luggage out of harm's way. 'My fault entirely.' The woman gave him a black look.

'I've been shopping,' he explained to Jess, sitting down beside her. 'My young niece, Amanda, regards me as a Father Christmas figure whatever the season. I'm on my way to Goathland, near Whitby, to spend the weekend with my sister and her family. And you?'

'Oh, I had the foolish notion that I needed a change of scenery. Now I'm not so sure. I feel guilty leaving the Cornwells to cope with the workmen.'

'I'm sure they'll manage perfectly well,' Hoyle said, smiling. 'I think Dora enjoys being in charge.'

'Yes, she does. Even so . . .' Jess knew she was simply making excuses to justify her return to Laurel Villa. 'Well, I musn't detain you any longer.' She gathered up her gloves and handbag.

'No, please don't go! At least let me show you the town.

We could drive to Oliver's Mount, the Spa, Peasholm Park. Unless, of course, you have made other arrangements.'

He did not add that he had looked forward to a few hours alone in Scarborough, a necessary interlude of peace and quiet between his wife's carping and his sister's over-powering conversation. Now the notion of a quiet inter-lude seemed an unnecessary waste of time with Jess beside him.

'We could have lunch somewhere . . .' He felt suddenly as shy and awkward as a teenager asking a girl for a date.

He believed that he had loved her from the moment she stood on tiptoe to press that butterfly kiss of gratitude on his cheek. But possibly it went back even further than that. Perhaps he had loved her from the first moment he saw her. He had certainly known he loved her the day he had loaned her his umbrella.

After lunch, they walked around Peasholm Park lake, stop-ping to watch a group of excited youngsters throwing bread for the ducks. There, Hoyle admitted that he, too, felt somewhat guilty, having left his wife in a nursing home.

So Mr Hoyle *was* married. 'I hope that she – your wife – is not seriously ill,' Jess said, suddenly ill-at-ease.

'No, not at all. I should not have forsaken her otherwise.' Hoyle grinned boyishly, enjoying the antics of the ducks. 'Actually, she seemed relieved to see the back of me. She has this love affair with television, you see.'

Adeline Peterson put down the receiver, and went through to the kitchen where her husband was busy chopping mush-rooms.

'That was Bill on the phone,' she said, 'to break the news that he's bringing someone with him – a client . . .'

'Oh?' George Peterson stopped what he was doing. 'Well, fair enough. If Bill wants to mix business with plea-sure, I suppose we can oblige the extra chappie with a spot of dinner – a loaf of bread, a flask of wine, and thou . . .'

'Don't be ridiculous, George! The client isn't a –

he. She's a woman. Someone he met, quite by chance, as he was quick to point out. Apparently, they've been all over Scarborough in Bill's car, sight-seeing! Hmmm, I wonder . . .'

'Really? A woman, eh? Well, good luck to him!' George, rubicund, bespectacled, wearing a striped butcher's apron, padded across to the Aga to inspect the beef casserole; tasted, added more salt, and listened, tongue-in-cheek, to his wife's commentary.

'But don't you think it rather odd?' Adeline, a plump woman, wearing slacks and a baggy sweater, her hair drawn back into a French pleat, perched on the edge of the table, nibbled a fragment of raw mushroom, and frowned as she attempted to come to grips with the surprising new development.

'I wonder if Bebe knows that Bill is whooping it up with a strange woman? I'll bet a hundred pounds to a hayseed, she doesn't! I mean, it's so out of character! Bill, of all people, risking the wrath of "She who must be obeyed". God, I wonder what *"She"* would say if she knew! Have a convenient relapse, I suppose! Send out an SOS message. Arrange for the Last Rites!'

Adeline's dislike of her sister-in-law, the woman whom she contemptuously referred to as Bebe, went back a long time.

She had been a mere child when Bill became engaged to marry Beryl Blair. A sudden memory of her sister-in-law as she had looked and behaved almost forty years ago, invaded Lina's mind – a simpering ninny with a penchant for romantic novels, lace party dresses, pointed shoes, and floppy hats adorned with artificial roses.

She had loathed everything about her from the word go. Most of all Beryl's proprietorial air towards her brother, the way she had criticised his taste in clothes, books, music. Everything about him which had not conformed to her own pathetically low intellectual standards.

Bill, Adeline remembered, had been bright, adventuresome, hopeful, a bit of a rebel before Bebe came on the scene. It was bad enough, she considered, that their father had crushed his idea of becoming an engineer and forced him to enter the legal profession, without saddling the poor dear with a made-to-measure wife.

Poor Bill. How resigned he'd seemed on his wedding day, hovering in the shadow of his radiant, possessive bride. Beryl had clung like a leech to his arm at the reception, making certain that her thick gold wedding ring was well on display. That ring had seemed to Lina, at the time, more like a glinting gold handcuff, shackling Bill to his wife's side for life.

The mist came down suddenly, like a thick woollen blanket, almost blotting out the road across the moors. The car seemed to be floating in the kind of swirling fog beloved of horror-film buffs. And yet William had never felt happier, with Jess beside him, listening to Chopin's Etude in E Minor, on the car radio.

It had not been easy persuading her to come with him to 'Mountain Ash'. She had put all kinds of obstacles in the path. It had taken every bit of his lawyer's skill and patience to convince her that she needed a break, that his sister, and George, would make her more than welcome.

He had enjoyed enormously their pub-lunch of bread, cheese and pickles, knowing that Beryl would not for one moment have considered lunching in such a place. And this, he thought, sitting near a roaring coal fire in a raftered room hung with genuine horse-brasses and faded photographs of long-disbanded cricket teams, was what he had missed most with Beryl; not, as his sister imagined, sexual intimacy, but quiet conversation, warmth, and companionship.

Looking into the heart of the fire, Jess admitted to certain misgivings about the alterations to Laurel Villa. Would her great-aunt Jessica have approved the modernisation programme?

'You mustn't let that worry you,' William said. 'Times change.'

'Yes, but not always for the better. I hate the compromises that one is forced to make, nowadays, as a matter of expediency.'

Hoyle knew exactly what she meant. Compromises were the price one paid, at a premium, for what one believed to be peace of mind. The kind of compromises he had lived with for such a long time that he had almost forgotten what it felt like to be free of guilt, of self-doubt.

The thought of the compromises he would be obliged to make when he retired, filled him with dread. That time was drawing perilously near.

He thought of his few precious hours with Jess, as a shining pearl necklace strung on a gossamer, yet tensile thread. Now familiar landmarks, farms, houses, a signpost looming through the mist, marked the end of their journey.

'We're almost there,' he said reluctantly, pressing the right-hand indicator: manoeuvring the car through gateposts into a pebbled driveway, wishing that they might drive on together through the foggy night to some tender glimmering of a new dawn.

Obviously not a person to stand on ceremony, Adeline Peterson tucked her hand confidingly into Jess's elbow.

'I hope you're hungry,' she said. 'George has made a casserole. We always have something substantial when we know Bill's coming. That frosty-faced housekeeper of his feeds him nothing but nursery slops! If I were Bill, I wouldn't give her houseroom. But then, she probably wouldn't give me houseroom, either.

'Have you met the estimable Mrs Bartram, by the way? No? Lucky you! Of course, Beryl thinks the sun shines out of her backside! No wonder. She treats "la Belle Dame Sans Merci" like the empress of Russia!'

'Beryl? You mean Mrs Hoyle?'

'Oh God,' Adeline said apologetically. 'I really am sorry. I talk too much; don't always stop to think what I'm saying!'

'This is a lovely house,' Jess said, diplomatically changing the subject, glancing round the stone-flagged hall with its scattering of rugs, and a copper container filled with autumn flowers on a polished oak chest at the foot of the stairs.

'Yes, it is rather nice, isn't it?' Lina said mistily. 'George and I bought it for a song just after we were married. It was originally a farmhouse – hence the stone floors. Please do come and look at the kitchen – unless you'd rather go up to your room first. We usually eat here, en famille, though we've built on a rather swish dining-room extension for the summer visitors. Oh, this is my husband! George, Mrs Carmichael. May I call you Jessica, by the way?'

As George and Jess shook hands, Lina blundered serenely on, speaking in a kind of verbal shorthand. 'Oh, where's Bill? I thought . . .' She laughed. 'He must have gone upstairs to see Mandy. I hope she doesn't give him a very rough ride. There was no controlling her when she knew he was coming. He spoils her dreadfully, of course, But then, so do we. Have you any children, Jessica?'

'No, I'm afraid not.' She knew then that neither had Mr Hoyle. Parents spoke often and enthusiastically about their offspring, the childless simply listened and said nothing.

Adeline sighed deeply. 'They're a mixed blessing, believe me.' She appeared to be thinking aloud. 'Perhaps we should send Mandy to a boarding school. We'd miss her dreadfully, of course, but she's rather outgrowing the village school. Not that there's anything wrong with it, but Mandy has this thing about dancing: wants to become a ballerina, of all things. Can you imagine? And, to be quite honest with you, although George and I love this place, we do often feel rather cut off from civilisation. Quite frankly, I miss Bevensea with its shops; concerts – the theatre. The tendency is to become too complacent, to drift away from the mainstream; to lose touch with the world.'

At that moment, William appeared holding the hand of an excited child whose mouse-brown hair was drawn back in a skimpy pony-tail.

'Look, Mummy,' she cried ecstatically, 'Uncle Bill's

bought me a red dressing-gown with a rabbit on the pocket! Isn't it smashing?'

'Absolutely gorgeous,' Adeline enthused. 'But surely you're not going to wear it at the dinner-table?'

'Why not?' Mandy stuck out her underlip aggressively.

'Because, knowing you, you'll probably end up with gravy stains down the front of it! Kids! Who'd have 'em!' Lina glanced conspiratorially at Jess, obviously proud of her daughter, who, to Jess's way of thinking, was a little on the lumpy side for a budding ballerina.

Next morning, William and Jess stood together on the headland overlooking Whitby harbour.

The Petersons, with their wilful child in tow, came to Whitby every Saturday to do their week's shopping. Jess had felt somewhat embarrassed by Adeline's insistence that she and Bill should go sight-seeing together, especially since Mandy had caused a commotion in the Tesco carpark at not being allowed to accompany them.

'No, Mandy,' Lina said firmly. 'Uncle Bill is taking Jessica to look at the parish church, and you know how you hate looking round churches. Besides we'll be meeting them later, for lunch!' She had added the final, sobering threat. 'If you don't behave yourself, young lady, I'll take you to have your hair cut!'

That did it! The budding ballerina made no further demur.

The overnight mist was rapidly dissolving, cut through with delicate sunlight. They had climbed from the town by way of a series of shallow steps – a hundred or more – cut into the hillside; had talked of Bram Stoker's *Dracula*; conjuring up the storm of Stoker's vivid imagination, the dark shape of a dog swimming ashore from a stricken vessel; laughing at the very idea of vampires – bloodsuckers – alive in a modern world. 'And yet,' Hoyle said, with that touch of dry humour Jess liked so well, 'the world's still full of them, you know, when you come to think about it. They go by different names now, of course: insurance agents; car salesmen; solicitors.'

159

She had asked him then about the steep, narrow runnel alongside the steps, and he told her that, in olden times, coffins were lurched up that way, on handcarts.

Now she thought of all those people who had taken that bumpy road to eternity, lying at peace in the old graveyard of the parish church with its interior of indescribable beauty – not in any way gloomy or enclosed, but as light and airy as the deck of a sailing ship.

'What are you thinking?' William asked gently.

'Oh, so many things, it's hard to say. The past – the future . . .' Jess clasped her hands. 'Especially the future. About – the divorce. I've given the matter a great deal of thought, and . . .'

'Yes?' he said, encouragingly.

'Well, I've decided to go ahead with it.'

'Have you, my dear? I'm so glad.'

At that moment, William experienced a momentary illusion of renewed youth and vigour, a sudden lifting of the heart, remembering that, fifteen years ago, he would have taken those hundred steps or more, at a run, and stood upon this headland gulping in deep breaths of fresh air, filled with a thrilling sense of achievement.

He now knew that his running days were all over and done with, and felt suddenly as stiff and unbending as a tombstone crusader in a marble suit of armour – and yet . . .

Looking at Jess, he thought that if only he could tell her what lay in his heart, without fear of her withdrawal, he might undergo some brief, shining, spiritual and physical metamorphosis, like a butterfly emerging from its wrinkled larva.

And then he thought wryly, as they made their way down the steps to the harbour, that he resembled not so much a butterfly as a stick-insect plagued with rheumatism in its knee-joints.

CHAPTER 11

The ceiling seemed very high and remote. Circles of light swam like obscure suns above the bed where she lay. She felt drowsy, yet acutely aware of sounds and movements, the rustle of a starched pinafore, the shifting wheels of a metal trolley.

She had not expected to feel so disorientated, so whoozy. She had never had an anaesthetic before. Lying flat on her back, Liz slid her hands lightly down her narrow thighs. Somehow she dared not touch the tender flesh enshrining her empty womb.

It was all over now. The child which she and Steen had created together no longer existed. She felt a flicker of pain, a queer, warm seepage of blood, the unaccustomed bulk of a sanitary pad between her legs. Her mouth felt dry yet, curiously, her hair was wet at the temples.

She remembered walking down the drive of Laurel Villa, adroitly side-stepping the ditches the workmen had begun digging, thinking that Jess might believe that she had planned the abortion to coincide with her absence, but that was simply not true. The letter from the Pregnancy Advisory Clinic, giving the time and place of the operation, had arrived by the Saturday morning post. It was sheer luck that she would not be needed at the theatre during the coming week. Meg Makepeace had been scheduled to play the female lead in *The Devil's Disciple* to Jolyon King's Dick Dudgeon.

Perhaps it was better that Jess had not been there when the letter arrived. Mrs Cornwell had been curious of course, and more than a little piqued when she had walked into the kitchen, carrying an overnight case, saying that she did not want any breakfast.

'Off on a jaunt, are you?' Dora had shaken the cornflakes packet as a kind of reproach.

'Something like that,' she'd replied lightly. 'Tell Jess I'll be home tomorrow, or the day after.'

She had known, by the pursing of Dora's lips, what she

was thinking – huh, off to meet some man or other – and wondered, waiting at the bus-stop, what Mrs Cornwell would have said if she had told her the truth, that she was not as sophisticated as she pretended to be, but lonely and frightened, wanting Steen so badly that her need for him tore at her like a physical pain, an incurable cancer of the spirit.

Lying quite still, tears trickling sideways from her closed eyelids, she heard a rustling sound. One of the nurses said gently, 'These flowers have just arrived.'

'Flowers?' Painfully, Liz opened her eyes. 'For me? But nobody knew . . .'

The cone of striped florist's paper contained a fragrant mass of pink carnations. The card read: 'I am certain now that Emily Brontë did not have a lover.' There was no signature, but she knew who had sent them.

On Sunday, Jess went with the Petersons, and William, to matins in the village church. She had wanted peace, a touch of the Brontesque, and here it was – moors, sheep, and all, a kind of Wuthering Heights landscape, only less formidable.

Even the hotel, facing the village green with its flock of grazing ewes, seemed to 'wuther' gently against a backdrop of rolling hills climbing up from the deep Aire valley.

George had booked lunch at the intriguingly named 'Mallyan Spout', where, after the service, they repaired for pre-luncheon drinks in the hotel lounge.

Sipping a glass of sherry, she tried to picture Hoyle as a young man. He must have been quite handsome, she decided. His smile would not have changed much throughout the years, and he seemed to be smiling quite often in the company of his effervescent sister, George, and their tiresome offspring. And yet she felt in no way excluded from the family gathering – rather the opposite. Adeline's artless chatter washed over them like bathwater. William said little, neither did Jess, and yet she had the feeling – a curiously warm and comfortable feeling – that he was some-how keeping watch over her.

Slowly the flesh and blood man was beginning to emerge from the shadow of the correct family lawyer. Human beings, she realised, assumed the behavioural patterns established by their role in society: the dominant influences of their lives. She wondered how deeply Beryl Hoyle affected her husband's life – 'la belle dame sans merci'.

After lunch, Mandy, bored with grown-up talk, wheedled her patient, good-tempered father into driving them to Grosmont to visit the steam-train railway.

William explained to Jess that, in summertime, the trains ran daily excursions from Pickering to Grosmont. Now the engines were laid up for repairs and maintenance, the work carried out, on a voluntary basis, by a team of steam-train enthusiasts.

'Yes,' Adeline cut in, 'and if Bill lived a bit nearer, he'd be among them – wouldn't you, darling?'

'How well my sister knows me,' he replied, laughing as he took Jess's arm to help her down a steep embankment.

Mandy was already streaking ahead to look at the trains, followed more slowly by George, whose girth precluded his moving any faster.

'Oh, go on Bill,' Adeline chuckled, 'I know you're dying to play "puffer trains". Jess and I will wait here. There's no way I can walk the cinder track in my best shoes – which are giving me gyp, incidentally.

She said more seriously, watching William as he hurried to catch up with George, 'Poor old Bill, he never got what he wanted or deserved from life. Perhaps I shouldn't say so, but he married the wrong woman. Jealous, narrow-minded people must be hell to live with.'

'Yes, I suppose they must be,' Jess said uneasily, not wanting to discuss Mr Hoyle's private life, deeply aware of Adeline's underlying motive. She had to say it. 'Our meeting *was* accidental, you know.'

'Oh, my dear! I never for one moment imagined . . .'

'No, of course not. I'm sorry. It's simply that your

brother has been so — so kind, so helpful . . . The last thing I want, or intend, is to jeopardise his career. In case you are wondering, I shall ask him not to mention . . . all this . . . to his wife. Not for the reasons you may imagine; simply to safeguard his own peace of mind. As you so rightly said, jealous, narrow-minded people must be hell to live with . . .'

Hoyle drove back to Bevensea by a secondary coast road, dawdling along as though he could scarcely bear the journey to end.

They stopped for lunch at the same pub with the horse-brasses and the cricket-team photographs. But this time the place seemed different. Or perhaps, Jess thought, it was they who were different; they were the ones who had changed during the past few hours together.

And then she thought, No, not 'they' but she. *She* was the one who had changed from a ghost-ridden woman into a far more relaxed human being, thanks to Hoyle's compassionate understanding. Now the thought that he might suffer for his kindness, troubled her deeply.

As though he had read her thoughts, William said quietly, 'In case you are wondering, I shall not tell my wife of your visit to Goathland.'

'Really?' She smiled her relief, 'I'm so — glad.'

'Another compromise towards peace of mind,' he said slowly. 'Yours in particular.'

When they reached Bevensea, she said, 'It might be more expedient if you dropped me off a little way from the villa.' She did not add that Dora might raise her eyebrows at seeing them together. In any case, she realised that Hoyle would understand why, without explanation.

She said, at the last moment, 'It has been such a lovely weekend. I can't thank you enough . . .'

It seemed to Jess, as she watched the car drive away, that she and Hoyle had somehow drawn strength and comfort from each other, had fed each other's deepest, inner needs with a dawning awareness of those needs. Above all, with gentleness, music, and laughter.

Happily, Dora was far too preoccupied with other matters to ask questions.

The air was filled with a hovering cloud of dust particles. Workmen were everywhere. They could scarcely hear each other speak above the din of hammering and drilling.

'I had no idea it would be as bad as this,' Jess shouted above the tumult.

Hoyle could not have driven up to the house in any case. Apart from the deeply dug ditches, the drive was blocked with contractors' lorries, rolls of cable and mounds of sewerage pipes.

'Ah well,' Dora said stoically, '"soonest broken, soonest mended", that's my motto. By the way, Miss Fremont's taken herself off somewhere or other. Didn't say where she was going, just said to tell you she'd be back tomorrow, or the next day.'

Jess closed her eyes momentarily, lanced with a deep feeling of regret that she had not been here when Liz needed her.

'She's gone off to meet some man or other, if you ask me.'

Suddenly Jess knew why she felt reluctant to tell Dora about her weekend in Goathland. Perhaps it was human nature to add two and two together and come up with the wrong answer.

'You won't be able to have a hot bath tonight,' Dora went on. 'They've ripped out the boiler. Funny, isn't it? I hated the sight of that old black thing, but I cried my eyes out when I saw it being dumped into the back of the plumbers' van.'

Liz put her feet to the ground for the first time since the operation. The sanitary pad between her legs felt bulky; uncomfortable.

When she protested, 'You'll have to wear one for a little while yet,' the nurse warned her. 'There's always some bleeding after an abortion. Don't worry, it will clear up in a day or two.'

The slowly oozing droplets seemed a silent reproach to Liz, as if her aborted, unwanted child still clung to her for sustenance; the life she had denied it.

Oh Steen, she thought bleakly. Steen, where are you?

She began to cry then, covering her face with her hands; shoulders shaking with the intensity of her sobs.

'That's right,' the young nurse said matter-of-factly, 'have a darned good cry. You'll feel better.'

She was not the gentle nurse, the one who had brought her the flowers.

'It's all part and parcel of an abortion,' the girl continued. 'Nothing to be ashamed of. You're not alone, believe me. All our patients go through it. Every woman experiences the initial feelings of guilt and loss. Frankly, that's why doctors go to so much trouble to counsel the women who come here, to warn them about the after effects. Not that they listen in nine cases out of ten!'

Liz almost hated the nurse at that moment. Loss, she thought bitterly. She had lost everything in the world worth clinging to, her child, her lover, her joy in living. Suddenly she saw herself as a woman totally lacking in courage, who had thrown away, on an impulse, with a kind of stiff-necked pride, the thing that mattered most to her – Steen's child. The living proof of their love.

He strode along the tarmac to the waiting plane, tall and buoyant, briefcase in hand, wearing dark glasses, hair slightly ruffled by the breeze, thinking he would ring Liz tonight from his New York apartment.

He had been wrong in believing he could forget her. Time and distance could never change the way he felt about her. He knew that now.

He could visualise exactly the way she looked, moved, spoke; that warm sexuality of hers which spread honey on the dry toast of life.

Showing his boarding pass to a pretty stewardess, moving down the aisle to his seat, staring out of the window at the familiar pattern of the airport buildings, he remembered the way Liz had looked at him that last morning, her eyes enormous in the pale, hurt oval of her face: remembered the funny, puttering sound the train had made as it drew to a halt in that typically English railway station, the way the breeze had tangled in her hair, reminding him of autumn leaves.

There was nothing he could have done or said then to make their parting less painful.

There had been other women in his life from time to time, brief physical affairs which had meant nothing to him, even less, he suspected, to the women involved. But Liz – Liz was different. He had known that the minute he looked at her across a crowded room. They had been drawn together by a kind of personal magnetism impossible to resist or deny.

Now he needed to see her again, to hold her, to feel the warmth of her body against his, to glimpse again that secret, amused smile of hers which had tugged at his heartstrings; that tiny, flickering smile which had twisted his heart with pain when he told her he must leave her.

And yet he had never really left her at all. She had been with him every waking moment of his life, ever since he had held her in his arms for the last time.

He thought, staring moodily at the deeply blocked shadows of the airport buildings, the blinding brilliance of the runway, of the times he had caught tantalising glimpses of her in Central Park, the times he had hurried, heart in mouth, to catch a stranger by the shoulders, the times he had seen her in an elevator as the doors closed, and he had pounded breathlessly up flights of stairs to find, when the doors opened, that the girl he had thought was Liz had a different face, a different smile.

How many times, he wondered bleakly, had he imagined her laughter in a New York restaurant? How often had he walked wearily into his apartment, high above the jewelled lights of Manhattan, to catch a memory of her perfume?

The haunting ghost of her was with him even now, gazing from the plane window, looking down with him at the shimmering foam-flecked sea, the slim, orange span of the Golden Gate Bridge far below.

He knew, without doubt or uncertainty, that he loved Liz Fremont as he had never loved a woman in his life before, as he would never love any woman again.

One look at Liz convinced Jess that she had not come through her ordeal unscathed. Her eyes, dulled to the colour of peat-brown water, ate up the pale triangle of her face. She resembled, Jess thought compassionately, a sepia line and wash drawing by Michelangelo; a brown and white madonna, with her faultless bone structure and face-framing mass of tawny hair.

She wore a pencil-slim brown tweed skirt, polo-neck sweater and a suede blouson jacket. That she had dressed up, like a little girl going to a party, touched Jess deeply. The childlike image was further enhanced by the way she walked, legs slightly apart, so that her movements lacked their usual fluidity and grace. She carried, apart from her overnight case, a bunch of pale pink carnations.

As Jess hurried forward to meet her, she said breathlessly, 'I don't want Mrs Cornwell to see me, to start asking questions.'

'She's not here at the moment. Let me carry your case for you.'

'Don't fuss, Jess! I can manage perfectly well on my own!'

'No, I won't fuss. I promise!' So what am I to do, she wondered. Pretend that nothing has happened?

'Do you mind if I come up later?' she asked lightly, thinking that she had, perhaps, missed her own vocation in life, as an actress.

The idea struck her forcibly with the strength of its validity as she stood at the foot of the stairs watching Liz go up to her room. She had acted so many roles during the past years. Katharina in *The Taming of the Shrew* had been just the beginning. Since then she had played an elderly Juliet to Douglas's ungainly Romeo, an understanding wife to an increasingly moody and acerbic husband, a small, defeated whipping-boy, a kind of female father confessor, an Indian squaw.

What role should she play now? And who, if anyone, would applaud her performance?

Later, in Liz's room, she said concernedly, 'Shall I make you some tea?'

'I don't want any tea! For Christ's sake, Jess! I don't want anything at all except . . .'

'Except Steen? I know. I understand.'

The room was filled with shadows. Beyond the undrawn curtains the lights of the esplanade sprang up one by one. Car lights raked the ceiling. Liz was sitting in the leather armchair close to the glowing gas-fire, shoulders hunched, face shadowed by her hair. The pink carnations lay wilting upon the table near the window. She had not bothered to put them in water.

'You know what is so funny, so bloody, excruciatingly funny about all this, don't you?' Liz said harshly, 'I thought I had got him out of my system! God knows, I tried hard enough! I believed, somehow, that when they cut my child away from me, they would cut him out of me too. I really thought that when I opened my eyes after the operation, I would wake up absolved; free from this torment!'

Jess gathered together the pink blossoms.

'Do you know what kept on running through my mind? Suffer little children to come unto me!'

'Don't Liz! Please don't!'

'Don't – what?'

'Punish yourself like this!'

'Punish myself? But I deserve to be punished? Don't you see? I'm a murderess! A female Herod! A killer of the innocent!'

'Stop it!' Jess turned on her sharply. Anger as well as compassion was necessary at times to cope with the unbearable waste of human life. 'Grief is one thing, but what you are doing to yourself now is not only wrong, it is wicked! Useless! All the guilt feelings in the world won't change a thing!'

Kneeling down, grasping Liz by the shoulders, shaking her, Jess said passionately, 'What matters now is that you should go on with your life! You must, Liz! You *must*!'

'And suppose I don't want to go on?'

'To hell with that! You have no other choice! Remember that you are a valuable human being too!'

And this was not acting. This was the bedrock of Jess's faith, this belief of hers in the sanctity of human life, however twisted or misbegotten. The reason why she had endured, with hope, the past twelve months of her life with Douglas, trying never to judge too harshly his inability to come to terms with the futility of his own past: those deeply implanted genes of selfishness and intolerance which made him the man he was, until he had forced her out of his life with his hatred and contempt of her meekness of spirit which he had somehow mistaken for weakness of purpose.

Suddenly, in the near darkness, fighting against tears, Jess felt the touch of Liz's hand on hers: saw by the fireglow, the trace of a smile on her lips.

She sighed then, and gathered Liz into her arms, whispering soft words of comfort as a mother would to a grieving child.

Liz felt like a child going back to school after an illness – measles or chickenpox – except that she wasn't a child, and she hadn't been ill. She felt that a great gulf, an unbridgeable chasm separated the woman who had walked up those steps of the Pregnancy Advisory Clinic and the woman who returned to the theatre a week later.

Nobody looked at her strangely as she went in through the rear door, past the set-designer's office, props, and the scenery workroom where the carpenters were busy constructing a balcony. She was part of the scenery, too, as familiar as the blocks of wood and the make-believe palm trees propped up in a corner.

170

When she popped her head round the door of the green room, nobody flew to her, hands outstretched, making sympathetic noises, telling her to sit down, to take things easy. They simply registered the fact that she was there and went on with what they were doing – talking, reading lines, arguing, drinking coffee, laughing, seeing no change in her, not realising that she was different, that part of her was missing.

'Want some coffee?' Jolyon asked laconically, shambling across to the percolator.

'Please.' Liz shrugged off her shoulder-bag. She felt intensely cold despite the muggy heat of the room. The below-street-level windows, she noticed, were misted on the inside, the basement railings beyond rimed with frost.

'Someone's been trying to ring you like crazy.' Jolyon handed her the coffee in a plastic container. 'Muppet's been tearing her hair out. Nobody seemed to know where you were. All very Marie Celeste.'

'You knew where I was. I told you. Laurel Villa,' Liz said defensively.

'Ah yes, darling. But there's no Mrs Carmichael listed in the 'phone book.'

'I'd better ask Muppet.'

Muppet was the nickname of the large cuddly lady in charge of the box office, whose penchant for wearing colourful mohair sweaters had prompted the sobriquet, who was sitting hunched upon her swivel chair, decorative glasses sliding down her nose, attempting to sort out the pile of seating plans and answer the telephone at the same time.

Edging the mouthpiece between shoulder and chin, she biroed three crosses on one of the plans; said briskly, 'Yes, that's fine, sir. Three seats, Row E, 20 November. *Private Lives*. You'll pick up the tickets? Fine. Thank you. Yes, fine. Thank you.'

Replacing the receiver, she grinned at Liz, displaying a top set of beautifully modelled false teeth complete with gold fillings. 'Oh, there you are,' she said breathlessly.

'Thank God you're back. He's been driving me crazy.'

'*He?*' Liz felt her knees go weak. '*Who?*'

'He didn't give his name. Just left a number for you to ring. Wait a sec.' Swivelling round on her chair, Muppet laid her hand unerringly on a memo pad near the rolled-up mounds of tickets on a shelf behind. 'Said it was very urgent. Yep. Here it is.' She pushed back her glasses. 'Caller, American International Enterprises, Madison Avenue, New York. I've made a note of the number. Ask for extension 419. Oh, and there's a second, private number. He said to ring anytime, day or night.'

Steen!

CHAPTER 12

It seemed ludicrous to Douglas Carmichael, at times, that his passionate affair with Avril had not become the subject of commonroom gossip. Surely everyone, unless they were blind or deaf must know by now. And yet they continued to play their complicated game of make-believe.

When the final bell went, he would gather up his books and papers, nod briefly to whoever happened to be in the staff-room, and stride across the carpark to make a pretence of cleaning his windscreen or rearranging his books in the plaid holdall which he invariably used instead of a document case. His unpopularity ensured that none of his colleagues would dream of approaching him for a last-minute conversation, to proffer hospitality, or invite him to join them for a drink later on.

Then a few minutes later, Avril would emerge, usually with a group of her students with whom she would spend a little time chatting before drifting unhurriedly to her battered Volkswagen; calling out – in case the caretaker's ears were flapping, or the headmaster happened to be looking out of his study window – 'Goodnight girls! Goodnight Douglas, see you tomorrow,' or 'See you on Monday,' as the case may be. And he would wave his hand vaguely, dismissively, in her direction, so that an onlooker would gain the impression that he could not give a damn if he never set eyes on her again.

The charade followed its usual pattern on this cold, late October evening. When it was over, Douglas stood alone in the carpark, fingering the letter.

His first reaction had been one of shocked disbelief that Jessica, of all people, had delivered him into the hands of the philistines.

Brought up in a community where the women did their housework as if a factory overseer was breathing down their necks, he had long since reached the conclusion that he knew as much about running a house as he did about prizefighting.

Cooking for himself was bad enough. Washing up, afterwards, a mess of greasy pots and pans, had totally defeated him, so that he no longer even attempted what he had always supposed to be the simplest meal on record – bacon and eggs. The first time he had done so, the bacon emerged rock hard from the frying pan, whilst the eggs had turned somersaults, spattering his shirt front with immovable grease stains.

The washing machine, lurking balefully beneath a littered work-surface, had also defeated him. His First Class Honours degree in English Literature, his Cambridge education, and all those swingeing debates on Human Rights had done nothing whatever to educate him in the simple procedure of pouring in the right amount of washing-powder or setting the dials at the correct temperature, with the result that his shirts and underpants had emerged green-streaked from the machine, whilst his revered cashmere sweater had shrunk to doll-like dimensions.

All this, he thought sullenly, was Jessica's fault. He had felt stunned, utterly bewildered when he had returned to the bungalow that night to find her clothes missing; gaps in the bookshelves – as if a servant had left suddenly without giving notice.

He had not believed her when she told him she was leaving, had thought her incapable of making a new life for herself.

But this letter! Divorce! He had believed that Jessica would come back to the bungalow sooner or later when she realised that she could not exist without him. In the narrow world of his upbringing, women played the minor role, as his mother had done. As the weaker vessels, women remained subservient to their menfolk. The old patterns had changed little in the windswept Welsh mining village of his childhood with its stark pit-heads and towering slag-heaps, cobbled lanes, smoke-blackened houses, Methodist chapel, pubs, and the inevitable working-men's club where the men swilled away the coal-dust from their throats while the women stayed at home to mind the children.

174

This was the world from which he had struggled to escape, and yet he remained shackled by the powerful influences, the ugliness and limitations which his childhood had brought to bear on his adult life.

The charade, which added a fillip to their relationship, had been Avril's brainchild.

She had considered the possibility of starting something with the aloof English master from the moment she set eyes on him.

'Heavens! You don't stand an earthly there,' Sadie Brown, the red-haired geography teacher, told her. 'He's an odd fish, our Douglas! Well, you've only to look at him! Besides, he's married!'

'Really? So what?'

She and Sadie had been sharing a flat at the time, until Avril could find a place of her own. Sadie had indicated that the arrangement would be, of necessity, a temporary one. She had her own fish to fry. So, come to that, had Avril. Sadie's 'fish' was called Jimmy, an intense, bearded young man, who appeared at weekends, complete with guitar and duffel-bag, several bottles of wine and, apparently, an insatiable sexual appetite for his delectable girlfriend which kept the pair of them confined to the bedroom for the whole of Saturday and most of Sunday, until it was time for Jimmy to go back to Durham.

Then, out of the blue, Sadie had announced her intention of moving to Durham to be with Jimmy who, surprisingly, was not the drop-out Avril had imagined him to be, but a university lecturer.

'So you might just as well stay on here,' Sadie told Avril. 'I'll fix it with the landlord if you like. He's Asian, poor pet, but most of them are these days.' She'd winked knowingly, and burst out laughing. 'He never asks questions, but then he doesn't speak very good English!' She'd raised a quizzical eyebrow. 'By the way, how are you getting on with "The Lone Ranger"? What do you make of his wife? Rather an odd choice, don't you think? Must be years

175

older than he is. Quite attractive, though, in a middle-aged kind of way. He treats her like dirt, of course, so watch out, my pet! Personally I think him a bit of a bastard!'

Avril could not have cared less about Sadie's opinion of Douglas Carmichael. Not that she meant the relationship she envisaged to provide more than a mild diversion. Conquest was all she had cared about at first; the thrill of the chase, the line and the lure; selecting the best method of attack. She had planned that attack as cunningly as Henry V before Agincourt.

If he played hard to get, so would she. And so she had treated him coolly, disdainfully, dressing as outrageously as she dared, knowing that he was becoming increasingly aware of her whenever they passed each other on their way to classes; aware of her musky perfume, her cropped-off fringe and the dark weight and sheen of her uncut hair which she either plaited or allowed to swing loose down her back.

Even so, she had begun to think she was getting nowhere fast; to chafe beneath her carefully assumed façade of indifference, until one evening after a staff meeting in the headmaster's study, as she was getting into her car, he appeared at her side, laid a restraining hand on her arm and said abruptly, 'We must talk! There's a lay-by a mile down the road.' Her heart leapt at the sound of his voice, and yet she had remained cool, seemingly shocked and distant, 'I don't understand,' she said. 'What is there to talk about?'

'You know damned well! Now drive . . .'

She had, of course, often noticed the lay-by set back from the main road behind a barrier of trees, a place where the drivers of heavy-goods vehicles would stop to eat their sandwiches and read their newspapers. But the lay-by had been empty on that occasion — on that splendid, dusky summer evening with a windswept sky; branches soughing gently, making soft, whispering sounds, the encroaching darkness lit by a solitary star.

'Well,' she had said, switching off the ignition, feeling the swift tug of desire in the region of her belly, 'start talking.'

But they had scarcely talked at all. With a deep sigh, she had simply lifted her face to his, had felt his hands warm upon her body as he searched frantically upwards beneath her lightweight covering of Indian cotton; his tongue flickering in the dark aperture of her wide-open mouth. And she had never thought, never realised that she could want a man so desperately.

'Let us go to my flat,' she had managed to say eventually, shaken by his urgency and passion, the feel of his hands at her breasts.

That had been the start of the affair.

Faced with his dilemma, Douglas lingered on the carpark. Events had not always run smoothly with Avril. The pressures of the affair, the secrecy and subterfuge had built up, at times, into explosive situations. Both were moody, short-tempered, quick to fly off the handle.

Possessed of a temperament which would not allow her to play second fiddle, Avril had often turned on him in a jealous rage, maddened by what she saw as his weakness, his reluctance to leave his wife: 'Wanting the best of both worlds,' she called it, thrashing him with her tongue, spicing her rhetoric with ugly, four-letter words, revealing the bitchiness of her second-rate mind; taunting him at the same time with the softness of her naked body, swishing back her hair; the rope of beads, the size and colour of aniseed balls, jingling against the hand-beaten silver cross she invariably wore; driving him mad by her occasional refusal to let him touch her; or to discuss his fears about his job or about the possibility of their liaison being discovered.

One night, 'You and your bloody job,' she had flung at him contemptuously, 'I'm sick to hell of hearing about it! Sick, sick, sick of your rotten bloody lies and excuses! There are other jobs, for Christ's sake! Other places! My God, what a pathetic little turd you really are!'

And then, because he was drunk with all the wine and whisky they had consumed, he had struck her, causing her to stagger backwards with the unexpectedness of the blow. She had sprung at him then, like a tigress, snarling her hatred of his weakness and cowardice, daring him to hit her again, and he had sunk his fingers deeply into her hair, taking a savage delight in her shrieks of agony as he twisted her head this way and that, uncaring of the pain she inflicted in retaliation, the kicks she rained on his legs, the blows to his chest with her tightly screwed fists.

He had wanted to kill her at that moment, to silence once and for all the stream of invective jetting from her mouth. And then he had done a shameful thing. He had been sick down the front of her.

'Ugh! Beast! You filthy beast!' Uttering a cry between a shriek and a wail, she had flung open the door and ordered him out of her flat. Suddenly he had found himself on the landing, edging along the wall for support, stumbling towards the deep well of the staircase, clutching the banister, feeling his knees buckling, tasting the sour tang of vomit on his tongue.

The door of her flat had re-opened suddenly, and she had rushed out, dragging his coat on the ground like a matador's cape. He had looked up, startled, as the coat descended and landed squarely on his head, shutting out the sight of her angry, passionate face, muffling the sound of her voice screaming at him to get the hell out of her life, to go home to his bloody wife . . . to get the silly bitch pregnant for all she cared.

Inevitably, they had gravitated together again, drawn by their overwhelming sexual need. When Jessica went to Bevensea Bay, he had rung Avril, whose temper had cooled by that time. But he had never forgotten the events of that night when he had become shockingly aware of Avril's basic ugliness and his own bestiality.

'Liz! Darling! My darling!'
    'Steen?'
    'Oh Liz! I've missed you so! How are you? Not – angry?'
    'Why – angry?'

'I don't know. You sound so far away!'

'I am – far away.'

She had longed for this moment, the sound of his voice. Now she scarcely knew what to say to him, the father of her aborted child, across an ocean of regret.

'Liz! Where have you been?'

'Here,' she said. 'In Bevensea Bay – where you left me.'

'Ah, so you *are* angry? I thought so! I could tell by your voice.'

'No, Steen – not angry.'

'What then?'

'Practical! I'm just trying to be practical. Nothing has changed. Why prolong the agony?'

Christ! Why was she saying all this? She had waited with bated breath, trembling limbs, for the New York connection. And now she was saying all the wrong things.

'All right Liz,' he said tautly, 'I understand how you feel. I know what you're thinking. Just answer one question. If the answer is no, I'll hang up, never bother you again!' He paused. The line crackled. 'Do you love me? All I want is a simple yes or no. You see, darling, I still love you. More than I can put into words. More than anyone, anything else on earth!'

She felt the slow movement of tears down her cheeks. Suddenly the realisation of how much she loved him flooded through her with the brilliance of a sky filled with moonlight and cold autumn stars.

'Yes, I *do* love you,' she said. Her voice caught on a sob, 'so much that I could die from it.'

'That's all I wanted to know.' The line crackled more alarmingly. She thought she had lost contact with him. 'Steen,' she cried out, '*Steen!*'

'Listen, darling. I want you to come over here as soon as possible.'

'To New York?' She was using the phone in Miss Tidey's room, amid a welter of cables the workmen had left behind, kneeling on the floor, shoulders hunched to the instrument, speaking close to the mouthpiece. 'You mean – *New York*?'

'I'll rent an apartment for you . . .'

'What about my contract? I have a contract. I can't simply walk out.'

'I realise that. The contract. When does it expire?'

'I don't know the exact date. Not offhand. Sometime in the new year.'

'That's fine, then. No problem . . .'

'How can you say that?' She brushed back a wisp of hair with shaking fingers. 'That's what I meant. Nothing has changed.'

'You mean – Dominique?'

'What did you think I meant?'

'So you *are* angry?'

She thought of a child denied life because of a simple failure of love when it mattered most; of a living, breathing child the man she loved obviously adored; a woman who had taken supremacy over herself, and knew that she *was* angry.

'Liz. Suppose I say that I have decided to tell Dominique the truth? I've got to. There's no other way. I want you here with me. Always! Liz, can you hear me?'

'Yes. Yes, I hear you.'

'I mean what I say. I've thought about it all the time.'

'And – Miguel?'

'He's only a child. He'll soon forget.' Steen's voice hardened. 'I'm not talking about an affair, Liz. This will be a lifelong commitment. I want you to marry me.'

'Oh, Steen!' Her lips were trembling. She could hardly speak.

'We'll talk again soon. Very soon, my darling. Goodnight, sweetheart. Goodnight.'

Suddenly her world had opened out again, all-embracing in the width and extravagance of its optimum shimmer and delight, because Steen loved her. Soon the pain and confusion of the past few months would possess no more substance than spindrift on a wave, the fragrance of a withered rose.

And yet . . .

She dreamt, that night, of a lonely, lost little boy crying for his father.

Jess looked with shining eyes and a sweet feeling of relief at the newly glazed and repaired conservatory. The tangled mass of overgrown creepers, as solidly interwoven as fibre matting, had been taken down with some difficulty, and a few choice epithets from the workmen engaged in the task.

Now, the work finished, the dining-room seemed far less gloomy despite the grey November weather. The heavy gasolier had been replaced by an Italianate chandelier of the moulded-wood variety. She could not have afforded crystal. But the new fixture would blend in well enough, and she had chosen the green shades with extreme care to match the moss-green wallpaper she had ordered. Green, with a watered-silk effect.

The necessary alterations, she considered, had in no way destroyed the essentially Victorian character of Laurel Villa. Wandering from room to room, experimentally snapping on electric light switches, she wondered what Great Aunt Jessica would make of it all – especially the kitchen.

She could scarcely believe what she saw. The transformation left her feeling as breathless as that transformation scene in *Cinderella*.

The window bars had been removed. The floor was covered with tough, springy blue-grey vinyl. Working surfaces complemented the predominantly blue colouring. Cupboards were white; the deep, functional sink-unit, stainless steel. The alcove which had once harboured the rusted range now contained a modern electric cooker set against a background of pale-blue tiles.

The introduction of wash-basins to most of the rooms had worried her, but people in this day and age could not be expected to cope without modern amenities. And then she had hit upon the idea of screening the washing facilities from view behind ceiling-high partitions.

181

Entering her great-grandfather's study, she wondered what the old lion would say if he could see it now, with a modern gas fire on the hearth and a screened-off wash-basin in the far corner.

And yet the room remained essentially the same. The bay window still frowned upon the gravelled drive. Now that the workmen had finished hammering and sawing, drilling, and laying cables, the carpet had been refitted; rugs relaid, and one of the towering glass-fronted bookcases brought back as a reminder of the man who had built this house and left upon it the imprint of his dominant personality.

Joshua Tidey. Jess had still not come to grips with him. She wondered what he had really been like – looked like. Had he been the stern Victorian martinet of her imagination – a kind of Edward Moulton Barrett with muttonchop whiskers – or simply a shrewd, hard-headed businessman with a natural affection for his family who had nevertheless remained a little aloof and withdrawn from the pressures of household matters?

In that case, why had his daughter destroyed his photographs? Why that clinical inscription on an exclamation point of Aberdeen granite in the Greyfriars cemetery?

Had he kept a mistress on the sideline? Many a Victorian husband had been guilty of that, Jess thought: leaving the management of the house and children to a patient, forbearing wife who closed her eyes to her lord and master's culpability in that respect. And what part had Annie Petch played in the Tidey family saga?

Today was Sunday. Dora and Alfred had gone across to Mews Cottage after lunch, to put the finishing touches to their home. Liz had gone for a walk along the beach. Jess knew why – to come to terms with the future, her role as Steen Bancroft's wife.

She had listened quietly when Liz poured forth her reaction to his telephone call, happy because Liz was happy, not venturing to voice her concern that Steen had not been straightforward with Dominique, not wanting to shatter

182

Liz's euphoria. And yet it had worried her that divorce from a Catholic wife might prove more difficult than he imagined. It troubled her even more that Bancroft could contemplate leaving his son, who, despite his brave words, he obviously loved dearly. Nor could she help regretting Bancroft's reappearance at a time when Liz was just beginning to come to terms with the abortion. Left alone, Liz, by the sheer strength and will of her dazzling personality, her driving ambition and love of acting, would have weathered the emotional storm of the past months. And now . . .

Engrossed in thought, Jess went upstairs to see how far the workmen had progressed with her flat – her oasis beneath the slates.

Two of the dividing walls had been taken down; the parapet lowered, letting in more light, giving a better view of the sea from the windows.

One day, she thought, looking out at the wide vista of Bevensea Bay, she would weather her own emotional storm, come to terms with her past life with Douglas. When the house was finished, there would be other things to occupy her mind. She wondered about the people who would come here to live – people whose problems would become as familiar to her as those of Alfred and Dora's. She wondered what they would be like, those unknown guests of hers, if they would be happy here, and remembered, walking downstairs to the kitchen to begin preparations for tea, that she had not seen Mr Hoyle since that weekend in Goathland; had deliberately kept away from his office. But why? Because she had sensed something between them she could not quite come to terms with. Something disquieting. A kind of hiatus?

Liz walked close by the sea's edge where the waves came in, like curdled cream, upon the gleaming wet sand.

Steen had rung several times since their first, halting conversation, building up a picture of their life together in New York. He had found a play for her, a revival of Ibsen's *Ghosts*.

'Mrs Alving?' she'd asked eagerly.

'No, darling. Regina.'

'I see.' Disappointment had tugged at her.

'It's a great part, Liz. In any case, Mrs Alving needs a more mature actress.'

'You mean a more experienced actress? A well-known name?'

'Yes. I knew you'd understand.' And she had known that this was Steen Bancroft, the perfectionist, speaking – a man who would never allow his personal feelings to out-weigh his commonsense approach to his work. 'Don't knock Regina, darling. After all, we are talking about a Broadway production.'

'I'm not knocking Regina.'

'Good. We're starting auditions in January, going into rehearsal, hmmm, let me see, the first week in February.' She could almost see him, brow furrowed, hair untidy, riffling through the pages of his desk-diary.

'It's not certain, then, that I shall play Regina?' she'd asked wistfully.

He laughed briefly. 'Don't worry, honey. You'll play her!'

'You mean – you'll pull strings?'

'Like a puppeteer!' A crackling on the line. His voice again. 'Hey, Liz darling, what is all this? You trust me, don't you?'

'Of course I trust you.' She wanted, needed to trust him. Her future, her whole life depended upon that trust. A trust he had once broken.

A grey November mist hovered over the sea's face, almost blotting from view the harbour; touching her skin with ghostly fingers: the greyness filled with dancing flecks of light, like darting silver fish.

Another call. 'I've leased an apartment for you, darling. Overlooking Central Park.'

'But you already have an apartment . . .'

'Don't complicate matters! We can't live together until things are settled between me and Dominique. I thought you realised that.'

184

'You've told her, then?'

'I have sown seeds,' he said carefully.

'Sown seeds?' What did that mean? She wondered if it meant that he had implanted so many seeds of discontent in his wife's mind that she had begun to doubt the validity of their marriage vows.

'We are virtually separated now. I haven't been home to San Francisco in weeks. Dominique knows there's something wrong.'

'I see.' So there had been no clear-cut declaration of his intentions, just the slow strangulation of a marriage.

'I don't think you *do* see, darling. You said you trusted me. Trust me, then, to know the best way to handle the situation. Liz, how many times do I have to tell you that I want you here with me always? God, how I hate these bloody phone-calls: the distortion of distance!'

'Yes, I feel that too.' She closed her eyes against the agony of not being able to touch him, to feel his arms about her.

She had almost told him, then, about the abortion. But the time was not right. She could not speak of it across the crackling miles of their separation.

Watching the sharp implosions of her footprints in the sand, Liz thought about her career. To play Regina Engstrand, on Broadway, was the chance of a lifetime. Naturally, she would rather have been offered Mrs Alving. But Steen was right. The part of Mrs Alving called for a seasoned veteran of the theatre, a name to draw in the crowds.

Her pulse quickened at the thought of Broadway: an apartment overlooking Central Park. Above all at the thought of being with Steen again, drawing inspiration from his presence: that quick, urgent vitality of his she loved and needed so much, knowing that this time it would be forever. Forever . . .?

She thought suddenly of Jess: their conversation in the graveyard of the parish church. Her own words: 'I thought it would last forever.' And Jess's reply: 'Nothing lasts forever. I've discovered that . . .'

185

Nothing?

She stood near the harbour and watched the sea splintering against the bastion walls; listened to the dull crump of the tide on the moss-slimed rocks at her feet; the keening cries of the seabirds weaving high above her, filling the air with their noisy clamour.

Soon she must tell the director of her decision to leave the company. Don Kent would be shocked when he knew she was going. Plans for the new season were already under review – rather like a school timetable – dates and names being pencilled in.

He would, of course, quickly gloss over his feelings: say she must do whatever seemed expedient to further her career. She could almost visualise the puckering of his high-domed forehead with its yellowish fringe of hair, his eyes narrowed to slits by the continual irritation of rising smoke from his lip-held cigarette, the nervous twitching of a muscle in his right cheek.

Part of her would regret leaving all this – the Bevensea Theatre Company which had been her cradle, her proving ground: this town in which she had known both joy and despair; the people she had grown to love and respect. But the future beckoned to her like a jack-o'-lantern, a tantalising will-o'-the-wisp light dancing before her.

She knew, as she retraced her steps, that it was time to move away from her past life, to move on to a dazzling future filled with hope and promise.

She might even have a child. What was it Dr Sanger had said to her? 'Woman, you have a fine, child-bearing body . . .'

She suddenly remembered that she had not even bothered to thank him for the carnations.

CHAPTER 13

The Hoyles invariably went away, at Christmas, to a luxury hotel of the sort which catered for the wealthy, indolent and lonely: those possessed of a penchant for rich food, powerful central-heating, and organised leisure pursuits.

In the summer, of course, Beryl insisted upon holidays abroad; luxury coach trips to the south of France, to Italy or Switzerland. (One met such *nice* people.)

Now her preoccupation with television was pleasurably interspersed with mulling over the mass of colourful holiday brochures garnered by the reluctant William from a local travel agent.

Sitting up in bed, wearing a pink brushed-nylon nightdress, with a fine, hand-knitted woollen bed-jacket about her shoulders, the brochures spread fan-wise on the rose-embellished duvet, spectacles perched on the end of her nose, comparing prices, and the glowing descriptions promulgated by the PR officers concerned in 'selling' accommodation as advantageously as possible, she scarcely noticed the carefully controlled expression of misery on her husband's face as she vowed and declared that she simply could not make up her mind between the Hotel Splendide in Bournemouth and the Miramar in Torquay. (This to the background accompaniment of the Terry Wogan chat show.)

Inevitably, Hoyle's thoughts drifted to a raftered pub; a warm fire, Jess beside him; a group of old men playing dominoes at a corner table, the feeling he'd had there of an added dimension to life, a hitherto unknown sense of companionship and rapport.

'William! I asked you a question,' his wife's voice cut into his thoughts. 'You might at least show *some* interest!'

'I'm sorry, my dear . . .'

Christmas, Dora said, would be upon them before they knew where they were.

Christmas, Jess thought. Dora was right. She had

scarcely noticed the passage of time. Liz would be playing 'Light' in Maeterlinck's *The Blue Bird*. And Liz, who seemed incandescent with happiness these days, would play the part to perfection.

In her oasis under the stars, Jess sniffed the unique smell of newly laid carpets. Wandering from room to room, she wondered what her home would look like it when it was finished, when all the lamps were lit, the furniture in place, and her books arranged on the built-in shelves near the fireplace.

Later, Alfred clumped into the kitchen, carrying a fir tree which he had dug up from the spinney at the sea-edge of the garden.

'I was careful not to disturb the roots,' he said, 'so that I can replant it after the holidays. I've no patience with folk who murder trees for money. I mean to say, what use is a tree without roots? Come to that, what use is anything without roots?'

Roots, Jess thought wistfully. Alfred had hit the nail on the head. Everything, everyone upon the face of the earth, needed roots; a feeling of security. A tree without roots was every bit as useless as a barren woman.

'Have you thought where you'd like it to stand?' Alfred set down his burden on the sheet of pliofilm he had arranged so that the container in which he had settled the tree should not mark the floor.

Jess tilted her head thoughtfully, 'Near the foot of the staircase, I think. Yes, that would be the perfect place for it.'

Instinct told her that a Christmas tree, with lighted candles, would have graced the hall when Clarice was the mistress of Laurel Villa. The house would have been fragrant, then, with the scent of roasting goose and hot mince pies; and there would have been mulled wine ready for the waits who would come to sing carols on Christmas Eve.

When Alfred had lumbered the tree into position, he dusted his hands on the seat of his trousers and felt in his pocket for a notebook and a stub of pencil. 'I've had a word with Sid Curtis,' he explained, 'you know, that bloke I told you about who does a bit of furniture removing in his spare time. He can come round on Wednesday morning, if that's all right with you.'

'Wednesday will be fine.'

'I'd better make a list of what you want shifting then.' Alf moistened the point of the pencil with his tongue. 'Would you mind going over it again, just to make sure.'

'Well, my bedroom furniture – except the big wardrobe – I doubt if that would go up the stairs – great Aunt Jessica's carved chest, and the bureau: that little blue velvet chair . . .' She ticked off the items on her fingers.

Alfred smiled. 'I'm glad you'll be settled in, in time for Christmas,' he said. 'Funny the way things turn out. Last year at this time, Dora and I knew that Geoff hadn't much longer to live. We were both at rock bottom then, wondering how we'd cope. It shook my faith, I can tell you. And now . . .'

Jess looked away, remembering the bitter arguments about faith she and Douglas had engaged in; how often she had come up against the brick wall of his atheism, the way in which he had dismissed, as sentimental nonsense, her observance of the old rituals: claiming, when she became emotional, that women were incapable of conducting an argument without losing the thread of it.

But if there was nothing more in life to cling to than a daily succession of household chores, cooking food to nourish a covering of dust, without some kind of faith or hope for the future, why bother to live at all?

Sid Curtis, strong of arm, a whippy middle-aged man who reminded Jess of a bookie's runner, aided and abetted by Alfred, had had the furniture in place, drunk several mugs of tea, and smoked ten cigarettes within the space of two hours.

When he had taken his leave, Jess went upstairs, like a child playing house, to put the finishing touches to her flat.

Gently fingering Annie Petch's Bible, she laid it on her bedside table.

'For where your treasure is, there will your heart be also.'

Annie's old room, with its narrow bed, horsehair mattress, yellow furniture, and strips of haircord carpet, had been incorporated into Jess's new kitchen. But whenever she washed up at the stainless-steel sink she would think of Annie's rickety wash-stand with its chipped ewer and basin, soap-tidy, and cracked toothbrush holder.

Remembering that she owed this oasis to William Hoyle, on an impulse she picked up the telephone and rang his office.

'This is delightful,' Hoyle said, his eyes lingering on the deep delphinium blue of the velvet buttoned chair, the colour of which had been picked up in the curtains and settee cover.

The room, he thought, reflected Jess's instinctive good taste. Lamplight glowed warmly on the choice pieces of antique furniture arranged against the plain, blue-grey walls. He noticed, in particular, how artistically she had grouped together Clarice's watercolours above the fireplace: felt deeply touched that she had gone to the bother of cutting wafer-thin cucumber sandwiches, and baking fresh scones for him, and thought how lovely she looked in her soft blue wool dress.

William looked tired, Jess thought, and dispirited. 'Have you been busy at the office?' she asked, handing him the plate of sandwiches; pouring tea from Clarice's silver teapot into the fluted Dresden china cups.

'Extremely so.' He sighed imperceptibly. 'Some of the cases have been exceptionally involved and complicated.'

'Are you spending Christmas with your family?'

'I'm afraid not. My wife and I are going to Bournemouth.' He pulled a wry face. 'The pleasures of the simple life have never appealed to Beryl. She much prefers large hotels with overheated dining rooms.' He shook his head wearily. 'I'm sorry, I should not have said that. How boorish and petty-minded you must think me. But what about you, Jess? How will you cope with Christmas?'

'I shall simply keep on reminding myself of the times I wished I could spend Christmas in peace. Now my wish has been granted.'

'But you'll have company if you feel like it?' Suddenly he could not bear the thought of her being alone, possibly unhappy during the so-called 'festive season'. 'You'll have the Cornwells, and Miss Fremont . . .'

'Yes, but Liz won't be here for very much longer,' Jess said wistfully. 'She's going to America in the new year. Dear Liz. I'll miss her terribly. We've grown very close in the short time we've known each other. But there's the future to think of; that's what the new year is all about, isn't it?' She spoke brightly, almost too brightly, Hoyle thought as she rose quickly to her feet, crossed to the bureau, and returned with a sheet of paper for him to read, on which was typed, 'Mrs Jessica Carmichael, Laurel Villa, 28 The Esplanade, Bevensea Bay, offers spacious accommodation to let. Home cooking, sea views. Freedom in which to breathe.'

'I'm not sure about the last sentence,' she admitted. 'Does it sound too high-flown?'

Hoyle laughed delightedly. 'Not to me. Reading this, I'd jump at the chance of "Freedom in which to breathe". It sums up exactly what you have in mind .'

He knew then that it was almost time for him to leave. Questions would be asked in the house if he was late for what Beryl grandiosely termed 'dinner'· Glancing at the carriage clock on the mantelpiece, he said reluctantly, 'I'm so sorry, I must be on my way now. But I have something for you, downstairs in the car; it isn't much, just a small housewarming present. I hope you'll like it.'

They walked together to the front door. Hoyle hurried out to his car and returned with a flat, oblong parcel wrapped in red and gold striped paper. 'Don't open it now,' he said awkwardly. Then, clasping her hands, longing to kiss her, he murmured, 'Well, goodbye, my dear. Happy Christmas.'

* * *

His gift to her, a delicate watercolour of the moors near Goathland, done in beautifully understated colours of umber, grey, white and purple, reminded her of so many things – the way he had smoothed her path for her, that loan from petty cash when she scarcely knew where her next meal was coming from, the care he had taken of her that day in Scarborough: standing with him on a hilltop overlooking Whitby Harbour, his gentleness and dry sense of humour – the day he had lent her his umbrella.

Hoyle, she realised, had become an integral part of her life. William. Bill. Her very dear Bill, twenty years older than herself, and married to someone else.

Could the warm feeling at her heart whenever she was with him, possibly be construed as love? If so, this was a different kind of love from any she had known before – that pulsating 'star that outshone all the suns of all men's days': the kind which had allowed no resting place, no peace of mind.

Having failed with Douglas, the best that she could now hope for was an ideal concept of love expressed in non-physical terms: better still, expressed not at all.

She could not bear the thought of walking blindly into another impossible situation, laying herself open to more pain – a second death of the heart.

Liz's happiness was destined to shatter suddenly. It happened one afternoon after rehearsal.

'Have you a minute?' Don Kent had waited in his office until she left the auditorium. His face was the colour of chalk apart from the patchwork of purplish threadveins high up on his cheek-bones, etched there like a map of the London Underground.

'Yah! Sure!' She had no inkling of what was coming as she perched on the edge of his desk, insouciantly swinging her legs. 'Well?'

'There's no easy way for me to say this, I'm afraid.'

'Is it about my contract?'

Kent's eyelids drooped. Eyes half closed, he considered

her carefully. How lovely she looked, how vibrant and invincible – the finest young actress he had ever worked with.

'Well, come on, let's have it!' Don had a way of making mountains of molehills at times. A thwarted actor's penchant for over-dramatisation, Liz thought.

Kent knew what she thought of him, knew exactly how he must appear to her – a decimated Falstaff babbling of green fields.

'The fact is,' he said hoarsely, 'I've just been on the phone to New York.'

'And?' Liz smiled, hiding her impatience.

'I'm sorry. There's been an accident. A terrible accident!'

'What do you mean – an accident?' Suddenly Liz stopped smiling, stopped swinging her legs.

'A plane crash!' Kent moistened his lips with his tongue, fearful of her reaction to the news. Filled with a burning compassion for her, he said slowly, 'It's Steen Bancroft. He was on that plane. I'm afraid he's dead!'

'*Dead! Steen?* What the hell are you talking about?' Anger took hold of her, a fierce, all-consuming anger against the man seated behind the desk. 'If this is your idea of a joke!' She stood up quickly. 'I spoke to Steen late last night. He wasn't planning to fly anywhere. Do you imagine he wouldn't have told me?' She laughed scornfully. 'I happen to know he's spending Christmas in New York.'

Then, seeing the way Kent flinched from the whiplash of her anger, she said dully, 'I don't understand.' She pushed back her hair with trembling fingers. 'I mean – where? Where was he going?'

'To San Francisco. It wasn't planned. His son was taken ill. I gather his wife sent for him.'

'I don't believe it. It simply isn't true!'

'Liz, darling. If there's anything at all I can do to help . . .' Kent scattered papers, overturned an ashtray in his anxiety to comfort her, moving clumsily round his desk, hands extended.

'No!' She stepped away from him as if he had attempted

193

to burn her with a lighted cigarette. 'I don't need help. Why should I? I don't believe a word of it! Steen would have told me! It's a damned, wicked lie!'

'*Liz!*' He tried to hold her, but it was no use. He watched her running away down the corridor, her hair streaming about her shoulders.

Hurrying after her, he wondered what she would do when she stopped pushing away the truth, when the full realisation of his words hit her. But she was already out of the building, dodging traffic, heading blindly across the road, swallowed up by a blur of whirling snowflakes.

Steen! She must talk to Steen! She would ring New York right away. There were phone boxes in the foyer of the post office on the corner near the public library. She would ring the overseas operator, put in a reverse-charge call.

Between New York and Denver, the woman on the phone told her. The plane had crashed somewhere between New York and Denver, en route to San Francisco. She sounded dreadfully upset. Liz knew she was crying. Strange, hearing an unknown woman's sobs across the miles that separated them. 'Everything's in chaos here right now,' she'd said. 'Well, you can imagine, can't you?'

And yes, Liz thought, hanging up the receiver. She could imagine everything quite clearly now – that phone call from Dominique which had ended Steen's life; his desperate desire to be with his son.

She could picture him, bare-headed, worried, boarding the plane, thoughts of herself expunged from his mind as he answered the summons which had shattered both their lives.

Walking unseeingly towards the esplanade, blinded by tears and falling snow, Liz knew that Dominique had won after all. Knew that Steen would never have asked his wife to divorce him.

'. . .Each in his lonely night, each with a ghost . . .'

Looking up, she thought that she had never really seen snow before the way she saw it now – a blinding involvement of vicious flakes slanting down in a fierce concentration of noiseless white fury, blotting out the sky, the whole world. Blotting out everything, both happiness and despair, numbing the face, the hands, the brain, the entire body, until all that was left in the world was the white anaesthetic of the whirling, indifferent snowflakes.

The winterbound esplanade became suddenly a circus of flashing blue lights. Red and white cones marked the scene of the accident. Besides the panda cars, an ambulance had been sent for, not that the crew could do anything for the time being except wait, and watch the police take measurements.

The esplanade had been silent, empty before, apart from the woman and the driver of the car. Now a crowd of sightseers had arrived on the scene – God alone knew where from, the driver thought as he attempted to explain what had happened.

'Take it easy now, sir. Just go through it again . . .'

The scene unrolled slowly, like a silent movie, in his mind's eye. But telling it again meant reliving the horror. He had just turned the corner on to the esplanade. Snow was falling thickly at the time, clogging his windscreen wipers. Then he saw the woman, standing still in the middle of the road, seemingly transfixed by his headlights – just standing there. He'd swerved, braked. But it was no use. She had made no effort to move. No, he hadn't phoned the police. Someone else had done that, a man with a dog. He had just sat there in his car, too shocked to move.

The other man, the one with the dog, said in his statement that he had been on the beach when he heard the squeal of brakes, had come up those steps yonder just after the accident happened. There'd been deep skid marks in the snow, and the woman was lying in the road near the offside wing of the car. No he hadn't touched her. He'd just asked the driver if he was all right, then he'd tied the dog to the railing and run to the nearest phone-box to put in a 999 call.

'Why the hell are we all waiting around doing nothing?' the driver demanded irritably. 'How much longer are you going to leave her lying there?' He was sitting in the ambulance, shaking like a leaf.

'Sorry, sir. We can't move her until the doctor's been.'

'Oh for Christ's sake, man! Anyone can see she's dead!' And he had killed her. He covered his face with his hands to shut out the slow-motion horror movie unrolling through his brain.

'I know, sir, but that's the law.'

The man with the dog said he'd gone back to the scene of the accident after making the phone-call. The driver of the car had seemed pretty shaken. Yes, he'd taken a look at the woman, though he'd realised from the first there was nothing to be done for her. He'd been in the war, and there was something about a dead person. Well, you just knew, that's all. Anyway, he'd shone his flashlight on her face. The strange thing was, he'd recognised her. No, he didn't actually *know* her, but he'd seen her many a time, at the theatre. An actress, she was, and a bloody good one. He had thrown up, then, in the gutter.

Sanger had spent a busy morning at his surgery, coping with the infinite variety of complaints that human flesh is heir to. More prosaically, several young mothers with querulous, sneezing infants – kids who should not have been brought out at all on such a freezing cold day. (Would they never learn?) Apart from which there had been the usual crop of elderly ladies with pinched faces and tired eyes who, for various reasons – loneliness, poverty, or the care of senile, incontinent parents – were unable to sleep properly.

Next on the list came a man Sanger knew well and respected, a gentle chap who had lost his wife recently, who appeared to be suffering from a serious iron and vitamin deficiency: who had obviously lost interest in life since the sudden, regrettable death of his partner, and now lived alone in a house far too big for one person. 'Sit down,

Mr Sloane,' he said quietly. 'What can I do to help you?'

After Mr Sloane came a hopefully pregnant young bride, badly wanting a baby but scared, Sanger suspected, by the old wives' tales she had listened to.

His face softened as he confirmed her pregnancy and advised her not to worry. 'Now I'd like you to attend prenatal classes to master the art of relaxation and deep breathing,' he said gently. 'And I dare say you'd like your husband to be with you during the actual birth?'

'Oh yes,' she was already breathing more easily. 'Thank you ever so much, doctor.'

When the girl had gone, Sanger leaned back in his chair to stare out of the window, reflecting upon the problems of his next patient for whom he also felt a great deal of compassion.

He had met Rachel Sweeting at the Belvedere nursing home the day her sister died. He had felt embarrassed as the tall, bizarre-looking old woman in her black cloak and witchlike hat had hurried towards him, saying he reminded her of someone, clutching at his hands in that strangely possessive way old people often do, in need of comfort, he not knowing of her bereavement until a young nurse had gently led her away to the almoner's office. He had then realised that the poor old creature was probably suffering from shock, and wished that he had known about her sister, had been more sympathetic, more understanding.

In the way of things, he had forgotten all about her until, later, she had come to his surgery and told him, without undue emphasis, that she believed herself to be insane.

Deeply shocked when she begged him to have her committed to what she termed an 'asylum', he had tried the light approach to her fears, speaking to her as he would have done to a frightened child. 'Oh come now, Miss Sweeting, it can't be as bad as all that.'

'But it *is*! You don't understand, doctor, I'm a thief! Yes, a *thief*! I steal things quite deliberately . . .' She had burst into tears.

That was the day Liz Fremont came to see him about an

abortion, Sanger recalled. He remembered the incident clearly because Liz had entered his surgery as Miss Sweeting had departed — weeping, and he had kept on looking down at his desk diary to hide his sudden angry awareness of his own ineptitude.

Morning surgery over, Sanger drank a cup of black coffee before setting off on his house calls.

Later, he ate lunch in a Chinese restaurant in the town square, finding pleasure in using chopsticks, savouring the crispy duck and sesame prawns; did some personal shopping, and returned to a packed waiting room.

About to finish his afternoon surgery, the phone rang; a call from the police station which his receptionist had put through to him as a matter of urgency. There had been a fatal road accident at the harbour end of the esplanade. How soon could he come?

Sanger glanced at his watch. 'Give me a quarter of an hour, sergeant,' he said wearily.

He had no idea, at the time, what awaited him. How could he possibly have known?

My God, he thought disgustedly, where the hell had all these people come from? What macabre impulse drew the human race unerringly to the scene of an accident? Pushing his way through the crowd, he gained some small pleasure from elbowing them aside harder than was strictly necessary.

And then he knew.

The woman lay where she had fallen. Misery engulfed him, an acute feeling of personal loss and grief as he knelt down in the road beside Liz, and saw, through a mist of tears, the way the snow had settled in her hair, and on her tightly closed eyelids.

He stayed on at the hospital until the early hours of next morning. Then, eyes red-rimmed with weariness, he walked unsteadily to his car, switched on the ignition and wondered if there really was a God, or if life was simply a crazy game of chance played upon a kind of galactic chessboard with human beings as the pawns.

The wind was bitter, the ground icy. The wind had scourged the snow into strange patterns. The carpark was chequered with brilliant patches of light from the hospital windows and the illuminated Greyfriars Hospital sign near the gates at the end of the long drive leading to the main road.

Drawing up at the traffic lights marking the junction of the dual carriageway, flicking on the wipers against the dancing heralds of a fresh blizzard, Sanger thought briefly of his wife, Margaret; conjuring her face, testing his many and varied memories of her, knowing that none of them possessed the power to hurt him anymore: imagined he saw the pale ghost of her scurrying away on the wind, and watched her go without regret.

Something had happened to him – a softening of certain attitudes of mind as he recalled the first time he had met Liz Fremont, the way he had punished her for the shortcomings of someone else. He had thought, at the time, that the someone was Margaret. He thought differently now.

He had waited at the hospital until the formal identification had been made: had made that his excuse to stay on, knowing that he could not bear to leave Liz alone in that bloody awful mortuary.

In the event, the police had asked the theatre director, Don Kent, to make the formal identification, and Sanger had been able to offer the shaken man at least a little moral support.

Afterwards, they had sat together for a little while in almost complete silence, drinking coffee, Kent chain-smoking between sobbing intakes of breath, muttering repeatedly, 'What a bloody waste. What a bloody awful waste!'

Then, suddenly, lifting his head, Kent had said, 'It was all my fault for breaking the news to her the way I did! I should have used more tact; chosen a better time. But then, is there ever a "better time" to tell a woman that her lover is dead?'

Lighting a fresh cigarette from the half-smoked embers of the last, 'I should have gone after her,' he muttered, 'knowing the state she was in.'

'What the hell do you mean?' Sanger sprang to his feet. 'For Christ's sake, man, are you trying to tell me that this wasn't an – accident?'

'No! That is, I don't know!' Kent stared up at Sanger intently. 'How the hell could anyone possibly know what was in her mind at the time?'

Sanger sank back in his chair and covered his face with his hands, unable to put into words his gut feeling that Liz had deliberately not moved away from death.

She must have seen the car coming towards her. He wondered if, standing there in the falling snow, waiting – she had glimpsed a solution – some bright, eternal springtime of the heart.

CHAPTER 14

Jess wandered aimlessly from room to room, pausing now and then to look out at the snow lying in blue-white drifts beneath a pale dying sun, noticing the way the branches of the trees were etched, in delicate brush-stroke patterns, against the amber-tinted sky. Like a Chinese watercolour.

Liz's parents had been to clear their daughter's room. Jess had left them to their forlorn task of emptying the drawers and wardrobe of her personal belongings, and turned her hands towards providing tea for them when they had finished the packing. Not that they would feel much like eating. Even so, the effort must be made. The show must go on, she thought, wincing at the solecism.

Liz's father, a bespectacled man with greying hair and a Ronald Colman moustache, had told Jess that they were taking Liz back to London for burial. 'Her mother couldn't bear the thought of leaving her here,' he explained, twisting his hat in his hands. And yes, Jess said, that would be the best thing to do, thinking how few men wore hats these days, a neat suit and collar and tie. Mr Fremont must have resurrected his navy suit as a mark of respect for his daughter. Her heart had gone out to him, a decent man trying hard not to break down beneath an almost insupportable burden of grief; the trauma of the inquest; the verdict of accidental death.

'You were good to Liz,' he said, 'I know because she wrote to tell us that she had moved in with someone kind.' He swallowed hard. 'I'd like to thank you for all you did for her.'

'It wasn't — kindness. I loved her,' Jess said simply, wondering if Liz had told her parents about the abortion. But no, she knew Liz better than that. She would not have told them anything about her personal life, her brief love affair with Steen Bancroft.

'Yes, well I'd better go up to my wife now,' Arthur Fremont said, embarrassed because Jess had mentioned the word love.

Buttering scones in the kitchen, Jess thought about Mrs Fremont, whose grief was terrible to see, whose tears had made runnels in her heavy pancake makeup.

And now they were gone, those two bewildered human beings who had produced the briefly shining star that was Liz.

She had asked Alfred to take away the Christmas tree. There would be no twinkling lights, no celebration this year. Dora, who had never shown any particular regard for Liz in life, had reacted unexpectedly to the news of her death. Breaking down in floods of tears, 'It wasn't that I didn't like her,' she wept. 'I didn't understand her, that's all. I was brought up to think of actresses as well, you know, a bit different from ordinary folk.'

Liz *was* different, Jess thought. But then, creative artists, whether actors, writers or painters, must, by the very nature of their creative impulses, feel and think differently from other people.

On the night Liz died, a young traffic officer had come to the house to break the news and make enquiries about her next of kin. Jess had almost fainted in his arms when he told her, as gently as possible, about the accident.

Later, when he had gone, apologising profusely for upsetting her – as though it was his fault that Liz was dead – Jess had searched in her handbag to find the card William Hoyle had given her with his home address and telephone number, remembering that he had told her to ring any time if she needed him. And how badly she had needed him then.

Beryl Hoyle answered the call. 'My husband is not available,' she said coldly. (Hoyle was in the bathroom at the time.) 'Who is this?'

'A – client, Jessica Carmichael. I – I just wanted a word . . .'

'That is out of the question! My husband and I are going to Bournemouth first thing tomorrow morning. In any case, he never talks to clients after office hours.'

Beryl had hung up then, without even the courtesy of

saying goodbye. 'La belle dame sans merci'.

Now, as daylight faded and the amber sky deepened and darkened, Jess moved away from the drawing-room window, and wandered to Clarice's parlour to clear away the tea things.

The Cornwells had gone to Broscombe Bay to visit Alfred's elder sister and make arrangements for the Christmas holidays. Evelyn always came to them on Christmas Day, Dora explained; stayed the night, then on Boxing Day they would go back to her place for a cold lunch, high tea, and a game of cards.

'Eh, what a lot of fiddle-faddle,' she'd said impatiently. 'Evelyn might just as well come to us for the whole of Christmas – but oh no! The sky might fall in if we suggested anything different.'

And yet, Jess thought wistfully, how wonderful to become set in familiar patterns – the gentle patterns she had known as a child, when her grandmother, Stephen, and her parents were alive, when the house in Reading had seemed, on Christmas Eve, full of mystery and surprises; the rooms decorated with holly and mistletoe, and the Christmas tree shining into the darkness from the sitting-room window.

Now she thought of the patterns which must once have existed beneath this roof: the carol singers; church on Christmas morning; her great-grandparents and their three children, Donald, Franklyn and Jessica, driving to the parish church to attend divine worship.

Families had clung together in those days. Nowadays, people simply drifted apart. She envied those people who had somehow managed to preserve the old way of life.

She had just begun to clear away the tea things when the doorbell rang . . .

Sanger drove slowly along the esplanade. Gone were the black skid marks, flashing lights, the traffic cones, the crowd of gaping sightseers whose breath had whirled into the air like smoke. Gone the huddled figure of the woman lying in the road. Fresh falls of snow had ironed out, had rendered impersonal the scene of the accident, yet Sanger would never pass that place at any time in the future, without remembering Liz.

He wondered as he drove, if he too was guilty of the macabre impulses which had drawn the crowd of sightseers to that particular spot. Ever since that night he had experienced a restless urge to come close to the people and places Liz had known, had even gone so far as to lunch at the theatre in the hope of seeing Don Kent, or Jolyon King – who had played the part of Branwell in the Brontë play. His heart had missed a beat when he saw the studio portrait of Liz in the corridor. This urge of his, he had thought then with a sick feeling of disgust, was akin to the morbid probing of a sore spot to discover the seat of the pain.

Paying for the food he had ordered and did not really want, he remembered that last night at the theatre, the crowd in the crush bar, William ordering the drinks; laying mental bets that Jessica Carmichael would bring up the subject of her great-aunt. When she had done so, he had been deliberately rude to her. Was he, then, the sadist Liz had accused him of being? The Mark Sanger of a few days ago would not have even troubled to ask himself that question. It now seemed to him that Liz's death had directed a harshly uncompromising spotlight into the recesses of his soul.

He had not known, that night at the theatre, that Liz lived at Laurel Villa. He had discovered that later when the police had searched her shoulder-bag for information – letters, an address book – anything to provide a clue to her next of kin. Now he wanted to visit the house again, to talk to Jess Carmichael about Liz, to apologise for his rudeness in the crush bar. He knew that he had deeply upset her. Moreover, Hoyle had known it too, although he had made no comment. Later, however, when he had suggested their going back to his place for a couple of drinks, Hoyle had made the excuse that he was tired and wanted an early night, and Sanger had known that he had somehow forfeited Bill's friendship.

Now he saw, in the encroaching twilight, the high perimeter wall of Laurel Villa; branches of trees adumbrated against the amber sky, pinpricks of light shining on to the drive as he got out of the car, walked up the front steps, and rang the bell.

The last person Jessica expected to see was Mark Sanger.

Worn to the bone with grief and fatigue, she felt like a bleached sea-shell on some vast, inhospitable shore. Incapable of pretence, 'What do you want?' she said harshly.

'Simply to talk to you.' He spoke quietly, with a humility that surprised her. 'May I come in for a few minutes?'

'I can't imagine what there is to talk about. Oh, very well then, but only for a few minutes.'

He stamped the snow from his shoes and followed her into the hall. 'What a difference,' he said, startled by the transformation.

'Oh yes,' she said dully, 'I'd forgotten. You haven't been here since my great-aunt died. You had better come through to the parlour. Liz's parents left a little while ago. They came to clear her room . . .'

'That must have been an ordeal.' He noticed the tea things on the table, a half-eaten scone, a crumpled serviette, a lipstick stain on the rim of a cup.

'It was.' Jess picked up the poker to stir the fire. Sanger noticed how pale she looked, and grief-stricken.

'That night at the theatre. I behaved abominably.'

'Tell me, Dr Sanger, by what right do you treat women so unfairly?'

'You don't believe, then, that people can change?'

'Yes, I do believe that. I know I have. A great many things I once believed in no longer exist.'

'I'd like to talk about Liz,' he said, watching the flames licking the wood.

'What is there to say that you don't already know?'

Sensing her hostility, 'I'm sorry,' he said. 'I just need to come closer to her. Ridiculous, of course. I'd better be going.'

Jess knew that she was being unfair to him. Now she was the one meting out punishment. The man needed absolution, not bitterness or condemnation. She did not want to add pointlessness to the tragedy of Liz's death.

'Her room is on the second landing, the third door on the right,' she said. 'I'll switch on the stair lights for you.'

'It isn't that I want to pry. I'd just like to . . .'

'I know. It's all right.'

He did not switch on the light in Liz's room. With the room in darkness he might be able to imagine she had never left it. He wished to God she had not. The fear that he had been in some way responsible for her death gave him no rest, no peace of mind. If only he could tell her that his brusqueness had been a shield against his own fears and inadequacies.

He was not akin to those people who visited shrines to the famous to mull over relics. He had no wish to touch the pillow on which her head had rested, to sit in her chair or look into her mirror, simply to feel that she had not left him in anger. And then it came to him, something he could not touch, see or account for, a warm lingering trace of her perfume.

Jess asked no questions, made no comment when he came downstairs. 'Would you like a drink?' she asked. 'Whisky?'

'Yes. Fine.' He paused. 'Thank you.'

'Liz loved this house,' she said. 'She told me she felt safe here. Comforted.'

'Is that why she came? Because she needed – comfort.'

Jess remembered the day in the churchyard. 'More than that. I think what she most needed was love.'

They talked then, as they might have done that night at the theatre – quietly and sensibly – had he not been so bloody arrogant: talked about her plans for the house, the advertisement she intended to place in the evening paper. Then Sanger thought about two of his patients who also, quite desperately, stood in need of love.

* * *

When he had gone, Jess cleared away and washed up the tea things, banked down the fire, switched off the hall lights and went upstairs to bed. All day long she had tried to remember the words of a poem; something relevant to Liz and Steen Bancroft which, if only she could bring them to mind, might help to alleviate this empty, drained feeling of loss. But the words would not come, and she was too exhausted to think any more.

As those words would not come, neither would sleep. At two o'clock in the morning, she got up, put on her dressing-gown and went through to the sitting room.

Everything was still. Silent. As if the world had frozen suddenly in space and time had ceased to exist. As if the stars had all gone out.

And then, unaccountably, as if someone had whispered in her ear, the words she had struggled to remember suddenly came back to her:

> Do you think there's a far border town somewhere,
> The desert's edge, last of the lands we know,
> Some gaunt eventual limit of our light,
> In which I'll find you waiting; and we'll go
> Together, hand in hand again, out there,
> Into the waste we know not, into the night?

The journey had been a nightmare from start to finish. Enraged because the hostess refused to serve refreshments until the coach was on the motorway, Beryl had cried out in a petulant voice, 'If I don't *soon* have a cup of coffee, I shall faint dead away!'

'Please Beryl, don't excite yourself,' William said uneasily, 'you'll make yourself ill.'

'And I thought this was supposed to be a *luxury* coach! Ha! Where's the toilet? I want to use the toilet!' (Beryl refused, on principle, to refer to a toilet as a lavatory. The more basic terminology offended her deeply.)

She edged her way then, to the rear of the coach, and mercifully disappeared for a quarter of an hour or so to relieve herself, powder her face, tidy her hair, and re-arrange her purple feathered hat.

By the time she returned, complaining about the state of the toilet, the lack of soap, paper, and space, the hostess had begun serving coffee, and the coach was buzzing smoothly along the M1.

How long, oh Lord, how long? William thought wearily, delving into his overnight bag for his strength and stay – a paperback copy of *The Complete Works of Conan Doyle*.

Flopping down heavily beside him, Beryl muttered sententiously, 'Oh, for heaven's sake, William, don't tell me you're reading *The Hound of the Baskervilles* again! Why on earth keep reading something you've read a hundred times before?'

Even if he attempted to explain to her that Doyle provided a kind of sheet-anchor in a troubled world, his gratitude for the company of Holmes and Watson, Beryl would never begin to understand his deep-seated longing for companionship.

Resting the book on his knees, giving up all attempt at reading as his wife babbled on beside him, he thought that when he retired, he might join the Sherlock Holmes Society. How wonderful it would be to travel to the Reichenbach Falls in the company of other Holmes devotees, to cling to the guard-rail at the exact spot where Holmes and Moriarty had engaged in mortal combat . . . A mild sort of lunacy, and yet . . .

The dream faded when Beryl complained that the coffee had made her feel sick. Then he had been obliged to rummage through the overnight bag to find the bottle of travel sickness pills that Dr Frobisher had prescribed for her.

When the pills took effect and Beryl sagged beside him, snoring slightly, he thought about Jess Carmichael; pictured her holding on to the guard-rail at his side, laughing as the spray touched her face; sharing his foolish idyll, understanding his deep-seated desire for companionship and love. Yes, love! Not necessarily physical love. He honestly did not know if he would any longer prove capable of making physical love to a woman. But love, he considered carefully, real love was – in the words of the song – a 'Many Splendoured Thing' – its roots deeply embedded in so many altruistic meanings of the word . . .

Then as the coach wound its way through the clogged streets of London, and halted interminably at the various traffic lights, William knew, beyond a shadow of a doubt that, given the chance, he *would* make love to her; wanting her so much, how could he possibly fail?

Jess! Jessica! Thinking of her, his lips curved to a gentle smile of remembrance of all that she meant to him. And then, suddenly Beryl snorted, awakened, and demanded to know if they had arrived yet at the Hotel Splendide.

'Not quite yet, my dear,' William said kindly.

He thought: 'Sit, Jessica. Look how the floor of heaven is thick inlaid with patines of bright gold . . .'

And this was how the nearly dark night London sky, with its flickering lights and great underlying mass of neon-lit clouds, seemed to him at that moment, as the floor of heaven thick inlaid with patines of bright gold.

The Hotel Splendide was everything that William had feared it would be: opulent, heated to near suffocation.

When the coach drew up outside the pillared portico, a jolly Mine Host figure, portly, with greying hair and a florid complexion, bounced down the steps, like a rubber ball, to greet what he termed his 'little flock'. This was Major Huntingdon whose job it was to ensure the comfort and welfare of the about-to-be-fleeced baa-lambs.

Obviously inured to coping with chattering crowds of tired but excited ladies in fur coats, zip-up boots, and feathered toques, he managed, with complete aplomb, to find a variety of mislaid umbrellas, handbags, and overnight cases, while the driver off-loaded the luggage stowed in the yawning belly of the coach.

Ohs and ahs of delight escaped the lips of the ewes at their first sight of the massive tinsel Christmas tree at the foot of the elegant branching staircase, the enormous *jar-*

dinières of lemon and gold chrysanthemums ensconced in spotlit niches, and the tantalising glimpse of the dining-room discerned through plate-glass doors; the hot-food smell drifting out upon the strains of the Palm Court orchestra.

Leaning heavily on William's arm, Beryl whispered greedily that she could eat a horse after all those nasty damp cheese and tomato sandwiches they'd had on the coach. The expectation of food had brought high spots of colour to her cheeks. Limping along the thickly carpeted landing to their room overlooking the promenade, she began to chatter longingly of roast beef and Yorkshire pudding. To William's chagrin, she buttonholed the porter carrying their luggage and asked him, in a breathless voice, if he knew what was on the menu for this evening.

Crossing to the french windows leading to a wrought-iron balcony, William looked out at the stars, crisp and cold and silver above the neon street lamps. Fidgety and ill-at-ease, he dreaded sharing a room with Beryl and saw the small balcony as a means of escape.

Turning away from the stars, he tipped the porter and noticed, with a sinking feeling in the pit of his stomach, the 23-inch colour television set complete with remote-control switch beneath a shelf containing tea-and coffee-making equipment. Beryl, having divested herself of purple feathers, had already laid claim to the bed nearest the television. The puffy pink duvet was strewn with her discarded mink coat, suede gloves, Jacqmar scarf, and crocodile handbag.

After a long and careful perusal of the menu, Beryl chose melon floating in a sea of port wine, roast beef and York-shire pudding, glazed carrots, roast and mashed potatoes, and sherry trifle. William knew that his choice of grilled sole had seriously displeased her.

'Are you trying to show me up?' she hissed across the pink lamplit table. 'No wonder you never put on an ounce of flesh. Grilled sole and cheese and biscuits! Faugh! Why don't you have some trifle?'

'I'm not terribly hungry,' he murmured, feeling like a hermit crab robbed of its shell, dreading what the night might bring in the wake of his wife's mindless self-indulgence – getting up in the early hours to administer Alka-Seltzer; rubbing her back between the fleshy shoulder blades to bring up an accumulation of wind – rather like burping an oversize baby.

After dinner, when he suggested they should take a short walk along the promenade, Beryl said indignantly that she had no intention of walking anywhere in her precarious state of health.

'You go if you want to,' she said stoically, 'I'm going up to our room to watch television.'

'Just as you wish.'

'You won't be gone long, will you?'

'No, not for very long.' Thankfully, he made his escape.

How good the fresh air tasted. Crossing the road, he rested his hands on the cold iron railings. Looking up at the sky, he wished that Jess were here with him now, on this lonely, starlit night.

CHAPTER 15

Jess first noticed the youngsters hanging about near the public library, her attention drawn to them because the girl – a frail-looking child with long fair hair – looked pinched and mottled with the cold.

What kind of parents, she wondered indignantly, allowed their children to wander about, in the bitter cold, wearing jeans, tee-shirts, and thin cotton anoraks?

The town was crowded with shoppers engaged in a Christmas Eve spending spree. The stores were packed solid with people choosing last-minute presents, while frantic assistants tried desperately to cope with the Yuletide bonanza. It had puzzled Jess, as a child; it still puzzled her – the strange anomaly between the Christian and the pagan aspects of Christmas.

She did not know if Dora would like the present she had chosen for her – an elaborate coffret containing dusting powder, soap, and spray-on cologne, or if Alfred would appreciate the tie from Somersets. It seemed odd not buying a present for Douglas this year, although she had felt compelled to send him a Christmas card.

Walking out of the store, checking her shopping list, turning up her coat collar against the searching, sleet-laden wind, she stood still for a moment, washed over with a sudden, intense feeling of loneliness.

It was then she noticed the children again, standing this time near a butcher's shop window, looking at the raised pies and ready cooked chickens. They appeared to be arguing. The girl was crying. She went up to them. 'Are you lost?' she asked. 'Is there anything I can do to help?'

'We don't need no help,' the boy muttered harshly, turning away. Then the girl wailed despairingly, 'I'm hungry! I want my mother!'

The boy took her hand. 'We're fine,' he said briefly. 'Come on, Colleen.'

'I was just about to have tea,' Jess said casually, with a feeling that something was terribly wrong. 'They do nice

212

afternoon teas at the Greyfriars Café: toasted teacakes, scones and jam; cream cakes.' She smiled encouragingly. 'Why not join me? My treat!'

'We don't want no tea.' Johnny McEvoy didn't trust grown-ups any more. But he had reckoned without his sister. '*I* want some tea,' she cried, sobbing in anguish at the treat denied her. Then because Johnny, too, felt desperately hungry, and responsible for his sister's welfare, 'Oh, all right,' he grunted, 'you win. Let's get it over with.'

They found a table tucked away near the service-hatch. Jess studied the menu. 'You could have baked beans on toast, if you like.'

'As well as the cream cakes?' Colleen frowned anxiously, looping her hair over her ears.

Johnny scowled at his sister, but Jess noticed, when the meal arrived, that both youngsters attacked the food as if they were starving. 'We'll have toasted teacakes and strawberry jam, as well,' she told the waitress.

'Don't forget the cream cakes,' Colleen reminded her. The waitress smiled.

There was something wary and defiant about the boy, Jess thought, reminiscent of a fox at bay. She knew instinctively that he would hate being questioned, but she had to find out where they were from. When she asked, both children answered at once. 'None of your business,' Johnny snapped. 'Newcastle,' Colleen blurted, then covered her mouth fearfully with her hands.

'You're a long way from home,' Jess said quietly. Tears spilled down Colleen's cheeks. Johnny sprang to his feet. 'You didn't fool me for a minute, missis! I knew what you were after, all along! Old nosey parker! Come on, Sis, we're getting out of here!'

People were looking round, eyebrows raised. Colleen's tears spilled even faster. 'Where to, Johnny? Where are we going?' She'd had her fill of being cold and hungry. They'd slept in a barn last night, and eaten the last of the food Johnny had brought with them; besides, her stomach ached, and she felt sick.

Jess said quietly, 'Please sit down, and listen. I'd be blind and stupid not to realise there's something wrong. The best thing would be to take you . . .'

Johnny interrupted fiercely. 'We ain't going to no bloody police station! We ain't going home, neither, not after what that old bastard did . . .' He choked back the words abruptly, angry with himself for having said too much.

'If you had allowed me to finish,' Jess said patiently, 'I was about to suggest taking you home with me. Listen, Johnny, your sister's in no fit state to go anywhere, except bed.'

She did not stop to consider if she was doing a wise thing. The police might have to be notified later. But not now.

'Huh, I know your sort! Bloody do-gooders! Don't listen to her, Colleen. She'll hand us over to the cops as sure as eggs,' Johnny said scornfully.

'No, I won't do that. Not tonight.' Jess looked steadily into the boy's angry young face. 'You'll have to trust someone sooner or later. Well, are you coming with me, or not?'

Johnny hesitated, torn between loyalty to his sister and the compelling eyes of a stranger. 'Yah, I guess so,' he said reluctantly, 'but only till Colleen's had a sleep. As soon as she's rested, we'll be on our way.'

Jeez, what a house, Johnny thought, knuckling his fists carelessly into his anorak pockets, impressed by the lions guarding the front steps, but wary still, and ill-at-ease, secretly scared of what he had done; pushing to the back of his mind the way the old bastard had grunted and rolled over after he'd smashed the 'tranny' on to the back of his skull. What if the old bastard was dead? If he had killed him?

Dora was in the kitchen, putting away a borrowed iron. Absorbed in what she was doing, worrying about an official-looking letter which had arrived by the afternoon post – something to do with the divorce, she reckoned – she did not hear Jess come in, and started when she saw her standing in the doorway, holding on to a couple of rough-looking children with dirty faces.

'Where on earth did they come from?' she asked in amazement. 'I didn't hear any carol singers! Why didn't they ring the bell?'

Dora, Jess realised, was in one of her worried, hypercritical moods: on edge because her sister-in-law, with whom she did not quite see eye to eye, was coming to stay, and because this would be her first Christmas without Geoffrey.

'They're not carol singers,' Jess said, wondering how to explain. 'I'm keeping them here for the time being. They're lost.'

'Lost?' Dora stared doubtfully at the children. 'Then why didn't you take them to the police station?'

'Because they're tired, and a long way from home.'

'Huh, sounds fishy to me,' Dora said snappishly, whereupon the overwrought Colleen burst into a fresh flood of tears.

'Colleen can sleep in my spare room,' Jess said hastily, as Dora and the boy glared at each other, 'Johnny can sleep on the settee.' She could have cheerfully strangled Dora at that moment.

'They're not sleeping anywhere until they've had a bath,' Dora said positively. 'Just look at the state they're in! You're just plain daft, Jess, in my opinion, keeping them here. Why, their folk must be off their heads with worry. Take my advice. Ring the police right away! They'll know what to do.'

Johnny McEvoy could stand no more. 'Why don't you shut your face, you silly old bat?' he burst forth. 'We ain't lost. We ran away. And you're wrong about our folks! All our Ma cares about is tarting herself up for that bloody nightclub! As for our so-called Dad . . .!' He stared defiantly at Dora. 'Well, go on, old lady, take a look at my sister's jeans! See what he did to her! The blood's dried up now, but it wasn't dry when we ran away! It was running down her legs! So shut up! Just shut up, will you?'

The thunderstruck Dora, who had read about child sex

abuse in the newspapers, had watched countless TV documentaries on the subject, and condemned as 'heartless monsters' those fiends who betrayed the trust of innocent children, seemed suddenly an avenging angel.

Uttering a hoarse cry of sympathy, she swept Colleen forcibly into her arms, hugging her until, almost breathless, the child pulled away from her and announced, bawling with pain, that she wanted to 'go toilet'.

'And so you shall, my pet,' cried Dora, 'and have a nice hot bath! You too,' she said less graciously to Johnny, injured because he had referred to her as a 'silly old bat'.

When Dora had taken Colleen to the new downstairs cloakroom, Jess said quietly, 'Now Johnny, I think you'd better tell me all about it, don't you?'

'I've already told you!' Johnny was still defiant, wary, hostile, fidgety; twitching his shoulders, no longer a child nor yet quite a man; poised in that curious imbalance between the two. Jess's heart went out to him, understanding his dilemma: the child forced by circumstance to assume the responsibilities of an adult.

'You said that as soon as your sister was rested, you'd be on your way,' Jess reminded him, speaking calmly, 'which means you must have some plan in mind.'

'Yeah. Well, what of it?'

Jess knew that she must somehow get through to him; break down his stubborn wall of resistance. If she had had a child of her own, a boy like Johnny, how would she have tackled the situation?

She drew in a deep breath. 'Look, Johnny,' she said coolly, 'the facts are clear-cut. Your sister has been interfered with. She's in pain. She's probably still bleeding internally. What she needs now is medical treatment.

'No! Hear me out! You're not a child, Johnny. You know as well as I do the psychological as well as the physical harm that may have been done to her. It's no longer a question of whether or not you trust me. It's gone far beyond that. What you think of me doesn't matter a damn. All that matters is Colleen's welfare. So why don't you stop acting

216

like a kid and tell me the truth?'

Close to tears, Johnny said harshly, 'I was taking her to find our real Dad. I thought, if only we could get to him, he'd know what to do. That's what I had in mind after I saw that bloody old bastard messing about with her!'

He buried his face in his hands. 'God, it was awful! That great fat lump! When I heard her cry out, I got up out of bed, an' . . . Well, never mind what. But it was all my fault! I'd fallen asleep when I should have stayed awake! Ma was working late, being Christmas, an' *he*, our stepfather, was pissed out of his mind! I'm glad I hit him! Really glad! The stupid, fat bugger got what was coming to him, that's all!'

'Then what happened?' Jess asked compassionately.

'I told Colleen to get up an' get dressed. I got dressed, too, then I emptied my money-box an' filled a carrier-bag with stuff from the fridge. Then we started walking. Next morning, as soon as it was light, we caught a bus to Scotch Corner. After that we thumbed a lift . . .'

'And your real Dad, where does he live?'

'Hull. Somewhere near the docks. I thought if we could get there we'd be safe, but our money and grub ran out an' Colleen started crying. I told her that Bevensea isn't a stone's throw away from Hull, but you know what girls are?' Johnny dragged his hand across his eyes.

Dora came back at that moment, her face as white as chalk. Drawing Jess aside, 'The child's still bleeding,' she said anxiously. 'What on earth shall we do now?'

'There's only one thing we can do.' Jess flicked through the phone book, found Mark Sanger's number, and dialled his surgery.

Mr Sloane closed the door gently but firmly behind Mrs Catskill – a tall, gaunt woman with iron-grey hair and what he thought of as 'wandering' eyes which appeared, all the time she was talking to him, to be taking in the dust on the furniture, a slightly askew picture on the wall, and the tarnished silver in the glass-fronted cabinet.

It was when she had taken the liberty of straightening

the picture that he knew he could not possibly accept her invitation to spend Christmas Day in the company of the Catskills en masse – his neighbour's dejected husband Albert, their married daughter Muriel, Muriel's spouse, Harold, and their three teenage children, Jason, Wayne, and Marilyn.

'It's very kind of you to invite me,' Mr Sloane said mildly, not wishing to cause offence, 'but I . . .' (difficult to put into words that he would far rather be left alone) 'I'd be poor company, I'm afraid.'

'Nonsense!' Mrs Catskill said briskly. 'You need taking out of yourself! Mrs Sloane wouldn't have wanted you moping here all alone, I'm sure.' (As if Mrs Catskill, of all people, could possibly understand what Maisie would have wanted).

'Even so, I'd rather be on my own, if you don't mind.'

'Oh, well, if that's the way you feel.' Ada Catskill bridled indignantly. 'But don't say you weren't asked.' Curiosity got the better of her. 'But what will you *do* all on your own?'

'I've just started reading *David Copperfield*,' he admitted.

'Oh well, if you like that kind of stuff,' muttered his about-to-be-evicted-next-door-neighbour. 'What I really meant was, what are you going to do about *food*?'

'Food?' Mr Sloane had not given the matter much thought, although the doctor had warned him that he was not paying enough attention to his diet, that he needed plenty of fresh fruit, fibre, vegetables, fish and white meat. 'Well, I've ordered a chicken, and I've got plenty of that bran-stuff; a couple of pounds of apples.' He sighed wearily, 'I shan't starve.' (All the time edging Mrs Catskill towards the front door.)

Ah! Peace at last! Settling down in his chair, aware of the slow ticking of the grandfather clock, he began reading again: 'It was a close and stifling little shop, full of all sorts of clothing, made and unmade, including one window full of beaver-hats . . .' A smile curved Mr Sloane's lips, his

218

thoughts drifted back to Somersets in the old days, the way he remembered it before the war changed everything. His eyes closed. The book slid, unnoticed, from his hands.

'Would you mind stepping into the manager's office?'

The young man's hand on her arm felt in no way heavy or restrictive. When she turned to look at him, Miss Sweeting saw that he was smiling slightly. 'I – don't understand,' she said faintly.

'I think you do, madam.' He continued smiling, but his hand tightened imperceptibly, filling her with dread. 'I have reason to believe that you have, in your possession, goods which you have not paid for.' He spoke very quietly, very softly, 'I'm sure you'd rather not make a scene out here in the street. Let's step inside, shall we?'

Never before had Douglas condescended to follow a woman round a supermarket, pushing a shopping trolley, but Avril had pooh-poohed, as male chauvinist arrogance, his initial refusal to do any such thing. 'The trouble with you is, you've been spoiled rotten,' she said scathingly. 'First your mother, then that stupid cow of a wife! So stop moaning and start pushing!'

She was dressed in her winter outfit – handwoven poncho, high-heeled red boots – with her hair hanging, rope-like, over her left shoulder. Smouldering inwardly with resentment, he watched her flinging groceries haphazardly into the wire basket, as though she were laying in food for a siege instead of a three-day Christmas break.

Curiously enough, he deeply resented her reference to Jess as a 'stupid cow', and wondered, as the mound of comestibles grew steadily higher, why he cared so much about the divorce. Why, on that cold October evening in the school carpark, fingering the letter from the Bevensea County Court, he had experienced a sudden overwhelming desire not to drive to the lay-by, to point the green Metro in the opposite direction. He now knew why. Hearing the news, Avril had immediately started making plans for their future. They must both apply for other jobs right away. He'd better sell the bungalow: move in with her for the time being. Then, when he was free of Jessica, they would get married; go somewhere else to live – London perhaps, or Birmingham. She would have a baby right away. And he had seen the walls of the trap closing in on him: himself as a kind of brood stallion serving an insatiable mare, sapped of energy and willpower by Avril's incessant physical demands on him. He had known then that something he had always suspected, was true. He did not want children. He did not even like them very much.

'That comes to £35.25,' the girl at the check-out said off-handedly as Douglas delved into his wallet to find his Access card.

When they were in the car, Avril uttered a shrill scream of laughter. 'You'll never guess what,' she giggled, 'I forgot all about bread, butter, and that kind of stuff. Coffee, milk, tea-bags! Well, go on sweetie. I'll wait here for you! Hey, what's the idea?' Her laughter turned to anger as Douglas slammed the car into reverse gear and backed savagely out of the parking place, almost colliding with an incoming vehicle. 'Hey, you bloody bad-tempered bastard! What about the bread and stuff?'

'You should have made a list!' Thirty-five poundsworth of convenience food, he thought bitterly. Rubbish! Frozen food, tinned stuff, rich cream gateaux, and he wouldn't even be able to have toast and coffee for breakfast. Jess would have made a list.

CHAPTER 16

On Christmas morning, worshippers – suitably clad in warm clothing – were shepherded to the waiting mini-bus by Major Huntingdon, Beryl among them, a reluctant pilgrim whose puckered face at a window reflected her anger that William had elected, at the last moment, not to accompany her.

How dare he stand there like a graven image, smiling and raising his hat, leaving her all alone to face a service she had no wish to attend anyway? She had simply said she wished to go to church because certain other people were going: Colonel and Mrs Smythe, the wealthy Misses Benton-Umpleby – above all, Lady Kagmire-Loach who had actually nodded to her over her kedgeree and lightly boiled egg. Now, everyone who mattered would think that William was a bloody agnostic.

When the bus had departed, William walked slowly along the promenade. Looking up at the sky he noticed that the light feathery clouds were tinged the palest pink, the colour almost of flamingoes in flight. He could hear the restless murmur of the sea washing in on the shore, the sound of Christmas bells on the cold clear air.

Turning his footsteps down glissading paths between stark winter trees, treading the delicate wind-broomed lumber of dead leaves and pools of crinkled ice, he attempted to come to terms with the rapidly dwindling and dulling facets of his life. Later he would pay the price for this brief escape from bondage. Strangely, he did not care.

On an impulse he stopped at a row of phone boxes on the promenade, every one of which had been vandalised. It would have meant a great deal to him to hear Jess's voice across the miles of their separation.

Slowly he walked back the way he had come, but the flamingoes had taken flight, the clouds had thickened and darkened, the sea no longer murmured but thundered – and all the bells hung silent in their towers. At least there remained the comforting bulk of Holmes and Watson in his overnight bag.

221

In the hotel lounge, he flicked over the pages and began reading:

> My first impression as I opened the door was that a fire had broken out, for the room was so filled with smoke that the light of the lamp upon the table was blurred by it . . .

Excitement had been intense as the fire-brigade arrived to cope with the blaze. The inevitable sight-seers had gathered to witness events, the windmill figure of Mrs Catskill well to the fore.

Standing in the cold, gesticulating wildly, she held forth about the shortcomings of her next-door neighbour to a young woman who lived further along the crescent. 'I mean to say, if the vicar hadn't called when he did, and rung the brigade, we might all have gone up in flames! It doesn't bear thinking about!'

'Poor old chap,' said the more compassionate neighbour, 'he's been very doddery since his wife died. Must be awful for him living all alone in that big house.'

'Huh!' Mrs Catskill removed a dewdrop from her nose with a surreptitious movement of her right hand, 'Well, I'm sure *I've* done my best for him. Stubborn old fool!' She angled her shoulders against the cold December wind. 'No one could have been kinder, though I say so as shouldn't – and what happened? Threw cold water in my face . . .'

'I'm glad the vicar went in the ambulance with him,' the other woman remarked, 'though I don't suppose he thought to take – well, you know, things Mr Sloane might need if they keep him in hospital.'

'*If* they keep him in hospital! I should jolly well hope they *will* keep him in hospital! Perhaps this will teach the authorities their duty! The man's a menace! Anyway, there's no way he could come back here. The house is full of smoke, I daresay. I tell you straight, the best place for Mr Sloane is in an old folk's home. Why, I'd never know a moment's peace of mind if they sent him back here. It's up to the vicar to see that the authorities do what's right. I mean, that's what vicars are paid for, isn't it?'

The nice young store detective had really been very kind and polite to her, Rachel Sweeting thought, sitting in her rocking-chair near the window, looking out at the ice-filmed garden, and so had the manager of the super-market in saying that, because this was Christmas, the season of goodwill, he had decided not to press charges this time, adding a warning that from now on, under no circumstances whatsoever, must she enter the store again.

The season of goodwill, Rachel thought blankly, remembering Christmas as it used to be in the old days, wishing she might somehow return to the magic of child-hood; forget about poverty and old age, and this sad little room with its preponderance of useless furniture. With a thickly beating heart, she wondered if, when word got about that she, a doctor's daughter, bearer of a well-respected name, was nothing but a common thief, the landlady would turn her out: tell her to find somewhere else to live.

Live?

The word seemed suddenly meaningless, rather like the word 'ink' which, the more one thought about it, seemed equally ridiculous. 'Live' meant, in one sense, to be full of power and energy, not obsolete and exhausted; in another sense to be alive, possessed of animal or vegetable life, to subsist, to live by one's wits; to escape destruction . . .

Rocking herself gently, Rachel thought about destruc-tion, self-destruction – Death. To sleep – perchance to dream eternally of orchard trees weighed down with fruit, the scent of meadowsweet in summer hedgerows, the sound of ringing laughter, the warm touch of familiar hands.

It was then she remembered the sleeping capsules that nice Dr Sanger – who reminded her so much of her favour-ite actor – Claude Rains – had prescribed for her. To die, to sleep, perchance to dream . . .

* * *

The little girl had been badly torn internally, Sanger told Jess who had come with her and the boy to Greyfriars Hospital. Colleen was now resting comfortably, but there was no possibility of her leaving hospital until the welfare people had been notifed.

'Yes, I understand,' Jess glanced anxiously at the boy sitting stonily in the reception area, 'but I doubt if her brother will.'

There were times when Sanger wished he was a road-sweeper.

'You look tired,' Jess said quietly, thinking how odd that less than a week ago the last person she would have trusted or turned to was Mark Sanger.

'I am a bit,' he admitted. 'It has been one of those days.' He smiled, and the smile wrinkled his eye corners, making him seem less formidable. 'It can't have been easy for you either, shouldering the responsibility of those two youngsters.'

'I'm just thankful I happened to notice them.' She sighed. 'But I'm afraid Johnny resents my interference. Poor kids, they're not going to have much of a Christmas. I can't help worrying about their mother, how she'll feel when she finds out what happened.'

'No, William, I don't want any lunch! I couldn't face that dining-room, not after what you did! Oh dear, the shame of it! Sitting there all alone in that hard pew. I hope you realise you've ruined my Christmas! But then, you didn't really want to come at all, did you? I remember thinking, when I was looking through the brochures, that you weren't the least bit interested. Well I hope you're satisfied!' Beryl unpinned her hat and threw it on the bed.

'I think you're over-reacting.' William said patiently. 'I'm quite sure you weren't sitting alone . . .'

'Over-reacting?' Mrs Hoyle pressed her hand to her bosom. 'Oh, my heart! How do you think I felt when Lady Kagmire-Loach asked me if you were a Roman Catholic?' Aggravated past bearing by her husband's lack of penitence, determined to thrash out the whole matter, she started to delve into his past dereliction of duty – beginning with her recent illness, the way he had left her alone in the nursing home to spend a weekend in Goathland; putting that wretched sister of his above herself. How he had gone to the theatre with Dr Sanger, not caring tuppence that she might have suffered a relapse; spilling forth angry words in a bubbling, disjointed torrent; saying it was obvious – had been obvious for a long time now – that he cared more for his work than his wife's welfare.

Moreover, she spat at him, she would not tolerate having clients ring up after office hours with their problems . . .

Hoyle frowned. 'I don't understand what you mean. To whom are you referring?'

Flustered, red in the face, frustrated that he had not reacted sympathetically to her histrionics, 'How the hell should I know?' she cried, 'I can't remember her name . . .'

'Then I suggest you try,' William said coldly, refusing to succumb to his wife's emotional blackmail, seeing her objectively, not as his wife but as a spoilt, overweight woman with whom he had been lumbered for the past thirty-odd years.

Looking up at him, suddenly equally cold, putting two and two together, 'Why, what is she to you?' she asked suspiciously, 'this Jessica Carmichael or whatever her name is?'

'Why didn't you call me to the phone?' The pent-up misery of the fruitless years he had spent catering to his wife's whims and fancies exploded suddenly into anger. 'How dare you interfere? Didn't it ever occur to you that the call might be important?'

Hoyle regarded his profession, his office, his clients as sacrosanct. Throughout the years he had drawn a strong demarcation line between his professional and private life. Beryl had every right to behave as she wished, to nourish her fantasy of ill-health, to cosset her hypochondria, to fill her days with bridge parties, shopping for expensive clothes, planning dull holidays, watching television, reading romantic fiction, if she so wished. He held no jurisdiction over her preoccupation with trivia, which he had perforce accepted and tolerated as long as her pursuits kept her reasonably contented. What he could not, would not tolerate was her interference in his professional affairs.

'You haven't answered my question. What is this Jessica Carmichael to you? How did she get hold of our ex-directory number unless you gave it to her?'

'I did give it to her, for good and sufficient reasons . . .'

'What reasons? Why is she so special?' Beryl's head came up sharply. 'Don't think I haven't noticed how strangely you've been behaving lately!' Her eyes narrowed, 'Ever since . . .! So *that's* it! That's why the weekend at Goathland! You went there with *her*! Well, go on, deny it! I dare you! My God! To think that all the time I was lying there in the nursing home, you were carrying on with another woman!'

Beside herself with anger, Beryl seized William's arm. 'Look at me when I'm speaking to you! I want the truth!'

Hoyle scarcely heard. Jess had called for help and he had not been told, had not been allowed to answer that call. Shrugging off his wife's grappling fingers, he began opening drawers, emptying his half of the wardrobe.

'What the hell do you think you are doing?' Beryl's anger was laced suddenly with nervous apprehension.

'That must be obvious.' He went into the bathroom to collect his shaving gear. 'I'm leaving you.'

'Leaving? But you *can't*! What will people think?' She resorted to tears. Unmoved, William continued packing. 'I – I don't feel at all well . . .' Her hands fluttered to her chest. Closing her eyes she flopped down heavily on the bed. 'I think I'm going to faint.' No response. Beryl opened her eyes, baffled by her husband's indifference. Then, realising that none of the old ploys would work this time, bitterly jealous, frightened by the way he moved calmly about the room gathering together his belongings, working herself up into a state of hysteria, she returned to the attack.

Lumbering to her feet, 'Very well then,' she cried shrilly, 'go home and sulk, and much good may it do you! Ruin a perfectly good holiday! You'll have a thin time of it with Mrs Bartram away. There'll be no one to cook for you!' Suddenly a dreadful thought struck her. 'Oh, my God! You *planned* all this! *She'll* be there! That woman! I see it all now!'

'I doubt if you do,' Hoyle said quietly, with a fleeting sense of compassion for his wife's stupidity. 'If you had listened more carefully. I said nothing about going home. I meant that I am *leaving* you. There is a subtle difference.'

Her jaw slackened. 'You mean . . .? But you can't! I won't stand for it!'

'I shall, of course, make adequate provision for you. Your lifestyle will not suffer . . .'

'No, but *yours* will! I'll see to that! I'll drag your names through the mud!' Beryl's voice rose to the shrillness of a factory whistle. 'You and your bloody principles! I'll show you up for what you really are! A . . . lecher! A . . . whited sepulchre!'

William strapped his suitcase. Picking up the telephone he asked the receptionist to order a taxi. He would be down in a few minutes.

Desperately afraid now, trembling, her face bloated with tears, marshalling more ammunition from her depleted arsenal, Beryl stormed, 'You are simply punishing me because of that bloody telephone call! Because I found out about your nasty, underhand love affair! Well go on, deny it!'

'Goodbye, my dear. I'll be in touch. Enjoy your holiday. You will, you know . . . possibly even better without me. Think of all the sympathy you'll elicit,' Hoyle said evenly.

A triumphant thought struck Beryl. 'You *can't* go! This is Christmas Day! There are no trains on Christmas Day!'

'I realise that. I shall travel by taxi to London. Stay there overnight. Tomorrow I shall make my way to Goathland to spend a few days with George and Adeline. You see, my dear, your threats carry no weight. My "nasty, underhand love affair", as you choose to call it, does not exist outside your imagination.' He paused, wanting to be entirely fair

227

to Jessica. 'It is perfectly true that I have fallen in love with Mrs Carmichael, though I very much doubt if she returns my feelings. The subject has never arisen between us.'

Vivaldi, Jess thought. At this time last year she had been in Manchester, cooking Christmas lunch and listening to Vivaldi on Radio Three, worrying about the strange feeling of numbness in her finger ends. Now her brain, her whole body felt numb with tiredness and mental exhaustion.

She had imagined that moving away from her old life would bring the peace of mind she longed for, a solution to her problems. It now seemed that she had merely exchanged one set of problems for another. Her marriage was virtually over – a date had been set for the divorce hearing. Liz Fremont was dead. A sexually abused child was in hospital, and she had failed to break through Johnny McEvoy's stubborn shell of resistance.

The boy was in the sitting-room watching television – one of those inevitable Disney films the media dished up – ad nauseam – during the festive season. She had looked in on him a few minutes ago, before starting preparations for lunch. Dora had invited her to Mews Cottage for luncheon, an invitation which she had cancelled at the last minute, knowing that Dora and Johnny were scarcely compatible, not wanting to spoil the Cornwells' Christmas.

Johnny had glanced up at her, a sullen expression on his face. He was slumped in a corner of the settee. 'All right?' she'd asked, and 'Yeah,' he muttered, turning his eyes back to the screen. She had wanted to say something special to him then, that gallant fair-haired boy whose favour she could not win: tell him not to worry, that all would be well. But she knew she would simply be wasting her breath.

In the kitchen, she turned on the radio. The voice of a choirboy threaded the air with silver: 'Once in Royal David's City'. Tears spilled down her cheeks. Wiping her hands, she went across the landing to her bedroom. Picking up Annie Petch's Bible, turning the pages, she came to the Gospel according to St Luke. Luke, her favourite saint.

Luke, the physician. 'Fear not, little flock; for it is your Father's good pleasure to give you the kingdom.'

Eyes blurred with tears, she noticed microscopic writing in the margin, too small to read without her glasses; reminiscent of the Brontë children's minuscule handwriting. Finding her glasses, she puzzled over the words: 'Born and died this 24 day of December, our infant son, Joshua. The Lord giveth and the Lord taketh away. My little lady is also in a bad way. The doctor came.'

So Annie Petch had given birth to a child. Whose child? But Jess knew. Deep down she knew who had fathered that child.

Turning the pages, she saw that there was more writing. Annie had used her Bible as a diary.

At that moment, Johnny called out to her. 'Are you there, missis?'

'Yes, coming.' Jess closed the book. He was on the landing, shrugging into his anorak. 'What is it? What's wrong?'

'I'm off,' he said defiantly, 'to look for my Dad, and don't you try to stop me!'

'I'm not your gaoler,' she said quietly. 'How are you going to get there – to Hull? There are no trains running today.'

'I dunno. Walk, hitch a lift, any which way I can.'

'Just a minute. It's freezing out. You need something to put on over that tee-shirt. I have a sweater that's too small for me. It's old but warm. I'll find it for you; make you some sandwiches. You'll need money, too. Here, take this.' She emptied her purse.

He coloured up, embarrassed. 'I'll pay you back one day,' he muttered. 'Thanks, missis.'

Later, shoving the parcel of sandwiches into his pocket, he said gruffly, 'Don't suppose you'll be going to the hospital to see Colleen. Not now.'

'Whatever gave you that idea?'

He shrugged awkwardly. 'Dunno.'

Jess smiled. 'Have you forgotten that I'm a "bloody do-gooder"?'

'Yeah.' He grinned suddenly, and his smile was like the melting of ice on a warm spring morning. 'Well, so long.'

She hated the thought of his leaving, this strangely defiant, brave little kid she had grown to like so well. 'Don't forget, I'm here if you need me. You'll keep in touch? Let me know how you get on?'

'Yeah, sure. I'll give you a bell tonight. Tell Colleen . . . well, you know. Don't let her think I've forgotten her. Just tell her I've gone to look for our Dad.'

How strange, Jess thought, watching him trudge away down the drive, that the only way to come close to the people one cared for was to set them free. In her letting go of Johnny McEvoy, they had, miraculously, drawn closer together. The barrier of mistrust which Johnny had built up between them no longer existed.

He turned to wave briefly before turning into Lymington Road, a jaunty, indomitable figure in his jeans and anorak.

Suddenly she remembered the words of an old Scottish ballad: 'I Know Where I'm Going'.

> Some say he's black, but I say he's bonny,
> The fairest of them all,
> My handsome, winsome Johnny . . .

She was just about to close the front door when her eye caught a flash of green; a car bonnet snouting through the gates. The bonnet of a green Metro. Standing stock still, she caught sight of the man at the wheel.

Douglas!

CHAPTER 17

After a sleepless night alone at the bungalow, he had driven through thick fog on the outskirts of Manchester.

On the Leeds–York motorway, the fog had cleared and a gleaming sun mirrored the road to a sheet of burnished pewter, patched dangerously with black ice. After Leeds, the sun had disappeared, heightening his sense of isolation. Then the blizzard had begun, driven by the keening north-east wind.

Battling on through appalling weather conditions, he had missed, near Scarborough, a vital signpost and found himself on minor roads threading a series of villages and remote farmhouses dotted among rapidly whitening fields. Passing a huddle of houses, he noticed the lights of a Snow-cemmed pub shining on to a pebbled carpark.

Head bent, he entered the fuggy atmosphere of a bar-parlour hung with faded photographs of bygone cricket teams, where a group of old men, playing dominoes near a roaring coal fire, stared at him briefly before returning to their game.

'Now, sir, what can I get for you?' The landlord, brisk and cheerful, wearing a crew-neck pullover, rested his hands on the counter. 'Whisky? Certainly, sir. A stranger hereabouts, are you?' Showing an interest in his customers was part of his stock in trade, but Douglas, in no mood for sociability, resented the man's friendly interrogation, hated having to admit that he had lost his way.

'I'm not surprised in this weather.' The landlord chuckled throatily. 'Perhaps I can help. Where are you heading for?' When Douglas told him, 'Ah, you should have turned off at the roundabout a couple of miles back. Not to worry, you'll soon be home and dry.'

Warming himself by the fire, Douglas reflected bitterly on the reasons for his journey – the cold, empty bungalow, an empty larder; remembered the food he had paid for which would never now be eaten, all those rich, creamy gateaux Avril had crammed into the waste-bin; the bottle of peaches in brandy she had hurled against the wall, the way the blood from her cut hand had swirled away down the waste-pipe. Shocked by her violence, he had slammed the front door behind him, hurried to his car and driven home, wondering what to do next. He had even considered driving to Wales to spend Christmas with his parents. The very thought made him shudder: the oxlike patience of his mother, the toadlike presence of his father, the claustrophobic confines of the two-up, two-down house, the cracked yard, the outside lavatory: the questions his pale, anxious mother would ask, his father's jeering remarks.

Face to face with his own future, weighing up all the pros and cons, he had come to the realisation that there was only one person he could turn to. Jessica.

Following the landlord's instructions, he drove back to the roundabout, found the Bevensea signpost, and came eventually to the Town Hall square with its silent shops and winking Rotarian Christmas tree, experiencing a Scrooge-like hatred of Christmas with its tawdry street decorations.

Driving slowly along the esplanade, he came at last to the open gates of Laurel Villa; noticed the thin figure of a youth striding down the drive, shoulders hunched, wearing jeans and an anorak, and saw Jess standing on the steps, staring at him as if she had seen a ghost, arms hugged about her body. Unsmiling, her hair blowing in the wind.

Getting out of the car, he walked slowly towards her.

At the cottage hospital, Sanger engaged in a brief conversation with the Reverend Roger Bullivant, whose prompt action in dragging Mr Sloane from a smoke-filled room had undoubtedly saved the man's life.

Bullivant, thin and earnest, exuded an air of intense nervous zeal. He was most probably, Sanger thought, a man of high, foolish integrity who regarded his parochial duties in the light of a burning mission to do good – even to those who did not wish to be done good to – the kind of priest who would encourage his parishioners to call him by his Christian name, engage in mild, innocent flirtations with the ladies of the flower-arranging rota, and enjoy speaking to women's luncheon clubs. Sanger wondered briefly if he was bisexual.

'You know, Doctor,' Bullivant said, with a curiously fast and co-ordinated blinking of his eyelids, 'I have felt worried lately about Mr Sloane living alone in that big house, and what happened to him bears out my feeling that he is not fit to cope by himself any longer. Now, my intention is to . . .'

'What actually happened?' Sanger interrupted, well aware of Bullivant's intentions; unwilling to enter into collusion.

'Oh, I gather he fell asleep. The book he was reading must have slipped from his hands on to the fire. Thank heaven the front door was not locked – otherwise . . .'

'Quite so.'

Bullivant continued eagerly, 'He hasn't been feeding properly, you know, since his wife passed away. I have tried to talk sense to him, without success, I fear. Mr Sloane can be very stubborn, yet one feels a deep sense of responsibility in such cases.' He sighed regretfully, and blinked even more rapidly. 'Now I feel the time has come to . . .'

'To put him into an old people's home?' Sanger had begun to dislike the man intensely.

Wounded by Sanger's brusqueness, slightly offended, 'Well, yes,' Bullivant admitted prissily, 'although I prefer the expression "sheltered accommodation".'

Sanger smiled grimly, 'Call it what you like, it amounts to the same thing.' He glanced at his wristwatch, 'Now, if you'll excuse me, I have another patient to attend to.'

With a brief nod, he strode along the corridor to the emergency ward to which Miss Sweeting had been admitted after the disgusting ordeal of the stomach pump.

Looking down at her grey, shrivelled face upon the pillow, Sanger silently condemned his own stupidity in not referring her to a qualified psychiatrist. In allowing his compassion for the old woman to cloud his better judgement he had, apparently, misread the signs of acute mental disorder.

His mind flicked back to the day in his surgery when, distressed by his suggestion that she should see a consultant psychoanalyst, she had wept into a scrap of lace-edged linen, and begged him to deal with her personally. 'I'm sure that *you* can help me better than anyone else,' she sobbed. 'That's why I came to you. Because I *trust* you.'

Puzzled, he had asked why himself in particular? Why she had changed doctors. 'Because my father was a doctor,' she said proudly, drying her eyes, 'and one *knows* about such things. You see, when I first noticed you at the nursing home where my sister, Lavinia, died, I asked one of the nurses who you were, and thought, now *there* is a man one could trust implicitly.' She smiled wistfully. 'Besides, you reminded me of someone.'

He had asked her then about her compulsion to steal; when it had started, and why. When she admitted, in a shaking voice, that she simply stole what she could no longer afford to buy, he had come to the conclusion that what she needed was supplementary benefit to eke out her slender retirement pension.

'Oh well, doctor, if you really think . . . But no! I'm sorry, I couldn't possibly. I have my pride, you see.'

'Pride makes a poor bedfellow, Miss Sweeting,' he said quietly, thinking of the many elderly people who allowed pride to stand in the way of accepting the government benefits to which they were entitled.

'Yes, I suppose you are right. Very well then, Dr Sanger, I place myself entirely in your hands.'

'Don't worry,' he said, making a note in his diary. 'I'll set the wheels in motion. How are you sleeping by the way?'

'Very badly, I'm afraid. I – I'm so anxious all the time.'

'Yes, I understand.' He had scribbled briefly on a prescription pad. 'Now I want you to take one of these capsules half an hour or so before retiring. Just *one* you understand?'

'Thank you so much,' she said gratefully. 'You know, doctor, I'm beginning to feel better already.'

He had shown her out, thinking, believing that he had done his best for her. And now . . . Had it not been for the landlady finding her in time when she had called for the rent, and phoning for an ambulance, Rachel Sweeting would surely have died. But *why* had she done it? What, in God's name, had made her swallow all those capsules at one go?

Douglas!

A convocation of memories swam together in Jess's mind as she looked at him. He seemed much thinner, uncertain of his welcome. How strange that, in so short a time, she had forgotten the details of his face, the exact colour of his hair. Perhaps she had simply wanted to forget all the things too painful to remember. Now that he was here, she wondered if happiness could be resurrected – like Lazarus emerging from the narrow confines of the tomb; if the story of one's life might be rewritten on clean, unsullied pages; all the mistakes of the past gently erased as if they had never existed.

Smiling uncertainly, she moved forward to meet him.

'I had to come. I wanted to see you. To talk things over,' he said.

'I'm glad you did.' Relief welled up in her. She took hold of his hand. 'We'd better go indoors. It's freezing out here.' Parting St Martin from the beggar, she led him into the hall.

Startled, his glance took in everything from the glowing stained glass to the richly carved chest with its red-shaded Chinese lamp.

'Well, what do you think of it?' Jess asked, proud of her home, knowing how much hard work had gone into the transformation.

Apparently she had said the wrong thing. He looked shocked, disapproving. 'I thought you said . . . I gained the impression that the place was falling apart,' he said, frowning.

'So it was, three months ago . . .'

'You told me you intended getting rid of it. I didn't notice a For Sale sign tacked to the gates.'

'I – I decided not to sell the house after all, but to try to earn a living from it.' She could tell by his face that he did not believe her.

'Do you take me for a fool? You knew all the time what

you intended. So that's the reason why you walked out, why all this divorce nonsense?'

'No, that isn't true.' The old feeling of dissemination was creeping back.

'You told me there wasn't any money, that there wouldn't be until the house was sold,' he said accusingly.

'You don't understand. It wasn't like that at all. In any case, I thought you'd be pleased about the divorce, that you wanted your freedom to marry . . .' The name stuck in her throat.

'Avril?' he said bitterly. 'That's all over and done with, for good this time. I never want to see her again.'

'So that's why you came?' Jess regarded him thoughtfully. 'Tell me, who made the decision to end the relationship? You, or Avril?'

'What the hell does that matter?' He felt sour, misunderstood, envious of his wife's inheritance. He pushed back his glasses with his forefinger.

'It's important to me.' So much for new beginnings, she thought bleakly. But this, after all, was the season of goodwill. 'Please don't let us quarrel, Doug. There have been so many misunderstandings between us. Couldn't we forget them for the time being? You are here now. That's the important thing.' She wished that he had not pushed back his glasses. But old habits die hard.

Dora pattered across the yard from Mews Cottage, and let herself in by the back door. She was carrying a plastic bag full of toys for Colleen – Geoff's Christmas presents from last Christmas which he had been too ill to play with. She had wept bitterly over those toys, but Alfred was right when he said that some other child might as well have the pleasure of them.

Her eyes puffy with tears, she pushed open the hall door, realised, too late, that Jess had a visitor, a lanky, discontented-looking chap wearing a tweed suit, and horn-rimmed glasses.

'Oh, I'm sorry. I'll come back later . . '

'No! Please don't go! Dora, this is my husband. Douglas, this is my friend and neighbour, Mrs Cornwell.'

'How do you do?' Resenting the intrusion, Douglas made no attempt to shake hands. Dora bridled indignantly. 'Huh,' she muttered disapprovingly, 'I'm surprised to see HIM here.'

'It was a surprise for me too,' Jess interposed hurriedly, knowing Dora's penchant for saying exactly what she thought; afraid she might say too much; aware of the danger signals. 'How's Alfred?' she enquired brightly, pouring oil on troubled waters, gently easing Dora towards the kitchen. 'And your sister-in-law?'

'Evelyn? She's just about driving me up the wall! To hear her talk, you'd think Alf was still in short trousers! Calls him "Alfie". Alfie! I ask you!' A pause, then, 'Where's that lad, by the way? Upstairs glued to the television?'

As Jess explained that Johnny had gone to Hull to seek his father, Douglas wandered about the hall with the air of a visitor to the Victoria and Albert; weighing everything up; estimating the value of the house, the furniture, the pictures, shoulders hunched, hands sunk in the pockets of his brown tweed jacket.

'Does that mean you won't be going to the hospital this afternoon?' Dora asked, glancing balefully at Douglas. 'Now *HE's* here?'

'Of course I'm going. My husband will give me a lift, won't you, Douglas?'

'What?' Sunk in gloom, Carmichael had scarcely heard the exchange, thinking that his wife appeared to be sitting on a bloody fortune, whilst he . . .

'The hospital, after lunch. You will come with me?' Jess reiterated. He simply lifted his shoulders, disinterestedly, and turned away to examine more closely the foliated stained glass.

'Just you be careful,' Dora hissed, sotto-voce, worried by the unexpected development, alarmed by Jess's lack of composure. 'Don't listen to *HIS* soft soap!' Dora reckoned she knew why Douglas Carmichael had come. It was as plain as the nose on her face – to talk her ewe lamb into going back with him to that bungalow in Manchester.

'Thanks, but you needn't worry . . .' Jess knew what Dora was thinking. The same thought had already occurred to her.

'Oh well, as long as you've got all your buttons sewn on! Oh, I almost forgot! I've brought a few toys for you to give to that little lass, Colleen. There's a teddy-bear, a crayoning book, a game of Ludo. I knew you wouldn't want to go to the hospital empty-handed.' Her eyes filled with tears.

'Thanks, Dora.' Bending forward, Jess kissed her gently on the cheek. 'And don't worry. Believe it or not, my buttons are well and truly sewn on this time!'

But they might not have been, she thought, had Dora not come at exactly the right moment. She had already begun to flounder beneath the weight of Douglas's physical presence.

Hoyle saw, from the taxi, the streets of London spinning past the windows; the city shorn of its pulsating crowds of sightseers.

Even Trafalgar Square was almost deserted, except for the pigeons. He noticed with pleasure the magnificent domes, theatres and temples of the greatest city on earth, all quiet and shining in the cold, pure air of a December afternoon: buildings adumbrated against the pale winter sky. And yet the scene with Beryl had disturbed him more deeply than he cared to admit.

He had often wondered what it would take to make him break free of his bonds, to move away from the shackles of his old life: the last straw that would finally break the camel's back. He knew now.

When Beryl had told him about the telephone call, he had known that their marriage was over – finished and done with. He could not have tolerated another moment of his wife's mindless insensitivity.

He realised that the burning sense of anger and injustice which had goaded him into his decision to leave Beryl, this sublime feeling of freedom, would not last for very long. Sooner or later would come the harshness and recriminations he dreaded. Beryl would not let him go as easily as this. He had not stopped to consider what he would do with his life from now on, apart from dissolving the law partnership which had been his raison d'être for the past four decades. It pleased him to think that, despite his initial aversion to becoming a lawyer, he had been instrumental in helping people. At least he would be spared the terrifying prospect of pruning his rose-bushes. Possibly he would end up puttering about with old railway engines. Above all things, he would never go back to the Georgian house on the hill.

He had no reason to suppose that Jessica loved him or would ever come to do so. She would probably never realise that he had moved away from his old life because of her, because, in loving her, he had glimpsed a new dimension to living. And this was the most painful aspect of his thinking – that in leaving Beryl, he had in one sense cut himself off from Jessica, too. Whatever happened, he must not jeopardise her peace of mind. He knew his wife too well to believe that she would not carry out her threat to drag Jess's name through the mud.

He closed his eyes suddenly against a gripping pain in his left arm, and cried out involuntarily as the pain moved, like a searing flame, cramping his chest muscles, tearing the breath from his body . . .

Sanger was at the hospital. Jess caught sight of him hurrying towards the women's ward. How tired and strained he looked. The thought crossed her mind that he was still punishing himself because of Liz. Had he been in love with her? Was he still in love with her memory?

Colleen was tearful at first because Johnny had not come to visit her. The poor little kid, Jess thought compassionately, how awful it must be for her, cut off from her own people, even in a brightly decorated hospital ward with a shining Christmas tree and a Manger.

She said quietly, 'Johnny asked me to give you his love. He's gone to Hull to look for your father.'

'Honest?' Colleen clung tightly to Geoff Cornwell's teddy-bear.

Jess smiled. 'He promised to ring me tonight.'

Sanger walked into the ward at that moment. 'I hoped you would come,' he said. 'I'd like a word with you later, if you can spare the time. My office is along the corridor.'

Douglas had elected to wait in the reception area. Jess wondered if he intended staying the night at the villa. If so he would have to sleep in the spare room. She wished she knew exactly why he had come.

Life with Douglas had been tantamount to a series of university lectures on English literature, Left Wing politics, social history and economics. She felt that she had passed out with flying colours. So where was her diploma?

Sanger leaned back in his chair. 'You don't look at all well,' he remarked. 'Is anything wrong?'

'I'm a bit tired, that's all,' Jess prevaricated. She added unwillingly, 'I have a lot on my plate at the moment. My husband has turned up unexpectedly.'

'So?'

'Never mind. It doesn't mattter. You wanted to talk to me?'

'Are you in a receptive mood?'

'Try me.'

'You may not cotton on to the idea, but I have two patients, besides Colleen, who might appreciate a visit.'

'Tell me more.'

'The person I am most concerned about is an old lady who attempted suicide. She's had a rough time, believe me.' Sanger paused reflectively. 'Her sister died some little time ago; her only remaining relative from what I can gather. Her name is Sweeting, Miss Rachel Sweeting – a highly intelligent woman – which is probably why she thought dying preferable to – existing. The other is an elderly gentleman, Mr Sloane, who very nearly died from smoke inhalation when he had the misfortune to set fire to his house. Not intentionally, I might add.'

Jess frowned suddenly. 'Mr Sloane?'

'You know him?'

240

'No, not exactly, but I think I know who you mean.'

'Well, then?'

'You really think I could help?'

'I would not have bothered to ask you otherwise.' A hint of the old Sanger asperity. 'I'm sorry,' he apologised, 'I'm rather tired myself at the moment. This has been a trying day. About your husband. Is he the patient type?'

'Hardly.'

'I didn't realise you had a husband. I gained the impression that you were a widow.'

'No, we parted company last September. That's why I came to Bevensea, to make a new life for myself.'

'What's he doing here, then?'

'I'm not quite sure. Hoping for a reconciliation, I imagine. We haven't talked about it yet. There hasn't been time.'

'You sound terribly defensive. Are you telling me, in that lady-like way of yours, to mind my own bloody business?'

'Perhaps.' Jess refused to be drawn on the subject. 'Now, about those patients you mentioned . . .'

People looked different in bed, Jess thought: fragile, far more vulnerable.

The collar of Mr Sloane's pyjamas was wrinkled. His face and body seemed to have shrunk. Blue-veined hands lay, fingers outspread, on the white hospital counterpane. His eyes were closed, although he was not asleep. A tiny pulse throbbed in his neck.

He had closed his eyes against the sight of the afternoon visitors coming into the ward, afraid he might weep that Maisie was not among them, knowing that, had she lived, she would have been the first person to enter through the swing doors, bringing with her a pair of well-ironed pyjamas with unwrinkled collar, a box of tissues, oranges – he so longed for oranges to ease the parched feeling in his throat. But then, had Maisie lived, he would not have been in his present predicament. There would have been no need for *David Copperfield* as a palliative against loneliness.

Maisie had loved Christmas. On Christmas Eve, they

would have gone shopping together to buy a turkey, holly and mistletoe. The house would have been filled with the scent of freshly baked mince-pies . . .

'Mr Sloane,' Sanger said gently, 'I've brought someone to visit you. This is Mrs Carmichael, a friend of Dora and Alf Cornwell.'

Octavius opened his eyes; lifted a trembling hand. 'A visitor. How kind. How very kind. Have we met before?'

'No, but I've seen you quite often.' Instinctively, Jess held Mr Sloane's hand. 'It was really just a matter of time before we were introduced. How are you feeling?'

'Much better. Everyone has been so kind to me.'

'Is there anything you need? Anything you'd like me to get for you?'

'Oranges,' he murmured, 'I'd like a few oranges.'

Jess smiled. 'You're in luck then. I treated myself to a dozen Jaffas on Christmas Eve. I'll ask Alfred to bring them tonight. I don't think that he and Dora know you're in hospital.'

'It was all a bit sudden.' Mr Sloane smiled faintly. 'Entirely my own fault, of course. I foolishly allowed *David Copperfield* to fall on the fire.'

'Poor David! Gosh, it's years since I read that book. Tell me, which character do you like best?'

'Oh, Mr Dick, whom everybody except Betsy Trotwood, and David, of course, mistook for a fool.'

'Ah yes, Mr Dick. Tell me, did you ever see the original film, with Edna Mae Oliver as Miss Trotwood, and Frank Lawton as David? It was shown recently on TV . . .'

'Yes, yes, I did,' Mr Sloane said eagerly. 'Oh, what was the name of the actor who played Uriah Heep?'

'Let me think. I know! Roland Young! And W.C. Fields played Mr Micawber . . .'

'You certainly made a hit there,' Sanger said drily, when Jess had taken her leave of Mr Sloane. 'Most of our visitors talk about nothing but the washing-machine having gone on the blink. But not you! Oh no, not you! All you could do was gas

242

on endlessly about an old Hollywood film: that dreadful Mr Murdstone and his double Gloucester cheeses.'

'Well, it's difficult to know what to talk about to a complete stranger,' Jess riposted, enjoying the verbal cut and thrust, beginning to like and appreciate Dr Sanger.

'Hmm. I reckon you'll have a much tougher passage with Miss Sweeting,' Sanger commented, leading the way to the women's ward. 'I'd better warn you beforehand, this is a very sick lady indeed.'

Looking at Rachel's bleached face on the pillow, 'I've seen her somewhere before,' Jess said, frowning, trying to remember where. Suddenly she did remember. Of course, in the fishmonger's that day several weeks ago. But how different the old lady looked without her 'witch's' hat and dramatic Wagnerian cloak.

Jess's approach to the old lady, Sanger noted, was entirely different from her approach to Mr Sloane. Watching her closely, he wondered by what instinctive grace she knew exactly the right words to say to Miss Sweeting. Not that she said anything much at all, simply, 'I'm here. Hold on to me. You are not alone, you know. Not now, and you never will be again.'

And Rachel did hold on to her. Tears spilling down her faded cheeks, the old woman clung to Jess's hands as to a lifeline, until the bell rang, signalling the end of the visiting hours.

> Stands the church clock at ten to three?
> And is there honey still for tea.

Douglas had never cared for Rupert Brooke, whose poetry he scornfully lumped together with that of the jingoistic Rudyard Kipling. He might have felt differently had Brooke died of a bullet wound. To have succumbed to blood poisoning – septicaemia – following an insect bite, seemed to him a feeble way for a man to die; a diminution of Brooke's literary ability.

Closing the book with a snap, he inadvertently creased the pages of 'The Old Vicarage, Grantchester'. Then, being a man who disliked human error, he re-opened the book and smoothed out the crumpled pages.

Jess was seated in the chair opposite. The room was warm, extremely comfortable. Moreover, she had proffered him the expected invitation to stay in this massive house of hers with all its long corridors and hidden staircases.

Christ, he thought bitterly, this – inadequate – wife of his whom he had always assumed would not know Stork from butter, had apparently fallen on her feet, while he . . .

The poetry-reading session had been his idea; an attempt to invoke memories of the past. But she had remained, throughout, curiously alert and on edge, unlike the old Jess who had gazed at him with a kind of wistful intensity whenever he had read to her.

So what had gone wrong? He had chosen Brooke on purpose to please her – an unselfish gesture, he considered, but she had not relaxed for a moment, and he had so far failed to pin her down to a serious discussion about the future. He blamed this house for the change in her. Ownership, money, had gone to her head like a strong wine, he thought bitterly. Money. He wanted, deserved a share of her good fortune. Whatever happened, he must play his cards right.

His affair with Avril was over and done with. Even so, he could not put her out of his mind. He wondered where she was, if she had remained at the flat or gone home to spend Christmas with her parents. Looking at Jess, he made constant mental comparisons between the two women. Jess was cold: Avril warm, exciting, tantalising, teasing. He remembered the compact shape of her sitting astride his eager thrusting body, the viperish flickering of her tongue in his mouth, the way her hair flowed and moved, the soft feel of it between his hands, the trembling of her finely honed body as her pulsating climax came, the way she would cry out with pleasure as he quickened his stroke.

Spitted on the horns of his dilemma, he knew that Avril was the only woman he would ever love – if all that squandering of physical energy could be called love. He also knew that Jess was worth a dozen Avrils. Truth to tell, he had always stood a little in awe of his wife's serenity and good manners, her decency of spirit, and yet this age gap between them, which had seemed not to matter at first, had gradually become an obsession with him, so that he had begun noticing, to her detriment, the first signs of ageing: having to wear glasses to find a number in the telephone directory; the first grey hairs; memories which went back further than his. And yet, God dammit, she was still a very pretty woman, with whom he might make love in the dark.

He wondered, as she rose to her feet, how she would respond to his lovemaking. There had been no physical contact between them since that night at the bungalow when he had used her as a substitute for Avril. The memory excited him. He had felt very strong, very purposeful, that night, thrusting into her, making her cry out, against her will, when her climax came. Was that the reason why she seemed so on edge, because she knew that he could have her again, if he so wished? Standing up, he placed his hands on her shoulders, forced her to look at him. 'I want you, Jess,' he said, 'and you still want me. That's true, isn't it?'

'I don't know. I'm not sure. I – I don't want to be hurt any more.'

'Oh, Jess!'

Closing her eyes as he bent down to kiss her, she savoured, for a fleeting moment, the touch of his lips on hers: felt, with swiftly beating heart, the stirring of the old familiar longing to be loved once more to 'the level of every day's most quiet need, by sun and candlelight'.

Suddenly, the telephone started ringing. Pulling away from his arms, she hurried to answer the call.

'Sorry to ring so late, missis,' Johnny said breathlessly, 'but everything's OK. I found our Dad, an' he's coming back with me tomorrow to sort things out.'

In Jessica's bedroom, Douglas stripped off his clothes and slipped, naked, beneath the flowered duvet, certain that she would come to him, savouring the thought of her sub-mission, cursing the hiatus of that mistimed telephone call, curious about who had rung her, and why. Another man? She had been jumpy all evening. The sly bitch! Suddenly jealous, he felt the hardening of his flesh, and lay on his back – waiting . . .

He awoke, sweating from the terror of his nightmare. The bedside light was still on. The hands of the clock had moved to five minutes past one.

Shivering, he recalled his dream: his father's voice, loud and coarse, jibing at him as he slid into a tin bath filled with tepid water; his mother's face, a network of worry lines, floating above him, a disembodied spirit clad in a white shroud; her coffin resting on trestles in the front room over-looking the slag-heaps.

He had got up, naked, in his dream, to look into his mother's coffin, had smelt the choking scent of death in his nostrils; seen her face as a skull, a grinning Death's Head, cushioned upon a white satin pillow, a face devoid of flesh, stripped to the bare essentials of bone, and hair.

He had started to run, then, away from the house where the coffin rested, stumbling through a lunar landscape of slag-heaps devoid of human life, where foetid water drip-ped silently from iron pipes, and no birds sang.

Teeth chattering, he got up, pulled on his trousers, and hurried through to the sitting-room. The room was in dark-ness. Where the hell had Jess got to?

Noticing a thin edge of light beneath the spare-room door, he strode towards it, beside himself with anger at her rejection of him. How dare she, the stupid old bitch, make a fool of him? Cursing savagely, he tried the door. It was locked. He called out to her to let him in; kicked the door, rained blows upon the panels with his fists.

The line of light disappeared, leaving him in almost total darkness.

CHAPTER 18

Busy in the kitchen next morning when Douglas made his appearance, Jess knew, from bitter experience, what she was in for. Times without number she had come up against him in this mood of sullen resentment which had, all too often, reduced her to a babbling nervous wreck. All that was over now.

Surprisingly, she had slept quite well and awakened clear-headed, knowing what needed to be done, envisaging a great bunch of colourful balloons, the strings of which she held in her own two hands, imagining the bright bubbles, cut adrift, sailing free against the pale winter sky.

'You have a fine day for your journey,' she said, mentally girding her loins for the battle to come. 'I thought you'd like a decent breakfast before you set off.'

'Journey?' He had not intended speaking to her until she had applied balm to his wounded ego.

'I naturally assumed that you intended returning to Manchester today.' She was playing the scene as Liz would have played it – as unemotionally as possible. 'The volcano will have cooled by this time, I imagine.' She laughed, 'Really, Doug, you must break this habit of rushing to seduce me every time there's been an eruption. It isn't very flattering you know.'

Douglas stared at her as if she had become mentally deranged. He said abruptly, in the schoolmasterish voice she had learned to dread, 'What in Christ's name are you mumbling on about? I came to discuss the future. *Our* future. So far we haven't discussed anything of importance. Your fault, not mine!'

She continued blooming eggs the way he preferred them. 'You mean about the divorce? My selling this house; returning to Manchester as your unpaid, undervalued housekeeper? I'm sorry, Doug. I could never accept that. It wouldn't work any better now than it did before. I'm sorry, but that's the way things are.'

Placing the eggs on a willow-pattern plate, adding crisply

grilled bacon, slipping bread into the toaster, she said, 'Sit down and have your breakfast before it gets cold.'

'I don't want any breakfast.'

'Oh! That's a pity. Seems such a waste of good food.' The days of pleading, of begging him to eat were over. Picking up the plate, she scraped the contents into the pedal-bin. 'In that case there's nothing to delay you.' Turning away, she ran hot water, squeezed washing-up liquid into the sink. 'Still, I daresay Avril will feed you when you get back to the flat.'

'She won't be there,' he said bitterly. 'I told you it's all over between us. She's probably gone to Nottingham to spend Christmas with her parents.'

'Then you must go and find her. Patch up your quarrel. Go cap-in-hand if necessary. Difficult in your case, I know.' Jess turned to look at him. 'You see, Doug, you and she belong together, I accept that now.'

'Why didn't you come to me last night?' he demanded hoarsely. 'You knew I was waiting for you . . .'

'Naked and unashamed?' She smiled sadly. 'The trouble is, you made me feel ashamed of my body a long time ago. If you had thought about it more deeply you might have spared us both the humiliation of last night. I understood your motives, of course – the passionate physical reunion, the meaningless panacea for all marital ills.'

'Christ almighty! I wanted to talk sense to you . . .'

'The sensible thing would be for you to make a fresh start,' Jess said quietly. 'To sell the bungalow. There'll be no financial entanglements. I shall not expect alimony.'

'My God! You've got it all worked out, haven't you?' he said bitterly. 'And I thought. . .'

'That all you had to do was to turn up on my doorstep; read poetry to rekindle the old spark in me? But I knew all the time that you were thinking of Avril.'

She spoke wistfully, remembering the potency of that spark – a long time ago. Herself and Douglas smiling into each other's eyes after their brief registry-office wedding, the violets he had given her, glossy-leaved, bound with pale-yellow raffia.

If he had taken her in his arms at that moment, if she had seen in his eyes some faint glimmer of nostalgia for all that had been lost between them, things might have been different.

Searching his face for that one flicker of recollection, of regret, she knew that he had forgotten all the warm, human incidents of the past – playing Petruchio to her Katarina; Saturday afternoon trips to the public library to borrow the books they could not afford to buy; working out their slender finances together, putting away money – so much for rent, gas, rates, electricity, and holidays – into various little honey-coloured stone jars in the kitchen cupboard.

'You had better go now,' she said, turning away to hide her emotion. 'Goodbye, Doug. Good luck.'

She heard his footsteps moving away from her, hurrying downstairs; the distant slam of the front door. Looking out of the window she saw the green Metro slowly disappearing from view along the wide, empty esplanade.

Keeping busy, as an alternative to weeping, she tidied the flat, creating order within emptiness, moving quickly and decisively to pre-empt a sudden unassailable feeling of loneliness, a deep sense of regret that Douglas had left without a kind word: that she had, of necessity, cut the fragile strands of their uneasy relationship, a marriage which had brought neither happiness nor fulfilment to either one of them. What else could she possibly have done?

Duster in hand, she wondered if Liz and Steen Bancroft would have been entirely happy together with the guilt of a broken marriage, the bewilderment of a small, unhappy child forever between them, diminishing their joy in living.

And what of Johnny and Colleen McEvoy, the two scraps of humanity who had suffered so appallingly from the trauma of a broken marriage? Would they begin a new life with their real father? She hoped so for their sakes. But if their father had no room for them in the new life he must surely have carved out for himself, what then? Would they end up in the care of social workers, welfare officers – the tender, sexually abused young girl and her defiant, aggressive elder brother?

Wandering from one empty room to another, Jess thought about the two old people she had met yesterday at Greyfriars Hospital, the comfort they had seemed to derive from the touch of her hand on theirs, the way they had looked at her, those victims of loneliness and loss, as if they had somehow lost faith in a world which they no longer understood, which had failed to understand them.

Suddenly the phone rang, cutting through the silence like a rapier.

'Mrs Carmichael – Jess – is that you?'

'Dr Sanger?' She scarcely recognised his voice. He sounded fraught, strangely upset.

'May I come to see you in, say, half-an-hour?'

'Yes, of course . . .'

'Sorry to butt in like this. Possibly you and your husband had something planned?'

'No. My – husband left early this morning . . .'

'Oh. I imagined that he would be spending the whole of Christmas with you.'

'I imagine he thought so too.'

'You mean . . .'

'Dr Sanger, why do you want to see me? Has something happened? Is something wrong?'

'I'm afraid so. I'll explain later.'

Waiting near the the drawing-room window, Jess noticed that the water she had put out for the birds was covered with a thin film of ice, that the tyre marks of the green Metro had frozen into tiny humps and ridges.

When Sanger's car turned in at the gates, she hurried to the door to let him in, He looked tired, strained, as though he had scarcely slept.

She had lit the gas fire in the drawing room, and made a thermos of coffee. 'You look half-frozen,' she said. 'Come and get warm.' Pouring the coffee, she handed him a cup, wondering why he had come, what could possibly have happened to diminish his usual, somewhat aggressive self-confidence.

Hazarding a guess, she said, 'You've come about Colleen McEvoy, haven't you? Something has happened to her!'

Sanger shook his head. Setting down the coffee cup, he ran his hands wearily through his shock of thick, dark hair. 'No, it isn't Colleen.' Looking up, smiling wanly, he said, 'She's fine. Apparently her father – one Rory McEvoy – a cheeky Irishman with a Dublin accent one could have cut with a knife – strode into the hospital in the early hours of this morning, bludgeoned the staff into submission, bundled his daughter into a Mexican blanket, put her into the back of his car, and drove off with her, and the boy, into the wild blue yonder. Can't say I blame the man. In his shoes, I'd have probably done the same thing.'

'I'm so glad.' Jess's heart lifted momentarily. 'But if not Colleen . . . ?'

'It's Bill Hoyle, I'm afraid. Apparently he has suffered a heart attack. I received a frantic phone call from his wife a couple of hours ago. I must go to London as quickly as possible.'

'London?' Jess slopped coffee into the saucer of the cup she was holding, unaware that she had done so. 'I don't understand. Why London? Mrs Hoyle told me, on the phone, that they were going to Bournemouth.'

Sanger regarded her thoughtfully. Getting up, he took the cup and saucer from her shaking fingers. 'I'm not quite sure myself,' he admitted. 'Beryl wasn't very coherent, but then, she never is. I simply gathered that Bill had decided to spend the rest of the Christmas holiday in Goathland.'

He frowned suddenly. 'Quite frankly, it's a wonder Beryl turned to me for help. I can only assume that she couldn't think of anyone else offhand. But that isn't the only reason I came.' He paused. 'I need your help. Remember the two old people you met yesterday?'

Jess nodded. 'Yes, of course,' she said dully.

251

Sanger glanced at his watch. 'I haven't much time. The thing is, they'll be discharged from hospital tomorrow. They'll need somewhere to go, someone to look after them. Would you consider having them here on a temporary basis?'

Pacing restlessly, he continued, 'Mr Sloane's house is still unfit for habitation. As for Miss Sweeting, I dare not risk her being left alone again for the time being. Well, what do you think?'

Jess said quickly, compassionately, 'Mr Sloane can have Joshua's study, and I could easily make up a bed for Miss Sweeting in Clarice's parlour. That way, they wouldn't have any stairs to climb, and I could keep an eye on them during the day. I could sleep in the drawing-room, in case they needed me during the night.'

'My dear girl!' Sanger raised her hands to his lips. Catching Jess's surprised look, just as quickly he released them. 'You have no idea what this means to me – what it will mean to them.' He glanced again at his watch. 'Well, I'd better be on my way.'

'You will let me know, as soon as possible, about Bill?'

'Yes, of course. I'll ring you tonight.'

At the front door, Jess remembered that day in William's office when she had first glimpsed the man behind the façade of the family lawyer. 'You know, Mark,' she said quietly, 'Bill once told me that he wanted to be an engineer, to build bridges. I've thought about that a great deal, the disappointment he must have suffered in never having realised that ambition. I told him there are different ways of building bridges. I really meant that he had built one for me. Does that make sense?'

Sanger nodded. 'Yes, it does.' He had not realised, until that moment, how much Bill Hoyle meant to Jessica.

None but the lonely, the very cold and lonely, Jess thought, without homes, jobs, without memories, or hope for the future, could begin to understand what it had cost her to watch the man she had once loved to 'the level of every

252

day's most quiet need, by sun and candlelight', driving away from her along the wide, empty esplanade.

For the sum total of one's life was surely anchored upon memories, the things which used to be and were no more – a woman perched upon a stile, her husband's arm placed firmly about her waist, a laughing boy holding a pail of freshly picked blackberries, herself gazing into the camera with untroubled eyes, all the seemingly inconsequential moments of one's life that one took for granted, until they ceased to exist.

The need to love and to be loved remained the strength and stay of the human heart. But when love failed, as the cruse of oil had failed, and one understood the necessity of letting go of love, how else could one possibly do it other than lightly – as lightly as children blow away the stamens of a dandelion clock?

Tomorrow would dawn a new day. Tonight she needed to be alone with her memories. She had come early to bed after Sanger's phone call to say that William was out of danger.

When the shops opened after the Christmas holidays, Jess went into town to buy fresh food; light, nourishing food to tempt the appetites of the old people who were coming to stay. Remembering the kind of food she had once cooked for her mother, she filled her shopping basket with free-range eggs, plaice fillets, fruit; packets of Complan. How odd, she thought, buying the plaice, that she had first seen Miss Sweeting in a fishmonger's, that day she had pretended to find a pound coin on the floor.

The matron of the cottage hospital had rung up to tell Jess that her charges would arrive after lunch, by taxi. 'They are still rather shaky,' she said, 'and Miss Sweeting, in particular, will need watching. But ring me immediately if you run up against problems, if you find you can't cope.'

Jess had furnished their rooms as comfortably as possible. Shortage of beds had been the main problem until Dora offered her the loan of Evelyn's bed from Mews Cottage.

Having done her duty by her recalcitrant sister-in-law over Christmas, Dora said huffily, 'Just fancy, a woman of her age taking up this health food fad! Well, I told her straight in the end. "Evelyn," I said, "you've already lived your allotted three score years and ten, plus a few more besides. What difference will a few slices of white bread make one way or the other?" And what do you suppose she gave Alf and me for Boxing Day lunch? Nut loaf, that's what! Did it on purpose, if you ask me, knowing that nuts get under my top plate!'

As the furniture lifting continued, so had Dora's running commentary. 'So that husband of yours took himself off, did he? A good job too, if you want my opinion. Saw him driving off the first thing Boxing morning. Now there's a bad-tempered chap, I thought, slamming the car door the way he did, and belting away without so much as a backward glance. Eh, what a queer Christmas this has been one way and another. I just hope we'll all have better luck in the new year. Do you suppose Mr Sloane and the old lady will want to eat in the dining room? If so, I'd better give it a swipe round with Pledge.'

She screwed up her face and the duster she was holding. 'Seems funny, doesn't it, Mr Sloane coming here to stay? Truth to tell, I feel guilty about him, and so does Alf. Well, I mean to say, if we'd known the fix he was in . . . But that's the way of the world, I suppose. When you get used to seeing folk every day of the week, you never stop to ask yourself if they're all right, if they need help. It was the same for Alf and me when Geoff died. The neighbours didn't realise how ill he was. Then suddenly it was too late. And we'd never have asked for help in any case. I mean, what could they have done anyway? I expect it was the same with Mr Sloane, after his wife died. He wouldn't have wanted strangers crowding in, making a fuss.'

'Each in his lonely night, each with a ghost', Jess thought, wondering why the quotation seemed familiar to her. Ah yes, of course, Rupert Brooke.

Mr Sloane's face resembled a faded sepia photograph of a First War soldier returning home from the horror of the trenches, Jess thought compassionately as she helped him out of the taxi. He was still smiling bravely despite his recent brush with death. His skin resembled the colour of putty, his breathing was laboured; hands shaking; legs seemingly unable to support the weight of his attenuated body.

'It's all right, Mr Sloane,' she heard herself saying, 'you are quite safe now. You mustn't worry any more.'

Then Alfred took over from her, tucking his hand under Mr Sloane's elbow, guiding him indoors to his room; talking about the old days, bringing a tinge of colour to the man's cheeks.

Miss Sweeting, wearing her Wagnerian cloak and broad-brimmed black hat, struggled, unaided, from the taxi, and stood back a little as Mr Sloane went indoors, gazing up at the house, a faint smile hovering about her lips, a tender expression on the stretched canvas of her face.

Jess wondered what was going through her mind as she hurried back to help her.

'Won't you please come indoors?' she asked gently.

'In just a moment, my dear. You see, I feel I know this house so well. I remembered, the minute I saw it, that I had been here before.'

The old woman frowned slightly with the effort of remembering. 'No! Don't tell me! Let me think! Ah yes, the stained-glass doors! St Martin and the beggar; the arches, the staircase . . . Of course, I was very young at the time, too young to realise that those lions could not possibly eat the bread I pushed into their mouths.'

Jess's heart missed a beat. 'You mean you *knew* this house? The people who lived here?'

'Oh yes.' Miss Sweeting smiled her still perfect smile. 'My grandfather, you see, was the Tidey family's physician.'

CHAPTER 19

For the first time in almost four decades, Beryl Hoyle found herself without a shoulder to lean on. Despite her propensity for taking the lead in what she had always considered a disappointing relationship with a prosaically minded husband who had failed to understand her sensitive, romantic nature – when the inescapable truth dawned – that William had actually left her – she broke down in tears of self-pity, siphoned from the well of jealous misery deep inside her.

Suddenly, she who had become inured to being the centre of attention, found herself in the position of a field marshal minus troops. What on earth would she say to Lady Kagmire Loach; Major Huntingdon, to explain William's departure? How could she possibly enter the dining-room alone? Knowing she could not, she picked up the house telephone and ordered dinner in her room. Tucking into a sizeable portion of turkey plus trimmings, she began conjuring up excuses to account for William's defection – a sick relative in the north of England perhaps, or a burst water pipe; ceilings coming down . . . No, a sick relative sounded more plausible.

When a knock came at the door and the major, accompanied by a police constable of the Dorset division, entered the room, Beryl rose to her feet, hand pressed to her breast, and uttered a shrill cry of terror, unnerved by the appearance of the uniform. Ah, but what comfort lay in being the centre of attraction once more; being helped back to her chair, having the major run down to the bar for brandy; her smelling salts waved under her nose; a strong uniformed arm about her shoulders.

The taxi-driver had acted with commendable coolness in an emergency. Realising that his passenger had become seriously ill, the man had driven straight to the nearest hospital and given details of his fare – where he had picked him up and so forth. Carrying on the chain of events, the Metropolitan Police had contacted the Dorset constabulary to alert Mrs Hoyle.

'Where is my husband now?' Beryl murmured faintly between sips of brandy. When the constable told her, Charing Cross Hospital, 'You must take me to him at once,' she said dramatically, imagining a thrilling dash to London in a police car. When the young constable admitted, albeit sheepishly, that she would have to make her own travel arrangements, her mouth hardened into a rigid line of disapproval. 'Make my own arrangements?' she cried indignantly. 'A woman in my state of health?'

'There, there, Mrs Hoyle . . .' Uttering soothing words of comfort, Major Huntingdon told her not to worry. He would ring at once for a taxi. Helping her into her mink coat, 'Is there anyone you wish me to contact on your behalf?' he asked urbanely. 'A near relative, perhaps, to help you through the ordeal?'

Despite her outward manifestations of grief and alarm, Beryl's brain ticked over coolly, analytically. 'No,' she said faintly, 'I must manage on my own – somehow . . .' The last person she wanted meddling in her affairs was Adeline Peterson. It was then she thought of Dr Sanger who would know exactly what to do if William died. She had already considered that possibility with a clinical calmness which might have shocked those who saw her as a stricken woman on the verge of a nervous collapse.

When Sanger arrived at Charing Cross Hospital, Beryl, awed by the atmosphere, overcome with fatigue, feeling utterly wretched and misunderstood, blurted out her troubles to him, as to a father confessor.

'I see it all clearly now,' she wept. 'William must have known he was unwell at the time. It was so unlike him to simply pack his things and walk out on me.' Dabbing her eyes with an inadequate scrap of lace-trimmed Irish linen, she added bitterly, 'Of course I blame her. That *woman*!'

'Woman?' Sanger frowned, scarcely able to make head or tail of what she was saying between all the sobbing intakes of breath and fresh outbursts of tears.

Beryl babbled on indiscreetly, ridding her soul of venom.

'He had the gall to tell me he is in love with her! Faugh! A man of his age behaving like a lovesick schoolboy! I don't wonder he had a heart attack, carrying on a cheap love affair behind my back! Women of her kind should be shown up for what they are! Disgusting I call it, sucking up to men the way they do!'

In full spate she blundered on, 'I expect she thought she was on to a good thing – a rich man with a delicate wife. But you can take it from me, if William recovers, I'll put a stop to his nonsense! I'll never let him out of my sight again! It's high time he retired in any case!'

Later, when she knew that William was out of danger, Beryl deeply regretted unburdening herself to Sanger; asking him to come in the first place – a man she had always disliked, who had offered no soothing words of comfort during her ordeal, who had simply looked at her as if he actually disliked her. Why, she could not imagine.

She had elected to stay at a hotel near the hospital, where Sanger had also booked a room, which meant they could not very well avoid having dinner together. Not that the food was up to much, in Beryl's opinion.

Even so, she sailed into the dining-room wearing a pink silk two-piece and a string of pearls, and ordered soup, a mixed grill, and pêche melba, while Sanger, worried sick about Bill, ate next to nothing; simply watched, disgustedly, his companion's gold-filled teeth masticating the steak and lamb-chops, sausages, onion-rings, and chips.

'You're as bad as my husband, Dr Sanger,' Beryl said archly, raising a glass of Burgundy to her lips. '*He* ate next to nothing at the Hotel Splendide. I knew then that he must be sickening for something.'

'A heart attack can in no way be compared to some contagious disease,' Sanger reminded her, as she speared the last chip, and belched slightly.

'No, well, you ought to know. After all, you are a doctor!'

'If you'll excuse me, I must go back to the hospital now.' Sanger rose to his feet, nodded briefly, and left the dining-room.

Ah well, Beryl thought, watching him leave — when William is well enough to travel . . .

Nobody in Bevensea — apart from Sanger and that dreadful woman — would know how close her husband had come to making a fool of himself, a laughing stock of her. She dug her spoon with unnecessary violence into the pêche melba.

In Clarice's parlour, Miss Sweeting looked into the heart of the fire, thinking how much the comforting shadows flickering on walls and ceiling reminded her of home, of Pear Tree Cottage. The warmth of the room had somehow seeped into her bones, melting away the chilliness of old age and poverty. She felt really warm for the first time in years, safe and secure in this house, this room, surrounded with the kind of furniture she was used to.

Smoothing her hands along the soft velvety arm of the chair she was sitting in, she thought of Mrs Roach's dreadful chairs edged with fuzzy yellow piping, and wondered what would happen to her when it was time to leave this temporary refuge.

She knew all this was merely temporary. The matron of the cottage hospital had told her so, and taken the opportunity of implanting a seed about sheltered accommodation. There were some very nice places for the elderly in Bevensea, Matron had said, where she would be given a room of her own, and three good meals a day. All this spoken in the 'gentling' tone of voice one might use to a recalcitrant child refusing to take a dose of castor oil, with the promise of a sweet afterwards to dull the taste.

Well, Rachel thought regretfully, better an old folk's home than all that fuzzy yellow piping, sagging cretonne curtains, and that beastly Kool refrigerator. Then she thought that movement within the walls of sheltered accommodation would, of necessity, be somewhat restricted, and envisaged a slow, thrice-daily perambulation from bedroom to dining-room, a communal lounge with chairs pushed back against the wall — chairs filled with sad-eyed men and women, hands patiently folded, drowsing, nodding, dreaming away time.

Jess came in at that moment with Miss Sweeting's supper on a tray – home-made chicken soup, grilled plaice and parsley sauce. 'I'll fetch the pudding later,' she said, 'unless you'd rather come through to the kitchen.' Above all she wanted her guests to feel free to move about if they felt like it.

'Perhaps I could lend a hand with the washing-up?' Rachel's fingers trembled on the soup spoon. 'I would try not to break anything.'

'That's a splendid idea. I'll wash, you dry.'

'Perhaps we could ask Mr Sloane to do the putting away,' Rachel suggested. 'He told me this afternoon, when we were walking round the garden together – propping each other up in a manner of speaking – that what he misses most is a feeling of usefulness.'

Jess thought suddenly of William Hoyle. Freedom in which to breathe – and wondered when Mark Sanger would return to Bevensea, how soon would end her guardianship of these people he had trusted her to care for during his absence; what would happen to them when her role as guardian ended?

Nothing remained static. In the short time she had known them, she had come to care deeply about their future; hated the thought of their leaving. Curiously, she needed them as much as they needed her.

Mr Sloane was looking so much better now; breathing better. That terrible clay colour had disappeared; the haunted, desperate look about his eyes. She had Alfred to thank for that, for spending so much time with him; Dora to thank for gossiping with Miss Sweeting about recipes and knitting-patterns.

After supper, when the old people had eaten their creamed rice pudding and fresh fruit, and helped with the washing-up, Jess went up to her flat to watch the nine o'clock news on TV; found that she could not concentrate on the screen. Switching off the set, she glanced at the clock. Nine thirty.

Possibly Miss Sweeting would be in bed now, would not feel much like talking.

Pacing restlessly, playing tug-of-war with her conscience, Jess half-convinced herself that it would be wrong of her to disturb the old lady at this hour. But she knew, as she lost the battle with her conscience, and went downstairs, how much she needed to talk to Rachel. Even so, she hesitated before knocking.

'Come in, my dear. I've been expecting you. We have a great deal to talk about, haven't we?'

Jess put more wood on the fire.

'You'd like to know more about your family, your forebears? About this house? The people who once lived here?'

'Yes.'

Rachel said reflectively, 'I think that your great-grandfather, Joshua Tidey, was the handsomest man I ever saw in the whole of my life. Of course I was just a little girl at the time, perched beside my grandfather on the seat of his horse-drawn carriage, wearing a straw hat with floating ribbons . . .'

The old woman's eyes clouded suddenly. She held out her frail hands to the fire. 'But are you quite certain that you wish to hear the truth? Truth has a way of destroying illusions, you know, and I think you are a person inclined to labour under certain illusions, or do I mean – delusions? The English language is so frightfully tricky, isn't it?'

Miss Sweeting, Jess realised, was playing for time. Clenching her hands in her lap, she said softly, 'Whatever the truth, however painful it may be, I'd like to know. You understand – I *need* to know.'

Jess had looked upon Laurel Villa as an anachronism in a modern world, a bastion of Victorian respectability, the silent witness of a less stressful age. Possibly she had needed to look at it in that way, to keep on believing in a lost world of family love and security, a neatly rounded past with no jagged edges to cut into the fabric of the here and now; had visualised her forebears as remote and mannered as the characters in a Jane Austen novel,

Remembering a play she had once seen, how an illusion of the past had been created by the clever use of gauze and lighting to create a second-dimensional effect, she thought that her ghosts, too, had seemed to move silently behind an impenetrable veil, as remote and untouchable as mist on a spring morning. Now those ghosts had sprung to life, fleshed out in her imagination because someone remembered them; described the way they looked, spoke and moved; knew something of their circumstances; the events and tragedies which had shaped their lives. And nothing had been very different then from now.

Certainly they had dressed more elegantly, employed servants to do their bidding, had cushioned their lives with the trappings of wealth – horses, carriages, oil-paintings, silverware, richly coloured stained glass, coal fires and glowing oil-lamps. But those trappings, artefacts, had merely cloaked, not mitigated, their very real human emotions – unrequited love, hatred, and jealousy.

The rooms on the upper landing had originally been the nursery quarters. Later, this room in which Jess was standing, Liz's room, had been converted to use as Donalds and Franklyn's schoolroom, the two boys in the charge of a pale, earnest young tutor called Halliday. Glancing about her, she pictured it as it would have looked then, with starched lace curtains and an acorned blind at the window, possibly the same blind and curtains which Dora had relegated to the dustbin; a blackboard, globe, desks; imagined Donald and Franklyn sitting there, heads bent over their exercise books, the tutor, Charles Halliday, standing close to Franklyn, lightly smoothing his younger pupil's hair with trembling, womanish fingers.

The boy would not have realised the significance of the tutor's touch, but someone else had done so – Nancy Bellchamber most likely, the buxom nursemaid in charge of the much younger child, Jessica. According to gossip, Nancy, who had set her cap squarely at Halliday, had met with a series of polite rebuffs. Was it Nancy, then, smarting from the tutor's indifference, who had reported Charles Halliday's nocturnal visits to Franklyn's room?

Little more than a child herself, Rachel Sweeting had picked up snippets of gossip from the Pear Tree Cottage servants: snide comments which had meant nothing to her at the time. She had simply listened to the cook and the parlourmaid, with their heads together, whenever she had tripped into the kitchen to beg a piece of cake; had giggled when the cook had called her a 'little pitcher with big ears'.

Shivering slightly, Jess wondered if it was here, in this room, that her great-grandfather had confronted the tutor. Here, or in the room across the landing, that he had thrashed Franklyn – if Clarice had hurried upstairs to intercede on her son's behalf: if Jessica, hearing her brother's cries, had hidden her face in her mother's skirts.

Or possibly Joshua had meted out punishment in his study. Yes, that would be more likely. Jess imagined a trembling little boy standing in front of that formidable desk with its dagger-shaped letter-opener, not knowing, not understanding why his father was so angry; admitting, perhaps, that he had allowed the tutor to kiss him goodnight; seeing nothing wrong in that. Ah yes, it must have been the study. Possibly that was the reason why she so disliked that particular room, as if the events which had taken place there long ago had somehow tainted the air, the very atmosphere.

Staring out of the window at the sky filled with low-hanging clouds, Jess wondered if the events of that day had sown the seeds of Clarice's mental instability – a woman whose gentle nature could not withstand the emotional shock of having her sons suddenly packed off to a harsh Jesuit boarding school. One could merely conjecture, but Rachel had recalled her grandfather's anxiety about that time. As young as she was, she had known that there was something seriously wrong with the 'pretty lady' at Laurel Villa, by the frequency of his visits.

Was it then that Clarice had turned to painting her delicate watercolours; filled the conservatory with singing birds, and planted her grapevines? Had she, too, in her grief and loneliness, striven towards quiet oases of the mind?

And what of the child Jessica? Had that scene in the study, her favourite brother Franklyn's unjust punishment, sown the seeds of her festering hatred towards her father? Had she begun to plan, even then, what she would do in revenge?

As Jess moved about the house, vacuuming, dusting and polishing, so her ghosts moved with her, peopling the rooms, silently reliving the drama of their lives. She could almost see her great-grandfather, a handsome, vital, charismatic figure, striding towards his study, sending one of the servants to fetch Franklyn; Clarice sitting quietly at her easel, painting a picture of a summer garden; a girl with a proudly held, stubborn chin and long dark hair bound with a blue ribbon, kneeling near an ottoman, throwing brightly coloured beads into a wooden box – putting away childish things.

Had Joshua ever considered, when he had accepted his mayoral chain of office, that his wife might prove unequal to her demanding duties as mayoress? Had husband and wife become, by that time, almost strangers? Two people living under the same roof yet curiously remote and detached from one another? Their sons had, by then, returned home. Donald to enter his father's business, Franklyn to complete his education at the Greyfriars Academy for the sons of gentlemen. Had Jessica, fast growing into an awkward girl entirely lacking in social graces, already begun to betray signs of a dark, rebellious nature totally inimical to that of her flamboyant, extrovert father?

One thing seemed certain. It was an innocuous-looking, gilt-edged invitation from Lady Anstruther, wife of the lord lieutenant of the county, inviting the mayor and mayoress of Bevensea and their daughter to one of her famous houseparties, which had proved a watershed in the fortunes of the Tidey family; had brought within their orbit a servant girl called Annie Petch.

Just a scrap of gilt-edged cardboard – one of the many invitations Jess had discovered that day last September when she had begun to sort through her great-aunt's belongings. If only she had known, had realised then the significance of that particular invitation upon which was scrawled, in thick, black, purposeful handwriting, a postscript saying that provision had been made for the entertainment of the younger guests – including Jessica – in the west wing of the house, under the supervision of her own children's nanny, Miss Prosser.

How rebellious Jessica must have felt at being relegated to the west wing of Mandeville Hall; entering the house by a side door, while her parents went in through the main entrance.

And what of Annie Petch? Had she been one of the servants in waiting, summoned by the snap of the butler's fingers to show the guests to their rooms? Was it then that she had first caught Joshua's eye? Had a look, a glance, passed between them which sealed both their fates? As Joshua helped his delicate wife to their room, had a quiet, restrained servant girl looked questioningly into his face?

Who could know for certain what had transpired that day?

Had Annie Petch later been sent to the west wing to help with the children's party? Was it there she had noticed a dark-eyed young girl looking down at the lights of the dining-room windows spilling on to the green shaven lawns of

Mandeville Hall, the well-kept flowerbeds and the lily pond with its pouting Cupid? Had she mentioned, respectfully, that supper was ready in the nursery; felt shocked, disturbed by the girl's expression of utter misery, her loneliness and inability to join in the fun; realised whose child she was by a certain, uncanny resemblance to her father?

The answers to some of those questions must lay hidden within the pages of Annie's Bible which she had used as an occasional diary, and Rachel had said that the events of that houseparty were widely reported in the *Bevensea Mercury* at the time. Copies of those old papers would be kept in the public library. There had been a hue and cry when Lady Anstruther's diamond and sapphire brooch was discovered missing from her jewelcase. Constables had been sent for, a search of the servants' quarters instituted. When the brooch was found, secreted in a drawer in Annie Petch's room, the girl had been placed under arrest, had pleaded guilty at her trial, and sentenced to six months' imprisonment.

The curious thing was, when Annie was released from gaol she had been offered the position of housemaid at Laurel Villa. Why? The inference was obvious. Annie had shouldered the blame for someone else.

Nothing could change the impermeable patterns of the past. Soon after that fateful houseparty, Joshua Tidey had announced his resignation as mayor to a packed council chamber in the Town Hall.

Had tongues begun to wag? Had someone remembered seeing the figure of a young girl idling along the corridor near Lady Anstruther's room about the time of the theft, and wondered what she was doing there? Or possibly the nanny, Miss Prosser, had noticed that Jessica was missing from the nursery suite at the relevant time. Had Annie Petch, noticing the girl's febrile excitement, the unnatural brightness of her eyes, the trembling of her hands, realised that something was terribly wrong with the child?

When the hue and cry about the missing brooch began,

had Annie, guessing the truth, discovered the brooch in the girl's room before the police arrived? Knowing what it would mean to a man like Joshua Tidey to have his daughter branded a thief, his career ruined, his good name tarnished, had she acted quickly, desperately, in hiding the brooch in her own room?

Giving rein to her imagination, Jess drew vivid mental pictures of the past, the scene in the council chamber; heavily built men wearing dark frock coats, starched linen, gold alberts: prosperous men; Joshua rising to his feet to make his announcement, standing there in that solemn arena of leather and mahogany; walking from the chamber, head bowed, to the stunned silence of his peers, the light from the stained-glass coat-of-arms' window reflecting, briefly, on the chain of office which he had worn, that day, for the last time.

What else could a man of honour have done? He had given the reasons for his resignation as personal, refusing to discuss those reasons at the time or afterwards. But how bitterly he must have reflected upon those reasons: his wife's increasing mental instability, signs of which, he must have felt certain, were also manifest in his daughter's scarcely concealed hatred of him; what he saw as his younger son's homosexual tendencies.

Possibly he had later regretted letting his anger get the better of him over the affair with the tutor; punishing the boy, blaming him for something that was not his fault. But how else would a full-blooded male have regarded a soft, womanish taint in a son of his? And how would a vigorous man in the prime of life, a Victorian pater-familias with a natural, healthy sexual appetite, have regarded, night after night, the closed and locked door of his wife's bedroom?

When Annie Petch arrived at Laurel Villa after her six-months' sentence, it must have seemed that a ray of light, of hope, had entered the house with her. Rachel remembered her as a pretty, fair-haired young woman, possessed of a quiet delicacy and charm, both modest and unassuming

– yet strong – as a rapier is strong. Steel true and blade straight . . .

Annie's love affair with Joshua would not have been entered into lightly or wantonly. It must have been a slow, painful process, their drawing together, the realisation of how much they meant to each other. When Annie understood what was happening, had she told Joshua she must leave Laurel Villa? Had he, in his loneliness and despair, begged her to reconsider?

Annie's presence in the house had brought a great deal of comfort to his wife, who seemed more stable as a result of the girl's gentle ministrations when Clarice's brief but shattering bouts of madness occurred. Jessica, too, had seemed brighter, less furtive and restrained, knowing she could trust Annie; aware, perhaps, of the debt of gratitude she owed her in the affair of the brooch; realising at last that her mother would have suffered more than her father had the real culprit been brought to book. Possibly this was the warning that Annie had brought home to Jessica on that fateful occasion.

Had the servants noticed the blossoming relationship between master and housemaid? Possibly not. The affair would have been conducted discreetly, in the small hours, when the house slumbered; when the trees whispered, out there in the garden, in the stillness of the night, to the murmur of the sea in the background – the eternally moving, restless sea.

Jess imagined the slight, ghostlike figure of Annie Petch slipping down the back stairs to her master's room; trembling, knowing that what she was doing was wrong, yet unable to resist the powerful, overwhelming love she felt for Joshua. Understood the restraint she must have experienced the first time he kissed her, her nervousness and slow response to his initial lovemaking, finally to be swept away by her passionate response to his ardour.

The servants might not have known, or had turned a blind eye to what was going on. They could, however, scarcely have failed to notice the slight thickening of Annie's waistline, her bouts of morning sickness, her extreme pallor, the purple shadows beneath her eyes.

Then, one morning, Annie had awakened in her attic room beneath the stars, to a gripping pain in her belly, had seen, with frightened eyes, that her bed-sheets were stained red with blood. She would not have been the first servant girl in the world to conceive a child by her master, doubtless she was not the last. Had the other servants, the cook, the tweeny, who endlessly washed up dirty pots and pans in the kitchen, the parlourmaid in her room next door to Annies,' hearing her cries of agony as her premature labour began, gathered about one of their own class, with a half-tolerant acceptance of her foolishness?

Obviously a doctor was sent for post-haste: Dr Sweeting of Pear Tree Cottage. As chance would have it, Clarice Tidey had also stood in urgent need of his ministrations on that particular December morning long ago. But in the midst of her own agony, Annie had spared a loving thought for her mistress, whose trust she had betrayed, of whom she had later written, compassionately, in minuscule writing in the margin of her Bible: 'My little lady is also in a bad way.'

It was then Jess realised the transience of life; that all the words which had been spoken in anger, love, jealousy or pain a long time ago, and the people who had spoken those words, were all dead now, finished and done with, as if they had never existed: all their very human mistakes and follies laid to rest in the quiet earth of the old Greyfriars cemetery.

But who, she wondered, had erected that gravestone to Annie Petch's memory? Was it Joshua whose child she had borne, who had found in her a reason for living? Was it Clarice Tidey who had come to rely more and more, as time went by, upon Annie's loving support and sympathy? Or Great-Aunt Jessica, for whose sake poor Annie had suffered a six-months' prison sentence for a crime she had not committed?

After a disturbed night, Jess came wearily downstairs to find that Dora had taken over her role as cook. The trays were already set; coffee percolating, eggs sitting in fast bubbling water. She suddenly remembered that this was New Year's Eve. Tomorrow the old leaves of the calendar would flutter away like snowflakes in the wind.

'You look awful,' Dora commented. 'Why didn't you stay in bed a bit longer? You might have known I'd come over to get the breakfast ready.'

Still hedged about with fitful dreams threaded between hours of wakefulness, Jess said, 'I've never asked you this before, but I'd like to know more about my great-aunt. What was she really like?'

'I haven't time to go into that now,' Dora sniffed, bustling toast and boiled eggs on to the trays; filling the coffee-pots. 'Why don't you pour yourself a cup of coffee? I'll be back in a couple of shakes.'

When the breakfast trays had been delivered, Dora settled herself at the kitchen table. 'I've often wondered,' she said, buttering a slice of toast, 'why you have never asked me that question before. But then, I knew there was no love lost between you and Miss Tidey. To be honest, I thought you didn't care tuppence about her.'

'Of course I cared! It was the other way round. I thought she didn't care tuppence for me, her namesake. That was a bitter pill to swallow.'

Dora sighed. 'I don't think she cared for anyone, really, except her mother.'

'What did she look like?'

'A crow, if you want my opinion,' Dora said bluntly, 'dressed in black from head to foot, always in long skirts, with her hair done up in a kind of bun at the back, all wispy and untidy about her face – as if she were still living in the past. Alf and I would see her out in the garden, at times, clipping away at dead flowers with a pair of rusty scissors, wearing an old straw hat, and black lace mittens. Truth to tell, I was scared stiff of her, and yet . . .'

Dora's face softened. She said, reflectively, 'And yet, despite her queer ways, she could be kind and generous if she felt like it. I'll never forget that day we passed her gate. We had Geoff in his wheelchair at the time . . .'

'Yes?'

'Well, you know Alf. When he saw her pottering about in the front garden, trying to clear away the bindweed, he called out that he'd be glad to give her a hand, any time, if she needed help.' Dora's face was a study, 'And what do you think she said to him? "If I need help, I'll ask for it, and not before." Talk about a snub. God, I felt like a worm. But next morning, when I took the milk in, there was a cardboard box full of toys on the doorstep. We guessed who had sent them, but we daren't for the life of us thank her.

'That's why we agreed to look after her when she was taken ill, to save her the humiliation of being carted off to the geriatric hospital. Mind you, she wasn't all that grateful, and my heart bled for the poor district nurse. Whenever she came to give the old lady a bed-bath, Miss Tidey fought like a tigress. We thought, at first, it was just natural modesty on the part of a maiden lady – until . . . ' Dora's voice faltered suddenly.

'Until . . . ' Jess prompted, holding her breath.

'Well, I don't know that I should say. It may have been guesswork. But no – the district nurse and I agreed . . . '

'Agreed about – what?'

'Well, we came to the conclusion that Miss Tidey was not a virgin. She had obviously given birth to a child. There was this scar on her body, you see. The mark of a Caesarean operation!'

Suddenly Jess understood. That understanding came as a blinding flash, a revelation.

She now knew why her great-aunt Jessica had severed all connections with her family. Not because she was too proud, but too ashamed.

Poor Great-Aunt Jessica.

That mark upon her body must have seemed to her as terrible as the Mark of Cain. She had lived the whole of her adult life alone in this great, empty house, continually

271

haunted by that tell-tale blemish.

But what had happened to the child she had borne? Who was the father? Some ingenuous youth who, about to sail for France during the First World War, had swept her off her feet; made her pregnant before the wedding-ring was safely on her finger?

Oh no. Not that. Jess knew that Great-Aunt Jessica would never have given herself so cheaply to someone she had met at some social gathering or other.

Adding two and two together, Jess also knew that the person Jessica had loved must have been someone very close to her, a lonely, misunderstood person in desperate need of love, to whom she had given all that lay within her power to give, by way of recompense.

How much she must have loved that person to risk everything for his sake, her good name, her reputation, her standing in the community.

Her own brother, Franklyn Tidey.

'I hope I haven't said anything I shouldn't,' Dora said as Jess got up to stare out of the window at the steadily falling snow.

'No, of course not.'

'I'd best be getting along, then. Alf will be wanting his breakfast.'

'Yes. Thanks, Dora.' But Jess was not thinking of Dora, her mind was filled with thoughts of a proud, lonely old woman battling out her empty days of regret in these ghost-ridden rooms: filling her mother's handkerchief sachets with fresh lavender; caring for her clothes; creating a shrine to the memory of a beloved person whom the rest of the world had long forgotten.

She now knew why her grandmother Tidey had refused to talk openly about Great-Aunt Jessica, because she was bound up with shibboleths; cursed with the burden of narrow-mindedness – the way that ordinary people, in this day and age, were equally burdened when it came to the question of AIDS, drug addiction, homosexuality, lesbianism – incest.

Oh God, Jess thought compassionately, how shamefully her grandmother Tidey must have viewed, half a century ago, Great-Aunt Jessica's unlawful pregnancy; how thankfully she must have packed her bags and returned to Reading after the death of her husband, Donald.

Of course, poor Grandmother Tidey must have realised what was going on under her nose. Had she seen, inadvertently, one night, Franklyn entering Jessica's bedroom? Had she guessed that the brother and sister, lying in each other's arms, had broken every rule of decent human behaviour? Was that the reason why Grandmother Tidey would never speak of Jessica? All the pieces fitted together, at last, like those of a complex jigsaw puzzle.

But life had taught Jess that nothing was ever as cut and dried as all that. That, without compassion, a deep awareness of human motives, without forgiveness, the world would be a kind of desert devoid of understanding. And then she thought that one person, at least, had understood Great-Aunt Jessica's torment – her mother, Clarice Tidey, who, to ease her beloved daughter's burden of guilt, had ordered the servants to clear her sons' rooms of their personal belongings: Franklyn's in particular.

And now, Jess thought, the time had come to close the pages on the past, to lay to rest her ghosts, tenderly, without regret. Watching the slow fall of snow on the trees outside the window, she hoped that the ghost of her great-aunt Jessica would realise that it was better so.

CHAPTER 21

It was good to be back in Bevensea, Sanger thought, a town he had always appreciated.

Driving along the esplanade, the windows wound down despite the coldness of the day, passing the spot where Liz had died, he remembered her brief, shining presence in his life, which had been his torment and salvation. But memories were not enough to live by. He had begun to think in terms of a lasting relationship, had reached the stage of needing someone to share his life.

Ready to trust, to love again, he thought of Jessica's quiet understanding. That day he had gone to the house, for instance, by what amazing perception had she discerned his need to be alone in Liz's room? He admired her quick appraisal of delicate situations, her innate decency and generosity.

Remembering the time he had spent recently in the ungenerous company of Beryl Hoyle, comparing the two women, he knew that only a person of Jess's calibre could have prompted Bill's decision to end his marriage. The pressures had been building up slowly over the years. Nor would anything convince him that Bill and Jessica had engaged in the 'cheap and nasty' affair of Beryl's warped imagination. He doubted if Jess even knew how Bill felt about her.

He wondered, as he drew into the driveway and walked up the steps of Laurel Villa, how his patients were faring, how Miss Sweeting would react to the news that a place had been found for her in an old people's home.

Jess answered the bell. 'How nice to see you, Mark. Come in.' She wore a brightly coloured overall. 'We're through in the kitchen, making mince pies for tonight's celebration.'

'Celebration?' He had no idea what she meant.

'It's New Year's Eve. Had you forgotten?' She laughed. 'We're having a party. Dora and Alf are coming over. Alf and Mr Sloane are Scrabble fanatics, did you know that?

Why don't you come through for a minute?'

'Not now,' he said briefly. 'It's Rachel I really came to see. Alone, if possible. Is she in her room?'

'No, she and Mr Sloane are in the kitchen helping Dora make the mince pies. I'm doing the sausage rolls and quiche. The trouble is, Mr Sloane put rather too much mincemeat into the pastry and is having to take some of it out again in case it boils over and sticks to the tins.'

'Good God,' Sanger said bemusedly, 'don't tell me you've got him wearing a pinny, too?'

'Not exactly a pinny – a butcher's apron.' Was Sanger angry, Jess wondered, or simply tired and worried? She wanted to ask him about William, felt that this was, perhaps, an inappropriate moment. Possibly he thought that old people should not stay up late or eat too much rich pastry. 'I'm sorry if you feel that Rachel and Mr Sloane are doing too much,' she said, 'but they're so looking forward to letting in the new year – rather like children.'

'It isn't that,' Sanger frowned. 'It simply occurred to me that Miss Sweeting, in particular, might suffer a feeling of let-down when she leaves here. There's a place for her, you see, in one of our council-run homes.'

Jess looked at him in dismay. 'But you can't take her away now. It would break her heart. Why, she's a different person. Like the *Mary Rose*, restored, with all pennants flying!'

'My dear girl,' Sanger said impatiently, 'there's no way she can stay on here. It's a matter of finance. All she has is her Old Age pension. I'm doing my best to get supplementary benefit for her, but even that, I imagine, will not be sufficient to pay for first-class accommodation.'

Jess flashed fire. 'What nonsense! I'm surprised at you, Mark. Finance – money doesn't enter into it! Rachel is welcome to stay on here for the rest of her days as far as I'm concerned. Why, she's like one of my own family!'

Sanger thought, with a singing feeling of relief, that this was the reaction he had half expected – hoped for. It was then he knew that what he suspected was true. He had fallen

gently, quietly and deeply in love with Jessica Carmichael.
Not in the same way that he had fallen in love with Margaret. Not impetuously, impulsively, because of skin-deep
beauty and glamour, but something far beyond that – the
immeasurable sense of peace and permanency he experienced whenever Jess was near him. For the same reasons,
he imagined, that Bill Hoyle had fallen in love with her.

Bill!

Remembering Hoyle, Sanger resisted a strong temptation to take Jess in his arms and tell her what he knew to be
the truth. Instead, he turned away to take off his gloves,
knowing he must bide his time, that Jess was far from being
in love with him. Putting down his doctor's bag on a chair,
it would take time and patience, he thought, and a lot more
besides before he dare claim his right to be loved, to ask any
woman to share his life: a coming to terms with, and conquering of, his own shortcomings. The battle had just
begun. The crustiness, assumed as a defensive shell, had
now, unwittingly, become part of his nature along with his
arrogance and conceit which he still believed to have been
responsible for the death of a beautiful young woman; his
jealousy and lack of understanding which had driven his
wife into the arms of another man. Besides which, Bill
Hoyle's feelings must take priority.

Jess knew that Sanger felt drawn to her. An undeniable
rapport had sprung up between them. He was not, as she
had at first suspected, an uncaring man. Events had proved
that. And yet she never felt entirely at ease with him.
Perhaps she had glimpsed an element of Douglas in his
make-up. 'So is it all right about Miss Sweeting?' she
asked. 'You will let her stay with me?'

'I was looking at things from your point of view,' he
reminded her. 'I imagine that you intend making a living
from the house. How can you hope to do so if you start giving rooms away?'

'I never intended letting Clarice's parlour in the first
place,' Jess said defensively. 'In any case, Rachel is too
proud a person to want charity. Knowing her, she'll expect

to pay for her keep. But I really couldn't bear the thought of her spending the rest of her days in some centrally heated council home.'

'You've made your point,' Sanger said. 'Now, about Mr Sloane . . .'

'He's had a succession of visitors,' Jess said quickly. 'Insurance men wanting to establish the cause of the fire, a nice young neighbour who brought him a bunch of chrysanthemums and a Get Well card, and a rather dreadful clergyman, with a nervous tic, who collared me afterwards and went on and on about putting poor Mr Sloane into what he termed "sheltered accommodation".'

'What did you say to him?' Sanger retained a vivid memory of his own conversation with the reverend gentleman.

'Simply that as long as Mr Sloane has his own home, and if he wishes to go back there, when he's well enough, he should be allowed to do so. After all, he's not all that old. About the same age as – Bill.' Jess bit her lip. The question she was burning to ask would not wait any longer. 'How *is* Bill?' she asked urgently. 'How did he seem when you left him?'

'He's making good progress,' Sanger said gently. 'With luck, he'll have a good few years ahead of him yet.'

Jess said, in a low voice, 'I'm not sure what that means – "with luck". And if his – luck – ran out? What then?'

Sanger said carefully, 'I simply meant that if Bill, by some happy chance, discovered a sound reason for living; if he is given peace of mind, he could go on for quite some time yet; live a normal life. It's difficult to be precise. Of course he'll have to retire.' He paused. 'Of this, however, I am certain, if Bill is forced to continue in his present circumstances, to live with someone who will destroy his will to survive, I would give him two or three months at the most.'

'You mean – Beryl?'

'You've never met her, have you?' Sanger thrust his hands into his overcoat pockets, understanding her distress. 'There's something you should know,' he said bluntly. 'When Bill was taken ill, he had already decided to leave his wife.'

'Leave? But why? I don't understand.'

'Unfortunately I do. I've watched it happening over the years; the slow, undermining process, the selfishness and the greed; the emotional blackmail . . .'

'Please don't!' Jess turned her head away.

'I must. There's something more.' Sanger laid his hand on Jess's arm. 'Bill left Beryl because he is in love with someone else. Need I elaborate?'

'No, I suppose not. But I never dreamt . . .' Jess's voice trailed away as she remembered the man who had lent her his umbrella, who, in his concern that an old woman's coffin should not be laid to rest without a full complement of flowers, had sent two wreaths to her funeral.

In silence, she recalled the past few months of her life, every day of which had been somehow lightened, made easier, more bearable because of William Hoyle's quiet strength, tolerance and tongue-in-cheek humour. Until this moment, she had never paused to consider how empty her life would be without him.

Tightening his clasp on her arm, Sanger said quietly, 'I'm going to London next week to bring Bill home. Beryl, too, of course.' He paused imperceptibly, formulating an idea. 'I shall insist that Bill spends a few days at the cottage hospital. A matter of expediency to make certain he rests well after the journey, and to undergo certain tests. He will not necessarily be bedfast during that time. Do you understand?'

'Yes, I understand,' Jess said simply.

Octavius Sloane got out of bed, crossed over to the window, and stood looking out at the sea rocking quietly to a blue-grey horizon; noticed a fishing-coble butting against the tide towards the haven of the harbour.

He had lived near the sea all his life, but he had never come so close to it before, had never known the joy of waking up to its quiet rhythm. But that was the way with people who lived close to the sea – who were generally too busy, or too lazy, to notice, as he and Maisie had been.

They had paddled, of course, when they were young and daft – courting. An old-fashioned term nowadays, but all they had noticed, then, was each other – two young people, drawn to each other, faced with the possibility that they might wish to spend the rest of their lives together.

He remembered that he had proposed to Maisie, in a Victorian shelter, just before the outbreak of the Second World War; that she had wept in his arms, knowing that he had joined the Army that very day; that he would soon be taken away from her. Even so, she had accepted his diamond engagement ring with that kind of joyous pride of hers which had set her apart from all other women.

Dear Maisie.

They had married, very quietly, when the war ended, and bought the house in Lymington Crescent, confidently expecting an increase in family. They had both wanted children – lots of children, but their first baby had been stillborn, and the doctor said that his wife would never have another child, that there was something wrong with her internally.

And so they had become all in all to each other. 'Making the best of a bad job,' Maisie had called it.

Strangely enough, she had never cottoned on to the idea of adopting a child. 'No, darling,' she said adamantly, 'if I can't have your child – our child – I'd just as soon do without. After all, I have you. We have each other.'

And now, Octavius felt that he had come through a dark, narrow tunnel, into a new world filled with light and hope, because of his friends, the Cornwells, and a very special lady – Jessica Carmichael.

Suddenly he caught sight of Dora pattering down the steps of Mews Cottage, on her way to start breakfast; saw the postman's van drive in through the gates, and returned the man's friendly wave; knew that, during the past few days, he had begun to look forward to getting up each morning, to wave to the postman, to catch the fragrant scent of toast and coffee from the kitchen quarters.

They had had a splendid New Year's Eve party. Now, on

this shining New Year morning, Mr Sloane felt himself uplifted, a new person, remembering the way that Dr Sanger had joined in the celebration; the fun they'd had when, at a minute to midnight, Sanger had been bundled out into the snow to await the striking of the hall clock: how he had returned, shivering, as 'first footer', bringing in with him a sprig of evergreen, a piece of bread, a lump of coal, a handful of tenpence pieces – all part of the Northern ritual to ensure good luck for the coming year. And the first-footer must, according to custom, be a dark-haired man.

Afterwards, Sanger had proposed a toast to the health and happiness of those present, and raised his glass to 'Absent Friends'.

And then the doctor had broken to him the news that, if he continued to improve at his present rate – he, Octavius Sloane, would be well enough to return home next week, or the week after.

It was then Octavius knew that he did not want to go back to his lonely house in Lymington Crescent. He was so happy here. Happier than he had been for many a long month – since Maisie had died, as a matter of fact. Indeed, ever since he came to Laurel Villa, to this room overlooking the sea, he had been busy furnishing, mentally, every crook and corner of it with his own and Maisie's belongings; thinking how nice her oil-painting of summer roses would look above the mantelpiece; how beautifully her house-plants, her ivies and busy-lizzies, would flourish on the window-shelf.

But what if Mrs Carmichael didn't want him; considered him a fire-risk?

When the postal van had driven away, he peered nervously round the door of his room, knowing that Jessica usually came through, about this time, to collect the mail. And so it came to pass . . .

'Oh, good morning, Mr Sloane,' she said, appearing from the kitchen. Then, frowning, 'Is anything the matter?'

'Well, yes and no. That is, could you spare me a few

minutes? I have something rather important to say to you. The truth is, I want to stay on here, if you'll have me.'

'Oh, my dear Mr Sloane — I thought you would never ask,' Jess laughed, closing the door behind her.

That afternoon, Jess walked along by the sea's edge. It would take a great deal of courage, she thought, to accomplish what she had in mind — to walk into the hospital, take Bill by the hand and bring him home with her.

She was not, never had been a particularly courageous person, simply an ordinary woman with a penchant for rushing in where angels feared to tread, never getting anything quite right the first time. But this she knew, deep down, there would never be another time for herself and William.

Kicking up the sand with the toes of her shoes, she thought — foolishly perhaps — of the Parting of the Red Sea to allow the Israelites to pass; Dunkirk — all those little boats setting sail to bring back home, to England, the remnants of a beleaguered army.

Watching the sea curling in on the sand, she remembered Douglas's cruel dismissal of her as being too old.

Too old for what? Almost certainly to bear children. Noticing a seagull's wing half buried in the sand, a sad, dead thing which had once been a part of a bird in flight, a part of nature, she knew that she would always regret the inability to pass on something of herself to a rising generation, teaching her children to take notice of the world, to ask questions, to read and understand the importance, the power of the written word, to enjoy great paintings and try for themselves to create something of beauty; listen to music. To look up at the stars.

Rain, too. How much she would have enjoyed teaching her dream children to appreciate the gentle fall of rain on September leaves:

The leaves of brown came tumbling down, remember?
That September, in the rain . . .

She would have bought them little red umbrellas with shiny spokes, and watched them, splashing through puddles, with a quiet feeling of continuance, a quick, ecstatic resurgence of her own childhood.

But all that was imaginary. What she intended to do, tomorrow, was not: could not be glossed over with the paintbrush of her imagination.

If only she could be sure that what she was about to do was right. If only she might, somehow, be imbued miraculously with fresh courage.

Stopping momentarily to watch a group of youngsters kicking a ball on the sands, walking away, thinking that it was one of their cheeky voices she heard calling after her to stop, she hurried on all the faster, until the voice became suddenly louder, more urgent: 'Hey, missis! Hang on just a sec!'

Then, recognising the voice, she turned to see Johnny McEvoy racing towards her.

'Gawd, missis,' he said breathlessly, 'you didn't half take some catching up with!'

'Johnny! What on earth are you doing here?'

'Yeah, well,' he muttered shamefacedly, delving into his anorak pockets, 'I promised to pay back the money you lent me, an' here it is. Every last penny! 'Sides, I just wanted you to know that Colleen an' I are OK. Our Dad is taking care of us, see? He's not doing too badly now, round the Clubs, singing Irish folk songs an' playing his guitar.' He grinned amiably, 'We quite like the woman he's living with, too. Her name's Sally. She's a bit on the big and busty side, but ever so nice and warm-hearted. Well, you know what I mean. I guess her an' me Dad'll get married quite soon, then Colleen an' me will have a proper home!'

'I'm so glad, Johnny,' Jess said quietly, 'but I don't want your money. I'd far rather you kept it.'

'Naw, missis,' Johnny said awkwardly, 'that wouldn't be right. You see, if it hadn't been for your nosey-parkering, none of this would've happened.' He grinned again, like a sunburst. 'I sure gave you a hell of a rotten time, didn't I?'

'Well . . . 'Jess laughed. They sat down on a rock.

Johnny said, staring out to sea at a great timber boat awaiting the turn of the tide to enter the harbour, 'Our Ma's given Bert his marching orders. Turned him out, she did, when she found out what he'd done to Colleen. She wants us back now, but we'd rather stay with our Dad. Course, we'll go to see her, that's only fair, ain't it? But Sis is better off where she is. She's scared stiff of going back to Newcastle – scared of the house, her old room . . . '

Twisting his hands into knots, he continued awkwardly, 'I just wondered, missis, if, next summer, you know, during the school holidays, I could come over once in a while an' give you a hand with the garden? I mean, it ain't all that far from here to Hull, an' me Dad said he wouldn't mind.' Words failed him, but Jess knew what he meant. This was Johnny's way of saying thank you.

'Fine, Johnny,' she said. 'Of course you can.' She laid a tentative arm about his shoulders, this skinny urchin, this towrag of a lad who had fought for what he believed in and emerged triumphant from the conflict, half expecting that he would recoil from her touch.

When he did not, but merely grinned up at her and laughed, she knew, with a singing feeling of joy, that Johnny McEvoy's love, so hardly won, was no inconstant thing, as variable as the tide: that this was the child she would teach to look at life through her own eyes.

The cruse of oil had not failed.

FINALE

William saw, through the windows of his hospital room, the car park bumpy with rutted snow, the coming and going of the nurses in their pristine white caps, their cloaks billowing in the wind. A kind of Lowry painting, busy with human life. And yet he felt no sense of belonging to life anymore; as if the will to go on living had suddenly deserted him.

Beryl would arrive soon to take him to the Georgian house on the hill. He felt sick, defeated, at the very thought of going home. Home?

So much for his brief escape from bondage. The future he had envisaged as a gentle buffing and polishing of the dulled facets of his life made sharp and brilliant once more by the simple expedient of cutting himself free from his old way of life, had been snatched away, summarily, by a quirk of fate.

Beryl had won, after all. He might have known that there could be no escape from the past. No future happiness for himself: no possibility of ever coming closer to Jessica, as he had hoped and prayed that he might.

Gone now, blown away by the winds of chance were his dreams of one day visiting the Reichenbach Falls with Jess as his companion; puttering about with railway engines; building bridges; his half-formulated notion of buying a cottage at Goathland where he might look out upon the rolling hills of the Aire Valley, read to his heart's content: listen to music – Chopin, Elgar, Debussy.

He had envisaged that new life as a kind of prelude: the fine, resounding chords of an overture to living; imagined Jessica as the axis on which his fine, free, new life would surely revolve, had thought that someday, somehow, when the trauma of her divorce was over, they might meet occasionally, have lunch together in that pub with the horse-brasses and the cricket-team photographs.

Now his glorious, imagined prelude had faded to a slow fugue in the minor key. He wished to God that he had died on the back seat of that taxi.

Beryl and Mrs Bartram, he realised, would guard him from now on, as assiduously as a couple of prison warders, stripping him of pride and identity, the independence and freedom he prized so dearly, monitoring his every movement; feeding him slops – Bovril, steamed fish, and rice pudding.

Then, after a while, would come Beryl's punishing catechism concerning his 'affair' with Jessica. He knew his wife so well. Her stung pride and jealousy would allow him no respite, no peace of mind as she tried to ferret out every detail of their relationship: how often they had seen each other; where and when? And she would never, never believe that they had not made physical love together.

Oh Christ Jesus!

Too late now. Wearily, he turned away from the window and began packing his overnight case with his personal belongings, pyjamas, dressing-gown, shaving gear – *The Complete Works of Conan Doyle*. Above all things, he knew he could not bear to witness the arrival of his wife's taxi: Beryl picking her way up the hospital steps, her lips set in a rigid line of disapproval.

Jess saw him, at first, in silhouette, his tall figure outlined against the fading light of a winter afternoon, shoulders bowed down by an insupportable weight of sadness.

'Bill,' she said softly, compassionately.

He turned at the sound of her voice, and held out his arms to her. Not speaking. Simply holding her as if he could never bear to let her go.

Resting her head against his shoulder, an enfolding sensation of peace flooded through Jess – a kind of homecoming after a long and difficult journey.

But she knew there wasn't much time. Beryl might arrive at any moment, and Bill must not be subjected to any more stress. Mark had warned her about that. He had suffered enough; was still a very sick man. But she must make certain that he wished to do what she had in mind.

The taxi was waiting – Alfred beside it, ready to escort

285

Bill to Laurel Villa. She had made the drawing-room ready to receive him; had rung George and Adeline to outline her plan of action. They had been shocked by the news of Bill's illness. Beryl had not even told them about his heart attack. 'I suppose she might have told us had Bill actually *died*,' Lina said bitterly.

Holding Jess tightly in his arms, the words William had wanted, needed to say all along came at last. 'I love you,' he murmured against her hair.

Looking up, smiling into his eyes, 'And I love you,' she whispered, knowing at last what it felt like to love and to be loved in return – the simplicity, the rightness of being in love, with the right person, for all the right reasons.

When, very quietly, she asked him if he would be willing to come to her, he made no reply. Withdrawing from her embrace, he simply zipped up the overnight bag, and put on his overcoat: trustingly, like a child; his eyes filled with tears.

'Here, let me.' With loving hands, she tucked his muffler inside his coat, and stood on tiptoe to kiss his cheek, the way she had done that day in his office. 'Ready?' she asked lightly

'Ready.' Then, 'Beryl,' he murmured anxiously.

'You mustn't worry on that score.' She placed her hand lovingly in the crook of his elbow. 'Come along, darling.'

'But you don't understand. You don't realise.' His arm shook convulsively.

Understanding his concern, she conjured up the definition of the word 'bravely' – to defy, to meet with courage. She did not feel particularly courageous, but this thing must be settled with honour: her confrontation with Beryl Hoyle. And Bill must be safely on his way to Laurel Villa when that confrontation took place.

'You don't know my wife,' he said shakily. 'I – I don't want you to suffer the humiliation . . . '

'Don't worry about me. I'll manage.'

'Let me stay with you, Jess!'

'No, darling. Leave this to me.' She drew him slowly but

firmly along the corridor. 'Alfred's waiting to take you home. I'll be along later. Please, darling. Trust me.'

'Home,' he said wonderingly, with a dawning realisation of what the word really meant to him. Life, not death. 'Oh, Jess, my love.'

When the taxi had departed, Jess drew in a deep breath of relief, and walked up the hospital steps, and along the corridor to Bill's room to await the arrival of Mrs Hoyle.

How odd that she had never felt the slightest desire to confront Avril Messiter, to march into her classroom, or upstairs to her flat, to engage in a verbal battle over Douglas. Not because she had feared the younger, more sexually attractive woman, but because she had known that the battle was not worth the fighting – or winning. But this was different. She was fighting now, not only for her own future but Bill's.

Suddenly she felt very strong, very certain, very courageous.

Looking out of the window, she saw that the sky to the west was filled with a cumulus of soaring clouds; great columns of cloud straining upwards towards freedom. Clouds shot through and through with the golden spears of an early winter sunset, reminiscent of some many-towered Camelot.

Camelot. That legendary city of dreams, of knights in shining armour: the kind of chivalry she had discovered in the man she loved.

When the next painful interlude was over, when she had made clear to Beryl Hoyle that her time of domination was over and done with; when she had done everything within her power to ensure Bill's peace of mind, she would devote her life to his welfare, to making him well and strong once more.

Looking up at the clouds, she wondered when she had really fallen in love with Bill. Then, smiling, she thought that it happened that day he had loaned her fifty pounds to keep her from starvation; his caring concern for her welfare: the day she had come to trust another human being.

She would never betray that trust. She wondered, with a stirring of nervous excitement, if she was really too old to have a child of her own. Bill's child. Perhaps not. Now, anything, everything seemed possible once more.

The door slammed open suddenly, pushed back by an ungentle, unloving hand.

The moment of truth had arrived. Truth in the shape of a short, slightly breathless, self-important-looking woman wearing a purple feathered hat, mink coat, a Jacqmar scarf; carrying a crocodile handbag.

Turning away from the window, drawing back her shoulders, ready to do battle, 'Mrs Hoyle,' she said proudly, unflinchingly. 'My name is Jessica Carmichael!'

THE END